A BALANCE OF POWER

A BALANCE OF POWER

by

JIM PRIOR

HAMISH HAMILTON

LONDON

First published in Great Britain 1986
by Hamish Hamilton Ltd
27 Wrights Lane, London W8 5TZ

Copyright © 1986 by Hamish Hamilton Ltd

British Library Cataloguing in Publication Data
Prior, James
    A balance of power
    1. Great Britain – Politics and government – 1964–1979
    2. Great Britain – Politics and government – 1979–
    I. Title
941.085'092'4   DA589.7
    ISBN 0–241–11957–X

Typeset, printed and bound in Great Britain by
Richard Clay (The Chaucer Press) Ltd, Bungay, Suffolk

CONTENTS

LIST OF ILLUSTRATIONS

ACKNOWLEDGMENTS

Many people have helped with advice and some with encouragement to enable me to write this book. I'm quite certain that without the support of Adrian House and Rob Shepherd I should never have progressed beyond the first chapter. By the time of going to print Jane Lewis, Elspeth Muir and Heather Laughton knew the text practically by heart and as well gave much help in both style and content.

In many respects the book is both a joint effort and joint account of the lives and careers of Jane and myself. Without her neither the book nor the career could have happened and, if she doesn't mind too much, I wish to dedicate it to her.

Brampton, Suffolk   JIM PRIOR

PART ONE

POLITICS

CHAPTER ONE

TOWARDS WESTMINSTER

By the time my father made it clear to me that he thought farming was no way to make a living, and that politics would be a waste of time, it was too late. I had already started down both those slippery slopes at Charterhouse.

At the age of thirteen I was delivered to this bleak looking school in Surrey, not long after the outbreak of the Second World War. We arrived in time for tea and its gaunt Victorian buildings grew even more dismal after dark: it took six miles of funereal cloth to make sure that the blackout regulations were properly observed. In these years of austerity the traditional values of boarding school food were further debased by rationing; and some genius ensured that our meals were not only meagre but cold. The heater in which they awaited us stood near the door of the hall; the wind swept in from the flat and chilly expanse of the playing fields and blew out the flames. One of the more notorious specialities on the menu was 'gas pudding'.

Like all schools Charterhouse looked to its more distinguished old boys for inspiration. Not for nothing was one of them that survivor of the siege and hunger of Mafeking, the founder of the Boy Scout movement, Robert Baden-Powell. The headmaster, a remarkable man called Robert Birley, saw to it that we looked to his example and grew food of our own. Potatoes and other vegetables were planted and cared for; I myself was intrigued by the idea of keeping pigs.

The Government was just then encouraging people to set up pig clubs as a way to boost food production and help make the country self-sufficient. If you ran a pig club you were allowed to eat half the number of pigs you fattened. As an added incentive you had to give up only half of your own slender allocation of meat coupons.

I decided with some others in my house that we would set up such a club and would use the swill from the kitchens as the main source of feed – not that there was a great deal left over. We built the sties, started with four pigs, increased to eight, and then kept up to about twelve at a time. It wasn't all plain sailing as sometimes the pigs got ill and I had to nurse one batch through an epidemic of swine erysipelas.

Although I enjoyed games very much I wasn't exactly inspired by the work and found pig farming extremely satisfying; I looked forward to enjoying the pork, the ham and the sausages. What is more the headmaster – who was also my housemaster – seemed to share my enthusiasm. He was therefore as outraged as I when just as we were about to kill the first pigs Whitehall announced that school pig clubs could not qualify for the coupon concession.

Birley's response was, I later discovered, typical of his approach to people and problems. One day a boy in the house asked if his godfather might come to tea after the service at which he was being confirmed. Who was his godfather? John Llewellin, Minister of Food. Of course he was welcome, Robert Birley replied. I was also invited to tea and I knew what to do when I was told to sit next to the Minister. According to the headmaster, Llewellin was so shaken that he went straight back to London and changed the regulations. Robert always claimed that this was the moment when he realised I was heading towards Westminster. If so, he had a much better idea of my future than I did.

*

My parents were of course the dominating influence in my early life.

My father was a delightful man, lazy but quite successful. He was a typical middle-class Englishman of his generation. A country lawyer, he had served in the Great War, was concerned with the community, but was more interested in sport than he was in politics: he always looked at the back page of the newspaper before he looked at the front. In so far as he voted at all he was a Conservative.

My mother had a very strong social conscience. She would have been much happier as a Liberal – but she was not radical and could never have been a suffragette. She was extraordinarily active and visited the local hospital, the Norfolk and Norwich, every Sunday afternoon for about fifty years. Before the war she held short services on Sunday afternoons in the wards and latterly called on people who had no visitors of their own. It was quite surprising, when I later became Member of Parliament for Lowestoft, how many people used to tell me how grateful they were that she came round to see them.

Life at home was very old-fashioned. Before and after each meal we had grace, and after breakfast every morning except Sundays we had prayers to which the maids were invited. My father, less religious than my mother, read daily from a book of prayers until he came to the end and then started all over again. I don't believe he ever paid the slightest attention to what he read. He used to try to get the newspapers, preferably back page upper-most, on the floor in front of him.

On Sundays we were made to go to church in the morning. Lunch was cold because my mother would never ask the maids to do any cooking.

She felt they should have at least a chance of going to church: they never did. For an hour after Sunday lunch, from the age of four onward, I was made to sit down and learn my catechism or hymns, or a passage from the Bible. This continued until I went to prep school at Aldeburgh at the age of eight and a half.

The youngest of the four children by seven years, I was the last to leave home. By then, of course, there were no maids, just my mother and father and myself, but still the rituals persisted.

On arrival at the school with my parents for the new boys' tea party, my father asked the headmaster how much pocket money I should require for the term. 'Not much,' he replied, 'half a crown should suffice.' It was duly handed over and recorded in the boys' money book. After my parents had departed, the headmaster greeted a small and very miserable boy with, 'Prior, do you wish to buy a cricket ball?' I blubbered, 'Yes, sir.' 'That will be half a crown.' My term's pocket money was gone.

The school had about sixty boys, mostly drawn from Norfolk, Suffolk and Essex, but a few from further afield – from London and service families. Some have remained friends and we see them regularly. There's much to be said for going to a school which draws from your own locality, where you're likely to spend most of your life.

We were taught to swim in a bitterly cold North Sea; it was enough to put one off swimming for ever. A fisherman in a dinghy kept an eye on us as, shivering with cold, we ran into the water. I won the beginners' race at the end of the term but then sank and had to be rescued.

We used to return home by train from Aldeburgh on what was known as the Aldeburgh Snail as far as Saxmundham, changing into another train to Ipswich, and then a third from Ipswich to Norwich. My memories of the holidays are mixed. Sometimes my father would take me out with him when he had to visit a client in the country or one of the farms whose creditors had foreclosed; I remember tragic and distressing scenes as farmers and their young families were evicted from their homes.

Later on, during the war, the Germans decided to bomb a number of ancient cities such as Norwich, York and Bath: they were known as the 'Baedeker raids'. At Norwich we were completely unprotected to start with, although barrage balloons were later provided. As the bombers attacked, we heard the aircraft diving, next the whistle of the bombs and finally the bangs – sometimes close enough to make the house and its occupants tremble and to break the glass in the windows.

During the raids we used to spend the nights in the cellar where we had a three-bunk arrangement: I was on top and my father at the bottom. When the sirens sounded my father would often rush off to fulfil his duties as a special constable. But on one particular night he was stretched out on his bunk when I must have lashed out with my arm in my sleep. I broke a bottle of port and as it dribbled down the wall, my mother, a teetotaller, commented on the disgusting smell. But my father knew his wine well, and in what I thought was an exercise of great self control merely remarked, '1927; what a lovely bouquet; what a waste!'

After about two years my prep school moved away from Aldeburgh Lodge to a lovely house called Orwell Park. The beautiful grounds led down to the River Orwell, which is one of the great estuaries of Britain; fields and woods rise gently on either side of a wide expanse of water. Orwell Park had been the home of the Pretyman family for many generations. They had entertained William Pitt the Younger, who had spent part of his childhood at the house, and a number of his pictures were still hanging when the school took over.

Like all schools it had its ups and downs. It had to move twice during the war to avoid bombs and afterwards came back to find Orwell Park in a state of dreadful dilapidation, having been a base for Free French soldiers. Inevitably the school was very short of money; one of the short-sighted things they did was to sell the lead off the roof and replace it with ordinary tarred felt. When I became a trustee of the school some twenty-five years later the felt had all rotted and the first task we had to undertake was to raise a fortune to spend on essential repairs.

*

I suppose that from my parents' point of view Charterhouse was a very sensible school to choose for my brother and me. My mother was satisfied with its Christian credentials: one of its old boys – before it moved from London in the 1870s – was John Wesley, founder of Methodism. My father was equally pleased with its sporting achievements. Some held it to be the cradle of soccer as Rugby was of rugger and its reputation at cricket was soaring. Its academic record worried them less but it was safe in the hands of Robert Birley.

I don't think I've ever been so miserable in my life as when I arrived at Charterhouse. I'd never been there before and I knew nothing about it. My brother, who had left the school twelve years before, took me because it was thought that if my parents came I would be reduced to tears; with him I ought to be less homesick, but the tears still came.

We slept downstairs in large rooms which had been specially strength-ened with wooden scaffold poles supporting timber strapping across the ceilings, not a surprising precaution as the outlines of a crater were still visible outside, where a bomb had dropped a little time before. Char-terhouse was on the main line to London for many of the bombers and we heard them going over night after night.

The corps, chapel and games were of course compulsory, as was fagging for the youngest boys. Birching had been discontinued, but caning by the monitors was still in practice. Drinking, smoking and homosexuality were optional extras. They were strongly discouraged, if necessary by sacking, but sometimes went on in the woods round the playing fields.

Dismal as the school may have looked, especially in winter, it was anything but gloomy. This was partly due to the influence of Robert Birley and his wife, Elinor, who brought a civilised glow and sense of purpose into the house and the school, as they later did to such forlorn places as post-war Berlin and Soweto, and even to the languid playing fields of Eton.

After the pig episode, Robert seemed to regard me as not only reasonable at games – I managed to play cricket and football for the school – but also as an oddity to be encouraged. If the pigs were my first political effort, my appetite was whetted rather more seriously by the Report of the Fleming Committee, of which Robert was a leading member and which attempted to open up the public schools to entry from state schools. The concept was one that appealed to me and, since I heard a great deal about it from Robert, I took it to heart and subsequently initiated a debate on it in Parliament. This gift of Robert's for spotting the leanings and talents of boys, and encouraging them, helped to ensure that for most of us Charterhouse life was neither dreary nor dull.

There was one boy in my year who had failed to win a scholarship at Eton as his classics and maths were not up to the brilliance of his history. As an historian himself, Robert was determined that Charterhouse would not make the same mistake and a scholarship was awarded to William Rees-Mogg. William soon became famous throughout the school, not just as a swot, a precocious young bibliophile (he shared the headmaster's passion for old and rare books) and a scholar of exceptional promise, but for breaking all the conventions.

He was the only Carthusian to be made Head of the School without also being head of his house: he had been at odds with his housemaster. As a Catholic William was able to opt out of compulsory chapel: that lasted until he became Head of School when he decided that he would like to attend in order to read the lessons. Like a great many other boys he did not enjoy games, but in a school as philistine as Charterhouse at that time there was no escape – except of course for William. His participation was reduced to occasional umpiring: more usually he was seen sitting on the boundary discussing with a master some crudite aspect of the rules or technique of the game. He did so with all the dispassion that as editor of *The Times* he later brought to its leaders.

Another boy, two years younger than me, made an impact on the school in his very first year. Peter May was shy and unassuming. He could have been in the first XI that summer, but Robert Birley and others were against bringing him along too quickly. This was obviously the right decision and sometimes, when this now distinguished chairman of the selectors has rushed a young man into the Test or touring side, I have wondered whether he remembers well enough what those wise old heads thought best for him at school.

But by 1943 Peter was in the first XI and facing the fastest bowler in the country – Alastair McCorquodale of Harrow. Alastair was dubbed the 'fastest white man in the world' when he ran in the 1948 Olympics. He was a real toff, wore a very smart scarf round his neck and was having a very successful season. Undaunted, Peter took a hundred off him and the other Harrow bowlers that day.

Already he showed a quality which separates the ordinary from the superlative – it was in the movement of his wrists just as the shot was being played. This instinctively changed the direction of the off drive, or any shot in front of the wicket, so the fielder was left chasing rather than fielding the ball.

Peter was always completely unassuming and never allowed his great talents and success to go to his head. Nor did he allow the attentions of one of the older boys to unsettle him, although Simon Raven – a contemporary in my house who has remained a life-long friend – could be very persuasive.

Simon is now a famous author and novelist who has introduced many of his experiences more or less directly into his books. Personally I find the results a little confusing: while there is a good deal of fact in his fiction there is also a good deal of fiction in his memoirs. Fancying some of the more glamorous boys as he did – there is a lyrical description in one of the novels of hair bleached by the sun, smooth brown skin and an unbuttoned shirt at the wicket – I daresay he had romantic illusions about Peter May, albeit in vain. I came to know Peter well when we both went to Cambridge and he could get more mockery and amused disdain into the one word 'Raven' than anyone else I know.

Simon's proclivities are, I think, clear from his novels. They emerged at an early age and were uninhibitedly bi-sexual. He certainly regarded the prettier boys at Charterhouse as a challenge and although his romantic advances were no doubt accompanied by lust I don't think his seductions were evil.

Never reticent on these matters, it was not long before he began boasting that he had made his first female conquest. He had found a prostitute in Piccadilly. Needless to say we were bubbling with interest and excitement. We wanted to know exactly how he had engineered his pick up – after all, he was only sixteen. There was a ready answer – 'Oh, it was all quite easy. You have to put the end of your tie over your shoulder – that is the universal signal.'

Despite these occasional lapses of which Robert Birley must have been aware, I think he was pleased with some of his protégés' achievements. William won a Brackenbury scholarship to Balliol College, Oxford; Simon won a classical scholarship to King's, at Cambridge; Peter was obviously destined to play cricket for Cambridge, and even for England. Robert might have been forgiven for taking less interest in me but before I left to do my National Service he helped me get a place at Pembroke College, Cambridge. Although he was an historian and I specialised in biology, under his influence I started to read and think for myself, though not quite at the level of William.

Nowadays, many boys of seventeen or eighteen go through a rebellious phase, but I think most of us were different. We did not experience life in the trenches which twenty-five years earlier had led men of Harold Macmillan's generation to dedicate themselves to a better society. But we had learned to tighten our belts and live through the bombing; each week we listened in chapel to the lists of our fore-runners and friends who had fallen at the front; almost every day we heard on the wireless news of disasters, excitements or victory; we were appalled by the early reports in the papers of the holocaust in Belsen and Auschwitz; later we saw pictures of the apocalyptic destruction created by the atomic explosions at Hiroshima and Nagasaki.

Without pomposity or any false sentiment – in fact with an impish and infectious enthusiasm – Robert made us aware of the merits of morality and learning, of thought for other people and an inquisitive mind. Both William and I came under the benign spell of this man whose powerful intellect and strong social conscience placed duty to others very high in the order of obligation and he gave a liberal twist to my entrepreneurial bent.

*

The army had quite a number of surprises in store for me. I had enlisted in the 60th Rifles to do my National Service but was ordered to report to a depot near Derby which had no regimental attachments at all. Next, my posting to an officers' training unit took six months instead of six weeks to come through. Finally I discovered I was not destined for Woolwich or Sandhurst, but for Bangalore, in Southern India.

My morale was at rock bottom when I reached the good ship *Georgic* in the Liverpool docks, bound for Bombay. But there on the deck I encountered the smiling face and distinctive red hair of none other than Raven. The deepening friendship we forged on the unspeakable voyage to India has managed to survive not only our years in the army and later Cambridge, but also the numerous libels he has subsequently perpetrated against me in a series of novels.

In the sequence called *Alms for Oblivion*, Simon follows the fortunes of a group of boys from their schooldays through to their final careers. Simon's early affection for Peter May must have caused him to let him off lightly or omit him entirely: Robert Birley, William Rees-Mogg and I are less fortunate. There is no doubt that the interested reader is nudged into associating the characters of Somerset Lloyd-James with William, and of Peter Morrison with me; Fielding Gray, hero and victim, is Simon himself.

This is all very well at the start, and it is perfectly reasonable for Simon to expiate the peccadilloes of his youth in the pages of his fiction, but I am not sure it is quite cricket to endow William's and my fictional counterparts with exploits dredged up from the murk of his psyche. The danger lies in the skill of his writing – his evocation of the realities of public school life and the charade of our training unit once we reached Bangalore are so convincing that the reader may also be convinced that the inventions are equally factual.

It is quite true we found ourselves all too well grounded in Urdu, swagger-stick drill and the niceties of section attacks – and too little in duties in Aid of the Civil Power. It is also true that we very much enjoyed Chinese meals as a respite from curry and the beauty of the 'chichis' as the Anglo-Indian girls were called: they are some of the most attractive women in the world and were much sought after for their pale brown skins and beautiful figures. On the other hand Simon alone seemed to fear catching typhoid from the former or had real cause to fear catching some more disgusting disease from the latter. Even so he would have been wiser to confine himself to girls, but judging from his book I'm afraid that I failed to persuade him of this.

These were the last days of the Raj and they were an extraordinary mixture of grim reality and peacetime frivolity. We spent many weeks on tactical exercises in the jungle, based on techniques learnt in the recent campaigns against the Japanese; and although Independence was still a little way off there were periodic riots in Bangalore and elsewhere disturbances far more alarming. I don't believe it would have been possible to hand over power to a partitioned India if as nowadays the world's media were able to show it day by day on our television screens. The massacre and brutality would have shocked the world into some kind of intervention before it reached the climax which finally occurred and dwarfed the horrors of Northern Ireland and Lebanon today.

Simon and I completed our training as officers together and if it had come to the crunch I think we would have acquitted ourselves without shame. But it did not come to the crunch while we were there, so we threw ourselves into the activities of the Army Bureau of Current Affairs, known as ABCA, an organisation to which is attributed the Labour victory of 1945. I rather doubt ABCA achieved it, for although it may have propagated a socialist if rather warped and colourful prescription for the troubles of post-war Britain, it was regarded by most soldiers as no more than a welcome respite from more serious and warlike activities. Simon and I joined in its debates with uninhibited relish – just as we joined in quite high class cricket on coconut matting and the other social entertainments laid on by the dwindling relicts of the Raj.

As Simon sprinkles his novels with fact so he peppers his cricketing memoirs with the odd fabrication. In *Shadows on the Grass* he describes a drinking contest with another officer in which I am supposed to have taken part – and if I say I can remember very little of it I suppose this confirms his story. Suffice it to say there was a wager, a quantity of whisky was consumed, and although I emerged the winner, I have never liked whisky since. After Simon's account of the episode was carried in the *Observer* no one wrote to complain about it, so I presume that readers either did not believe it or forgave it as the exuberance of youth.

Despite our training and social activities I found that I still had enough time on my hands to develop a profitable sideline. It was possible to buy carpets in India and ship them home for sale at more than treble the cost. It is hard to understand now, but by the end of the war there was an enormous shortage of many household goods, including carpets. Apart from my limited cash I couldn't overdo it as I might have run into import problems and also my father had to find buyers. However, he encouraged my enterprise and I was able to make several hundred pounds profit.

My father had always been helpful in letting me have early responsibility for money – so much so that at the age of fifteen he opened a bank account for me and after that I paid all my own bills, including my school fees. It was an excellent discipline and training.

*

At long last, we were commissioned and I was sent to the Royal Norfolk Regiment, then serving in Germany. My first posting was to a garrison at Detmold. Apart from certain limited guard duties we had little else to do.

We then moved to Berlin, which was much more interesting, and I was on the advance party to take over in the Tiergarten. The soldiers spent much of their time in a tatty café-cum-night club opposite our quarters, called Maxims. The major from whom I took over was not a great disciplinarian; he kept his mistress in his quarters with him but told me that he discouraged the men from bringing their girls into theirs. The discouragement did not appear to be overwhelming. The men paid for their drinks and other pleasures with part of their cigarette ration, since tobacco was then the main currency.

While I was in India I had occasionally exchanged letters with Robert Birley, who was a prolific correspondent. He had left Charterhouse and was now in Germany as Adviser on Education to the Military Governor of the British Zone, General Sir Brian Robertson, who was an Old Carthusian. I could not help wondering, as did the *Observer* and a number of Labour MPs, how much the appointment owed to the old boy network. Nevertheless if there is such a network – and there certainly is – the Oxford tradition of bringing it into play on academic and ecclesiastical preferment is healthier than its Cambridge application to espionage and treason.

In Berlin I was able to see much of my old headmaster, between spells of guard duty and energetic games of regimental football. The time I spent with him and Elinor in the evenings left me with an understanding and vision of post-war Europe, implanting the concepts and ideals of the European Community. Robert never allowed me to forget my post-war experience in Germany and was a formidable correspondent during the EEC negotiations in both 1961 and 1970.

The Birleys lived in a grand house, with a large staff, among a number of other important military and diplomatic figures. As a young second lieutenant I was frequently entertained there in a manner to which I was hardly accustomed – both by Robert, who had the honorary rank of major-general, and by the General himself, no doubt on the strength of the Charterhouse connection. I was, however, far more impressed by the spirit of communion that the Birleys built up with the Germans than by all the high living.

Both in Berlin and later at the annual Königswinter conferences, started by Frau Milchsack but inspired by Robert, changing groups of fifty influential figures – politicians, lawyers, businessmen, service chiefs and academics – responded to his liberal beliefs. However important ideas and ideals might be, he was convinced that people were more important still and that it was often essential to adopt a pragmatic rather than a dogmatic approach to the problems of the world.

One effect of this further exposure to the influence of my ex-headmaster was a growing determination to make the most of any talents I had – and if possible leave some mark in the world. It did not look as though I was going to inherit very much, so anything I wanted I would have to earn for myself. I therefore decided that when I went up to Cambridge, instead of reading Biology I would take the more practical course in Agriculture. While I was in Germany I laid hands on every single book on organic chemistry which I could find, and as a result, by the time I got to Cambridge I had read far more than was actually necessary to get my degree.

*

Cambridge, at which I finally arrived in 1948, provided as many unexpected influences as Charterhouse and the army. My father saw Pembroke as an excellent games college – and so it turned out to be. Peter May arrived there to strengthen the football and the cricket. At soccer I played right half to his inside right for Pembroke and the Old Carthusians. Much of the time, though, Peter played for the University (for which I only got a trial) – and he was in both the football and cricket Cambridge XIs for three years running.

After my first year at Pembroke I changed to reading Estate Management as my father warned me there would never be any question of his being able to help me financially, and therefore I needed a professional qualification. The switch meant that I had to compress a three years' course into one and a half. I became a man in a hurry to start a career. I knew by this time that I wanted to enter politics but not until I had made some progress in farming and had a base from which to operate.

Early on at Cambridge I nearly ruined my political career before it had even begun. I was caught removing a hurricane lamp which was temptingly marking some scaffolding outside Trinity. Two of us were summonsed for pinching the lamp, the rest of the party having done a quick bunk. My head Tutor was very upset – didn't I realise that if convicted of a felony I would be barred from becoming an MP or entering the Civil Service? He therefore suggested that I had better be defended by a QC, who just happened to be a Fellow of Corpus Christi, the neighbouring college. He earned £15, but my road to Parliament remained open.

During one of the Cambridge vacations I had my first real insight into industry and living in an industrial community. I wanted to learn about tractors, their maintenance and repair, so I applied to attend a course at Dagenham for tractor mechanics.

Ford were very kind and accepted me although I had no background or sponsor for the course, and had neither skill nor any mechanical aptitude: nevertheless I enjoyed mixing with the other students.

I came away little the wiser about tractors, but a lot wiser about industrial life, for I was greatly privileged to stay with a family who had a flat over the Liverpool Insurance building, almost on top of the main gate at Dagenham. Two of the family worked in the factory and they had moved down from Birkenhead with Ford when Dagenham first went into production. They were skilled workers and loyal to Ford, but were troubled that, if they produced too much, they would work themselves out of a job. We used to argue the toss about productivity and I did my best to convince them that they were mistaken – the more they produced and the lower the cost, the more they would sell.

The lesson for me was that this deeply-held view simply had to be reckoned with: I remembered it constantly in later years when I attempted to guide the Conservative Party towards understanding the committed trade unionists whom we needed to attract to our side. These were the weeks when that much mocked character 'Pussyfoot Prior' began to form a judgment of how best to handle relationships on the production line.

The family taught me another great lesson after my very sheltered middle-class upbringing. This was about the intense patriotism of these, my friends. They were immensely proud not only of their work during the grim and dangerous conditions in the war, but even more of their only son who was killed whilst serving as a pilot officer. I don't think for one moment that they voted Conservative – certainly not in 1945 – but they did more to help my political education than they could ever have realised. To my very great regret I have completely lost touch with them.

Back at Cambridge, while Peter May excelled at cricket and football, and I struggled to achieve my professional qualifications, Simon Raven spent a number of years seeking to act out a role for which his props and his stage were insufficient. At school his act was under some sort of control, but by the time he reached Cambridge Walter Mitty was beginning to take over. He liked the idea of being a bit of a wag, rather racy, moneyed and, above all, a gentleman. He managed to complete his years at King's with some style, but in the end just failed in the first of his conventional ambitions – to become a Fellow of the college. I saw quite a lot of him and went to stay with his parents near Sheffield – and could not help speculating how much of his own home life was reflected in that of his fictional alter ego Fielding Gray. Certainly we went to a great many parties together, although I don't think he was at the May Week Ball when I first met a girl called Jane Lywood.

It was a significant meeting, although I don't think either Jane or I recognised this at the time. She was already engaged to one of my friends, but I had no idea that the romance was about to disintegrate. When the engagement finally collapsed I made an effort to see her again: if I hadn't I would have missed the best of all the advantages that I derived from Cambridge – and there were many.

*

My father had still not really changed his objections to my becoming a farmer. It was the last thing he wanted me to be after his unfortunate experiences as the Official Receiver in Bankruptcy in Norfolk in the 1930s. At that time life was really hard and rough; there was great poverty and the conditions for farmworkers were terrible. They had to work out in the rain with sacks over their shoulders, and if it rained too long they were just sent home without any pay. There was hardly a single farm-worker who, by the time he reached forty-five or fifty, did not have a bad back from lifting the very heavy sacks – in those days sixteen or eighteen stone was the normal weight for a bag of barley or wheat. The majority developed a rupture. Many also suffered from what was called 'farmers' lung' – brought on by dust, mouldy hay and their working conditions. Seeing all this, day in day out, had determined my father's views. He was shocked when I told him that I wanted to farm. He had hoped that I would follow him into the law. But that was not for me.

In October 1950, I started work in a land agent's office where I learnt to manage and advise on a number of clients' farms. I was given a great deal of responsibility, although my experience was limited. However, I was able to improve the profitability of some farms, which the local bank noticed – this was to prove very useful a little later.

One of the clients I looked after was John Hill, who had a big farm on the northern border of Suffolk, and after a year or two he asked me to work exclusively for him.

By now the ambitions I had felt stirring had grown a little clearer. I really believed it was possible to make money out of farming, and I began to persue my interest in politics. I also became extremely interested in seeing more of Jane Lywood: towards the end of 1953 I asked her to marry me and she accepted.

We were married in January 1954, at the Savoy Chapel in London during a snowstorm and spent our first night at Claridges. We told them we were on our honeymoon and booked a bedroom for the princely sum of £5. When we arrived at the hotel with rose petals falling around us, we were greeted with the salaams of 'My Lord' and 'My Lady' and were shown up to a magnificent bridal suite which seemed good value for our fiver. Jane started to put our clothes away and noticed a lot of dirty old luggage in the wardrobe. We rang to complain.

An embarrassed manager appeared. Jane asked for the luggage to be removed, to which request he replied, 'But you are Lord and Lady de Freyne?' 'Certainly not', was her answer; and a little later: 'And we are not moving.' I'm afraid the de Freynes probably had our £5 bedroom, but we had the bridal suite and I knew for certain that I had a wife to be reckoned with.

The next day we set off on a skiing holiday, but I had been kicked by a cow a few days before and contracted pleurisy. We therefore had to abandon the ski slopes and stay in Vienna, where Jane was promptly taken ill. It was an inauspicious start to a marriage which has happily proved to be one of mutual understanding, collaboration, stability and love. All through our lives we have needed each other, and that remains as true today as it has ever been.

I cannot remember which of my older friends I asked to the wedding though I must have invited the Birleys. By now they were at Eton where he was headmaster after his spell in Germany. His liberal approach to the problems of the world had caused consternation among the more die-hard Old Etonians and even before he arrived he was dubbed 'Red Robert': I don't suppose he voted anything other than Tory all his life. But he proved, once more, a successful headmaster, and when he left he took the most unusual and courageous step of his life, to become visiting Professor of Education at Witwatersrand University, Johannesburg. There, his uncompromising intellectual honesty and powerful humanity communicated themselves and their values to both sides of a divided society very different from Germany, yet equally – or even worse – distressed by its current situation.

Simon Raven could not have come to the wedding. He had now given up research at Cambridge to become an officer in the King's Shropshire Light Infantry. Wedded to the glamour and protocol of life as an officer and a gentleman he took great pride in his uniform and was loath ever to be separated from his gloves and his swagger stick. On one occasion it nearly led to a court martial when he refused to obey an order to take off his gloves to dismantle an engine on some motor transport course.

More appropriately, he later became an Intelligence Officer, but still was inclined to run into trouble. As a captain he was called on to make a special presentation to a visiting general, who was well known to be straitlaced and thought alcoholic consumption in many messes too high. But, when the general arrived, there was no sign of Raven. All the officers waited with the general and his staff for the captain to appear. Tension mounted. Eventually, a shuffling noise was heard down the corridor, followed by a shout from Raven to the barman for a quadruple gin and tonic. By this time steam was emitting from the general's ears.

Raven approached, a little flushed and fortified by the gin – no apology for being late – 'Well, General, shall we begin?' 'You will begin,' said the general, 'by calling me Sir.'

Seeing service in the exotic plains and forests of Kenya, Simon may not have been laying the foundations of a famous military career, but he began to gather very useful material for some of his infamous novels.

Meanwhile Jane and I settled down to married life in a rather more prosaic environment. Our first house had no electricity and was lit by Tilly lamps that needed constant refilling and priming. Our water had to be pumped from a well and it is surprising how quickly one empties the tank of a rural cottage – especially if there are babies to look after. We soon had two children: David, born at the end of 1954, and Simon in 1956.

My opportunity to get involved in politics came in early 1955 when my boss John Hill, whose farm I was managing, decided that he wanted to stand for Parliament. He was adopted as Conservative candidate for the South Norfolk by-election that January. I offered to help and before I knew where I was, I found myself speaking for him, going round canvassing and helping out in just about every way possible.

Then to my astonishment, a little after the general election of that year, I was driving a tractor along the road when someone stopped me and said they were looking for a new candidate at Lowestoft – 'You're a young man; you're just the type of person we want. Why don't you let your name go forward?' I didn't even know they needed a candidate.

I went home and talked it over with Jane. She thought that I might as well let my name go in – it wouldn't do any harm. Almost immediately I found myself the prospective candidate for the Lowestoft constituency. Everything had happened so quickly that I was selected as their candidate without having been approved by Conservative Central Office.

The local Party Chairman, a stalwart farmer, therefore went to London to persuade the Party Vice-Chairman then responsible for candidates, Donald Kaberry, that I should be allowed to go on the Candidates' List. His reaction was to ask, 'What does this young man know about politics? He's done nothing, he's not a local councillor, he's got no background in politics, he wasn't even a member of the Party at university. Are you sure that you really want him? You've already done pretty badly in the seat at Lowestoft; perhaps you ought to look for someone else.' The local Chairman must have been adamant that they wanted me.

Eventually I was asked to go to London to see Kaberry, which I did in fear and trembling. I started by saying, 'I do hope you're going to let me become the candidate because I've already been selected.' He looked at me, asked me a few questions, and then said, 'They want you at Lowestoft, so they had better have you.' I suspect that, like the rest of the Central Office, he had written off Lowestoft as a winnable seat.

At that stage I never thought that my life was going to centre round politics. Lowestoft was a Labour seat, and I thought that even if I won it once – which looked most unlikely – I would never win it again. So I didn't take it terribly seriously, although we worked hard in the constituency for the next few years.

By the time we had married, I had been managing farms for a few years and had been running my own Land Agency practice. Most of my work had been at Blyford with John Hill, but when I was adopted as a

Conservative candidate he told me to get my own farm, as he felt that it would be wrong to have a Conservative candidate working for a Conservative Member. It was good advice.

In 1957 the bank lent me £10,000. I took a mortgage out for a further £12,000 and with my own resources of about another £10,000 we were able to buy a 360-acre farm at Brampton for £23,000. I confess I did make an offer for the farm before Jane had seen the house – at the time, the productivity of the land and its profitability counted most for us.

Although the house was in need of repair and modernisation, it was a lovely sixteenth-century building with a moat round it. The farm has been a wonderful place to bring up children and also provided the secure base without which I could not have launched a political career.

Not long after we had moved in, I had a letter from Simon Raven to say he had left the army – 'very lucky to get out' was the ambiguous phrase he used, suggesting some unspoken difficulties. It went on, 'Can you lend me anything between £10 and £1,000? It is a combination of slow horses and fast women!' For old time's sake I sent him £15, which was meticulously acknowledged.

I forgot about it until by chance I read his review in the *Spectator* of a book on gambling, in which Simon described his experience at Aspinall's where he had picked up some sizeable winnings. It was a beautiful piece of writing and tempted me to ask, with tongue in cheek, for my £15 – after all he had won it at gaming and presumably had a fee for the review. I was unlucky. There were, to quote his letter, 'many more ahead of you in the queue'.

It was some time before Simon made any real money from his writing. Until he did, his publisher sent him a living advance each week on the sensible condition that he resided in Deal and never came to London except on business. Nevertheless, I am glad to say that this brilliant man, whose first two novels were published in 1959, made money at last. He repaid his debt with the first of a series of excellent dinners which we have had together ever since. At last he could afford to lead the life of a gentleman he had coveted for so long.

By 1959 William Rees-Mogg was still some way off becoming editor of *The Times*, but Peter May was captaining England in Australia: altogether he has led them in forty-one test matches.

The summer of 1959 was one of the best this century. Even the North Sea was warm enough to make swimming enjoyable, and we had a good harvest. It was too hot for Jane who was expecting Sarah-Jane, but when she arrived on September 5, I was able to say that two parts of our autumn treble were now in place: a good harvest, a daughter, and now for a win at Lowestoft.

By the time of the October general election, the Tories were at the height of their popularity, with Harold 'Supermac' Macmillan as Prime Minister. The Government had also recovered from the Suez affair, although Suez was the issue that people heckled me about at every single meeting.

My opponent was the highly respected, very decent Labour MP, Edward Evans, who had held the seat since 1945 and had increased his majority against the trend. Conservative Central Office was not even prepared to give us status as a 'critical seat', whereby certain marginal seats are helped with additional aid and finance.

*

In the outcome I won with a majority of 1,489. The contrast between the young man, who was the local boy, and the old man who was getting towards the end of his career, together with the national swing against Labour, finally proved too much for him.

The crowds cheered my victory but all his supporters just drifted away. They didn't stay with him, they didn't try to console him, and didn't even thank him for his services over the years. It was really sad. I went up to him to commiserate. He looked at me and said, 'Whatever you do, don't spoil them.'

After the count I went on the traditional victory tour which my older supporters had not savoured since 1935. The scenes in the small towns of Beccles, Southwold and Halesworth were very heart-warming. Little did I realise that this was the start of a long political career.

Edward Evans' view as an old Labour Member was that you were in Parliament to deal with national matters and shouldn't get too mixed up in local affairs. It was a significant remark because over the years a lot of Members of Parliament have gone in more and more for 'pavement politics'. The upshot is that almost everything locally has now come to be seen as the responsibility of the Member of Parliament. Sometimes one can help a constituent, but I have always taken the view that it was important that people should have a chance of talking over their problems and being listened to, however hopeless the case may be. Too often I have found that no one has listened to them, and the therapy of understanding and concern has been lacking. A letter from the House of Commons can help, even if the contents contain disappointing news. But the wise MP should avoid creating the impression that he or she can tackle just about anything.

Edward Evans had been a good local Member who drew his support from all sections and parts of the community. His wife had died, and now he had lost his Parliamentary seat. He had little left to live for, and was dead within a year or so. I took his sad end as a warning that I should never allow my whole life to become totally absorbed in, or overwhelmed by, politics. I have always tried to maintain other involvements and sources of interest, not only for my own sanity but also to retain some ability to 'switch off' from politics now and again, and to be able therefore to take a more detached, and I hope balanced, view of the political issues of the moment.

The 1959 general election on October 8 had produced a Tory landslide. We won 365 seats, which in those days included the Ulster Unionists, against Labour's 258. The opening of the new Parliament and the Queen's Speech was a very impressive occasion for a new young MP, who knew nobody, and whom nobody knew.

The Government benches were packed, and with an overall majority of 100 there was a mood of great confidence. Winston Churchill was there in his corner seat below the gangway. Hugh Gaitskell and Aneurin Bevan sat opposite Harold Macmillan and Rab Butler.

Yet the speech which was to impress me and haunt me for some years did not come from the Government benches: it came from Nye Bevan. What struck me was not that he had always been portrayed as the ogre of the right wing; it was not his famous remarks about Tory vermin which the *Daily Express* never allowed him or anyone else to forget; it was not even his impish sense of humour: it was a few simple sentences, as he leant across the dispatch box and pointed his finger at Macmillan and the front bench:

'What do they propose to do with their victory? A heavy responsibility now rests upon them.'

For me it was Bevan who stole Macmillan's thunder. I was already falling into that trap which no politician should allow – that of seeing merit in one's opponents.

CHAPTER TWO

FALL OF THE OLD TORIES

When I became a Member of Parliament, I had never been to the House of Commons before and knew no one there. Once I had become an official Parliamentary candidate, I could have visited the Commons for dinner and other meetings, but I wasn't going to tempt Providence.

So in October 1959 I went to the House as an absolute new boy, without any kind of reputation. I had only one suit, a light blue tweed. Jane said that when she looked at me from the Public Gallery I stuck out like a sore thumb amongst the serried ranks of pinstripes and black jackets with striped trousers.

It was a totally new and somewhat confusing way of life for me. I was not always certain who was on my side or who was a member of the Opposition. This made the obtaining of a 'pair' difficult, but I soon recognised an attractive new young lady Member – Mrs Judith Hart – and she used to be my pair from time to time, so that I could get away from the House on at least some occasions.

I thoroughly enjoyed my first five years in Parliament, but thought this was to be an interlude in my life. I was only expecting to be in the House for one Parliament and then be out again when Labour's fortunes revived. A whole group of us first entered the House in the 1959 election on Macmillan's coat-tails, and we naturally went round together, including Tim Kitson, who later became Ted Heath's Parliamentary Private Secretary, and Julian Critchley, who was to become one of the great characters of the House and has kept us amused ever since in his witty columns.

Margaret Thatcher had also been elected for the first time in 1959, but she wasn't really one of our set. Margaret made an impact early on with a Private Member's Bill which made it obligatory for the Press to be allowed into local council meetings. I heard her make the occasional speech and knew roughly what her views were, but at that time the few women in the Parliamentary Party tended not to be accepted so easily by their male colleagues.

Many of us did not expect to hold on next time round, and with a majority of 100 we took life fairly light-heartedly. Our approach came as a shock to some of the 'old school' on the backbenches. In the early days of the new Parliament Jane and I were invited to a drinks party, where we met Sir William Anstruther Gray, a respected senior backbencher, Deputy Chairman of Ways and Means in the Commons, and who was later to become Chairman of the 1922 Committee. Jane happened to mention that I hadn't got a pair for the evening but would not bother to go back to the House to vote. Sir William was shocked to the core. How could anyone be away from the House unpaired? It was unheard of not to vote on a two-line whip.

It was not yet the era when the newest member is on christian name terms with the Prime Minister and the Cabinet. We called Harold Macmillan 'sir', and talked reverently to him and 'Rab' Butler if either of them came into the smoking room. They were both very aloof as far as new young Members were concerned. They were a formidable pair, perhaps the most experienced duet in modern politics, both highly intelligent, both creative and liberal in outlook.

Harold gave the impression of being very patrician, happiest shooting grouse or dining with his aristocratic friends at Buck's or Pratt's. He liked to pose as the gifted amateur, although he was the complete professional. Rab on the other hand delighted in being the professional, brilliant as an administrator, with a delightful political touch and a little bit of impish deviousness. They distrusted each other: but Harold knew that Rab was not only indispensable but carried with him an important wing of the Party; and Rab knew that he had to be loyal to Harold, in his fashion.

The Commons was changing as the old guard slowly dropped out, until by the mid-sixties we were seeing a very different type of Member. It was the last Parliament in which the 'Knights of the Shires' would be the bedrock of the Tory Party's loyalty and support, and in which the old trade unionists on the Labour benches – given a few years in Parliament as a reward after long service to their union – performed the same role for their Party.

The 'Knights of the Shires' were a most unusual and sometimes eccentric lot. They may have been indisputably right wing in their basic attitudes and approach to life, but they were also intensely loyal, particularly to someone like Harold Macmillan. They recognised that he had a degree of flair and brilliance which others didn't have, and that he had pulled the Party out of the débâcle of Suez, resulting in our re-election with an increased majority. They were not at all happy about many of the decisions that were being made, yet with Harold Macmillan as Prime Minister and Derry Heathcoat-Amory, a gentleman personified, as Chancellor of the Exchequer, they broadly felt safe and therefore on the whole they ought to go along with it.

There was no question that more than a sprinkling of the old Knights could have contemplated belonging to the One Nation Group, which had been founded in the 1950 Parliament and which had included Robert Carr, Ted Heath, Iain Macleod, Angus Maude, Reggie Maudling and Enoch Powell amongst its members.

This Group met weekly for informal discussion and over the years its members have published numerous policy proposals. The old Knights would have been aghast at that sort of theoretical politics.

They believed in hanging, they believed in bashing the unions, and they believed, no doubt, in holding to a 45-hour or 50-hour week, but they certainly would not have done so on the basis of any intellectual or theoretical argument. They were not committed to a doctrine. They were pragmatists to a man.

They used the smoking room as their meeting place, hence the view that the Commons was 'the best club in London'. It was in the smoking room that the Whips had to find out their views and there that characters were blackened or sanctified. Some of them probably did not receive more than three or four letters a week, so there was no problem about dealing with correspondence. They led their villages and their constituencies, and made speeches when they had to. They were honourable, loyal, shrewd, and had a certain native wit.

But they were a dying breed. Many of them either left Parliament of their own free will or were knocked out in the 1964 election. Yet, before their demise, they had given me the opportunity, after just one year in the House, to become Secretary of the Party's back bench Agriculture Committee. In those days it was an immensely powerful Committee, probably next only to the back bench Finance Committee in importance. We used to meet each week in Committee Room 14, the same room used for the weekly 1922 Committee, because there were very few other rooms big enough to hold all the people who wished to attend.

The Tory Agriculture Committee consisted mostly of landowners and Members with some knowledge of farming. Only a few had any scientific or professional knowledge. It was therefore not all that difficult for me to build up a reputation and get to know the 'Knights of the Shires'.

I was lucky to be patronised by some of the senior backbenchers, particularly by Anthony Hurd (Douglas Hurd's father), a distinguished and highly respected man who had turned down office in Churchill's Government in 1951 and had written for years for *The Times* as their agricultural correspondent. I was also taken under the wing, though to a lesser extent, by John Morrison, the then Chairman of the 1922 Committee (later Lord Margadale and whose sons, Charles and Peter Morrison, subsequently became MPs).

By the early 1960s the Party, led by the many Knights of the Shires, was becoming restive about the apparent lack of understanding of agriculture by the Board of Trade and the Treasury. The problems caused by increasing farm production and the strong farming lobby were running up against the need to encourage industrial exports, particularly to Russia and Eastern Europe, and Britain in turn was required to import more of their produce in exchange, whether barley from Russia or soft fruit from Eastern Europe. The Treasury was also concerned about the ever-increasing cost of farm subsidies.

The Party Whips thought it was a good idea if I spanned the two areas, trade and agriculture. I was therefore appointed to become PPS to Freddie Erroll, who had been appointed President of the Board of Trade in 1961, whilst I also remained Secretary of the Agricultural Committee. This dual role meant that I was developing an insight into the Party when it was undergoing considerable change.

It was as Freddie Erroll's PPS that I had my first real meeting with Ted Heath, in early 1962. I accompanied Freddie, Christopher Soames, Minister of Agriculture, and Ted, Lord Privy Seal with special responsibility for European negotiations, to an important meeting of the European Free Trade Association (EFTA). EFTA's seven member-states (Britain, Austria, Denmark, Norway, Portugal, Sweden and Switzerland) were countries which did not join the European Economic Community in 1957, but which banded together to reduce progressively their tariffs on each other's goods and create a free trade area. The Portuguese, however, were the main stumbling block, wanting to benefit from the removal of other EFTA members' tariffs while retaining their own.

Ted's approach seemed to be to treat the Portuguese in much the same was as de Gaulle had treated him a few months before in the abortive negotiations on British entry to the Common Market. It was rather heavy-handed, with the Portuguese very much on the anvil. But as the hosts they had laid on a magnificent banquet and dance for the end of the meeting. They were desperate to get the meeting concluded and no one knew this better than Ted. We eventually found ourselves arguing the toss about reductions in tariffs on sardines and other trivia.

Ted got his way and the Portuguese were forced to relent rather than lose the banquet. The Trade Minister had a lovely wife and Ted started the dancing with her. After a while, I suggested that I should take over. I thought I was doing him a good turn, but he was enjoying her company too much for that. As I discovered then, and on many other occasions, he appreciates attractive women.

*

From the outset of my Parliamentary career I found myself happier and more comfortable on the liberal, or left, wing of the Party.

I made my maiden speech within a few weeks of entering the House during the debate on a Bill introduced by Reggie Maudling, then President of the Board of Trade, to alleviate local pockets of unemployment. Two small areas in my constituency were suffering 4 per cent unemployment: the average was about $2\frac{1}{2}$ per cent. I argued that it would surely be better to build more ships in the shipyards at Lowestoft rather than pay people the dole – maybe not a very fashionable view by the 1980s, but quite fashionable in those days.

Towards the end of my speech, I set out my own guiding political principle and the one which throughout my career I was to fight to sustain as the Conservative Party's. Describing myself then as 'one of the younger generation which never saw the mass unemployment which affected the country between the wars', I declared that 'I will never work or stand for any party which would support a policy of unemployment. We have a duty not only in economic terms, but also in social and moral terms to make certain of giving every man a fair chance of doing a decent day's work.'

Early on I succeeded in securing a full day's debate on implementing the proposals advanced in the Fleming Report to assist wider entrance to public schools. The idea wasn't at all radical. It was really a precursor of the assisted places scheme, but it still got me into trouble with the Government.

The then Minister for Education, David Eccles, summoned me to his Minister's room at the Commons, a pokey little office up the stairs behind the Speaker's Chair, at the top of the building. Eccles then proceeded to bully me for a long while, saying how the idea was all wrong. Then came his *coup de grâce*: 'Your trouble, Prior, is that you've got a pink conscience.'

Without wishing to be a rebel, or belonging to any group or dining club, as would happen with a new MP nowadays, I was found voting in favour of nearly every liberal issue of the day and taking part in most of the revolts against the Government. Some of us voted against our own Government on a motion to introduce a Peerage Bill, to support Anthony Wedgwood Benn's campaign to be allowed to renounce his hereditary peerage and sit in the Commons. But we did not win because Labour MPs had not turned out in full force. When I tackled some of them on their failure to show up, they replied that they were not all that keen to see Benn back in the Commons.

A Government-sponsored Bill was subsequently introduced to allow Peers to renounce their title and seek election to the Commons. Little did anyone imagine at that time that the main beneficiary of the 1963 Peerage Act would be the Conservative Government itself when it was faced with a leadership crisis later that year. All in all, the Conservative Party has a lot to thank Mr Benn for, and this was not the least of the benefits, which with characteristic misadventure, he managed to confer on us.

In the autumn of 1961, I was called to second the Loyal Address to the Queen's Speech following the opening of the new parliamentary session. This is quite an honour for a young MP, and indicates that the powers-that-be are considering you for future promotion. But I could not resist a touch of irreverence. The charge of nepotism had been levelled against Harold Macmillan: his nephew the Duke of Devonshire was a Minister at the Commonwealth Relations Office, his son-in-law, Julian Amery, was Minister of Air, and he was related to other Ministers through marriage.

As I reminded the House, Ipswich, Suffolk's soccer team, had just won the League Championship for the first time in its history. It was just as the Conservative philosophy dictated – here was the little team, the small man, carrying off the highest honours. And, there was an additional feature – the chairman of the club, Johnny Cobbold, was the Prime Minister's nephew.

*

By 1962 a good deal of the panache and sparkle of the early Macmillan years had evaporated. The right wing of the Party had gone along with Macmillan after Suez because he was astute enough to convince them of his credentials. But he was never a right winger on the economy and since 1959 he had upset the right on a range of foreign policy issues – the attempt to join the EEC and the effect this could have on Australia and New Zealand; his 'Wind of Change' speech in South Africa; and the granting of independence to many former British colonies, particularly in Africa.

The economy was not in good shape. Selwyn Lloyd's second Budget had continued his deflationary policy and there had been industrial unrest as the Government sought to restrain pay. The Liberal revival was at its peak – in March, Eric Lubbock had won Orpington, a previously safe Tory seat. Although we had an overall majority of around 100, the Whips insisted on keeping large numbers of us at the House, which did nothing to improve the Party morale – a lesson which John Wakeham, who as Chief Whip also had to contend with a three-figure majority after 1983, was wise enough to learn.

To add to our unease, too many Ministers did not impress at the dispatch box. Gaitskell, meanwhile, was becoming a very formidable and most impressive Parliamentary performer.

As the summer recess approached, we therefore expected some changes in the Government. But we were not prepared for July's political bloodbath, 'The Night of the Long Knives', as it became known.

Most of the new Members supported the sackings, but it was wishful thinking to expect a new look team to make much difference. And Macmillan's handling of the reshuffle seemed only to provide further evidence that his grip was slipping away.

The butchery during the Night of the Long Knives extended right through the ranks of the Government, even including the Parliamentary Secretary to the Ministry of Agriculture in the Lords – Earl Waldegrave – the father of William Waldegrave. I couldn't see how this knowledge-able and very friendly man could possibly be having a deleterious effect on the Government's image, but Macmillan clearly felt that he had to go.

But, when the Peer was called in to see the Prime Minister, they had a long discussion about their love of trees. Macmillan expressed himself on the beauty of trees at the different seasons of the year – in the spring the bursting of buds, the new green leaves; in summer the shade and quiet dignity of the beechwood, or the solitary park oaks; and then in autumn the rustle of dying leaves, and the colourings of the leaves with the cock pheasants dimly visible as they go to roost; and finally, winter, with the stillness of the wood and the gauntness of the trees. As Waldegrave left the great man's presence he was met at the door by Martin Redmayne, the Chief Whip. 'Am I in or out?' said Waldegrave. 'You're out,' came the reply. 'But you've been offered the Forestry Commission.'

Macmillan's most notable appointments were Reggie Maudling, who at the age of forty-five became Chancellor, and Iain Macleod, who became both Leader of the House and Chairman of the Party. Keith Joseph, at forty-four, became the new Minister for Housing, and Edward Boyle, at only thirty-eight, became Minister for Education. In the en-suing censure debate, Gaitskell was able to make great fun out of a new look Government in which Reggie Manningham-Buller, the Attorney-General, had been promoted to Lord Chancellor with the title Lord Dilhorne of . . . *Towcester* – the emphasis on the word 'Toaster' reduced both sides to unrestrained mirth.

Long after Harold retired I used to see him occasionally at Birch Grove. No one else combines the classical historian, politician and country gentleman in the way he does.

A friend went to interview him at Birch Grove, knocked on the door but could make no one hear. In due course he wandered around to the front of the house and through the window could see Harold up a step ladder looking at some book in his library. Fortified by the knowledge the great man was up and about, he returned to knock on the door. Eventually it was opened by the housekeeper. 'Oh, you've come to see Mr Macmillan, I'm sorry to tell you he's not very well today.' My friend was escorted into a room (presumably, being Macmillan's home, the saloon) and there was Harold, tucked up in a deep armchair, with a rug up to his chin. Characteristically he gave a magnificent interview.

*

Nothing seemed to go right for the Government during 1962 and 1963. In October 1962 William Vassall, an Admiralty civil servant, was imprisoned for eighteen years for spying for the Russians. There were rumours that Vassall had been protected by Tam Galbraith, a former junior Minister at the Admiralty and then at the Scottish Office. Galbraith resigned, but was subsequently exonerated. This incident had not been speedily or well managed by Macmillan, adding further to the impression that he was increasingly out of touch.

It was a miserable and unsettling period to be a back-bencher on the Government side. The breakdown of the EEC negotiations in January 1963 was a further blow. It was the age of the satire boom. BBC Television's *That Was The Week That Was* was all the rage. And it was not long before the lobbies were beginning to buzz with rumour of an even bigger sex scandal, this time involving a War Minister, the Russian attaché and their relationship with a prostitute.

Jack Profumo has paid a terrible penalty for the error of judgment he made when he denied to the House that there was any truth in the rumours. He had been quizzed about them in the middle of the night by a group of his colleagues. It is extraordinary that neither the Solicitor-General, Sir Peter Rawlinson, nor the Chief Whip, Martin Redmayne, nor the Party Chairman, Iain Macleod, were able to fathom the truth: an experienced lawyer (Sir Peter), an army man (Martin), and one of the brightest brains in the Party (Iain) grilled Jack assiduously and declared him as clean as a whistle. Most of us were initially reassured by their findings.

It was hardly surprising that Harold Macmillan should refuse to sack Profumo after this. First, he had been severely criticised for not backing his junior Minister in the Vassall affair; there had been accusations of disloyalty. It is understandable that he did not wish to face now the same accusations – Profumo, after all, was a more senior Minister and a popular one, with many friends in the Cabinet.

Secondly, the attack in the Commons came principally from the Labour MP, George Wigg, who, with hand on heart, used to rise from the front bench below the gangway and profess that his only interest and concern was the good name and reputation of the army, which he loved. George Wigg may have loved the army, but we on the Government backbenches did not love him. We were not going to allow someone whom we regarded as an old reprobate, abetted we felt by the new Leader of the Opposition, Harold Wilson, to destroy the reputation of one of our Ministers and undermine the Government's authority. The Whips were left in no uncertain state about our feelings. If Profumo was implicated he must go, and the quicker the better: but if he was not, we would back him to the hilt.

There is one personal postscript to the Profumo story. Jack had been a great friend of John Hare, the Minister of Labour in Macmillan's Government. They had been such close friends that when Jack disappeared after his resignation, and the Press were scouring the country to find him, they need not have looked any further than Little Blakenham, the Hares' Suffolk home, where John had created one of the most beautiful early summer gardens in England.

Some while before his death in March 1982, John Hare had attempted suicide. At his memorial service, Jack Profumo gave the address: it was beautifully done. How much one admired Jack's courage for the way he had re-built his life. No one was better able than Jack to understand John Hare's courage in facing the public again as he did, after his suicide attempt. Just before Jack Profumo went up to the pulpit, I saw Valerie his wife take his hand and give it a good squeeze. I could sense their feelings and emotions and found myself with very different sensations to those I had experienced nearly twenty years before.

And there was one other feature of that service which I shall always remember. John Hare had not been a good speaker in the Commons, nor a dynamic figure, but he had been respected and trusted by the union leaders. Tucked away at the back of the church at the memorial service was Jack Jones, the former transport and general workers' union leader, and the scourge of any Tory Minister.

*

The Profumo affair was accompanied by rumours of vast indiscretions by other Government Ministers, which it took Lord Denning's best-selling report to quash. To the new intake of Tory MPs, and there were nearly a hundred of us, it was as if those in whom we had placed our faith and hope had suddenly become rotten. It may seem hard to believe now, but that is how it appeared at the time.

There seemed to be a death wish in the Party. It entirely overlaid the economic recovery stimulated by Reggie Maudling's budget. The cynics would say a pre-election boom was being created, but Reggie was aiming for a breakthrough to higher growth and better productivity. We had also sought an accommodation with the unions to involve them in our efforts to improve the economy – together with Ministers and industrialists, leading trade unions were represented on the National Economic Development Council, set up in 1961. In fact we came near to success but, with a general election imminent, political considerations prevented the emergence of sufficient consensus.

I could not see how Harold Macmillan could have stopped the rot by the summer of 1963. It was sad to witness one of our best Prime Ministers this century dragged down in this way. He had tried to give his Government a new look with the Night of the Long Knives, but now the Party had its knife deep into him. Selwyn Lloyd remarked to me around this time that, like all Prime Ministers, Macmillan needed a bisque or two when in difficulty, but all his bisques had been used up, none more so than by his handling of the 1962 reshuffle. His period as Prime Minister was the most prosperous and settled this nation had known since the War and it is some justice that he has come to be recognised as a great elder statesman.

By the summer recess in 1963, I calculated that about half the back-benchers felt that a change of leadership was needed before the new session in the autumn. The difficulty is always to decide on who the new leader should be. The Prime Minister is so powerful that it is not easy for anyone else to become established as an alternative leader. Although Rab Butler was designated Macmillan's deputy, there was a question mark over his suitability as a leader – the qualities which had denied him the premiership in 1957 were still remembered, particularly by the right wing.

There was no sign, however, that Harold Macmillan had any intention of relinquishing the Premiership. Quite the reverse – a few days before the 1963 Party Conference he made clear his intention to lead the Party into the next election. This greatly depressed me. I could not see how we were going to recover under a Leader who I felt had become so played out and discredited.

The grouse moor image was becoming something to avoid, but I have to confess that two days before the Conference I had spent a happy day's grouse shooting on the army ranges at Catterick with my brother-in-law. We joked about the grouse moor image giving eligibility to a Tory leader. Little did I realise what the next few days would bring.

As Jane and I travelled over the Pennines to Blackpool for the Party Conference, we heard the dramatic news that the Prime Minister was in hospital for an emergency prostate operation. The next day came the announcement that he would be tendering his resignation to the Queen. There had been so many extraordinary, bizarre events over the previous year or so that the ramifications took some while to sink in. While I was sad that a great career was to end in this way, the sorrow was tinged with relief. We would, after all, be fighting the election under a new Leader.

The front-runners were Rab Butler, Quintin Hailsham and Reggie Maudling. There began a period of intrigue and rumour the like of which I had not experienced before and have not witnessed since.

Reggie Maudling, who was proving a successful Chancellor, was much better known to the younger Members. Reggie was brilliant, no one could go to the heart of the matter quicker than he. Civil servants who worked with him would describe how quick was his grasp of a subject and how little additional homework he required. When I arrived at Blackpool, I was invited to go to a meeting of Members who were Reggie's supporters. About twenty attended. Our general view was that Reggie probably wouldn't win, and our support would then switch to Rab. But if Reggie could make a great speech at the Conference, matters might just be transformed. We would therefore do our best to engineer a standing ovation. Alas, Reggie did not rise to the occasion, and therefore neither did we. He was not that type of speaker, which was probably greatly to his credit.

Of the front-runners for the Party Leadership, Quintin Hailsham probably had the biggest following. In the eyes of the public and in the Party generally he had been an outstanding Party Chairman and made a very significant contribution to the great election victory of 1959, particularly in restoring morale after the low point of Suez. The insiders, however, had clearly taken a different view and following the election Quintin was given the cold shoulder by Harold Macmillan. He considered himself very badly treated. He was appointed Lord Privy Seal and Minister for Science, instead of being given the senior post he could well have expected. When Alec Home became Foreign Secretary in July 1960, he was very nearly passed over as his successor, to be Leader of the House of Lords. Vigorous representations had to be made on Quintin's behalf to prevent a nonentity being appointed.

By 1963, however, there was a rapprochement between Macmillan and Hailsham. Quintin was appointed Minister with special responsibility for the North-East, in an effort to ease the region's economic and social plight; and he was also appointed Britain's special representative for the Moscow negotiations, which culminated in the Nuclear Test Ban Treaty, signed in August 1963. Quintin's political rehabilitation was further enhanced by the legislation that year enabling peers to renounce their titles. This had come about partly at Quintin's insistence, since his elevation to the Lords on the death of his father had denied him the chance to develop a blossoming career in the Commons.

In October 1963 Quintin therefore threw his cap into the ring immediately, announcing his intention to renounce his peerage. He and his supporters were lobbying hard – some of us felt rather too hard for his own good. Julian Amery rushed to Blackpool and, along with Randolph Churchill, rallied the supporters by making it clear he was Harold's choice. This choice was not altogether surprising, as Harold had calculated that the succession was between Rab and Quintin, and sadly he was determined to stop Rab if he could.

But Quintin's rampant self-publicity worried his friends and sickened his opponents. He had many of the best qualities – a true generosity of mind and spirit – but most of us thought there were sufficient rough seas ahead without having a pilot who would steer straight for the eye of the storm.

I do not think Rab ran an active campaign – if he did it certainly didn't touch me. I sense he was almost fatalistic about it all – that if he was to become Leader it would just happen, and there was not much he could do about it either way. He obviously had very strong support in the Cabinet from Macleod and Powell, amongst others. But he was too remote from the younger Members to have the wholehearted support which he needed and frankly deserved. And for most backbenchers it is easier – and more likely to be profitable for one's prospects – to follow the Leader's line, and Harold had seen to it that Rab had not been in fashion for a number of years.

The process of consulting the Parliamentary Party began at the Party Conference with the area Whips asking their respective Members whom each of us favoured. In due course we were seen individually by the Chief Whip in a room at the Imperial Hotel. Up to that time I had hardly ever ventured into the main Conference hotel. In those days it was regarded with a good deal more reverence than now. There were none of the area cocktail parties and only the very privileged were entertained by Ministers or the Party hierarchy. The bar was the preserve of the political correspondents whose numbers were very small compared with today's contingent from the various media.

It was therefore with some trepidation that I found myself summoned to the Chief Whip's presence. The Whips in those days were very regimental, exercising a military discipline by a combination of helping those who conformed and pouring obloquy on those who dared hold different views. They were stiff, but effective and had a degree of low cunning which had been developed at their public school or in the army.

> 'Who do you favour?'
> 'Reggie Maudling as first choice, but if not, Rab of course.'
> 'Not Quintin?'
> 'No, not Quintin.'
> "Thank you very much.'

Then:

> 'By the way, what about Alec if he decides to stand?'
> 'I don't really know him, and in any case he's in the House of Lords.'
> 'So he's not a runner?'

'Well, we don't know yet, do we?'
'But if he does renounce?'
'I suppose he would be possible.'

My interview with the Chief Whip was over, and I have little doubt that even at that early stage I was put down as an Alec supporter. I cannot understand why Iain Macleod, who after all was Party Chairman, ever allowed the Home bandwagon to gather momentum. It seems that he did not take it seriously, but if Iain, along with the others, had come out firmly against the move early enough, it could have been stopped. Again, if Rab had just let it be known that he would not serve under Alec, it would have sufficed. But by the middle of the following week it had become clear that Alec would be a candidate, and he was unquestionably the one with the fewest black balls against him.

The Macleod forces did not really try to organise themselves until the day before the final choice was made. I was telephoned to say that time was getting short and I should therefore ring the Whips' office. I spoke to Michael Hughes Young, the deputy Chief Whip, to be told that he thought the Queen had already summoned Alec to the Palace. That was that as far as any backbencher was concerned. Even then, had Rab and the others stood firm – not just Iain and Enoch – Alec would have been unable to form an administration. The way would then have been clear for one of the other front-runners.

Although in later years I was to become very close to Ted Heath and to hear much of his thoughts about people and events, he was always very reticent about the way in which the 'Magic Circle' was able to secure the Premiership for Alec. I know that Ted himself was close to Alec, having worked with him in the Foreign Office when Alec was Foreign Secretary and Ted was Lord Privy Seal, conducting the EEC negotiations. Alec liked and respected Ted and was always a great help to him, but it is still surprising that Ted worked hard for Alec to be Prime Minister. Perhaps Ted had recognised that, although his own time had not yet come in 1963, he did stand a chance of being Alec's successor, and that he would be much more out of the running if either Rab Butler or Quintin Hailsham had been chosen. This seems the most likely explanation of Ted's support for Alec, apart from the mutual friendship and respect which exists between them: but it does also reveal Ted in a more scheming guise than I was to associate with him on virtually any other occasion.

Although I greatly respected Alec Home and believe he did a fantastic job in restoring the Party after the humiliations of that 1963 summer, I was deeply sad that once more Rab Butler had been unsuccessful. Without doubt he must have been the most able politician and statesman never to become Prime Minister. His intellectual quality, the way he handled the House of Commons, his humanity and ability to convey compassion and understanding had helped enormously to change the public perception of Conservatives after our shattering defeat in 1945. He was certainly indiscreet, he may have been egotistical, but he gave great encouragement to me as a young backbencher and later as a Cabinet Minister.

The opening of the new, 1963–64 session of Parliament was postponed to give Alec time to fight the by-election in Kinross and West Perthshire. Once in the Commons he courageously faced the taunts of the Opposition. They were after his blood, scenting that an easy victory was now in their grasp. Alec made a desperately shaky start but the House always respects an honest and decent man.

Alec was not well known in the country. To the initial strain of coming back to a rumbustious and excitable House of Commons was added the need to get better known in the country. A series of tours were organised, particularly to marginal seats. One of these meant a foray through Norfolk and Suffolk and took in the attractive little town of Bungay in my constituency, and just inside Suffolk. A wagon was drawn up near the old Butter Cross, where in previous generations local farmers had sold their butter and other produce. A large crowd waited patiently for the inevitably late arrival of their new Prime Minister. In due course he did arrive, only to announce how pleased he was to be back in *Norfolk*. The groan from the crowd was audible enough for me to know I had a hard fight ahead of me when the election was called.

But it was clear that in other ways many people were coming to trust and respect Alec. He had renounced his ancient earldom and was fighting for his, and for their, political beliefs. And it nearly came off. Before many months were out Labour MPs were beginning to be a little more doubtful about their victory and were finding by early 1964 that the 14th Earl was becoming more effective as 'the 14th Mr Wilson', as Alec dubbed him, began to falter.

*

Alec Home let the Parliament run its full term. In the 1964 election, held on October 15, Labour won 317 seats, giving them a slender majority of 4 over all other parties. We won 304, better than had been expected, and the Liberals won 9.

Much to my surprise I held Lowestoft and, despite the national swing to Labour, my own majority had almost doubled to 2,704. I had held on against the odds when many former colleagues had lost. Returning to the Commons, this time to the Opposition benches, I began for the first time to realise that I might have a political career ahead of me.

Now we really did have to sit down and plan together for there were four children – our youngest, Jeremy, was born in 1962, our oldest, David, was eight years old – somehow the family had to be fitted in to the hurly-burly of political life at the top as well as the grass roots.

I was soon appointed junior front bench spokesman on Agriculture, and shortly afterwards became Party Vice-Chairman at Central Office, with responsibility for the candidates' list – ironic when I recalled my own experience before the 1959 election.

It was a task I enjoyed very much and I was in a position to have some influence over the Party's future candidates. But the extent of my influence was limited because the candidates' list was very long, and it would only be possible to permit a limited number of new entrants. The problem was always to try to reduce the list of deadbeats who were never going to be selected for even the most hopeless seat, but just liked to be able to say they were on the list.

I saw a good deal of candidates who were expecting to be Members and who had been on the list for some time. One of them arrived to see me with a rather languorous and droopy moustache. I could not believe that any selection committee of a safe Tory seat would ever adopt him looking like that. I made it plain that his chances would be greatly enhanced if he shaved it off.

I was to rue the day I gave him such sound advice. He took it and in 1974 entered the House as the Member for the rock solid Tory seat of Reigate. This was probably the only time that George Gardiner took my advice throughout his political career. He turned out to be an active organiser of the right wing in the House and I seemed to be his main target.

By the summer of 1965 another general election seemed imminent, as Labour would seek to increase their majority from four to a more manageable margin. Unless we could galvanise ourselves, we would face a hammering at the polls – Harold Wilson was now knocking Alec around twice a week at Prime Minister's Question Time, and we were trailing well behind in the opinion polls.

Alec Home had nearly pulled off a miracle in the 1964 October election. But leaders of the Conservative Party are loved only when they win. Alec had lost once, and looked like losing again. That was enough for most of us. We tended to overlook the inconvenient fact that whoever led the Party would face a Labour Party on the up, skilfully led by Harold Wilson and hungry to retain power. 'Thirteen wasted years' and the '£800 million balance of payments deficit' had been crosses which Alec had had to bear, and so also would any successor.

In July, *The Times*' headline proclaimed 'Sir A. Home to remain at the helm.' But most Tory MPs were already expecting that Alec would go. I was particularly amused when my Charterhouse contemporary, William Rees-Mogg entered the debate on the leadership, to some effect. On 18 July the *Sunday Times* published an article by William entitled 'The Right Moment to Change'. He argued that Alec had played a good 'captain's innings' and ought now to make a dignified exit – it was an appropriate metaphor from someone who had spent his schooldays umpiring or analysing cricket from the boundary edge.

I shall always believe that Alec Home finally decided to quit after a public opinion poll showed that most people thought Harold Wilson was the more sincere of the leaders.

A few days later, after a poor performance in the House, Alec announced his decision to quit at a regular Thursday evening meeting of the 1922 Committee.

It was perhaps fitting that it fell to one of the old school, Sir William Anstruther-Gray, to preside as Chairman on this occasion and thus herald the end of an era. Sir William had seemed a rather remote figure to the newer generation of Tory backbenchers – he had once talked of the Conservative Party's unique ability 'to push the ship of State uphill'. Characteristically, those who had most avidly been calling for Alec to go were now amongst those to look most shocked. Most of us, I suspect, were glad that the resignation had come, though I recall Greville Howard, the Member for St Ives, saying how shocking the whole business had been and how disgraceful it was that some Members had been plotting against the Leader. It was a day the Party would live to regret, he thundered to his 1922 colleagues. Before very long there were a number who would agree with him.

Alec had only come to the premiership in circumstances of pressure, duty and labyrinthine obscurity. 1963 had marked the end of the selection process dubbed the 'Magic Circle' whereby the Leader had emerged following a series of secret consultations amongst the leading figures in the Party. After the 1964 general election Alec agreed to set up a review of the method of selecting the Party Leader. Humphry Berkeley suggested that the selection should be made by a straight vote of MPs. In February 1965 the new system was adopted. Under the new procedure, on the first ballot the winner needed an overall majority of 15 per cent of those voting. If no one achieved this, there would be a second ballot, in which a bare majority would suffice. Having done the deed, Humphry left to join the Labour Party, and now resides with the Social Democrats, maintaining stoutly that his politics have never changed, it is just that the Parties have altered.

Seldom have I known a more unpopular Member than Humphry, yet the consequences of his efforts will be felt when most of us have been long forgotten. Not only did he play a leading part in bringing about the new method for electing a Tory Leader, he also introduced a Private Members Bill to change the law on homosexuality. For his pains he was vilified by a group of old Tory backbenchers, both in public and through a campaign of letters. His speech on the Second Reading of his Bill was one of the best and most moving I heard in all my days in the House. Although he was defeated in the 1966 general election, he had won the argument. Eventually in 1967, this long overdue liberal, reforming measure was enacted.

The three frontrunners to succeed Alec appeared to be Reggie Maudling, Iain Macleod and Edward Heath, but almost immediately Iain decided not to run. Enoch Powell then came in with a challenge from the right, so it was his name that went forward with Heath's and Maudling's.

Iain could not have won, since he had lost the support of the centre by not agreeing to serve under Alec in October 1963, and the right wing had always distrusted him since his time as Colonial Secretary. 'Too clever by half' was Bobbity Salisbury's description – grossly unfair, revealing more about its author than about Iain. But, like many childish remarks in politics, it stuck.

Iain decided to support Reggie, but Reggie had shown little interest in Opposition. We saw little of him in the House. Although he was angry with Wilson for the way he exploited the £800 million deficit, and for the subsequent run on the pound which he felt Wilson's constant harping on the £800 million deficit helped to cause, he just was not interested in petty opposition and opposing just for the sake of it.

Reggie was keen to be the new Leader but only if he could obtain it without too much hard work or personal canvassing. He left his campaign to his supporters and hoped that Iain's support would see him through.

Ted Heath's support was more widely based than Reggie's. Ted had won respect as Chief Whip during the Suez crisis and later when he led Britain's first attempt to join the EEC, and it was generally reckoned that privately Alec was backing him.

Enoch Powell attracted support from the right, but he was regarded as too much of a maverick by many, and his refusal to serve Alec in 1963 was held against him as it was against Iain Macleod.

In my role as Vice-Chairman of the Party organisation it would have been inappropriate to take an active role in the campaign, but I told the few who were interested of my choice. While most of the Parliamentary candidates were probably in favour of Ted, they were more 'Alec must go' than they were for anyone in particular taking his place. In the event, Ted polled 150 votes, Reggie 133 and Enoch 15. Reggie instantly withdrew in favour of Ted.

Reggie was profoundly shocked by the result, but chiefly because at the last minute Iain and his close supporters swapped sides and voted for

Ted Heath. Years after, Reggie, who became a great personal friend, told me that Iain had promised support and withdrew it without giving any reason.

I have no doubt that Iain's judgment was correct. I had supported Reggie in 1963, but decided to vote for Ted in '65. Reggie was a very agreeable man, and I was very fond of him, but he wasn't the stuff of which Prime Ministers are made. I think he recognised that too in the end.

At times he was lazy, not just over work or perhaps a speech in the House which he found a bore, but also lazy in picking his friends and making certain they were as basically honest and decent as he was himself. This lack of care and his obvious need of income was to mar a highly successful political career.

Ted won chiefly in July 1965 because of the way he had led our front bench team on the Finance Bill. Jim Callaghan's first and second budgets, in November 1964 and April 1965, introduced Corporation Tax, extended Capital Gains Tax and put up taxes generally. They had thus given us our first chance to hit back hard in Opposition. Ted took his chance to lead the assault.

It is curious how history has a habit of repeating itself. Some nine years later when the Party again found itself in Opposition, and was looking for a new Leader, someone who was pugnacious and determined to press home the political attack, it was Margaret Thatcher who took her chance. In 1974 the target was Denis Healey's first budget and Finance Bill. She was not even in charge of the Tory finance team, which was led by Robert Carr, but she did enough, as Ted did in his day, to convince the Party that she had the right qualities to become Leader.

Ted's handling of the abortive Common Market negotiations during 1962 and 1963 had also brought him to the notice of a wider audience – despite de Gaulle's eventual 'Non' to British entry, Ted's own performance was impressive.

He seemed the one man who was not afraid to take the attack to the enemy: here was the man we needed in Opposition to rebuild the Party for the new era, the Grammar School boy to replace the Old Etonian, the man to take on Wilson.

CHAPTER THREE

A NEW VISION

The day after Ted Heath became Leader, Willie Whitelaw, then our Chief Whip, phoned me at Conservative Central Office. 'Could you come and see the Leader at once?' It had never entered my mind that I should change my job. I had only been a Vice-Chairman of the Party, installed in Smith Square, for a few months. I had had very little to do with Ted.

I was ushered in to see him. The Leader of the Opposition had a terrible office in those days, a dark and sombre room with a big rec-tangular table at which the Shadow Cabinet used to meet and at which the Leader did all his work.

'Willie says you have to be my Parliamentary Private Secretary. He says I know nothing about farming or the rural constituencies, and your experience at Central Office will help. You've got to help me keep in touch with grass roots feeling and get me into the smoking room as much as you can.'

That was my introduction and my invitation. It was a style I was to grow accustomed to over the years – at times brusqueness amounting to rudeness, yet also the shyness of an introvert; and sometimes a reaction of great frustration that he could not always get through to people.

And yet there was nothing those of us who came to work closely with Ted would not do for him. He had quality and vision and, even if he never dared to show it, he had a softer side which we understood. This enabled us to share things with him that more than compensated for some of the supposed defects which others who never really knew him were always quick to spot. There were few dry eyes round the table at his Government's final Cabinet after the February 1974 election defeat, and I'm told there were even fewer amongst the Number Ten secretaries, the 'garden room girls', when Ted left Downing Street.

By the time of the Party Conference at Brighton in October 1965 we were trailing again in the opinion polls.

Ted's popularity was dropping fast. The Party was badly split on Rhodesia and it took all of Alec's prestige and statesmanship to get us through a difficult debate. The mood was sour. The situation was not improved by Harold Wilson rushing off to Balmoral to see the Queen, stealing the headlines during our Conference. Ted was furious, but I remember he couldn't resist saying, with a wry smile, 'Good Lord, no one's done this kind of thing since Harold Macmillan.'

Ted and Harold really hated each other at that time. There was a feeling of animosity and personal antipathy rarely experienced between the two main party Leaders. Ted, straightforward, honourable, honest and dogged; Harold, who seemed wily, insincere, devious and two-faced. It took a number of years for each of them to see the good qualities of the other. Later Harold was always the more generous of the two.

After the Conference we knuckled down to the tiring business of countryside tours to publicise and popularise the Leader, knowing that a general election could not be more than a matter of months away. These tours were a nightmare – speeches and handouts to be prepared, time-tables to be kept to, instant reaction to Government statements and any other events. We knew we couldn't be far from an election. But there was little time for reflection, nor time for a deliberate build up.

As our position worsened, so the criticism grew. On these occasions the Leader bears the brunt. There were many complaints about Ted's television performances; he appeared wooden, unconvincing – nothing like his performance during the EEC negotiations – and his speeches became humourless and monotonous.

The more the criticism grew, the harder it became to get him to relax. Experts were called in to give coaching. Today's generation of politicians have been brought up on television, but twenty years ago it was a new and mysterious experience, which many found difficult to master. But Ted was coached and briefed so hard before each TV performance that one felt he was always trying to remember what he had been told to do and say, and that he had no contact at all with the interviewer or the viewer. It seems strange now as one sees Ted's entertaining and relaxed TV performances to recall that this was once a source of much criticism of him.

In late January 1966, a by-election was held in Hull North, a marginal Labour seat won from the Tories in the October 1964 election. If Labour held it, they would undoubtedly call a general election. It was a notable campaign. Labour's Minister of Transport, Barbara Castle, announced the building of the Humber Bridge, which seemed to be a blatant piece of political window-dressing. The bridge took years to build and at vast cost.

On our side the idea had got round that canvassing was a matter of a lot of good-looking young girls accompanying the candidate, who ran from one house to the next. This, so it was claimed, had been the secret of Charlie Morrison's win at Devizes in 1964 and would do the trick for Toby Jessel, our candidate at Hull North. Peter Walker was the chief instigator, but for my part I didn't think it would make much of an impact amongst the fishing fraternity of Hull.

My own view of canvassing was rather more limited. If you can find some really good talkers, spend a bit of time with them, and with any luck they will do much of the work for you. Other than that it is a matter of finding out where your supporters are so that you can get them out on the day.

Jane and I watched the result on television with Ted in his flat at the Albany. It was a depressing night. Labour held the seat with a majority of 5,351, and a swing away from us of 4.5 per cent. We knew we would be facing an election at once and we were staring defeat in the face.

The preparation for Ted's speeches was in the capable hands of John MacGregor and Michael Wolff. John was Ted's political secretary, a man of outstanding promise, full of ideas and very hard-working. His promotion to the Cabinet, as Chief Secretary to the Treasury, in September 1985 was fully deserved. Michael was much more phlegmatic, at times a little morose, but in my book one of the outstanding men of his generation. His advice was always sound, his writing good: he had bottom and bottle. His sudden death in 1976 was a tragedy.

With these two I formed the speech-writing team, drawing in others as required and consulting the member of the Shadow Cabinet responsible for each particular area of policy. There wasn't time for elaborate policy-making. Although Alec had set up Policy Groups, which Ted had taken over, they had had no time to report.

I don't think it mattered what the policy was; we were in a 'no win' situation. It was a matter of damage limitation. Cecil King, then Chairman of Mirror Newspapers, told Ted that it could be a Labour landslide: he would do well to restrict Labour to a majority of no more than 100. The opinion polls showed Labour ahead by about 8 or 9 per cent and only narrowed slightly as polling day approached.

We heard a lot throughout the 1966 campaign about Harold Wilson's 'white heat of the new technological revolution'. Labour's National Plan was forecasting a planned growth of 4 per cent per year, the unions were co-operating well with the Government – in other words it seemed that the Socialist utopia was just round the corner. We bashed away. Ted shone at the daily press conferences, but 'give them a chance' and 'time for a change' after the 'thirteen wasted years' were powerful persuaders. Our advice to Ted was to build a reputation for telling people the truth, which would come in useful as Labour began to fail in Government.

Labour won 363 seats, which gave them an overall majority of 96. We were reduced to 253 seats, while the Liberals had increased their number to 12. I managed to hold on to Lowestoft by the skin of my teeth – my majority was down to 358.

It was a massive defeat for us, but it could have been much worse. Ted had fought a good campaign. He had done himself a lot of good with the political correspondents who followed him round. They stood and clapped him at his last news conference. He had proved that he had the quality which the British love above all else – how to be a good loser. It was unfortunate that he could not maintain this reputation some years later.

*

I had survived the Party's defeat at the polls, and my own political career really began to take off. My appointment nine months earlier as Parliamentary Private Secretary to the Leader of the Opposition was clearly a marvellous opportunity. I was now involved in all the Leader's consultations, in all the squabbles and the handling of the 'prima donnas', which are part and parcel of party politics, and which make it so difficult and yet so fascinating.

Ted's first task after the election defeat was to form a new Shadow Cabinet. The election had been imminent from the moment he had become Leader and there had therefore been no opportunity to introduce new faces. But with a full Parliament now ahead of us, it was time to rebuild.

This was a task primarily for Ted and his Chief Whip, Willie Whitelaw. My advice was asked on only one aspect. We still thought in terms of appointing a 'statutory woman'. 'Who should she be?' asked Ted. 'Margaret Thatcher,' was my immediate reply. There was a long silence. 'Yes,' he said, 'Willie agrees she's much the most able, but he says once she's there we'll never be able to get rid of her. So we both think it's got to be Mervyn Pike.'

With Heath, Macleod, Maudling and Quintin Hogg as the four main spokesmen for the party from the mid-1960s, there was never much chance that we should forget the great liberal-Tory revival which Rab Butler had fashioned in the 1940s and 1950s, and which Harold Macmillan had carried forward as Prime Minister. The emphasis on full employment, on fairness, on the compassionate society, placed our policies firmly in the middle ground of the political debate.

I did query one other appointment – Enoch Powell. It wasn't that I regarded him as an out-and-out right winger: he was on the right, but in those days there wasn't any great distinction between right and left wings in the Party. Nor did he have a particular group of followers. But he was causing trouble on Rhodesia, and had proved idiosyncratic as Defence spokesman – at the 1965 Party Conference his speech questioned the value of retaining our forces East of Suez, and therefore appeared to be counter to Party policy at the time. Enoch's defence strategy emphasised Britain's position as a European power.

Enoch had always been a very uncomfortable colleague. I could not see him fitting in with any team and warned Ted against him. He was always likely to resign over something. He had quit the Treasury with Thorneycroft in 1958 and then refused to serve with Alec in 1963. There would always be some difficulty with Enoch: he was an awkward character. But the view was that he was too dangerous to leave out. I doubt, however, if a row then would have led to the intense acrimony and disruption which came a few years later with Enoch's speech on immigration.

Another problem for Ted was that he and the Party Chairman, Edward du Cann, could not stand each other. Every time Ted seemed to be near to dismissing Edward, there would be a leak in the press that Edward was about to be sacked. So Ted would back off. This went on for months and didn't help Ted's position with the Party Organisation and the grandees on the voluntary side with which he had a prickly relationship.

There was a paradox about Ted and the Party. He was a left of centre Tory, yet he had the reputation of being extremely tough and determined to the point of obstinacy. What dogged him with a lot of the older backbenchers was the way he had pushed through the abolition of Resale Price Maintenance, enabling manufacturers to dictate the price at which their goods were sold in the shops. Ted saw this reform as a means of increasing competition and giving consumers a better deal. But his stand on the issue was an enormous handicap for him as far as many in the Party were concerned, since they reckoned that he was anti-small business and against small shopkeepers, who obviously could not afford to bring down their prices sufficiently to compete with the large chains buying and selling in enormous quantities. The issue kept coming up in the Party – it was impossible to attend a single gathering for about two years after the 1964 election without it being raised.

Nor did Ted's position on the other controversial issues of the day help endear him to many in the Party. He was liberal on race and on Rhodesia – it was extraordinarily difficult to handle the Rhodesian problem with the Party split all ways through no fault of Ted's. In 1969 his backing for sending the troops into Ulster caused a big row at that year's Party Conference, because of the Party's long-standing links with the Unionist majority. Others were antagonised by Ted's determination that Britain should join the European Community.

There were also a number of enemies he had made, particularly during his time as Chief Whip. People like Airey Neave were sworn enemies from day one of Ted becoming Leader. And if, like Ted, you're a man who doesn't make friends easily, you have to be successful. If you're successful, everything's all right; but, if you're not, they're after your blood very quickly.

*

We knew we had a whole Parliament ahead of us in Opposition. There would be time to plan ahead and bring forward fresh policies. All of us were determined to create a policy for a great reforming administration.

We felt that the country was suffering from a malaise which derived from its declining economic performance, and we believed that this decline was due to a failure to invest, a reluctance to work harder for a rising standard of living and an anachronistic reliance on our preferential trading links with an Empire which we had deliberately dissolved.

Ted Heath had several prescriptions for these ailments. First, he was in favour of Government intervention to modernise the country's basic infrastructure; and second, he felt that he could release human motivation by freeing the country of controls, abolishing restrictive practices whether by unions or management, reducing taxation and opening up new markets, particularly in Europe. His whole approach was inspired by his desire to create a confident, happy, open and liberal democracy.

This was a vision which inspired us all, but in opposition any party has to contend with the day-to-day pressures, dictated by the course of events. There is the dilemma – to go for the grand solution, or to concentrate more on opposing all that the Government of the day does and says.

*

In July 1966, within a few months of Labour's crushing election victory, a serious economic and balance of payments crisis forced Harold Wilson's Government to introduce an emergency package of deflationary and restrictive measures. Government spending was cut by £250 million, taxes increased by £176 million, and a six-month freeze was imposed on prices and incomes and given statutory backing.

Our reaction to the prices and incomes policy was divided. The more theoretical, right wing economists were adamant that this was against all economic logic and should be opposed at every stage: it was a gross interference with market forces and would be bound to fail. Others, particularly those who who had experience of Government, did not like the statutory, all-embracing power of the new Act, but they realised that some means of stopping the wage/price spiral was necessary and would have to be found.

Reggie Maudling felt that removing the obstacles to growth was unlikely to be sufficient in itself to create a better balance in the economy, and that therefore an incomes policy would have to be part of Tory policy. He hoped that it would not need to be a statutory policy, but based on as much consensus as possible through the National Economic Development Council, and through education and exhortation. Keith

Joseph was not a very powerful member of the Shadow Cabinet, but he was always very keen on the educational side of an incomes policy – that you tried to educate and persuade people of the dangers of inflation.

Iain Macleod had just taken over as Shadow Chancellor and, ever a politician to his fingertips, simply could not see how he could hold the Party together if we came out in support of an incomes policy. Ted saw the same political problem. He became very anti-incomes policy, almost going so far as to recommend employers to pay no attention to the Government's legislation, despite the fact that it was the law of the land.

We therefore became committed against statutory controls over prices and incomes. For good measure we pledged that we would sweep away not only the Prices and Incomes Board, but also Labour's new Industrial Re-organisation Corporation, which was likewise seen as gross interference in the operation of the market. The argument was seductively simple – all we had to do was to free the economy from the restraints imposed by Socialism and trade union power and all the other paraphernalia of Government intervention would become unnecessary.

I had no experience of Government and went along with the theory. But with hindsight, it is clear that we were already back onto the old roller-coaster of party politics: one party in Government becomes committed to a particular course of action, and this immediately results in the Opposition becoming equally committed to the opposite point of view. The result is unstable government as the policies chop and change, and a reluctance by industry to take the long-term investment decisions which require a degree of consensus between a country's main political parties. The irony of our posture in the late 1960s is that Ted was so determined to remove the constraints on Britain's growth, yet this form of adversarial politics was probably the biggest constraint of all and the one which Ted himself came to deplore.

A further classic example of our outright opposition to the Government was prompted by Labour's devaluation of the £ sterling in November 1967. I could not agree with Ted on this issue. I felt at the time, and much more so since, that Ted made too much of the sanctity of the exchange rate. He appeared to hold an absolute belief, an almost religious conviction, that the £ sterling should not be moved under any circumstances. His strength of feeling motivated him to deliver a furious attack against Harold Wilson who had glibly announced that devaluation made no difference to the £ in your pocket or purse.

Ted's argument was based on the belief that if the right economic measures were taken the £ sterling would automatically hold its own. Enoch Powell's support for a floating £ sterling only helped strengthen Ted's commitment to a fixed parity. None of us appreciated then the degree to which money would subsequently become footloose and move in vast quantities from one country to another, reflecting a combination of sentiment and relative interest rates. When the pressure of events brought the Conservative Government to float the pound in June 1972 – a policy which Ted had fought so hard to avoid – Tony Barber told me that had we tried to protect our parity, we could have lost all our gold and dollar reserves in about three days' trading. It would be a much shorter period today

*

After the 1967 devaluation we enjoyed a spectacular lead in the opinion polls, lasting throughout 1968, and won some resounding by-election victories.

Perhaps one of the less attractive features of the party political battle is that no one ever loses an opportunity to embarrass the other side, even though the longer-term consequences might not be best for the country. On March 14 1968 the Commons was sitting late, debating the Labour Government's Transport Bill. At about midnight Dick Crossman, the Leader of the House, asked me if I could find Ted as he had a message for him. He wanted Ted to know that Roy Jenkins, who had succeeded Jim Callaghan as Chancellor, would make a statement to the House the next morning about exchange control policy.

An international financial crisis had blown up, which necessitated a meeting of the Privy Council that evening. Within an hour, various rumours were sweeping through the Commons and there were speeches in the Chamber about the absurdity of continuing to debate a Transport Bill whilst the City was in chaos. In the end Jenkins was prevailed upon to make his statement at 2 am.

A few of us were sitting in Ted's room, discussing how he should reply to the Jenkins statement, when in rushed Robin Maxwell Hyslop, the Member for Tiverton: 'I've just heard George Brown tell Ray Gunter that he's resigned and will never serve under that bloody little man again.'

I was sent out to check the story. The best people to ask are always the policemen, particularly those stationed in the corridor behind the Speaker's Chair.

'Is George Brown resigning?'

'I don't know, sir, but I've just heard him tell Ray Gunter he'll never serve under that bloody little man again.'

Ted's advice was to make certain that everyone knew so that this time George Brown could not go back on his threat. I telephoned members of the lobby – most had gone home, expecting a quiet night, but a few others were already sniffing round the story. I spoke to the ubiquitous

Harold Davies, my counterpart as Harold Wilson's PPS and a good friend of mine. Was it true about George? He wasn't certain, George was now deep in his cups and not making any sense. I suspect that not for the first time Harold and Roy had taken a decision without consulting George, and this had proved too much.

George Brown did resign. Ray Gunter was to go within a few weeks. The Labour Government had thus lost two of its outstanding characters. For all George's unpredictability and bullying attitude on occasion, he was a patriot whose heart was very much in the right place. He probably did drink too much at times, he may have kissed one or two elegant ladies rather too fulsomely, he may even have slapped a bottom or two, but he did his job conscientiously and whilst he was a leading member in a Labour Cabinet the country felt reassured.

In this episode, there is no doubt that we had succeeded in our intention to see the Labour Party slip up on its own banana skin, but of course the implications for the country of Labour's incipient schism was far from amusing.

Ray Gunter was a straight man who believed passionately in the trade union movement, but who became disillusioned with the way that many of its leaders behaved. He felt they were letting down the Labour movement, and felt the same about many of his Cabinet colleagues.

We should have paid more attention to Gunter's views. His resignation began a drift away from the Labour Party for a man whose whole life and career had been built round the Christian Brotherhood of Man. He was one of the first leading Labour politicians to see what was happening to the Labour movement. Many subsequently reached similar conclusions, but unhappily Ray was ahead of his time and received only obloquy for his beliefs. Ray Gunter's departure brought Barbara Castle to the old Ministry of Labour, then re-christened the Ministry of Employment and Productivity.

*

Within a matter of weeks the spotlight moved on to one of the key elements in Ted Heath's programme of reform – the reform of bad industrial practices. This was to reveal how a Government could be pushed, by a combination of events and the Opposition, to produce a policy which ran counter both to its own basic beliefs, and to the views of a large part of its active supporters.

The public mood was increasingly against the unions. The economy was suffering a range of 'wild cat', unofficial strikes, particularly in the car industry. While there was strong public support for prices and incomes policy; our incomes policy was itself one of the main causes of the strikes. Everyone was in favour of an incomes policy but for someone else, not themselves.

In April 1968 we published our proposals to curb union power in 'Fair Deal at Work'. Besides the immediate, popular appeal, they appeared to provide an answer to the question of how we intended to prevent wage and price inflation without a statutory prices and incomes policy – we would tackle the unions' monopoly power and thus restore a better balance in wage bargaining.

The Labour Government realised that they were acutely vulnerable on the unions, a fear reinforced two months later with the publication of the report of the Royal Commission on trade unions and employers' organisations, chaired by Lord Donovan. Barbara Castle, a dynamic and strong Minister, decided she had to do something, and in January 1969 she published a White Paper 'In Place of Strife'. While accepting many of Donovan's recommendations for union reform, the White Paper also proposed conferring certain discretionary powers on the Secretary of State.

It was these proposed powers which provoked bitter opposition from the unions. The Secretary of State would have the power, on pain of fines, to require a union to hold a ballot before calling an official strike which would involve a serious threat to the economy or public interest; to order a 'conciliation pause' of up to twenty eight days in strikes which were unconstitutional (in breach of collective agreements), or where adequate discussion had not taken place; and to make orders to enforce recommendations on inter-union disputes.

It was clear that these proposals were unacceptable and deeply wounding to the trade union leaders and to many Labour backbenchers. A long and bitter struggle was in prospect. It was there that I think we made a major tactical error. We should have realised that the prize of a united approach would have done wonders for the country and still left the Labour Party seething with discontent. I believe that Ted and Iain Macleod should have spotted our opportunity and supported the Castle proposals.

Once more, however, we sought to maximise our own short-term political advantage. This let Labour off the hook. Harold Wilson was able to tell the unions they would get far worse from the Tories: if they did not like Barbara's proposals they had better come up with something themselves which would be sufficiently convincing to the public. Hence the TUC's special Croydon conference and Wilson's announcement afterwards that he had, after all, secured a 'copper-bottomed guarantee' from the unions.

Jim Callaghan played an active part throughout the whole affair. Whilst staying in the Cabinet, he snubbed any notion of collective Cabinet responsibility and let it be known that he was totally against his own Government's proposed legislative curbs. He was the Labour Party's Treasurer at the time and no doubt conscious of the need for the unions' political funds. He made clear his opposition to any legislative change. It couldn't work: it would lead to anarchy. The only way was by co-operation and understanding and that, he declared, was something the Tories would never understand.

Some ten years later Britain endured the 'Winter of Discontent' when Jim Callaghan was Prime Minister. The hospitals were picketed, the dead were not buried and lorry drivers decided who would get supplies. This time Callaghan was facing the rap. He made a number of strong speeches, but could not bring himself to advocate even a mild change in the law. On this occasion, it was Callaghan who let slip an opportunity, because we would have agreed on limited union reforms. Some of my colleagues would have wished for more, but as our front bench spokesman I could have held the line at that stage. Perhaps it was fitting that Callaghan should lose an election largely as a result of the abuse of union power. Wilson and Castle were apparently not too upset.

*

Membership of the European Community was so fundamental to Ted Heath's vision of the future that, when Harold Wilson did one of his most remarkable political somersaults and applied for British membership in 1967, Ted readily backed Labour's attempt.

Ted saw British membership as providing us with markets which would revitalise our own industrial effort, with the consequent income necessary to sustain rising standards of living. He also saw Europe as an essential platform from which Britain could once more exercise its influence in the affairs of the world.

My role in preparing for Britain's entry into Europe – Ted was determined that even if Harold should fail he would one day succeed – was to chair the policy group on the reform of the system of agriculture support. I kept in close touch with many organisations, including the National Farmers Union and the Country Landowners Association. To my delight the reform of agricultural support was one of the main planks in the 1970 election campaign.

Reform would have been necessary, even without our plan to join the European Community. The system of support for farmers, through 'deficiency payments', which had served the country well since the early 1950s was coming under increasing strain. The basic change needed was for the Government to cease subsidising the farmers, which had been done to protect them against competition from imported cheap food.

The intention of the new scheme which we proposed was gradually to replace these subsidies which cost the Exchequer £250 million a year, and to substitute instead a system of tariffs on imported food. Surprisingly the farmers, who are naturally conservative by nature and suspicious of any change, were not at all unhappy about our proposed new policy. The scheme we proposed was also much more in line with the European Community's system of agricultural support embodied in its Common Agricultural Policy.

*

Ted Heath's absolute conviction that Britain's future lay with Europe did not diminish his vision of the special role which Britain should play in the world. He fully accepted the responsibilities thrust on Britain by the legacy of the Empire, a view characterised by his approach on defence and race.

Ted strongly opposed the Labour Government's decision, announced in January 1968, to withdraw British forces from East of Suez by 1972. He believed that some forces could have been retained in the Persian Gulf to support, by acting in full co-operation with, the friendly states in the area. He also envisaged British forces based in Singapore and actingly jointly with forces from Australia, New Zealand and Singapore. A British presence was important strategically, to help protect our trading interests, create stability and give confidence to Britain's allies.

Ted's views on the need for a British presence East of Suez gave him, unusually, common cause with the Tory Party's right wing. Generally the right wing had more respect for Enoch Powell, but he appeared to favour British withdrawal from East of Suez. Ted and Enoch, however, were soon to call on their more traditional forces of support in the Party when they clashed on the issue of race.

Race had raised its head at the 1964 election. An openly racialist campaign, supporting the Conservative, Peter Griffiths, had defeated Patrick Gordon-Walker at Smethwick. When the new Parliament assembled, this led to Wilson calling Griffiths a Parliamentary leper.

We had introduced the first control over Commonwealth immigrants in 1962. Labour pledged its repeal, but in 1965 and again in February 1968 they further tightened the controls. However, large numbers of immigrants continued to enter the country: over 63,000 in 1963; 49,000 in 1964; 51,000 in 1965; 46,000 in 1966; 61,000 in 1967.

In April 1968 Enoch Powell decided to make his move. The situation gave the right a chance to combine their prejudice with political opportunism – they argued that we would be on to a sure election-winner if blacks could be stopped from coming, and preferably those already here could be sent home; they argued that Labour could not hope to emulate this approach. The fact that this policy was bound to create great fear in the black immigrant community, and to stir up both fear and prejudice in poor white areas, was not something to deter the unscrupulous right.

It was just this nasty, authoritarian element on the right that made many people fear the Tory Party. It was equally true that the Party under Ted Heath's leadership would have no part in it.

Our policy on immigration was not easy to explain. We had accepted that too many immigrants were entering the country. The concern about jobs aggravated people's worries – unemployment had increased, although it was far lower than the levels which were to prevail in the 1970s and 1980s. We also recognised that we had to deal with the social consequences of immigration in particular urban areas.

A series of discussions had begun in Shadow Cabinet, led by our Home Affairs spokesman, Quintin Hogg, with Ted, Iain Macleod and Edward Boyle, whose constituency of Birmingham Handsworth was one of the most affected, playing a major role. The purpose was to try to achieve a sensible position which we could hold against the right wing's campaign. This was reaching a crescendo by 1968, with the right wing press and Enoch very much in the van. The extreme right had been putting on a lot of pressure in the Party, particularly in the constituencies – all the talk from the constituencies was on the need for tougher action against immigration.

At one of the Wednesday meetings of the Shadow Cabinet a long, and not very productive, discussion took place. Powell was very restive and pushing for much tougher controls, but Macleod, Boyle and Hogg were not prepared to accept them. The left wing of the Party was not yet digging its heels in, but there was a beginning of a feeling that no compromise with Powell would prove possible.

The meeting adjourned without any decision being reached. A small group would work on a fresh policy statement to be discussed the following Monday. In the meanwhile no one would say anything on the issue. This was the agreed position.

But Powell had other ideas. His notorious 'rivers of blood' speech was delivered to a Conservative Political Centre meeting in Birmingham on the Saturday. He chose not to release it through Central Office because that would have alerted everyone in advance and efforts would have been made to stop it. Enoch might still have made the speech, but it would certainly not have been before a hell of a row. His colleagues would also have been able to get their views out at the same time as Powell, which might have helped undermine his speech in advance. But as it was, Enoch had a clear run from the Saturday, over Sunday and into Monday.

Most of his senior colleagues were angry and flabbergasted by Enoch's attitude over immigration. They remembered all too clearly how as Minister of Health he had stubbornly refused to improve a $2\frac{1}{2}$ per cent pay increase for nurses in 1962. Selwyn Lloyd, the Chancellor, and John Hare as Minister of Labour were begging him to make a better offer. But I was told that he had been adamant that, if nurses didn't wish to accept his pay award, he could recruit plenty of women from the West Indies and other places. So much for his immigration policy.

Ted sacked him before the Shadow Cabinet met on the Monday. If he hadn't dismissed Enoch instantly, a number of the Shadow Cabinet would have resigned, including Quintin Hogg and Edward Boyle. Not only had the language of the speech been quite out of line with his colleagues' thinking, it was an act of enormous disloyalty to them. There hadn't been much love lost between Ted and Enoch for a number of years. Powell knew he was chancing his arm a great deal. I don't think he cared. I think he was quite happy to be sacked, although I suspect he doubted whether Ted at that time was strong enough to do so.

From Enoch's point of view, his sensational speech had the desired effect. He became a national figure overnight. The Smithfield meat porters marched in support of him to the House of Commons. Mail began to arrive at Ted's office literally by the sackful. Ninety nine per cent of it backed Powell. But I wonder if Powell really knows or understands to this day the filth he collected to his side. A number of letters were so vilely written that it was offensive for the girls in Ted's office to read them: others carried their message by including excrement.

Party meetings at Rugby and Cheltenham were picketed by violent mobs, excited by the television cameras – as soon as the lights went on, so the mob reacted. We felt that Enoch had by design stirred the racial pot and the scum in society were quick to come to the surface.

Sacking Enoch was another cross for Ted to bear. Never a popular figure, he was now doubly unpopular. There was plenty of support in the constituencies for the right wing's anti-black position. The impression was created that he was not a strong man like Enoch, who knew the truth, was prepared to say it and would act upon it. Ted had a very difficult, very unpleasant time with the Party for some months. It was an unsavoury passage in the Party's history.

*

In politics, personalities are just as significant as policies and events. Although I despise nearly everything that Enoch Powell has worked for, I hope that I have never under-estimated his Parliamentary performances or his intellectual capacity. But the logic of his thought process was such that it carried him inexorably forward. No diversions were permitted. As

Iain Macleod once said, if you find yourself travelling on Enoch's train, make certain to get off three or four stations before he runs into the buffers.

Enoch was now on the back benches, but all his animosity to Ted was exposed. It was a feud rivalling those of mediaeval Sicily, and was to have a marked impact on politics over the next fifteen years. Within weeks of Enoch's sacking, Alec Home was betting that it would not be long, probably only a matter of months, before Enoch came out against British entry into the Common Market.

With Enoch's departure, the Shadow Cabinet worked much better together as a team. But a year later Edward Boyle decided to retire from politics. This was a great blow to the Party. Edward was very much on the liberal wing, with such a magnificent intellect that even those who detested his views admired him. There is a nasty element in every party, and for some politicians the time comes when they get so sickened by the constant infighting that they either explode or withdraw. But the loss of Edward Boyle was more than that of one man: it was a tilt to the right, because Margaret Thatcher, who had joined the Shadow Cabinet as Power spokesman in 1967 and had become Transport spokesman in 1968, now became Education spokesman.

I had wanted to see Margaret in the Shadow Cabinet. She was of the right, but not excessively so. She was by far the best of our women MPs and was beginning to build a following in the country. Politics, particularly at front bench level, was still a male preserve. I did not favour that and saw in Margaret someone who deserved to be in any Cabinet on merit. Her appointment was the start of the breaking down of the old approach to forming a Cabinet which included a 'statutory woman'. I was glad she was in the team and for many years we worked harmoniously. There was little rapport between Ted and Margaret, and I was often used as a go-between. But at least they did not quarrel.

As Ted's PPS I was concerned mainly with his dealings with the Shadow Cabinet and the backbenchers. There was also policy work, but this had to be done when I could spare time from running his office. In the early days, our staff were not very numerous – I was amused after Margaret Thatcher had become Leader when she decided to cut down the staff in her office and poured scorn on the numbers Ted had taken on. She soon found how necessary they all were.

Ted Heath was fortunate to have two political aides of great promise at this time. The first was John MacGregor, who has a first class intellect. John was something of a terrier, bubbling over with ideas and getting very excited when the political debate hotted up. The second, Douglas Hurd, was equally clever, but as an ex-diplomat was calm and collected. He had a romantic streak and found time to write novels. He also acted as political secretary for the whole period that Ted was Prime Minister, and was on hand to put in the politics when this was being ignored by Ministers or civil servants.

Having had a close association with his father, Anthony Hurd, as a young MP, I always found it a delight to work with Douglas. His political views were very much in the same mould as my own, but he was certainly more diplomatic and could resist the temptation to boil over or give way to the injudicious remark, so often my downfall.

The work in Ted's office also increased rapidly around this time and we decided we needed a second private secretary to take some of the weight off Douglas. One of those interviewed was Jeffrey Archer, who was very disappointed not to get the job. In breaking the news to him, I asked what he was going to do. 'I haven't decided yet,' he replied, 'but either become an MP or make a million.' It seemed a bumptious reply at the time, but Jeffrey was in the House a year later, having won the seat of Louth in a by-election and having pipped the august figure of John Davies, who was Director-General of the CBI at the time, as the Conservative candidate. Later on, when his financial affairs went awry, Jeffrey resigned his seat and was stony broke, but in the space of five short years had made his first million. I'm not certain his passion for politics is well directed, but he is a great entrepreneur. I enjoyed his book about the American dream, but he deserves credit for his own British dream.

I helped a lot with Ted's speech-writing, particularly at Party Conferences. Michael Wolff would write the various drafts, and I would try to sharpen these up and bring out the right points for the occasion. Ted would hold meetings to discuss major speeches starting perhaps weeks ahead, Ted would see the early drafts and make his suggestions. But Michael Wolff and I would invariably be left on the last night of the Conference to write the final draft.

Ted's approach was extraordinary. He was struggling to retain his control of the Party all through his years as Leader of the Opposition, yet he would hardly look at our final draft for this, his crucial, annual address to the Party faithful till around breakfast time on the day of his speech.

I used to put our last attempt under his bedroom door at about 4 am so that he could start working on it first thing in the morning. Quite often when I turned up a little after seven o'clock to see if his final version was ready for typing, he was still dressing. I found the whole business hair-raising. On one occasion I went to his room in my slippers, saying to Jane that I would only be away for a few minutes and would be back for breakfast. I ended up going to the Conference in my slippers, as I hadn't had a moment to go back and change. I was having to give the speech to the typists as Ted cleared each page. With the Press we had to keep up a pretence of being calm and in control. The only person who wasn't flustered was Ted: he was very much a last-minute man.

Because Ted was a bachelor, I would accompany him more often than I would have otherwise. When he was among friends, or was in the right mood, he could be marvellous. He gave a dinner at Number Ten for the Kent County Cricket Club – his home county – after they had won the Championship in 1970 – and made one of the wittiest speeches I have ever heard. I was sitting next to the *Daily Telegraph*'s former cricket correspondent, E. W. 'Jim' Swanton, who struck me as a crusty old right winger. After Ted's speech, he turned to me and said, 'I never knew that this man could be like this. It's completely changed my view of him.'

Ted also loved going to Rugby internationals. During his visit, in Opposition, to New Zealand, we saw Wales play the All Blacks – he would go far to watch Rugby – and there is no doubt that the Welsh players thought a tremendous amount of him.

In Australia we visited the mining district around Port Dampier and Mount Vernon. Ted went in the miners' clubs, and drank and talked with the miners and got on very well with them all. Our host on that tour was Charles Court, Minister for Development in Western Australia. He had heard from his state's Agent-General in London that Ted was aloof and not at all easy to get on with. Court found Ted's character a revelation and confessed to me that he had been given a wholly misleading impression.

Trade union leaders like Jack Jones and Hugh Scanlon had a great respect for Ted and came to like him in a way they never really felt for Harold Wilson. He could be good with the Press, but I don't think he ever found it easy. At times he was dreadful, seeming to be totally unbending when confronted with someone like Joe Haines.

He could also be extraordinarily difficult on social occasions with friends. On one occasion at Albany, he held a party for about forty of us and had specially invited the concert pianist, Moura Lympany, to play for us. Moura was a great friend of Ted's. She had been sitting with Jane, and Jane came across to tell me that Moura wanted to play as she had to leave soon for another engagement. So I had a word with Ted. 'Tell her she can't play,' was Ted's response.

Ted's difficulty was that he would win one group round – perhaps on the back benches, or amongst the Press – but then it was as though he said to himself, 'Well, thank goodness that's over, I won't have to worry about them again for a while.' So six months later he would be back to square one, and would have to make a special effort with them all over again. One had to see him at close quarters to understand his real nature and his true driving force. He had the ability to inspire and generate respect, which is given to very few.

*

By the early months of 1970 the benefits of devaluation, together with the sound policies pursued by Roy Jenkins as Chancellor, were beginning to produce results and we were heading for an election. Unemployment was no longer on the increase, inflation seemed under control and the general outlook more promising. We feared a give-away budget and were mildly encouraged when Roy Jenkins resisted the temptation. Although May's local election results were encouraging, our lead in the opinion polls had been slipping and a mood of depression was returning to our back benches.

May's Gallup poll confirmed our worst fears. Labour's crawl back seemed to have developed into a sprint: they had a lead of 6 percentage points, $41\frac{1}{2}$ per cent to our meagre $35\frac{1}{2}$. An election looked certain.

The next week Ted had an important speech to make to an Industrial Society Conference, an opportunity to rally the troops with our industrial relations policy. He was a flop.

There were rumours that Ted was to be the victim of a putsch. Ted's Shadow Cabinet colleagues remained loyal, but a number of disenchanted backbenchers were saying that we would be bound to lose a second time under his leadership: the sooner he was out the better. His own standing in the polls was invariably worse than the Party's, and he undoubtedly found it hard to get himself across to people. The potential rebels wanted Alec Home back – after all, he had not done badly in 1964. These rumours were to persist through the ensuing election campaign.

Ted was depressed and dejected, and it showed through in his every word and action. Before long Michael Wolff was on the phone to me: 'You've got to tell him to snap out of it; another performance like that and we are all lost. He's got to talk to Central Office and Tony Barber to get them moving on some national advertising to improve morale in the country. And Willie must do something about some of his Whips, who are going about with faces as long as a wet week.'

I set off to Ted's flat at Albany in fear and trepidation. I knew it was my job to be absolutely frank. There wasn't much future for any of us if we didn't pull it off this time. It was a time for plain speaking.

I knew that Ted was depressed, and who wouldn't be in similar circumstances? But he had great reserves of inner strength. Not much had come easy to him in life. He had fought hard for most things and because he was a loner he was dependent on his own strength and no one else's.

I delivered my message. We could win, the polls were probably wrong. But we could defeat ourselves, unless we set to and got the message through to Central Office and the Parliamentary Party: this would at least start a come-back. We were off to the Scottish Party Conference at Perth on the Saturday. This was the occasion for a rousing speech, and it had to be combined with headlines in the Sunday press and national advertising as well.

He largely agreed with me. I was sent scuttling off to see Tony Barber and Willie Whitelaw with suggestions as to what needed to be done. I got back to the House around ten o'clock and bumped into my opposite number, Harold Davies, Harold Wilson's PPS. He was waiting for a cab with another Labour MP.

'Where the hell are you off to?' I asked.

'We're going up to the Press Club in Fleet Street. Why don't you come along?'

We headed off together.

'We're in bloody awful trouble,' said Harold. 'Harold's going to call an election and it's all wrong, it shouldn't be called, it's the wrong time. I told Harold it was not good and we'll be out.'

In those days I must have seemed very sure of myself. I replied: 'Yes, I think you may well have made a mistake.'

At the Press Club we met Derek Marks, the chief leader-writer on the *Daily Express* and its former political correspondent. There we were, the two PPSs to Harold Wilson and Ted Heath. Wilson was about to call an election, yet Harold Davies was looking as miserable as sin and I was looking quite happy. I said that I thought Labour had got it all wrong, that our constituency workers were in fighting mood and that Ted was in great form.

Derek Marks believed all this and was soon writing about the Tories' confidence. The word soon spread round and helped us to sustain a make-believe situation. It had really all happened through chance and a few drinks on one night – I suppose the contrast between poor Harold Davies and me must have seemed remarkable. It was probably even more remarkable than the fact that we were out drinking together in the first place.

That weekend Ted gave a rousing speech to the Scottish Tories in Perth. He stole the Sunday papers' headlines. Central Office had made a prodigious effort, with nearly every paper carrying a full-page advertisement depicting a waste-paper basket full of Labour's broken promises. Ted followed up by getting the better of Harold Wilson at Prime Minister's Question Time on the Tuesday. The whole Party for a change was cheering loudly. As we came out of the Chamber together, Ted commented to me that it was a pity that their support had not been like that over the previous four years.

By this time our election manifesto was practically complete. Ted was too honest to wish to put anything in the manifesto he was not absolutely sure about. He wanted to be certain that there were no hostages to fortune, however tempting.

The more nervous the Party became about winning, the more they looked around for something they thought would be a smash hit. We had already had some experience of this with the weekend conference held that January at the Selsdon Park Hotel. On the Saturday afternoon there was little to report. But the Sunday press were hungry for a story. Ted and Quintin had told them that law and order was figuring prominently in our manifesto preparations. The Press concentrated on this the next day – hence the creation of the myth of 'Selsdon Man', implying that Ted was trying to take the party to the right.

*

The manifesto may have contained few surprises, but that cannot be said of the campaign.

Ted started with set speeches, while Wilson concentrated on 'walk-abouts'. By the end of the campaign the roles were very nearly reversed. There was considerable concern at the outset that Ted's meetings would be acccompanied by violence. We were still in the shadow of the fracas on immigration and the National Front had threatened to break up our meetings.

On the Sunday at the end of the first week we assembled at Ted's flat to discuss the campaign. We were trailing badly in the polls, but everyone agreed that meetings were well attended and that enthusiasm in the constituencies was high. Tony Barber reported that money was coming in well and Central Office was confident. Michael Fraser, head of the Research Department, was certain of victory, but I thought he was whistling in the dark to keep up our spirits. The opinion polls were always right and hunches wrong.

My main preoccupation was to hold Lowestoft. It had always been marginal, with my own majority cut to 358 at the previous election. The worsening national opinion polls and a good local Labour candidate made me nervous. Although I spent most of the campaign in the constituency, I was in daily contact with Ted before his morning press conference and spent four full days touring with him.

The daily forays were carried out by plane from Heathrow. The weather was hot, the plane journey generally bumpy, the whole affair was extraordinarily tiring and likely to make anyone tense. I joined Ted for his visit to Norwich. I had travelled to London late the previous night, and reported that the campaign seemed to be going quite well, but no one could really believe it because of the evidence in the opinion polls. He thought his walk-abouts had helped and had found the reception good.

We arrived at Norwich about 4.30 pm to be greeted by a small crowd at the airport. Two young children of one of my old school friends were thrust forward to get Ted's autograph. The Press looked on cynically. He signed, and the two children ran back to their father: 'What do we do with these, Daddy?' It was going to be one of those days.

How wrong we were constantly to think up these gimmicks for Ted: they always turned sour. But how were we to get across his real human qualities for the press and public? His music and his sailing were genuine interests, but lacked the common touch which Harold Wilson conveyed by smoking a pipe and talking about soccer.

These thoughts were going through my mind as we made our way to Norwich for Ted's walk-about. But the streets were almost deserted: it was early closing day! In all the planning of Ted's campaign, a simple, silly oversight had let him down.

Two days later, on the Friday evening in Manchester, Ted had one of his best meetings of the campaign – a confident and strong speech, enthusiastically received. But as he left the platform he was told the devastating news – Saturday's *Daily Mail* was carrying its latest NOP result, giving Labour a lead of twelve per cent.

Early on the Saturday morning, I was phoned by Douglas Hurd. Enoch Powell was to make a speech that evening which would be a thinly veiled attack on the leadership. The press would see it that way. What should we do? To ignore it would appear weak: to attack it would expose the disunity so close to the surface, and we couldn't afford to under-estimate Enoch's following.

Enoch was clever enough not to let it appear that he was in any way a contributory factor to a defeat, but those of us who knew the man were aware of what he was about. It was clear that Enoch had calculated that the election was lost and was making his bid for the leadership battle which would follow.

I discussed what our reaction should be with Willie Whitelaw. We agreed that there should be no comment until after the speech had been made and we had seen how the Press reacted. I phoned Ted to give him our view.

'Yes, I suppose you're right, but if we are to go down, we will at least do so honourably and with our flags flying.'

I spent that Saturday canvassing on a housing estate in Lowestoft. I was never more depressed and simply discounted the good response I was getting as being no more than politeness. It was very positive, yet I simply didn't believe it.

Katie Macmillan rang to say that her father-in-law, Harold, wanted to pass on some views. Harold was genuinely fond of Ted. He felt that Ted had been a good Chief Whip and had helped hold the Party together after the Suez débâcle, when Harold himself had succeeded Anthony Eden as Prime Minister. The night Harold took over, he invited Ted to champagne and oysters at the Turf Club.

Katie knew the score about Enoch and had been discussing it with Harold.

'I think you ought to tell Mr Heath that Mr Powell's behaviour is a matter for the Parliamentary Party after the election and they must decide then what if anything to do about it. In the meanwhile I advise Mr Heath to say as little about it as possible.'

I rang Willie with Harold's view. Before I could say anything he was shouting down the phone: 'Have you heard the news?'

'What news?'

'Gallup is coming out tomorrow showing the Labour lead down to one per cent.'

The polls were haywire: they couldn't both be right. If we stopped believing them and started to believe our own eyes and ears the whole picture was transformed. Powell would be forgotten. I went to bed a lot happier, and didn't care too much when Sunday's *Observer* concluded from its survey of the previous week's polls that 'only a miracle can save the Tories'. The Chairman of our Eastern Area, David Sells, reported to me on that Sunday that he had been all round the Eastern counties, talked to the press, seen the canvassing returns, examined the local opinion polls. All showed a swing to us. 'We are going to win.'

It was the first election in which the bookmakers played a big part. Charles Forte had phoned me to suggest that ten business friends were prepared to put £5,000 each on a Conservative win: at the time the odds were 10–1. I reported this to Central Office and it was thought best to wait till the last two or three days of the campaign and then get all the money put on at the same time so the press could see that the odds were shortening – 'money on Tories to win' would be a helpful headline. The right moment never came and the money was never put on. I lost Charles Forte a small fortune, but he didn't complain – he got the result he wanted.

The last three days were comparatively plain sailing. The balance of payments figures came out on the Tuesday. They showed a marked deterioration which Ministers tried to explain away by the purchase of four Jumbo jets in one month – if that was enough to upset the balance of trade, heaven help Britain. It all helped to cast doubt on Labour's claims. Our own 'quickie' opinion polls told us that doubts about Labour were growing and that people's voting intentions had narrowed, so there was little to choose between us and Labour.

On the day of the election, June 18, Jane and I did the usual round of visiting all the polling stations and talking to our hard-working supporters in their committee rooms. We were by no means certain of victory. We had a very strong and good candidate, Douglas Baker, against us and as the polls closed I told Jane that we had better prepare ourselves for possible defeat. The count at Lowestoft was always conducted slowly so there was no point in rushing to see it taking place. There was time to go back to friends, have a bath, a meal and see the early results come through on the TV before going off to the count. But my stomach still turns over when I think about it.

As the first results came in, Guildford and Cheltenham showed a 4 per cent swing towards us. Soon others followed. We knew we were in. My own majority was up from 358 to 5,523, but by the time the declaration was made my thoughts were already on the morrow. We won a clear, working majority of 30 seats in the Commons, with 330 seats against Labour's 287 and the Liberal Party's 6.

This was the end of a long and worrying five years in Opposition with Ted's position always vulnerable. It was the beginning of a new chapter in my life. It was not surprising that I slept little that night and by 7.30 on Friday morning I was on the train to London.

I went straight to see Ted at Albany. He was with Douglas Hurd and Michael Wolff, Douglas as calm and collected as ever and Ted looking incredibly relaxed but also seeming rather bemused that he should find himself about to become Prime Minister. When we left to go to Conservative Central Office in Smith Square at about midday, the traffic stopped in Piccadilly, cars hooted and people cheered. It was a moment of triumph but we were all close to tears. Disaster had been so close. Now Ted was to be given his chance.

At about three o'clock we heard that Harold Wilson had gone to the Palace to tender his resignation. A short while later Ted was asked to the Palace. Douglas Hurd, Michael Wolff and I went straight to Number Ten. Our job was to weigh up the right shape for the Government, who should occupy the many posts not yet settled, and also to liaise with the civil service, who were there to serve the incoming Prime Minister with as much hard work and loyalty as they had given to Harold Wilson a few hours before.

That evening was spent in planning in detail the positions in Cabinet and Government. We had so much to sort out that we decided to work through supper. But, perhaps all too predictably, warm beer and sandwiches, those symbols of the Wilson years, were all that remained in the larder. We hastily organised something much better: we felt that Ted's first meal at Number Ten should be a decent one.

Much had to wait on the arrival of the Chief Whip, Willie Whitelaw, who had to travel down from his constituency in Cumbria, although most of the senior Cabinet posts were already settled.

By Saturday afternoon the Cabinet was complete and I returned to Suffolk for a celebration party.

PART TWO

GOVERNMENT

CHAPTER FOUR

INTO THE CABINET

The nature of our election victory in 1970 put Ted in a powerfully dominant position. Any leader is bound to take some credit for a victory, but in Ted's case everyone felt he had personally plucked it from almost certain defeat.

At the start of the first Cabinet meeting, Reggie Maudling, who had been appointed Home Secretary and was Ted's Deputy, said how much the Cabinet and the whole Party would like to congratulate him on the success of the election campaign and on the courage and skill he had shown throughout his leadership. At the Carlton Club's dinner on the eve of the opening of the new Parliament, everyone was saying how splendid Ted was – often the very same people who a few weeks earlier were saying that he was no good and should go.

I was lucky to be in Ted's Cabinet from the start.

I spent Friday and Saturday at Number Ten conferring with Willie Whitelaw, who had been our Chief Whip since 1964, and Douglas Hurd, about the various appointments and the overall shape of the Government. The senior Cabinet posts were largely settled in advance, but Willie told me that Ted was uncertain about Agriculture. Willie wondered whether I could manage it, or would I be better starting off as the Minister of Agriculture's deputy, outside the Cabinet at Minister of State level? After all, it was a big step to go from being Ted's PPS into the Cabinet and in charge of a Ministry.

I told Willie quite plainly that I was very unwilling to accept a junior post. After all, I had been a front bench spokesman before becoming Ted's PPS, and I thought I could handle a Ministerial job. I was in a strong position because I had done an enormous amount to advise and sustain Ted throughout Opposition, particularly during the election campaign.

Reggie Maudling, as Ted's Deputy, was naturally consulted by Ted about the key appointments. He thought that I should take over from Willie as Chief Whip, but I would have hated that. Francis Pym was appointed Chief Whip and, as a great House of Commons man, was much more suited to it.

Ted did not have strong views either way, but when he heard my reaction to Willie's suggestion he thought I had better be in the Cabinet.

He asked me into his room and said, 'Well, I suppose you had better be Minister of Agriculture.'

The June 1970 Cabinet was deliberately kept small; there were eighteen of us altogether. It was Ted's wish as Prime Minister to have a small enough group so that we could all be involved.

There were few surprises in the senior appointments, since they were more Ted's equals and their responsibilities had been tacitly agreed in advance: in addition to Reggie Maudling as Home Secretary, Iain Macleod Chancellor of the Exchequer, Alec Home Foreign Secretary, Quintin Hailsham Lord Chancellor and Willie Whitelaw Leader of the House and Lord President of the Council.

One surprise was that Keith Joseph was appointed Secretary of State for Social Services instead of Robin Balniel, who had served as front bench spokesman in Opposition. With Margaret Thatcher as Secretary of State for Education, Keith and Margaret were thus in charge of two of the two big-spending departments of state.

A smaller Cabinet tends to be more cohesive, and Ted's Cabinet was certainly a good deal happier than Margaret's was to prove: whatever criticism may be levelled against Ted for his aloofness, he did all he could to keep us a happy and united team. We enjoyed ourselves, we were friends who got on well together and had a sense of comradeship which I haven't since experienced.

Ted always listened attentively in Cabinet, generally reserving his own position till he heard the discussion. Margaret's approach was nearly always the opposite, making her own view clear as soon as the relevant Minister, depending on which issue was being discussed, had said his piece. If a Minister tended to be the slightest bit long-winded, or if she did not agree with his views, Margaret would interrupt.

However, one could not always be sure about Ted's position even by the end of Cabinet: he would quite often go his own way afterwards. But, if Ministers were never quite sure in Ted's day what Cabinet had decided until we saw the Cabinet Minutes the next day, with Margaret it generally seemed that everyone in the country knew as soon as they opened their Friday morning paper.

*

On the Sunday after Ted had appointed me Minister of Agriculture, I was telephoned by Sir Basil Engholm, the Permanent Secretary at the Ministry – as Permanent Secretary, he was the senior civil servant, responsible for the management of the Department. For the first time in my life I was called 'Minister'. It is a curious and rather unnerving experience.

He had heard from Number Ten that I had been appointed Minister, and was phoning to congratulate me. He was looking forward to working with me and assured me that the Ministry was fully prepared for a new Government and a new Minister.

We returned to London from Suffolk on the Sunday evening. First thing on Monday morning the chauffeur-driven Ministerial car – in those days a black Rover – rolled up outside our flat. My driver, Charles Richardson, stayed with me throughout Ted's Government and became a wonderful friend and adviser, particularly when I was depressed or was in trouble. Sadly, he was to die before my second spell in Government.

I was whisked off to the Ministry of Agriculture, which is just off Whitehall at the northern end, near Trafalgar Square. There to greet me on the steps and welcome me to the Ministry was my Principal Private Secretary, David Evans.

The Principal Private Secretary is a young, career civil servant who has been identified as a future 'high flyer', and can eventually expect to reach one of the senior posts in Whitehall, perhaps as a Permanent Secretary running a Department. He or she is the Minister's link with the Department and the rest of Whitehall: all official business is channelled through the Private Office, minutes of meetings recorded, phone calls logged, and the Minister's diary arranged.

I always felt that arranging my diary as a Minister demanded the skill of a top-level diplomat. There was the constant conflict between my official duties – meetings with my civil servants, official functions and visits – and my political activities, House of Commons business, party political engagements and speeches, and constituency work. I was fortunate to find that Joyce Wheeler was my diary secretary in the Private Office: she was a superb organiser and shrewd judge of people. She was tremendously loyal and, unusually for a career civil servant, was able to work with me in the various Government posts I held until her retirement in 1984.

As soon as I arrived in my office, Basil Engholm came to meet me and talk over the immediate problems facing the Government. Urgent decisions were needed to tackle an outbreak of brucellosis and there was a scare that rabies had spread to Britain. The necessary meetings were set up, and then Basil left, handing me as he went a huge book which was the Ministry's briefing for the new Minister.

During an election campaign the civil servants in every Department or Ministry prepare two sets of briefs to present to the incoming Minister after the election. One set is prepared for a Conservative Minister, another for a Labour Minister. The briefing provides a detailed analysis of how the Party's relevant manifesto commitments for the Department concerned might best be implemented, the costs involved, and so on. In addition, there is a thorough update on all the key aspects of the Department's work which has to be carried on regardless, whichever Party happens to win the election.

I suspect that many new Ministers, suddenly finding themselves responsible for a Department of State, could be totally overawed by the officials' detailed briefing. Fortunately, in my first Cabinet post I knew my subject as a farmer better than most of my officials and so had few qualms about being too dependent on their advice or being overwhelmed by the volume of work.

But I soon discovered some of the political pressures on a Minister. Within a day or so of my appointment I was phoned by one of the Tory Party's most revered figures, Lord Margadale. He was furious that Harold Wilson, in one of his last appointments as Prime Minister, had appointed a socialist, Lord Taylor of Gryfe, to be chairman of the Foresty Commission. Margadale was telling me in no uncertain terms that this was a typical Wilson ploy, that Taylor had to go, and that I should deal with it right away.

I contacted Number Ten to see what could be done, but was told that Lord Taylor's appointment had been approved by the Queen. There was nothing that could be done: he couldn't be sacked within days of the Queen giving her approval. The landowners were furious.

But, within a year or two, Lord Taylor had turned out to be the landowners' darling. None of them could say a word against him. He was a pillar of the establishment.

And, when our controversial industrial relations reforms came before the House of Lords, there was Lord Taylor supporting our legislation and criticising his own Party. Eventually he left the Labour Party to join the SDP.

I settled into my new office quickly and saw no point in turning the place inside out with new furniture and decorations, as some Ministers do. In fact, it was my civil servants who felt that my room really needed to be re-decorated. I objected, but the civil service won in the end, although I refused to agree to a new carpet, which they had also wanted. It was agreed that the re-decoration should be done during the summer recess. Nevertheless it took so long that when they unrolled the old carpet they found that a mouse had made a nest in the middle and had eaten through several layers, so a new carpet was required after all. This wasn't the best advertisement for a Department responsible for pest control.

Another important aspect of a Minister's life is relations with the media. Within a few weeks of becoming Minister, we were faced with a dock strike. Almost immediately there was concern about loads of tomatoes from the Channel Islands going rotten in the ships, and cargoes of bananas being thrown overboard. I went to Smithfield Market and Covent Garden to see what supplies were getting through. At Smithfield I was heckled by some vociferous meat porters whose misuse of the English language was very marked; one paper had a picture of a meat porter with his trousers down and his backside prominently displayed towards me.

At Covent Garden there appeared to be a shortage of South African apples, but plenty of French, Italian and Spanish peaches. I was asked about the shortage of apples and made the rash comment that there were plenty of peaches. The peaches were cheaper than apples, but I had failed to understand that peaches were for the rich and apples for the poor. This gaffe caused me to be nicknamed 'Peaches Prior' for several years by the *Sun*, and led to comparisons in the House with Marie-Antoinette's supposed 'let them eat cake'.

During the election campaign a Central Office policy paper issued under Ted Heath's name had stated that by reducing taxes such as the Selective Employment Tax and controlling the prices charged by nationalised industries we could reduce the rise in prices 'at a stroke'. As food prices were still rising I was asked during a radio interview about reducing prices 'at a stroke'. My reply was that this 'should not be taken too seriously'.

This led to accusations of bad faith, a claim from Harold Wilson that I had turned Queen's evidence, and more calls for my resignation. My driver, Charles Richardson, heard the interview and tried to console me by saying that he couldn't understand what all the fuss was about: I had been quite right – no one had taken our promise to reduce prices seriously.

The *Daily Express* suggested that I needed a good dressing-down from the Prime Minister when he next saw me. To his credit all that Ted said to me was, 'I understand from the *Daily Express* that I'm to give you a dressing down. But bad luck, we all do these things.'

It did not alter the fact that I had made a silly remark and the press put me through the mill for days afterwards. It was the kind of experience which can easily destroy any Minister's confidence.

*

Despite my own inauspicious start, my two and a half years as Minister of Agriculture, Fisheries and Food was the happiest period of my political career.

I knew the farmers well, understood the fishing industry because Lowestoft was itself a fishing port, was on top of my subject and there-fore felt in a strong position within my own Department.

In these days of increasing sensitivity to conflicts of interest between a Minister's public responsibilities and his private investments, it may seem anomalous that as Minister of Agriculture I was allowed to keep on my farm, but it would have been ridiculous to expect me to sell it.

It was a busy and fascinating life. There was a lot of travelling round the country, and Jane was able to play an active role in it for she knew the ins and outs of a farmer's life. She was also extremely interested in another side of the Ministry – its active responsibilities towards the food industry.

Dealing with this industry was a new and absorbing challenge. The food manufacturers and retailers were effective lobbyists, and put up strong resistance, for instance, to my attempts to persuade them to introduce date-stamping of food in the shops. In that case they ultimately accepted it was in the shoppers' interest and began to implement the change on a voluntary basis: it eventually became compulsory in 1980.

The detailed brief which Basil Engholm handed me when I arrived at the Ministry of Agriculture set out exactly how we could implement the policy we worked out in opposition. I was warned that I would have no friends in the rest of Whitehall, but there was just a chance that I might manage to get it through, as it had been a major part of our manifesto – here was immediate confirmation that, besides the researchers for other parties, civil servants are the only people to read a party's manifesto in detail and take it seriously.

From the start the Foreign Office and the Department of Trade and Industry were against me. They both argued that our proposed policy was against the free-trade principles of the world's main trading countries, embodied in the General Agreement on Trade and Tariffs (GATT). Both Departments feared that our policy would result in retaliation against British exports, and that it would be particularly unpopular with some of our closest trading partners – the United States, Canada and New Zealand.

Fortunately the Government's overriding commitment to join the European Community meant that these difficulties had to be faced and overcome, where necessary, by some judicious concessions during the negotiations. In the case of lamb from New Zealand, we eventually agreed a levy of one old penny per pound, and the levies on Canadian and American grain were subsumed into the Community tariffs level once we joined the EEC.

In Europe, the knowledge that we intended to move towards a system of protection similar to the Community's helped persuade the six EEC countries that this time we meant business and were prepared to be 'Communautaire'.

I am convinced that we would not have been able to carry through our new policy unless we had been about to enter the Community, as the pressure on us from our main trading partners not to raise tariffs would have been too great. But had we not introduced our reform, or not entered Europe, British agriculture would have become much more vulnerable, with food surpluses being dumped on us and the Treasury fighting to resist the consequent increase in subsidies paid under the old deficiency payments scheme. The Labour Opposition fought us the whole way, arguing that we were putting a tax on food, although at the time food prices were remarkably stable.

Although the detailed negotiations with Europe were being conducted during my time at the Ministry, I only had to make periodic visits to Brussels or Luxembourg. Geoffrey Rippon, as Chancellor of the Duchy of Lancaster, handled all the negotiations, with the expert help of Con O'Neill who headed his team of civil servants and Freddie Kearns from my Ministry.

It was an intricate negotiation, involving not just our own agriculture and fishing, but also requiring difficult decisions which affected the Commonwealth sugar agreement and New Zealand butter and lamb. The New Zealanders have always held a special place in the affections of the British and we all felt that some special concessions had to be negotiated for them. Their team was led by Jack Marshall, the deputy Prime Minister, a man of great integrity and plenty of charm. He took the view that our countries were so close in interests that what was good for Britain must be good for New Zealand too. By taking this attitude he was able to shame us into a very good deal. By contrast, the Australians tried to bully us a bit, although they had much less of a case. They got less in consequence.

*

During Ted's premiership we were strongly committed to the post-war economic and social consensus in which the basic goal of economic policy was full employment. We recognised the need for an improved Welfare State. We believed in a society in which the social services should be expanded and more done about housing.

We were equally committed to working through the institutions which had been developed to implement this consensus approach. Ted himself was a former Minister for Labour, and therefore knew the union leaders well. He wanted to keep the unions closely involved through 'Neddy', the National Economic Development Council, set up by Macmillan's Government in 1961.

We were also the best prepared Party to take office since the War. But, however detailed the policy work undertaken in Opposition, it is not easy to discover all the nuances which a Government must take into account. Circumstances can change quickly and demand a more flexible response.

Perhaps it is not too fanciful to think of Ted, his Government and the institutions of Britain, as the captain, his crew and an ageing ship setting out with new charts on a voyage during which he planned to introduce new disciplines and to refurbish the engine and hull. But what neither Ted nor any of his officers could know was that we were heading for heavy seas – the storm of worldwide inflation, induced by rises in commodity prices beyond the control of any single government.

On the first leg of Ted's voyage he intended to remove the restrictive practices of the unions. But the unions and their members were not ready for it.

We tried to do far too much at once, putting our faith in the idea that sweeping changes in the law would rapidly change behaviour on the shop floor. We pressed on at great speed with our legislation, thinking we had done more than enough research and consultation in Opposition. We re-wrote the entire framework of the law on industrial relations, and had our Industrial Relations Act on the statute book by the end of our first parliamentary session, in 1971.

We would have been better advised to put our own proposals into abeyance and take up the reforms which the Labour Government had proposed in 1969 in their White Paper, 'In Place of Strife'. But apart from Robert Carr, our Secretary of State for Employment, scarcely anyone in the Party understood industrial relations or knew industrialists, let alone any trade unionists.

Ted was determined that a better balance had to be restored in col-lective bargaining by reducing union power: it was essential to prevent any renewed upsurge in wage and price inflation. He had given Geoffrey Howe the task of seeing how the legal framework could be amended. Geoffrey's approach was legalistic in the extreme, with no appreciation of what made the unions tick on the real world of the shop floor.

Robert was simply unable to resist all the pressures for rapid and radical reform. The party was anti-union, Ted was determined to tackle any obstacle to economic growth, and Geoffrey was at hand with his detailed legal proposals, which seemed to offer the panacea.

I knew nothing of industrial relations and went along with the majority view: the problems which our approach would cause were not readily apparent. In fact as our popularity waned in Government, I recall Michael Wolff commenting to me that the only thing stopping us from being even more unpopular was that we were seen to be taking on the unions.

*

By early 1972 we had suffered a number of pay disputes in the public sector. The most serious challenge had been a go-slow in the winter of 1970–71 by the electricity power workers. Its impact was so rapid and effective that even the union's own leaders were surprised. From the start of the dispute, and quite unpredictably, house and street lights had gone out and the power cuts hit hospitals, sewage works and other vital immediately set up an inquiry under Lord Wilberforce, the action was called off, and the result was reasonable for both the union and the Government. Most people thought that we had handled things firmly and well.

But the next winter, 1971–72, the miners presented us with a fresh challenge. The turning point came when the miners' pickets, led by Arthur Scargill and other trade unionists massed outside the Saltley cokeworks in Birmingham. At the very start of Cabinet that day, Ted told us that the Home Secretary, Reggie Maudling, would give an up-to-date report on the events in Birmingham. Reggie reported that the Chief Constable had said that he had sufficient police available to keep the works open, and that he was determined to do so.

But halfway through Cabinet Reggie was handed a note. He read out the bad news: in view of the mass picketing and fears that the police might be overrun, the Chief Constable had decided to close the coke-works' gates.

This unexpected turn of events had a profound effect on us. We had felt all along that we were badly unprepared to face the miners' challenge: although we had enough coal, there was a shortage of lighting-up fuel at the power stations. We turned again to Wilberforce, who had done a good job the previous year in settling the power workers' dispute.

On this occasion his findings appeared to go wholly in favour of the miners, giving them a wage increase of 22 per cent. To make matters worse, there was a further delay before the dispute could end while the miners' union debated whether the settlement, generous as it was, would be acceptable, Cabinet met before the NUM had come to its decision, and we had to use candles because of a power cut. We vowed that never again would we 'do a Wilberforce'.

*

This led to our second major mistake, which was to opt for a statutory prices and incomes policy in the autumn of 1972. Our decision had been prompted by the repercussions of Wilberforce. But it has to be seen against the background of Ted's overriding commitment to full employment.

During the winter of 1971–72, the numbers of unemployed had increased towards the million mark, a level unprecedented in the post-war period apart from the early months of 1947 when industry had run short of fuel in severe weather. In January 1972, although the jobless total adjusted for seasonal factors remained below one million, the unadjusted overall total exceeded that. The Commons had to be suspended during the Prime Minister's Questions following Labour's furious protests.

This in itself did not shake Ted, but he utterly despised and detested the pre-war Conservative Governments, who had tolerated between two and three million unemployed. It was therefore no surprise in which direction Ted decided our economic policy should go when he now had to choose between tolerating a continued high level of unemployment, in the hope that this would keep some control over wage claims and inflation – or trying to run the economy with a higher level of output and growth, and seeking some other means of control over wage and price increases.

The high unemployment route was counter to everything Ted believed in and had hoped to achieve for Britain. Tony Barber's 1972 Budget was a reaffirmation of our commitment to full employment and higher growth. It launched our expansionary strategy, cutting £1,200 million off tax rates in 1972–73 and considerably more in a full year. It was designed to achieve an annual economic growth rate of 5 per cent, some 2 per cent faster than would otherwise have been realised. Besides taking 2.75 million people out of tax and cutting £1 a week off income tax, there was a further cut in purchase tax, a new programme of incentives for investment in the poorer regions and the announcement that we wished to move towards a tax credit scheme, which would carry our reforms of the tax and benefit system substantially further.

All too often Cabinets have not been well enough briefed to take sensible decisions: probably only two or three departments know much about the issue under discussion. For example, how could most of the Cabinet produce an informed judgment on the very great difficulties of Rolls-Royce in 1970–71 when the company would have gone bankrupt had the Government not intervened. The Department of Trade and Industry and the Treasury were obviously involved; the Foreign Office had a view, as any decisions affected Lockheed, Rolls-Royce's principal customers in the United States; and the Ministry of Defence was concerned because of the worldwide defence implication for aero engines. But the rest of the Cabinet would know very little.

Ted Heath had understood that this was a problem for effective Cabinet government and set out to solve it by setting up a new body, the Central Policy Review Staff (CPRS). The CPRS, or 'Think Tank', existed to brief the whole Cabinet.

Ted was very fortunate to obtain the services of Lord Rothschild as the Think Tank's first Head. Lord Rothschild quickly assembled a group of able people, some from the civil service, some from outside Whitehall. The role of the CPRS was to give the Prime Minister and Cabinet a detached view of any problem before Cabinet, and of other problems which might arise. In effect, they were in the 'crow's nest', alerting those of us in the navigation room to possible troubles ahead.

Victor Rothschild's role was unique. He had a magnificent intelligence and was totally independent both in thought and financially. When it came to dealing with the devious ways of the permanent civil service, they were no match for him. Any country, and perhaps we more than most, could do with a dozen men of similar quality to advise, to guide, and to forecast.

If the significance of the Wilberforce inquiry's 22 per cent pay rise for the miners and our expansionary Budget needed any emphasis, Victor Rothschild provided it. His warnings were that while a boost to the economy would reduce unemployment sharply – the graph showing the forecast level of unemployment came down very nicely – this would only be achieved at the expense of higher inflation.

We could only keep this in check through some form of incomes policy, which in the prevailing mood would have to include a prices policy. Tripartite talks with the CBI and TUC were initiated in the spring. They lasted through the summer, and into the autumn. They very nearly succeeded in reaching an agreement including restraint of pay and price rises.

But on November 2 the TUC rejected our proposals. Jack Jones, then leader of the Transport and General Workers Union, the largest union, has since said that, if only we had gone on talking for another twenty four hours, we could have got an agreement. I honestly doubt whether this was really so, and I suspect that the union leaders have subsequently sought to appear in a more favourable light.

We would have much preferred a voluntary policy to help restrain pay increases, but after the talks had collapsed Ted felt that there was no alternative to a statutory policy.

A number of us in Cabinet worried about the political difficulties we would face, with accusations of having done a 'U-turn' and the problems it would cause on our own back benches. But having decided on the need for the policy, all of us agreed to push ahead with it.

We were reluctant converts as we realised the difficulties it would cause, with all the inevitable anomalies and inflexibilities. Following the initial Stage I pay and prices freeze from November 1972 to March 1973, we sought to overcome these problems in Stages II and III by devising the most sophisticated pay policy ever introduced.

*

Although Ted's Cabinet had the advice of Victor Rothschild's Think Tank, there were nonetheless gaps among his closest political advisers. In any generation there can only be a few really wise heads. In Opposition, Ted had the benefit of extremely able and loyal chief lieutenants, but fate was now to deprive him of their daily counsel, just when he needed them most.

The tragic death of Iain Macleod in July 1970, a month after he had been appointed Chancellor, was a body blow at the very outset of Ted's Government. He had the romanticism of the Celt from the Western Isles and yet the hard-headedness of the Yorkshireman who was interested in brass. This was a formidable combination in a politician. He could inspire and move people by a combination of speech and ideas, but never allowed his emotions to get too far ahead.

Iain made people feel that he cared about them, that he recognised and shared the ambitions and hopes they had for themselves and their family. He was able to associate with the ups and downs of everyday life and realised better than most the movements going on in society – that people were beginning to change out of the old working class, 'cloth cap', image and were starting to seek the home ownership and higher standards of education, which had previously been the preserve of the middle classes.

In the House he was a formidable speaker, a master of articulate and biting wit. Typical of Iain was his remark that it had taken since Magna Carta to 1964 for the statute books to cover so many volumes and only the time of the Labour Government since then to double them; and his judgment on Jim Callaghan as Chancellor – that for him the laws of averages had ceased to exist, he was always wrong.

Iain was particularly scathing about Labour's record on unemployment, castigating the Government every time the jobless total rose over half a million.

What would he have thought today? He would certainly have been a 'wet'. I fancy he would have been a good deal more effective at fighting his corner than we have proved to be. But then if he were with us, we might never have suffered the doctrinal swings that have bedevilled the Conservative Party in recent years.

Towards the end of our spell in Opposition, Iain appeared to be feeling the strain of his painful disability and was obliged to take massive doses of pills. He was past his peak and was no longer the Macleod whom many of us had known and worshipped in the early 1960s, with his power of speech and vision of a free, yet caring, society. He had remained up to his death the man whom Labour most feared.

Reggie Maudling, Willie Whitelaw, and Alec Home were now also absent when Ted needed them most.

Reggie was an extraordinarily good colleague, placid and wise, and never out to make life difficult. But as Home Secretary he was burdened with Northern Ireland until March 1972, when Ted created a new Cabinet post of Northern Ireland Secretary. Then in July that year Reggie felt he had to resign as Home Secretary, to avoid any suggested conflict of interest with the inquiries by the Metropolitan Police into the Poulson affair. Reggie was never to regain his stature in Parliament. He and Beryl suffered greatly in their private lives, but in a close friendship I never heard any complaint from one or the other, and their love was strong enough to withstand all the strains. His early death in 1979 was a much bigger loss to the Party and the country than most realise. How I wish he had been on the back benches after the 1979 election: the cause of 'wetness' would have had a very calm, but caustic leader.

Willie Whitelaw had been Leader of the House up to March 1972, and therefore very much at the centre of things. But he was Ted's choice for the new Northern Ireland post. It was absolutely right to accord the problem top priority by appointing someone of Willie's ability, but it did deprive Ted of Willie's immensely sound judgment at an increasingly difficult time for the Government. By the time Willie returned from Northern Ireland, in December 1973, it was too late even for him to pull something out of the hat.

Alec, as Foreign Secretary, and now in the House of Lords, was extremely loyal to Ted. But inevitably he was not closely involved in the domestic political scene.

Without Iain and Reggie, and with Alec fully occupied as Foreign Secretary, much of the political weight, or 'bottom' as Reggie himself would call it, was lost. There was no way that I, or anyone else – however close we were to Ted – could hope to replace them. They were political equals of Ted's, and could talk to him in a way that even Willie Whitelaw and Peter Carrington, whom Ted appointed Party Chairman in April 1972, found difficult. Willie and Peter were too close to Ted to give the truly independent and detached view which is invaluable in government.

Ted was brilliantly served in his political office at Number Ten by Douglas Hurd and Michael Wolff. But, as time went on, he relied more and more on a trio of senior civil servants, led by William Armstrong, head of the Civil Service, with Douglas Allen, Permanent Secretary at the Treasury and Conrad Heron, Permanent Secretary at Employment in support. They were able and loyal advisers, but they were not politicians. This added to the resentment already felt by a number of backbenchers that Ted was not paying sufficient attention to the Party, and fuelled the charge of corporatism which was increasingly being levelled at his Government.

*

In March 1972 Robert Carr succeeded Willie Whitelaw as Leader of the House of Commons and Lord President of the Council when Willie went to Northern Ireland. But in July when Robert replaced Reggie Maudling as Home Secretary it proved impossible for him to combine all three posts. In November, I therefore succeeded Robert as Leader of the House and Lord President.

The Leader of the House is responsible for the business of the Commons, and my principal task therefore was to help ensure that the Government's legislation got through and the Opposition were kept reasonably satisfied.

Willie Whitelaw's advice to me was that a good Leader of the House is never heard of, and my success would be in inverse proportion to the publicity which I attracted. This is why John Biffen, who until recent outbursts had remained comparatively unknown in the country, has proved such a successful Leader of the House since 1982. At the other extreme was Dick Crossman, Leader of the House between 1966 and 1968, who could never resist a headline and was a disaster at leading the House and getting the Government's business through.

I was in a difficult position from the start because earlier in the year, Ted had appointed me Deputy Chairman of the Party, a job which brought me into the front-line of the political battle. Yet as Leader of the House I needed to be non-partisan and to keep down the political temperatures in the Commons.

The task of planning the business is left largely to the Chief Whip, and to his clerks, who are often described in the press as 'the usual channels'. In my time in the House there have only been three Chief Clerks, Charles Harris, Freddie Warren and Murdo MacLean. All have been immensely successful and have understood that the smooth running of business depends on consulting fully the opposition parties; indeed, a mature parliamentary democracy is much about the rights and opportunities afforded to the opposition.

I was appointed Leader of the House over the weekend in the middle of the Commons debate on the Loyal Address. This debate follows the Queen's Speech at the opening of a new parliamentary session, which usually takes place in November each year. Having made a very poor speech to open the day's debate on Food Prices on the Friday, I had to wind up the whole six days of debate on the Loyal Address on the following Tuesday evening. I was new to the job, and I was known to be a protégé of Ted's. Our tripartite talks with the CBI and TUC had collapsed and we had unveiled our statutory prices and incomes policy – the very policy which we had castigated Labour for introducing when they were in Government. The Opposition were obviously going to give me a rough time.

I didn't disappoint them. My speech was dreadful – it was dull, without any spark. It was accompanied by derisive laughter from the benches opposite and dumb embarrassment from my own.

A bad performance makes the Minister and the Government look weak. I wondered that night as I talked it over with Michael Jopling, who had been enormously supportive as my PPS at Agriculture, and who was by then one of the Government Whips, whether I could ever make the grade.

Some Ministers regard their PPS as no more than dogsbodies to get them paired and attend the back bench committee of their particular Department, but a good PPS can be a valued adviser and candid friend, and at the same time learn the ropes himself, ready for a Government job in the future. All my PPSs have helped me enormously with policy matters as well as keeping me informed of Party opinion.

My speeches did improve, but I was never better than a good average performer. I was always a bunch of nerves. At one stage I used to drink two neat whiskies about fifteen minutes before getting up to speak, but even then I shook all over.

As Leader of the House I had to make a statement every Thursday afternoon, telling MPs the business of the Commons for the coming week. By tradition the Leader of the Opposition always responds first to the business statement, and invariably criticises the Government's allocation of Parliamentary time.

My second main task on Thursday afternoons was to give an unattributable briefing to the lobby in a little room symbolically as far away from the Chamber of the House as the building allows. This gives an opportunity for the Leader of the House to plant any stories or information he wishes in the knowledge that his name will not be mentioned. In their turn the journalists can ask any question they like in the hope that the Minister, knowing his name is protected, will be unusually indiscreet.

If one of my besetting sins for a politician was to talk too openly, I believe public life would be better understood and people more tolerant about our mistakes if we were not always so secretive and sometimes downright dishonest. The Parliamentary lobby is a case in point. Journalists who hover round the bars and lobbies of the House of Commons or who ring you up at all hours of the day or night will talk to you on 'lobby terms'. This means they cannot report what has been said to them by name, but they are at liberty to use the information either as background or unattributably. Much of the information out of Downing Street, Government departments or the Opposition Leader comes in this form. When one reads of 'sources close to the Prime Minister', it generally means Bernard Ingham – Mrs Thatcher's chief Press Officer. If one reads 'senior Ministers' or 'influential backbencher', it is nearly always possible to narrow down the source of the information.

I found the lobby briefings a terrifying business and dreaded reading Friday's papers, for all my colleagues would know the source of these ill-disguised indiscretions. Donald Maitland, Ted Heath's Chief Press Officer, was always present on these occasions. He has been a great friend, but I suspect I caused him as many an anxious moment as I caused myself.

And yet looking back through all the agonies my 'frankness' has caused me, I believe it proved a great advantage. The press generally recognised they were getting a true story and were not being misled.

Returning to my room from the lobby briefing one Thursday afternoon, I found a very angry Harold Wilson waiting to see me. For the Leader of the Opposition to come and see me immediately after my briefing must mean that this time I had committed a really appalling leak, for after all, I was not responsible for the Opposition. Harold looked furious, as he was personally affected. Water was pouring in through the ceiling of his office. He was not very amused to see how relieved I was by the nature of his plight.

I also got to know Bob Mellish, who was Labour's Chief Whip during my time as Leader of the House. We often met and Bob used to regale me with his tales of woe about some of his more independent-minded backbenchers. To tease him one day I expressed condolences about the health of Arthur Lewis, the Labour MP for West Ham North, who had not been well and who I knew was not a favourite of Bob's. Back came the reply, 'Thank you very much and I'm glad to be able to tell you it's something serious.'

The Leader of the House chairs the Commons Privileges Committee and in those days was also responsible for the Commons Services Committee. I used to dread chairing the meetings of the Privileges Committee. It is a Select Committee of the House which deals with any matters relating to questions of parliamentary privilege, such as an MP's right to name people in the House without fear of being sued. It is invariably packed with senior parliamentarians, often barristers, and in my time included Enoch Powell and Derek Walker-Smith QC, a former chairman of the Tory Party's 1922 Committee. The atmosphere was like a court of law, with one's every word being scrutinised for its precise meaning and selected passages from Erskine May (the guide to parliamentary practice) quoted at great length.

The Services Committee was an all-party committee which met once a week and dealt with all manner of complaints about the services of the House, ranging from security to the quality of food in the canteen, or the lack of accommodation for Members or their secretaries. If any of the officers of the House had a problem, they would come to see me. On one occasion the officer who handled MPs' car expenses reported that ten Members had claimed more than £5,000 for the year. The top figure was £10,000 which at 5p per mile meant this MP had claimed for 200,000 miles. It was either a fiddle or a mistake. Fortunately, this and other cases were dealt with tactfully without having to divulge any names to me.

As Lord President of the Council, which is one of the oldest offices under the Crown. I was responsible for the Privy Council and conducting business in the presence of the Queen. A number of matters come within the purview of the Privy Council, such as various appointments to Government, certain legal problems requiring confirmation by the Council and also granting Royal Charters. All the detailed work is carried out in the Privy Council Office, but many things required the Queen's approval. The meetings of the Council gave me and the three or four senior Ministers who attended on a mild form of rota a chance to meet the Queen and to discuss things with her informally.

Shortly after I became Lord President of the Council, I found that a great dinner of all Privy Councillors was to be held to celebrate the Queen's Silver Wedding anniversary. Originally it had been planned to have it in the Painted Hall at Greenwich, but Dick Crossman and Barbara Castle had complained that the price was too high and that they would boycott it; so it was agreed to have a less grand affair in the Royal Gallery of the House of Lords and risk the food being cold by the time it reached us.

The seating arrangements spread Privy Councillors around regardless of seniority. This seemed a good idea, but Harold Wilson took exception. After the dinner he said he would not meet the Queen in protest at the treatment an upstart like Prior had given him.

In fact, I had no say in the seating at all, it had been arranged between my predecessor Robert Carr and Sir Godfrey Agnew, who was the Clerk to the Privy Council. It was a number of months before I got on reasonable terms with Harold, but in the end we became good friends and often discussed the relative merits of Huddersfield Town and Norwich City.

The Lord President is also required to preside over a number of Cabinet Committees. I chaired the Legislation Committee, which deals with all legislation due to come before Parliament and identifies legislation envisaged for the next session. This committee was not usully controversial, although it could be, particularly if Quintin Hailsham, the Lord Chancellor, was on form. The barristers who serve as Parliamentary Counsel and who are responsible for preparing and writing the legislation would attend, and if they knew that Quintin was going to be present most of them would flock in to listen. He was always very entertaining and never let them down.

The work of the Civil Contingencies Unit was also my responsibility. The unit was composed of senior civil servants, one from each of the main departments, assisted by officials from the Cabinet Office. Their job was to plan what the Government should do in the case of national emergencies. The unit had come into its own after the six-week coal strike of early 1972, when we had found ourselves unprepared to deal with emergencies such as the provision of stand-by generators to keep hospitals running during power cuts. The theory was that the better prepared we were, the more likely it was that we would be able to resist, or even prevent, a serious strike.

The odds were always against us. Having concentrated on the strategic planning we were then faced with the practical consequences. Should we for instance allocate a large generator to a sewerage pumping station, as we were always being warned that London could be flooded by sewage? Or should we let it go to Nigg Bay, where an oil rig was being built but could be delayed for a year unless the welding was completed on time – and without a large enough generator the welding simply could not be finished in time.

On other occasions we had to recommend when the emergency powers legislation should be introduced, which power cuts should be implemented, when heating should be cut off, what temperature permitted, and so on. Margaret Thatcher is to be congratulated on avoiding most of these crises – much of my work at that time now seems no more than a bad memory.

*

In the early summer of 1973, I was contacted by an old business acquaintance who had been told a remarkable story by someone closely involved with the Eve nightclub, where he had been entertaining some business clients. According to his source, at least one Government Minister was involved. If the story broke it would be a source of considerable embarrassment to the Government, particularly as one of the Ministers was at the Ministry of Defence. My acquaintance suggested that I should meet his informant.

I was worried not only about the information itself, but how exactly I should handle the problem. I consulted Sir Burke Trend, at that time the Cabinet Secretary, who suggested that I should see the nightclub owner's wife, but that I should be accompanied by Robert Armstrong, who was then Ted's Principal Private Secretary.

The meeting was held in my room in the Privy Council Office. It was an imposing room, looking out on to Whitehall, with many paintings of great value hanging from the walls and with many historical associations.

Yet I doubt if the room had ever witnessed a more bizarre yet intriguing story than the one revealed to us that morning.

Our informant was an extremely articulate lady. She told us that one of the hostesses in the nightclub worked as a prostitute and had been seeing Lord Lambton, the Minister responsible for the Air Force at the Ministry of Defence. In fact, the girl, Norma Levy, had approached our informant because Lambton had been indiscreet about his identity and she realised that he was making himself vulnerable to the risk of blackmail. Norma Levy's husband had a criminal record.

As the lady talked, she recited a tale of intrigue and corruption, which involved the police, including the removal of one bright young policeman who had got on to the story but who had been quickly transferred elsewhere: there were allegedly a number of police officers involved who were rotten to the core.

She was not certain whether other Government Ministers were involved, but she shared Norma Levy's concern that Tony Lambton was being indiscreet and could be blackmailed very easily. All the ingredients of a really major scandal were present.

I sat and listened to this extraordinary and seemingly far-fetched story without being able to judge at first whether it was true or a pack of lies from start to finish. But as soon as the lady had left, Robert immediately made it clear that in his judgment she was an honest and intelligent witness.

Word had reached Downing Street of the impending disclosure of some compromising photographs – Norma Levy's husband had contrived to photograph his wife in bed with her clients, in extremely compromising situations. Within days the *News of the World* had got hold of the story.

Tony Lambton was carried to political oblivion, which was sad as he was a man of independence and intelligence. But tragically Lord Jellicoe was also swept out of the Government for what we all thought were totally unnecessary reasons. George Jellicoe was then Leader of the House of Lords and, as Lord Privy Seal, was responsible for the Civil Service Department. His name was in no way implicated in the same case, but had been mentioned to the police by a complete coincidence. There was no risk of blackmail photographs, and he himself had volunteered information about his private life to Ted Heath. George nonetheless felt that he had to resign. We were all very sad, including Ted.

After these resignations both the Party's standing and Ted's own popularity improved sharply in the June opinion polls. But it was shortlived. Some of us commented at the time that perhaps we needed a few more scandals.

The episode had given me a fascinating window on to the world of Soho crime and sex. It took a number of years for Robert Mark to clean up the Metropolitan Police Force, particularly its Savile Row division.

Perhaps one of the most extraordinary aspects of this whole episode had been to watch a doyen of the world of Whitehall like Robert Armstrong squeeze the last detail about a totally different world out of a rather remarkable lady, who turned out to be impeccably reliable and intensely patriotic.

*

Ted is one of the few leaders of his generation who really had a vision of the society he wished to create. His objective was to release a fund of new investment and energy by breaking through the old 'stop-go' cycle which had bedevilled all post-war governments. He accepted fully Government's role in boosting the rate of economic growth, modernising Britain's infrastructure and launching great national projects – the third London Airport and new seaport at Maplin Sands and the Channel Tunnel were part and parcel of Ted's plans. He was passionately committed to seeing Britain's economic performance revived and our national pride restored.

A central element in this vision for the country was the passionate belief that Britain should honour her world commitments with Ted's own brand of compassionate Toryism. This was best demonstrated in the summer of 1972 by his response to Idi Amin's expulsion of the Asians from Uganda. As United Kingdom passport holders they were entitled to settle in Britain, but there was enormous pressure from the Tory right and in the right wing press for Ted to renege on Britain's commitment to these unfortunate people. We were witnessing a repeat display of the ugly prejudices which had been paraded following Enoch Powell's speech on immigration and his sacking four years earlier.

It came at a bad time for Ted, as the Party was still badly shaken by the reverberations of the miners' strike earlier in the year and we were trailing Labour in the opinion polls. But Ted remained firm to his own beliefs and his stand during those difficult months helped shift the Party, and the country, decisively away from the prejudices of a few.

Ted's courage and vision were equally evident in tackling another legacy of Empire – the problems of Ireland. He accorded it top priority, appointing Willie Whitelaw as Secretary of State for Northern Ireland in 1972, and eighteen months later – when many other problems were all demanding his attention – by personally taking charge at the Sunningdale talks on the future of Northern Ireland. It was very much due to his determination that a new accommodation was reached between Unionists and Nationalists in Northern Ireland, and between London and Dublin. The new power-sharing executive, in which Brian Faulkner and his Unionists and Gerry Fitt, with his SDLP colleagues, worked together, offered the first real ray of hope since the Troubles had erupted.

Ted's great ambition was that Britain should take her rightful place in the European Community, not as a supplicant, but as a leading country. His whole design was to lift this country out of the inertia and years of decay which he felt characterised the last years of Harold Macmillan's premiership and the Labour Government which followed. He was supremely confident that we could do much better for Britain, regarding European entry as the springboard.

Certainly it was this that gave him his enormous motivation and idealism for the European Community and our membership. Those early days of 1961 and 1962 when he led the abortive negotiation and by a combination of brilliant negotiation and idealistic fervour convinced doubting farmers and wavering Empire loyalists alike was leadership of a very high order. In the early seventies as Prime Minister his determination to go for growth was based on the frustration of seeing France, Germany and others improving their infrastructure and modernising their industrial base, whilst Britain lagged behind in a morass of complacency.

No one should under-estimate what Ted was seeking to achieve for the country, or his enormous courage in trying to make it happen. No one other than Ted would have taken Britain into Europe.

Before the 1970 election campaign, Iain Macleod was very keen that we should commit ourselves to a referendum on British entry to the EEC. He thought this would remove much of the opposition within the Party and would make it impossible for Wilson to come out in favour of one, a trick he was convinced Wilson would play unless we moved first. It took at least two meetings with Ted and Alec Home to shake Iain off this point. Even then, during the first week of the campaign he came very close to saying that he thought there ought to be a referendum.

The argument against Iain was that we were fighting the election on a pro-EEC platform. It would be a matter for Parliament to decide, on the basis of the terms which we were able to negotiate.

In Cabinet, Minister after Minister would set out all the difficulties and recount the insoluble problems – whether it was our relations with Australia and New Zealand, or the much more emotive Commonwealth Sugar Agreement or British Agriculture, or farming, or fishing. But Ted had the sheer determination to find the answers and overcome all the difficulties.

It was always obvious that the arithmetic of the vote in Parliament on British membership of the European Community was going to be difficult. We knew that a number of our Members were implacably opposed, like Enoch Powell, Neil Marten and Harmar Nicholls. Their vote if combined with all the Opposition's support would defeat the Government, which would not only have prevented membership of the European Community but also led to the fall of the Government.

We could rely on the small band of Liberals, but what of the pro-Europeans on the Labour benches? We knew that Roy Jenkins, Shirley Williams and others were in favour of Britain joining the Community, but many who had supported Harold Wilson's abortive attempt in the late 1960s would vote against us. These included Denis Healey, who came out against membership in an effort to curry favour with the left wing, whom he had upset so much as Labour's Defence Secretary between 1964 and 1970.

All through this anxious time we made great efforts privately to keep Roy Jenkins and his group informed, and they in turn advised us what was possible and how we could play our hand. Tony Royle, who was a junior minister at the Foreign Office, played a part in this. He did it very well and the work was well rewarded as in the major vote on the principle of entry we had a majority of 112.

The Bill to implement our membership was a much tougher proposition with a number of very small majorities, down to four on some occasions. When the Bill was finally through and the vote had been reported to the Speaker, Francis Pym, the Chief Whip, gave vent to his feelings. Much to the amusement and delight of us all, this cautious and phlegmatic character danced a jig on the floor of the House.

British membership of the European Community is the most significant political development for Britain since the Second World War: the tribute for achieving this should go entirely to Ted Heath.

CHAPTER FIVE

END OF A VISION

Once Ted Heath had made the landfall of Europe, he may well have felt that the next few years would be plain sailing. But the storm of inflation was fast approaching.

Victor Rothschild's Think Tank warned Ted of the dire trouble ahead. He produced a paper for the Cabinet Economic Committee on oil prices well before anyone else had foreseen the risk of a big increase. The gist was that Western Europe could not expect to go on with such low oil prices, which were then around $1\frac{1}{2}$ a barrel. By 1977 we could be paying up to $4 per barrel of oil. This was too much for the Department of Trade and Industry which was then responsible for energy policy. The DTI's paper argued that, while oil prices probably would increase, Lord Rothschild's forecast was a gross exaggeration. In fact, by December 1973, a matter of months after this exchange, oil prices were approaching $12 per barrel.

The continuation of our prices and incomes policy was essential to sustain our overall economic policy, yet we could not afford to risk another showdown with the miners. The Party had received a terrible beating from our own supporters for what they saw as our surrender to the miners in February 1972: we simply had to avoid any repetition. I had learned over the years that large sections of the Tory Party were never so happy as when they felt they were bashing the unions; but never so miserable as when they felt that they had been beaten by them.

The miners' next pay award was due in November 1973. During the summer Ted Heath and Sir William Armstrong tried to find a way to accommodate the miners within the terms of Stage III without providing a loophole for all other pay claims. The provision for pay awards to include extra increases for 'unsocial hours' was designed specifically to meet the miners' demands, though others would undoubtedly try to seize the opportunity. Ted and Armstrong thought that they had reached a satisfactory agreement with Joe Gormley, the National Union of Mineworkers' President. The Cabinet were never given any inkling about the talks between Ted and William Armstrong and Joe Gormley, but we were under the impression that the 'unsocial hours' clause in the pay policy was flexible enough to allow a settlement.

I did not know Joe well in those days, but I got to know him very well afterwards and believe that he was too wily an old fox to have given the kind of firm pledge which they seemed to think that they had been given. I cannot believe that Joe would have tied himself down so firmly – his line would have been that the offer wasn't too bad, he would do his best, but of course he couldn't promise anything and he would have to carry his executive with him on whether to recommend accepting the offer.

By the autumn of 1973 we had therefore well and truly boxed ourselves in. We thought that we had made all the adjustments necessary in Stage III of our pay policy to meet the miners' demands, but we were proved wrong. The miners rejected the offer, yet we could not disown our own legislation.

With a statutory pay policy, there was no room for the usual bargaining. If we had offered the miners a lower figure at the outset and then conceded the 'norm' afterwards, we would appear disingenuous – it would have been an obvious charade. With hindsight, we probably should have given the miners more to bargain about. Union leaders need to show their members that they are working for them and earning their salt. Many complained to me in later years that a pay policy takes away much of their power over their members.

Yet we simply could not afford to be seen to 'ease up' in any way in our counter-inflation policy.

We had set our face against the option of higher unemployment, and the inflationary surge in world commodity prices, during 1973 gave a further turn to the screw.

I sat in during some of Ted's talks at Number Ten on a pay policy with the union leaders. These were always conducted in a friendly and reasonable manner – even the ashtrays which Ted had removed from the Cabinet table at the start of his Government were reinstated. Jack Jones and Hugh Scanlon seemed to have considerable regard for Ted, but the talks were strangely listless. The explosion in world commodity prices presented the country with a serious crisis, but Jack always seemed more concerned about the price of cabbages than anything else.

Our reaction to the miners' overtime ban which began in November was dictated by the traumatic experience of the 1972 miners' strike. We were determined not to get caught out again, but now we went to the other extreme. In December, we put industry on a 3-day week and introduced restrictions on lighting, heating and broadcasting long before they were strictly necessary. Had the miners' overtime ban continued, we had coal stocks to last through until April, but there was an overriding strategic imperative to conserve our coal stocks at the highest possible level. That winter's oil crisis, prompted by the Yom Kippur War, precluded any idea of switching some power stations from coal to oil: with a world oil shortage, the supplies simply did not exist.

But, having taken such drastic action from the very outset, it was subsequently more difficult to convince people that the situation was really as serious as we had claimed, a feeling which the Labour Party naturally exploited.

It was my task as Leader of the House to announce, each Thursday, the Commons' business for the following week. The House is generally full as the announcement is made at 3.30 after Prime Minister's Questions, and it provides MPs with a further chance to ask questions and grind a few axes, so long as they justify their question on the grounds that it is to do with next week's business. We were endeavouring to keep the temperature down – in every sense – as we had more than enough troubles wihout upsetting the House of Commons, and I had therefore announced a particularly innocuous week's business.

Harold Wilson, as Leader of the Opposition, rose to complain about it, and then asked me when, in view of the parlous state of the economy, the Chancellor would introduce his autumn budget. On these occasions I nearly always had Ted Heath on one side of me and Francis Pym, as Chief Whip, on the other. Usually they would offer some characteristic advice: from Ted, 'Have a go at them'; from Francis, 'Don't get involved in the merits.' But this time there was not a murmur from either. I got up quickly and stated firmly, 'There will be no autumn budget.'

To my amusement and astonishment, the Stock Exchange, which had been languishing, put on 14 points in after-hours dealings, and the *Daily Telegraph*'s highly respected political correspondent, Harry Boyne, declared the next morning that it was obvious there must have been a full discussion at Cabinet for me to be able to answer so unequivocally. I happened to see the Chancellor, Tony Barber, later that day. He smiled. 'You're a countryman, aren't you; how long does the autumn last?'

It was during the 3-day week that I first became aware of Margaret Thatcher's absolute determination to fight her corner. As Lord President of the Council, I chaired the Ministerial meetings overseeing the handling of the crisis. We had introduced an Order which, by mistake, failed to exempt schools from the cuts in heating which had been introduced to save fuel. Tom Boardman, Minister of State at the Department of Trade and Industry, had been responsible for the Order. A meeting was held in my room, attended by Margaret, as Secretary of State for Education, Tom Boardman, myself and two or three officials. Margaret was absolutely furious because she had not been properly consulted. She laid down the law to Tom Boardman in a way that I had never heard it laid down before. I was most impressed. In fact, one of her officials had been at the meeting of the Contingencies Unit which had made the decision, but had not said anything.

I was amused to find, the very next morning after Margaret's great

performance, that the *Sun*, of all papers was condemning her in its leading
article for being so hard-hearted over the decision to cut heating in the
schools and saying that this was in line with her reputation as a 'milk
snatcher'. This was hard luck on Margaret, but probably the last time the
Sun ever attacked her.

Ted was determined till the very last that a negotiated settlement
should be sought. At the start of December he recalled Willie Whitelaw
from Northern Ireland to bring his considerable bargaining skills to bear
on the issue. It was hard for Willie to get himself into the picture so
quickly, but he was convinced that had he been allowed a bit more leeway
he could have settled the dispute: by that late stage, however, there was
simply no leeway left.

At one point it seemed that we had found a means of settling the
miners' claim without letting every other group gain bigger pay rises.
The idea was to pay the miners for 'bathing and waiting time'. But
Harold Wilson heard about it and put it forward himself as a possible
solution. He must have known that we would disown it. Joe Gormley has
never forgiven Harold.

A siege mentality had taken hold of the Government. There were
further talks at Number Ten with union leaders, but the chances of
success were slight. Those of us who were hawkish felt that the only way
out was to call a general election. There seemed every justification as the
oil crisis had transformed the country's economic prospects – spending
cuts had had to be rushed through before the Commons rose for
Christmas and the balance of payments had suddenly been knocked for
six.

At Conservative Central Office, the Party Chairman, Peter Carrington,
and I knew that Ted would be very reluctant to call an election: he was
very concerned about holding an election during a national crisis, fearing,
quite rightly, the political divisions which would be stirred up in the
country.

All the advice Ted was receiving was to take a hard line. From Conservative Party headquarters, Peter Carrington and I were urging a tough
approach, in tune with the Party's sentiments at the time, although neither
he nor I was a hawk as far as the unions were concerned. It was the same
message that Ted was hearing from the Treasury and from William
Armstrong. Willie Whitelaw and Robert Carr at the Home Office were
the only voices urging Ted to be conciliatory.

William Armstrong's feelings were particularly strong and influenced
me. For this brilliant, highly objective civil servant to be taking so determined a position was most unusual. He told us that what was at issue was
the sort of society in which his grandchildren would be brought up, and
that it was imperative that the rule of law must not be flouted. If he was

emotional, I was also becoming emotionally committed too. Emotions do run high in politics, and there is not necessarily any harm in that: but I do not think I served Ted well at that time by allowing myself to go along with my emotions, and not to standing back and trying to see things more objectively.

By the Christmas recess, Peter Carrington and I were strong advocates for announcing in early January an election on February 7.

*

It had been agreed that as Chairman of the Contingencies Unit I should keep in close contact with Ted over Christmas. It was important that we should be seen to be in control of events. The country might be on holiday, but the Government had many problems and there was a national emergency in force. I had reported to him by phone, and he then suggested that I should visit him at Chequers, not so much to get through a lot of work as for appearance's sake.

I travelled down to see Ted at Chequers on December 27. His hospitality was, as always, generous. We did no serious work. He was rightly relaxed, and no doubt contemplating how he would play his hand over the ensuing weeks. It was quite clear that he did not wish to become embroiled with me over questions of a possible election.

Every time I got round to the need to prepare a manifesto the subject was changed. It was almost as if he wished to be incommunicado as far as decisions on election preparations were concerned, although both Peter Carrington and myself were becoming convinced that it was the only answer. We couldn't face yet another humiliating climb-down with the miners, the Party was only just recovering from the 1972 débâcle. We had unwittingly played ourselves into a corner and an appeal to the public on who governed Britain looked the best answer.

After lunch there was not much point in my staying any longer, but I decided not to leave too early as this would create the wrong impression. I was asked whether I would like to see a film, so after lunch I sat in solitary state and watched *The Belstone Fox*. It tells the story of a fox which is kept and mothered as a pet by the huntsman's family, and when put back into the wild draws the hounds across a railway line where many are slaughtered. I sense now, looking back on it, that Joe Gormley was proving himself to be the wily old fox. And we were soon to chase him to our own disaster.

This frame of mind in Government explains how we missed an opportunity which came on January 9 at the regular monthly meeting of the National Economic Development Council attended by Ministers, industrialists and union leaders. Sydney Greene, the NUR leader and then chairman of the TUC's economic committee, put forward the TUC's offer to restrain other pay demands if the miners could be made a special case. But we spurned them.

Len Murray had very recently succeeded Vic Feather as TUC General Secretary, and Willie Whitelaw, who had only just taken over at Employment, had not had time to get to know the union leaders. As a result the Government had no inkling beforehand of the TUC's proposition. The usual practice, before suggesting such a major initiative at a forum like Neddy, would have been to discuss the idea privately first, so that all concerned could take the necessary soundings. It has been said that the idea was kept under wraps for fear that it would leak, but if that was so I am sure it was a mistake and should have been handled differently.

Tony Barber, chairing the Neddy meeting as Chancellor, did nothing to encourage the TUC to believe that their offer would be taken up. But he didn't rule out the idea altogether and immediately consulted Ted and others. Given our attitude by this stage, it is perhaps not surprising that the offer was rejected. The TUC had talked of 'special cases' many times in the past, but were never able, or willing, to hold the line.

Around this time Frank Chapple, the power workers' leader, came to see me, and in his usual forthright way made it clear that, if the miners were a special case, so were his members. We thus urged Ted to stick to a tough line. With hindsight, however, our rejection of the TUC offer was clearly a missed opportunity. It would have got us off the hook and put the unions on best behaviour – had their self-restraint failed, we would then have been in a much stronger position to take whatever steps might have been necessary.

Late in the afternoon of Thursday, January 17, the day on which we would have had to announce an election for polling on February 7, I went to see Ted at Number Ten: 'If it's any consolation, I'd like you to know that all the Labour Members were coming up to me in the tea room to tell me that we have let them off the hook. They're throwing their hats in the air – they haven't been in that kind of mood for weeks.'

Ted retorted, 'It's all your bloody fault. If you hadn't allowed Central Office to steam this thing up, we would never have got into this position.'

'If you had told us definitely that you were against an election, it wouldn't have been steamed up,' I replied. We had already marched the Party's troops up the hill, ready for combat, and then had to march them down again; it would be much harder to march them up a second time.

Within a week the miners had voted 81 per cent in favour of an all-out strike and in the end Ted felt there was nothing else he could do but go to the country. We had no room for manouevre, any opportunities to find a settlement had been lost, the miners were going on an all-out strike and the world economy had been thrown into turmoil by the oil crisis.

I was guest speaker at a Press Gallery lunch at the Commons on Wednesday, February 6. My comment that 'the miners have had their ballot, perhaps we ought to have ours' was the signal that the hawks' view had finally, perhaps belatedly, prevailed. The next day, Ted called the election for February 28, three weeks later than we hawks had wanted.

At my last business questions I announced the dates of the reassembly of the new Parliament. There then followed a few minutes of party political banter. Andrew Faulds, the Labour MP and an actor, asked me whether I would 'make speedy arrangements to have erected on one of the plinths . . . in the Members' Lobby a rubber statue of the imminently ex-Prime Minister, bearing the words, carved in stone: "The wrecker".' I had been longing to have a go at Faulds for months and replied that I hoped he would have 'a good chance to go back to the job which he occupied before and take part in another film such as *Young Winston*, in which he played the part of a mounted Boer'. As I walked out of the House, Harold Wilson stopped me to say that he wished he had thought of making that remark to Faulds.

*

Harold Wilson probably thought he had as much chance of winning in 1974 as we thought we had in 1970. We had a useful lead in those wretched opinion polls. I could not see how we could lose on the central issue of 'Who governs Britain, the duly elected Government, with the authority of Parliament, or the mineworkers' union?'

There were no violent scenes on the picket line during the election campaign. In the previous miners' strike in 1972, there had been considerable violence, and again during the dockers' strike in the summer of 1972. But the miners were clever enough tacticians to play everything quietly. They instituted a Code of Practice on picketing, which restricted pickets at any site to six, and whether at the mines, power stations or docks they were as quiet and well-behaved as mice.

The campaign itself was a nightmare. Even at the best of times February is a bad month in which to try to make people feel optimistic. But people were being laid off from work, there was a batch of depressing economic statistics and some very high profit figures from the banks and the oil companies, which undermined our claim to fairness as the reason for a pay policy.

The biggest bombshell came on February 21, a week before polling, in the shape of an interim report from the Pay Relativities Board. The miners' claim had been referred to the Board on February 8. Their report appeared to show that the miners could have more money for washing and winding time, that the figures on which the NCB had been working were wrong, and that the dispute, and hence the election itself, were both unnecessary.

In one television interview after another I tried to refute the Relativities Board case. But it was all to no avail. The damage was done, the seeds of disbelief and muddle had been sown. It began to look as if we had been opportunistic in calling the election. The electorate had been suspicious of Wilson in the last day of the 1970 election, but now the tables had been turned against us. Two days before polling Campbell Adamson, the Director-General of the CBI, was highly critical of our Industrial Relations Act, which was gleefully exploited by the Labour Party.

A few days after Christmas 1973 the white swan, which lived on the moat at our Suffolk farmhouse, had flown away. We had originally rescued it as a cygnet from vicious parents on the nearby river Waveney, and it had joined the pair of black swans we already had on the moat. When the cygnet grew into a lovely white bird we could not resist calling it 'Enoch'. I can't think why he took wing, because he lived in perfect freedom and harmony with his black friends; it may have been because the black swans were starting to nest. Four eggs were laid and were due to hatch out on election day, February 28. The omens escaped us at the time.

After Ted had called the general election, Enoch Powell promptly announced that he would not stand in an 'essentially fraudulent' election. Enoch had long been disaffected with Ted and the Conservative Government. It was not just the old sores over immigration which still rankled, it was more the direction of economic policy and, of course, our membership of the European Community.

I suppose that Enoch has made two great miscalculations in his political career: one was the result of the 1970 election which he had expected us to lose, the other, the outcome of our approach to the EEC was our membership of the Community. He thought that a combination of the Labour Party and the right wing of the Conservative Party would be sufficient to keep Britain out – most of the Labour Party were worried that membership would deny them the right to introduce socialist measures, while the right wing Tories had romantic visions of Commonwealth, cheap food and a power for Britain which was fifty years out of date.

Enoch's speech during the February 1974 election campaign denouncing Ted and advising people to vote Labour was, on the other hand, undoubtedly an important factor in the final result.

*

Although my majority was reduced to 3,604 as a result of a 2 per cent swing to Labour, I held my seat at Lowestoft. In the Commons, we lost our overall majority and with 297 seats we were no longer even the largest party. But Labour, with 301 seats, had fallen short of winning a majority of seats and we had actually polled 240,000 more votes than them in the country. The other parties had gained at the expense of us both – the Liberals won 14 seats, the Scottish Nationalists 7 and the Welsh Nationalists 2, while in Ulster the more hard-line Unionists won 11 of the 12 seats.

Was it possible that with the help of the Liberals we could hold on as a minority Government? They had had a very successful election campaign, polling 6 million votes, increasing their share of the vote to 19 per cent and recording their best performance since the 1930s. Jeremy Thorpe had led them with style and panache. Would he negotiate with us?

As the last results came in during Friday, Ted decided that at least he should talk to Jeremy, but the problem was to find him. By this time a group of us including Ted were having a decidedly wakish dinner at the Wolffs'. Ted was completely shell-shocked. We had ordered oysters from Prunier's, as these were his favourite, but he barely seemed to notice them as a couple of dozen slipped down his throat.

We kept telephoning Barnstaple to talk to Jeremy, but he was out on a candlelight victory procession and could not be contacted. Eventually the next day a meeting was arranged.

The weekend was dreadful. We had lost the election and yet there was obviously no great enthusiasm in the country for a Labour government. Although Jeremy himself was quite keen and would have relished the post of Home Secretary, his Parliamentary Party would have split. David Steel and Cyril Smith were not interested in any coalition with the Tories. By the Monday it was clear that only a Government including members of all parties would be acceptable to the Liberals, and neither we nor Labour could stomach that.

Once Ted had reported to us that the talks with the Liberals had broken down, there was no more that he could do other than hand in his resignation to the Queen. For us to hang on longer and perhaps even face the House of Commons was not an alternative, since the miners' strike was still on and we were beginning to give the impression that we were bad losers.

The door of Number Ten was to close behind us for the last time and few thought that we should be back again for ten years at least. The miners' strike, the oil price increase and the commodity boom had taken their toll, but oil was beginning to gush out of the wells in the North

Sea. All that Labour needed to do was to govern quietly, blame us for the mess we had left behind, have a further election and they would be set fair for a lengthy spell in office.

On the night of the election down at our house in Suffolk a fox broke into the swans' enclosure and killed the pen. Some of the family were far more upset about this loss than the loss of the election. I suppose they were keeping things in perspective.

To this day, I am convinced that the three week delay in calling the election was crucial. But, if my enthusiasm had helped Ted to win in 1970, my impetuosity in 1974 had contributed to his defeat.

*

The new minority Labour Government was buoyed up by a victory which they had never expected and would clearly use every trick in the book to ensure a working majority at a further election. In the meanwhile they were able to govern with the connivance of Liberals and Ulster Unionists. The circumstances of our defeat gave us no grounds for comfort that we could regain office at an early election. It was not in our interests to cause too much trouble: we were in no position to win and felt that the executioner's rope was already round our neck.

In May 1974 Ted Heath decided to make Willie Whitelaw Chairman of the Party. Peter Carrington as chairman and myself as deputy had advised on an early election and lost. It was right we should be replaced ahead of a certain election that autumn. No doubt too that Willie was the right man to unite the Party and hold everything together at a very difficult time.

Peter Carrington is a great diplomat but was never very happy at Central Office. His liberal instincts made him dislike some of the hard-nosed characters in the constituencies. He had never experienced the cut and thrust of party politics in the Commons or on the hustings. He was a marvellous man to work with, a droll wit with a very quick mind. He would have been a contender for the leadership all through the 1960s and 1970s had he chosen the Commons rather than the Lords. But to be a Prime Minister you have got to want the job very badly, and I don't think Peter wanted it enough.

The battle lines of the great ideological argument within the Party, which has raged ever since, were being drawn up. The months immediately after the February 1974 election were a period of 'phoney war', with no more than skirmishes, but soon the monetarists would feel free to go on to the attack. In our desire to break through the vicious circle of 'stop-go' after the winter of 1971–72, we had misjudged the level of demand and allowed the money supply to expand too fast. In his own rethinking in Opposition, Keith Joseph had latched on to 'monetarism' as the panacea, and during 1974 was steadily building a denunciation of our entire approach.

In September 1974 we got wind, a few days beforehand, of Keith's plans to make his most outspoken attack yet on our policy in Government: this at a time when Labour was set to call an October election and would pull out all the stops to secure an overall majority in the Commons. A number of us tried to stop Keith giving his speech. I even had a word with Margaret Thatcher, who by then seemed to have become one of Keith's followers, 'You know this is a disastrous speech – can't you stop him giving it?' Margaret replied that it was the work of Alfred Sherman: she felt that Keith did not always understand the political impact of arguments, but that she did not have much influence over him.

Sherman had been appointed Director of the new Centre for Policy Studies, which Keith, Margaret and Geoffrey Howe had been instrumental in establishing soon after we had left office. Ted had agreed to the CPS being set up, and gave it his support, writing to people to ask for funds. Its declared objective at that stage was to examine the role of the entrepreneur and how the creeping effect of Socialism could be pulled back. It was envisaged as being broadly based and was never presented to us at the outset as some new pressure group for monetarism, which is what it soon became.

Ted thought it would be a good idea if Keith and Margaret could get to know more about industry, as he felt that they had no real understanding of it. He hoped that by arguing with, and listening to, senior businessmen, they would realise how difficult things were and that there was no simplistic answer to our economic ills. Val Duncan, then Chairman of Rio Tinto Zinc, was asked to hold a series of dinners, to which two or three other leading industrialists would be invited. Marcus Sieff of Marks and Spencer and Hector Laing of United Biscuits were among those who attended. Peter Carrington and myself made up the group. A number of these dinners were held before the second 1974 general election, but after that no more was heard of them.

*

Predictably Labour called an October election, with polling on the 10th. At the outset of the campaign most of us were anticipating a heavy defeat.

But the electorate were obviously attracted to Ted's idea of a 'Government of national unity'. It seemed to make a lot of sense, although none of us was quite certain how on earth it could be made to work in practice. It was a reflex action to the traumas through which the country was passing, and there was little confidence that either of the main parties had all the answers itself, or could govern effectively.

Not many of us distinguished ourselves in the campaign, except perhaps for Margaret Thatcher. As our environment spokesman it fell to her to put forward our two specific policies – the abolition of the domestic rates and the pledge to hold mortgage interest rates at 9 per cent – which undoubtedly saved us from a disastrous defeat. Though pegging the mortgage interest rate would have seriously distorted the market, Margaret soon overcame her initial reluctance to become a fervent and effective exponent. She has been valiantly if vainly trying to abolish domestic rates ever since.

Labour with 319 seats won only a meagre 4-seat majority over all other parties. My own majority in Lowestoft was further reduced to 2,062. In the Commons, the Party lost 20 seats, leaving us with 277. The Liberals won 13 seats, the Scottish Nationals further increased their strength to 11, and the Welsh Nationalists to 3. Of the dozen Northern Ireland seats, 10 were won by Unionists, including Enoch Powell, who returned to the Commons as MP for South Down.

Our defeat was nothing like as heavy as most of us had feared. But within twenty-four hours I told Ted that his only chance of carrying on as Leader was if he submitted himself to an early election through the 1922 Committee. He replied that he didn't intend to submit himself to a leadership election because he was determined to fight the right wing, I told him that if he refused to go he would probably end up giving them exactly what they wanted. Maybe I delivered my opinion more bluntly than I should have, but I had always been candid with Ted.

I felt that there was no chance that he could sustain his position. An early decision to submit himself to re-election was probably his only chance of holding on, though I doubted if he could in any circumstances. My impression was that Ted by then was only hearing the advice he wished to hear, including some from sources to which previously he had paid scant attention.

I was surprised by the number of people who were saying that they disliked him, and by the degree of bitterness and the spiteful determination that he had to go. The executive of the 1922 Committee met at the home of its chairman, Edward du Cann, on October 14, and decided to press for a leadership election. The executive had been dubbed the 'Milk Street Mafia', after a more public meeting at Edward's City office at Keyser Ullman, in Milk Street.

Again Ted demurred, but the Parliamentary Party's unease over the procedure for new leadership elections caused him to set up a review committee under Alec Home. The conclusions of Alec's review committee, however, were not at all helpful to Ted. There should be a provision for annual leadership elections in the Parliamentary Party. If there was a second ballot, new candidates could stand at that stage.

The most likely of Ted's challengers was Keith Joseph, the most senior 'dissident' who had been in Ted's Cabinet. No one had then realised that, however decent the man, his political antennae were too insensitive. But they very soon did, for within a few days, on October 19, Keith made a speech in Edgbaston which demonstrated almost unbelievable ineptitude for someone in the running for the Leadership. He referred to social classes 4 and 5 as being the least able to bring up children without resort to the state, and appeared to suggest that they should be encouraged through birth control to have fewer.

In fairness to Keith, he realised very quickly that he lacked the requisite qualities and threw in the towel. This posed the dissidents with quite a problem. They did not really want Edward du Cann – he was recognised as having been disloyal to Ted Heath, and his City activities, with Lonrho and Keyser Ullman, were not universally accepted. He soon announced his decision not to run.

At this stage most people would have given up the struggle and for a time settled for Ted, who by now had enlisted new blood into his team, including the trusty old campaigner, John Peyton, and Peter Walker, who was re-engaged as Ted's campaign manager. But we reckoned without the persistence and almost obsessive scheming of Airey Neave.

Airey was a man of great courage – he had escaped from Colditz – and bitter determination. He was an implacable enemy of Ted's, from the 1950s when Ted had been Chief Whip, and they had a great row. Someone who had been determined enough to escape from Colditz was unlikely to be put off by losing a couple of potential candidates, so the next in line was pushed forward. This was Margaret Thatcher.

Up to that time, I do not believe that she had thought of herself as a candidate for the Leadership. My conversations with her gave me no inkling to that effect, and, although she was ambitious, I do not think she felt that her time had come. However, Airey ran a brilliant campaign – I was in a good position to judge because at that time Margaret had the little box of an office immediately opposite mine in the Shadow Cabinet corridor at the Commons, and this became Airey's headquarters. There was a constant flow of MPs to see them, and I began to realise that these were drawn from a wide cross-section of the Party.

Although Margaret knew I would not support her, I was on reasonable terms with her – so much so that during the battle for the Leadership I attended her constituency annual dinner and dance as guest of honour.

Airey Neave's exercise was carried out by a combination of promises and flattery, and was brilliantly masterminded. Margaret's stature in the

Party had been enhanced by her performances at the dispatch box as Robert Carr's deputy opposing Labour's Finance Bill. Her courage in opposing Ted went down well in the Party and in much of the press. Other potential candidates, who were remaining loyal to Ted but who it was known would come in on the second ballot if Ted were defeated, were quietly being accused of cowardice by the Neave camp. The fact that a vote for Margaret was the only way to secure a second ballot was also turned to advantage.

There was only one really bitter outbreak of in-fighting, prompted by a story which Peter Walker had raked up from somewhere that gave an account of Margaret hoarding food during the miners' strike. The intention had been to brand her as a 'hoarder' as well as the 'milk snatcher', but most of us thought this seemed an eminently sensible thing for her to have done.

On the day of the first ballot, February 4, 1975, I was on a political tour of the East Midlands. I had allowed plenty of time to return to the Commons to vote, but the train was one and a half hours late. I arrived at the House in time to be greeted by the sight of Alan Clark, the maverick right wing MP for Plymouth Sutton, rushing out of Westminster Hall shouting at the top of his voice, 'She's won, she's won.'

Margaret received 130 votes to Ted's 119 and Hugh Fraser's 16. Thank goodness my vote would not have made any difference. It was one of the most miserable days in my life.

The next day I received a visit from Humphrey Atkins, by then our Chief Whip, telling me in enthusiastic and forceful terms that I should stand for the leadership. This surprised me, as I had not thought of him as someone who would favour me, and in any case I presumed that he would support Willie Whitelaw.

My main supporters were my former PPSs, Michael Jopling and Barney Hayhoe, the former retiring to bed with 'flu for the rest of the the week between the two ballots.

I received a number of approaches to withdraw. Ian Percival, the lawyer on the right of the party, suggested that Margaret as Leader and myself as Deputy would be a winning team and the votes could be delivered. I cannot believe he came without Airey Neave's permission, but it did not look a very comfortable arrangement, and I declined.

On the second ballot on February 11, Margaret won 146 votes, Willie Whitelaw 79, myself and Geoffrey Howe each won 19 votes, and John Peyton 11. It was clear that Geoffrey Howe and myself would be the also-rans, but I was a little surprised that I ran so badly. I discovered when I later spoke with Geoffrey that he too had been persuaded to stand by Humphrey Atkins.

Margaret had won convincingly. The party was greatly relieved to get the whole business over and done with.

I have no doubt that Willie lost his chance of being leader and perhaps Prime Minister as a result of his loyalty to Ted during this period. If he had been free to enter the leadership stakes immediately after our October election defeat, he would almost certainly have been elected. No one can fault the absolute loyalty that Willie gave to Ted and then Margaret. He has had a very distinguished career and by dint of old-fashioned virtues and a marvellously warm personality has held the Party together on many occasions.

There was no way that the Party was going to be generous to Ted Heath after three General Election defeats out of four. The right wing hated Ted and the scenes of rejoicing when he was beaten in the leadership contest by Margaret Thatcher left me feeling very sad.

*

After his resignation as Leader he remarked to me: 'The backbenchers all complain that I've never kept in touch with them. But more of them came to Number Ten whilst I was Prime Minister than ever before.' I am certain that this was true. He was a very generous host, but being a good host is about more than choosing good wine and good food. It's also about enjoyment and talking, making people feel happy and at ease. He was never very good at that.

In the same way he had actually been quite punctilious about going round the tea-rooms at the Commons, but the difficulty always was getting him to talk and be natural. There was that element of reserve, of shyness, which came across as rudeness.

Over the years I grew very fond of Ted Heath, although I cannot say that this has ever developed into a great and close relationship. In many ways he is a very private, rather shy and unapproachable man who can be given to rudeness and show boredom quickly if he finds people uninteresting or he is suspicious that they are trying to use him in some fashion.

In no way is he gregarious, and this is surprising in a man who has been Prime Minister, Chief Whip and Member of Parliament for a number of years in a constituency that was never too safe.

I am quite certain that the more Ted saw of the party establishment or for that matter the establishment in general, the more he became convinced he could beat them, as of course he did; and the more successful he became, the more he came to despise them as well. This is evidenced by his reactions when Margaret became Leader, and the establishment turned against him. He never liked them and this was reciprocated.

As Prime Minister he was perhaps in too much of a hurry and ahead of his time. The country had not responded to his warnings against the perils of the unions rejecting reform and of high rates of inflation. It was to take a further ten years for public opinion to catch up and Margaret was to reap the benefit. Ted had been right to tackle the dangers but did not have time to solve them before he ran into rough weather.

Because of this, in public and particularly in the House of Commons, he appears to have become totally disenchanted with the world, but that is an unfair and superficial judgment of this exceptional man. He is a very talented musician, a considerable expert on pictures and porcelain, and of course has won perhaps the most challenging of all ocean yacht races, from Sydney to Hobart, with a standard boat of no particular merit. If he now becomes an expert gardener in his beautiful Salisbury home, it will come as no surprise. But above and beyond these personal interests, he is as informed and concerned about the fundamental issues of Britain and the world as he ever was.

Shortly after he retired from the leadership I went to have lunch with him. As I arrived and walked down the hall to his study, he saw me coming and got out a copy of his book on sailing and handed it to me. 'Is this for me to look at or keep?' I asked. 'To look at,' he replied.

I must confess I was disappointed, but he was never one to mince words. My delight was all the greater when he sent me the book for Christmas.

CHAPTER SIX

MRS THATCHER TAKES THE REINS

I had been at the centre of Tory Party politics for almost ten years, since Ted had appointed me as his PPS, but once Margaret Thatcher took over it all altered. It may seem hard to understand why I experienced so great a change – after all, I was in Margaret's Shadow Cabinet and then her Cabinet continuously until September 1984: surely that is being at the centre of things, or 'on the inside track'?

But in any Party, and in any Government, the Leader, or Prime Minister, inevitably relies on a very few trusted colleagues – usually a few Ministers and perhaps two or three aides. With Ted as Leader and Prime Minister, I was right on the inside. But, when Margaret became Leader, I became one of the outsiders, saying my piece, at times able to exert some influence, but all the time aware that the centre of decision-making and weight of the Party and Government machine lay with others.

Yet curiously Margaret was a Leader and a Prime Minister who in some ways remained on the outside herself. She felt able to divorce herself from decisions which she did not like, as if at times the Party, or her Government, were nothing to do with her.

Partly as a result of her approach as Leader, and partly due to the change in the Party since the early 1960s, the traditional ways in which the old 'inner circle' used to organise the Party – informally and discreetly, born of the values of duty and loyalty – could no longer work. Whenever Willie Whitelaw and Francis Pym used to get together, they still seemed to think that the Party could be run as they had run it ten or fifteen years earlier. Although they undoubtedly could wield some power and used all their skill to keep Margaret's Shadow Cabinet reasonably cohesive, it could never be the same again.

When Margaret took over I was shocked by her immediate dismissal of Michael Wolff, whom Ted had appointed Director-General of the Party Organisation. Michael had taken no part in Ted's campaign for re-election as Leader, but he became the scapegoat of a violent attack by Edward du Cann and others on the right. I saw Margaret and told her that she was misinformed and wrong to let him go. But she said it was the decision of Peter Thorneycroft, whom she had appointed as the new Party Chairman. Peter, however, maintained otherwise. On the evening

that Michael was sacked from Central Office I refused to vote for the
Party and stayed away from the Commons. Margaret's action was an
early demonstration of the iron hand in a velvet glove.

It was not only the political personalities and the methods of Party
management which were altering; the philosophy was changing also; and
by the mid-1970s, the economic argument was shifting perceptibly too –
to the right. Inflation had become a bigger enemy than unemployment.

The fresh intellectual arguments from the right, spurred on by Professor Friedman and the Chicago School in America, and initially by
Enoch Powell at home, were beginning to look respectable and were being
presented as the panacea by which all our problems could be solved. The
nostrum of 'sound money' was back in fashion. Some were so confident
in the new theories that they even suggested that the rate of inflation
could be accurately predicted from the rate of increase in a particular
measure of the money supply some two years earlier.

Harold Macmillan had tried to balance inflation and employment; Alec
Home had relied on Reggie Maudling's 'dash for growth'; Harold Wilson
and Ted Heath had resorted to statutory incomes and prices policies;
now it was to be the turn of the monetarists. The Conservative Party had
found a doctrine.

The basis of my difference with Margaret and Keith was not that many
of the policies which they espoused were wrong or unacceptable in themselves – after all, we were united in believing that there had to be a shift
from taxing earnings to taxing spending; that public expenditure must be
brought under control; and that every effort had to be made to free the
economy and individuals from the burden of statutory and bureaucratic
controls. What began to stick in the gullet was the growing belief during our
years in opposition that the only thing that really mattered was control of
the money supply and that Professors Milton Friedman and Hayek, as the
high priests of monetarism, stood above all others as our prophets and
gurus. As a Tory, I instinctively reacted against the dogmatic or simplistic
answers to what I believed were very complex and deep-seated problems.

I also recalled a conversation I had with Dean Acheson at a dinner
whilst accompanying Ted Heath to the USA in 1966. Averell Harriman,
another great anglophile, was also at the dinner, and the world scene was
amply reviewed. At the end, Acheson said quite simply, 'When I became
Secretary of State of this most powerful nation on earth, I really thought
I could change the direction of our policy in whatever way I wanted. I
now realise that it is given to no politician or statesman, however hard he
tries, to make more than 5 per cent, or at most 10 per cent, difference to
the course which events would otherwise take.' This too made me sceptical of colleagues' claims to have discovered some miracle cure which
had curiously evaded all other post-war Governments.

It was also Dean Acheson, as President Truman's Secretary of State, who had given historical perspective to the enormous challenge which all British governments had had to face since the end of the last world war: 'Britain has lost an Empire, but has not yet found a role.' Though this was true – maybe because it was true – it had made him highly unpopular for a while in this country. Yet, far from being anti-British, Acheson was enormously pro-British and the very acme of a rather dapper, very successful English country gentleman.

All my political life Britain had been struggling with the same daunting problem: how could we match our competitors in terms of growth and prosperity? The conviction which motivated me more than anything was the fear that because the record of Britain had been relatively unsuccessful in the post-war years, particularly in the 1960s and 1970s, we should now believe that there was some great political philosophy which could solve all the problems. A full appreciation of the historical perspective indicated that there was no simple panacea.

In the immediate post-war period the world had been hungry for goods, Germany and Japan were yet to recover, and Britain still had a great Empire almost solely dependent on us for manufactured goods. Perhaps it was hardly surprising if we had rested on our laurels as a result. Although much subsequent blame has been heaped on the shoulders of politicians and manufacturers alike, we also have to remember that we had suffered an enormous drain on our resources in the War, and then also had to contend with a period of massive change in the balance of world power and trade.

As a declining imperial force, there were legacies which handicapped us in our efforts to compete in the new, post-war world. Legacies which have had to be honoured, like Gibraltar and the Falklands, have made our ability to trade with Spain and South America so much more difficult. In other areas of the world, such as Africa and parts of South-East Asia, we have been regarded with suspicion, and there has been an uneasy love-hate relationship.

At home Britain had the in-built problem of a highly politicised trades union movement, harbouring so many prejudices and a good deal of downright bloody-mindedness. Britain's confrontational style of politics, and the swings from left to right, and back again, with changes in government, had held back the modernisation of many old and basic industries. Not enough was done to develop our technical skills, through training and re-training, and there had been too much experimenting with the educational system.

After the War, Britain had tried to build a decent and fair society. But this had ended up with us trying to run before we could walk, and building bureaucratic institutions more interested in their own future than the people they were employed to serve.

This was the scale, and variety, of the problems which I felt Britain faced by the mid-1970s. My own political beliefs, and my experience in Government, convinced me that there could be no easy solution, no single theory which might explain our ills or provide all the answers.

Yet as Britain's relative economic decline continued, more radical policies were beginning to have a wider appeal but there was no radical appeal in the plans of the Labour Government after 1974. Labour remained wedded to their old-style doctrine of nationalisation and were tied hand and foot to the trade unions, who paid them, controlled their Party conference and dictated policy. It may have appeared satisfactory when a large union like the Transport and General Workers was led by men of patriotism and moderation such as Ernie Bevin and Arthur Deakin, but the whole concept of a party and a government being controlled in this way is flawed and totally unsatisfactory in a modern democracy.

As some intellectuals on the left became increasingly disillusioned with Labour's lack of radicalism, they became increasingly attracted to the Conservative Party, which was now beginning to assume the mantle of the radical party. The Conservative Party had, since the war, placed its emphasis and based its philosophy more on individual freedom, but it was non-doctrinaire and totally pragmatic. This was a weakness in the eyes of many intellectuals, who despised the shifting of positions and apparent lack of principle which this entailed.

Ted Heath had first identified the need for more radical measures as early as the 1960s, but the country was not ready for the sweeping changes he sought to implement. By the later 1970s, however, attitudes were changing, a process accelerated by the harsher economic climate after 1974, following the sensational leap in oil prices.

Fairly typical of the mood around this time was an argument I had with Margaret which did become more ferocious than usual. In the end, I had to say that I was sorry but I had to leave. To add a little salt to the wound, I added that the reason I had to leave was to attend the re-launch of Harold Macmillan's book *The Middle Way*. She looked at me and said: 'Standing in the middle of the road is very dangerous, you get knocked down by the traffic from both sides.' Not particularly original, but it was an insight into her outlook.

*

Any Leader of the Opposition has a very difficult task. If too critical and strident, the accusations of being unpatriotic or destructive are quickly made; if on the other hand too compliant and positive, the Leader's own Party soon gets restless and demands more abuse of the Government.

Margaret was always at her best in responding to the more right wing of the Party, or seeking to bash the Labour Party and the unions. If she was never very successful in uniting her colleagues or the Parliamentary Party, the end result was not at all bad.

One of the interesting features about Margaret as Leader of the Opposition, and subsequently to a certain extent as Prime Minister, was the way she overcame resistance from her colleagues to her own wishes on Party policy. For someone who had the reputation for thinking things through and being over-keen on detail, she tended to make policy very much by shooting from the hip. The reason was that she did not find it easy to get her own way round the Shadow Cabinet table, so she tended to make policy – usually of the more extreme kind – on television, or at Prime Minister's Question Time in the Commons. She was afraid of being pushed off what she wanted to do if there was much consultation with her colleagues beforehand, so she reckoned it was better to make the policy and argue about it afterwards.

Her comments on people's fear about being 'swamped' by immigrants was a classic example. She knew that once she had said it on television, it would be difficult for the Party to avoid following her approach. Although she actually made no firm commitment about immigration during that particular broadcast, her use of emotive words swung the argument her way. It left poor Willie Whitelaw, who was then Shadow Home Secretary, with a most difficult job of trying to settle what Conservative policy actually was. He had to go to the Party's Central Council meeting at Leicester and make one of his 'on the one hand, on the other hand' speeches, trying to explain her comments away as best he could. Very few of us could have performed this trick as well as Willie.

At first some of us thought this tendency of Margaret's to make new policy on television was simply a matter of inexperience. But it was her way of making certain she got her way. We did not fully appreciate at first that she was the strong, determined leader which she subsequently turned out to be.

*

In the early days of her leadership Margaret had little experience of Foreign Affairs and took little interest in them. Her early approach as Leader was typified by a remark of Jonathan Aitken's which unfortunately for him appeared in a Middle Eastern newspaper: 'If you asked her about Sinai, she would probably think it was the plural of sinus.'

She had appointed Reggie Maudling as Foreign Affairs spokesman, but despite his long experience and immense wisdom she rarely bothered to consult him or take his advice. Her general view at the outset was apathetic on the European Community and a belief that we could exercise more power in the form of British nationalism; a strong pro-Israel view, in part the result of being the Member of Parliament for Finchley; and a simplistic and romantic sympathy for Ian Smith and Bishop Muzorewa in Rhodesia.

Margaret went on a number of overseas tours to meet other leaders, including Jimmy Carter soon after he won the US presidential election in 1976. On her return, she gave the Shadow Cabinet her normal account of her impressions, and ended up by saying that she had not been favourably impressed by Carter, but sometimes the job could make the man. 'Yes,' commented Reggie Maudling, 'I remember Winston's remark – if you feed a grub on royal jelly, it will grow into a Queen bee.' Some took it badly, some were hard put to contain their mirth. Margaret was po-faced. I did not fancy Reggie's chances in the next reshuffle.

*

The heart of any government's domestic policies lies in the economy, and at the heart of the economy is the Exchequer. Margaret had, however, appointed Geoffrey Howe as her Shadow Chancellor rather than Keith Joseph, who was not considered politically stable enough to hold such a key post. Geoffrey therefore had to contend with Denis Healey who was Labour's Chancellor throughout their five years in office from 1974.

In the House of Commons, or at the Party Conference, Geoffrey appeared stodgy and dull, with no fire in his belly. Denis exploited this mercilessly, most notoriously with his quip that Geoffrey's attacks on him were like being savaged by 'a dead sheep'. Denis put me in mind of Ian Botham – he always gave his opponents the feeling that they might bowl him out cheaply, but if he was in form the glorious shots would flow and everyone else was made to feel third-rate.

Geoffrey was far more suited to a small gathering, where the warmth of his personality could come through. As Shadow Chancellor, he chaired our key economic policy group after 1975, the Economic Reconstruction Group, and was a patient and courteous chairman. Amongst the members of the group were Keith Joseph, David Howell, the monetarist economist Brian Griffiths, and myself. At times I thought the monetarists on the group were spouting the most dreadful nonsense, and used to say as much.

But in those early discussions in Opposition, I did not feel that we were becoming exclusively or obsessively monetarist. The Economic Reconstruction Group paid a great deal of attention to improving the economy's competitiveness and industrial efficiency, and we were con-cerned about the best way to privatise parts of the state sector.

We decided that wherever possible we would take nationalised industries out of the public sector and make them more responsive and competitive. In the formulation and early implementation of the policy, the proceeds of the sale of assets was a very secondary consideration.

In Shadow Cabinet we devoted considerable time and effort to debating our economic policy. The zeal of the monetarists was tempered by the rest of us who were advising that we should remember that our experience in Government last time had been rather different from the approach which we had planned to adopt in Opposition: the realities of office had forced us to jettison a load of philosophical baggage.

During her first couple of years as Leader, Margaret did not appear to be the convinced monetarist she became by 1979. But as she seemed to grow progressively more dedicated to the doctrine I became increasingly worried about the importance being attached to it at the expense of other measures, and particularly by the complete rejection of any form of incomes policy. I did not want to go for statutory controls, but I believed that we had to have a policy to encourage voluntary restraint, and that we would need a pay policy for people who served Government, both in the public sector generally and in the civil service. No Government could avoid having a pay policy with regard to the seven million or so people employed in the public sector, whether it employed them directly or whether indirectly in local government or the nationalised industries.

I was not prepared to get myself into a position where I said I was against incomes policy, only to introduce it, or be a party to it in Government. That was precisely what we had done in the late 1960s and early 1970s, and yet here we were again in Opposition apparently wanting to commit ourselves to a total denunciation of pay policies.

This debate caused a great deal of controversy in Shadow Cabinet, culminating in the row over our proposed policy document, 'The Right Approach to the Economy'. Some colleagues, notably Margaret, wanted no mention of pay policy at all; others, including me, insisted that it was nonsense to believe that a pay policy was not essential, at the very least in the public sector, where the Government had a direct responsibility.

In the end 'The Right Approach to the Economy' did contain a reference to Government needing to have some view on pay. As we argued, '[Yet] in framing its monetary and other policies the Government must come to *some* conclusions about the likely scope for pay increases if excess public expenditure or large-scale unemployment is to be avoided; and this estimate cannot be concealed from the representatives of employers and unions whom it is consulting.'

The document was signed by Geoffrey Howe, Keith Joseph, David Howell and myself, with Angus Maude as Editor. But Margaret absolutely refused to allow the document to be published as a Shadow Cabinet paper.

So we were warned or, perhaps it would be fairer to say, put on notice. If only we had stuck more firmly to the words in 'The Right Approach to the Economy' in our first year in Government, at least a part of our early difficulties might have been mitigated.

*

Governments tend to create their own downfall and for several years it seemed that the Labour Government would be no exception. They lurched from crisis to crisis. In 1976 the IMF were called in to impose discipline and to save the pound. The Labour Government were also defeated on the key clause in their Dockwork Regulation Act, when two of their own backbenchers, Brian Walden and John Mackintosh, rebelled. In 1977 and 1978, they found themselves bogged down in Parliament with their abortive attempts to give devolution to Scotland and Wales.

We had scored some notable by-election victories during Labour's most troubled period in 1976 and 1977, but at times we were still inclined to sound too extreme and raise fears about renewed confrontation if we were returned to power.

On one particular occasion, when a combination of Margaret, Keith and Geoffrey had made it seem that we were swerving way out to the right, Peter Thorneycroft, the Party Chairman, came to the rescue of the moderates. He prepared a paper for Shadow Cabinet setting out the points which they had been making and the effect they were having. At the end of the paper he merely stated 'if we want to win, we should stop saying these things'.

Peter was very much a steadying influence who thought it was madness to go overboard for specific policy pledges while we were in Opposition and was not above giving Margaret strong advice, which she listened to for a considerable time.

By the summer of 1978, there were signs of economic recovery. We took it for granted that October would see us at the polls, and at that stage we were not very confident of winning.

On the day in early September that Jim Callaghan was expected to announce an October election, I travelled down to the annual TUC conference in Brighton to address a meeting of Conservative Trade Unionists that evening. I had prepared my speech, anticipating that it would be the opening salvo in the election campaign.

Before going to the meeting, Jane and I joined the BBC's Vincent Hanna in his hotel for Callaghan's TV broadcast. As we watched, we sensed that he was not going to go to the country after all. The minute he had said that Labour would soldier on, pandemonium broke loose.

I had to go off and address a few loyal Tory trade unionists. Instead of a hall packed with reporters and TV crews for the start of the election campaign, I found myself going through the motions for a couple of dedicated pressmen. I then headed back to the main conference hotel to find out what the union leaders made of Callaghan's decision.

They were deeply upset that he had led them up the garden path in the way that he had. They had been convinced that he would call an election. They felt that they had been misled, and never forgave him, which didn't help the Government the following winter.

Bill Kendall, the leader of the civil service unions' negotiating committee, said to me that evening: 'You want to thank your lucky stars there's not an election this autumn. You might just have won it, but I can tell you that whichever government is in office this winter is going to have a very rough time. We've had an incomes policy for three years and we're simply not prepared to take it for a fourth. There's going to be a lot of trouble around, and if you had been in office, it would all have been blamed on the fact that the Conservatives simply can't work with the unions.'

I asked him what was the difference between working with a Conservative Government and a Labour Government as far as the unions were concerned. He replied, 'Twelve months.'

I asked what on earth he meant. He explained: 'A Labour Government can get away with an incomes policy for three years, and a Conservative Government can get away with one for two years. So the difference is twelve months.'

Later that autumn it became clear that the unions simply would not accept Jim Callaghan's and Denis Healey's 5 per cent limit on pay rises. The ensuing 'Winter of Discontent' threw Labour into deep conflict with their supposed allies, the unions.

The scenes of factories and ports being blockaded by flying pickets, rubbish piling up in the streets and incidents where the dead were left unburied, demolished Labour's claim that only they could work with the unions. The *Daily Express* had a picture of a rat crawling out of an enormous pile of rubbish, which was effective and rather frightening propaganda. It now seemed that no Government could work with the unions and they would have to be brought to heel.

The Winter of Discontent showed up the very considerable friction between Margaret and myself. She wanted to take much tougher measures than I was prepared to support, and in fact tougher than anything we have since done in Government. I was telling her all the time that we should take things steadily, and not believe that we could solve all the problems by draconian legislation.

The Winter of Discontent also put Margaret much more in tune with the people. Her Party Political broadcast at this time was remarkably restrained, given her real feelings. It was written for her by Chris Patten, who had served as Director of the Research Department since 1974. Margaret never gave Patten the full credit for all that he did in Opposition. She had still not established her control over the Party by 1979, and he was helping to ensure that party policy was held to a much more central, 'One Nation' course at a time when she desperately needed to do so otherwise she might well have split the Party.

We had been impressed by Jim Callaghan's performance as Prime Minister. We thought that he was firm and straightforward. His debating skills in the House of Commons were very good indeed – even when his Government was defeated in the Commons at the end of March 1979, I thought he put up a good performance. So we were not surprised that he proved such a good election campaigner, though we thought he went over the top when he claimed that the Tories would lay bare the industrial heartlands of the country. We feared his ability to draw votes, particularly since he appeared to be a good, comfortable conservative whom people could trust in a way that they had never seemed able to trust Harold Wilson.

But the task of pulling Labour back from the brink proved too much even for Jim Callaghan.

*

In the general election on May 3, we won 339 seats to Labour's 269 and secured a majority of 43 over all parties in the Commons. After years of nursing a marginal seat I was relieved to see my own majority in Lowestoft increase to a healthy 7,821, at that time the highest I had ever enjoyed.

Our commitments made in the 1979 manifesto were not all that different from those we had made in 1970. In fact, the 1979 manifesto was reassuringly moderate in content and tone, even referring in its introduction to our wish 'to work *with the grain* of human nature'. Our plans to control inflation, reform the unions, restore incentives, strengthen the country's defences and so on were the staple of Conservative manifestos.

I assumed that quite a bit of what Margaret claimed we would do was Opposition rhetoric which would be moderated by the realities of Government. I failed to recognise, however, that the mood of the country had changed during the 1970s and it was ready for a more radical move to the right than in 1970.

I seemed to be more worried about the impact of our policies on people and on the social structure of the country than the people apparently were themselves. Margaret had caught the new mood; she was more in tune with people than I was.

CHAPTER SEVEN

HIGH AND DRY TORIES

'Where there is discord, may we bring harmony . . .' Margaret's choice of words on her arrival in Downing Street, quoting St Francis of Assisi, could scarcely have been less apt and from her lips were the most awful humbug: it was so totally at odds with Margaret's belief in conviction politics and the need to abandon the consensus style of government, which she blamed for Britain's relative economic decline over the past two decades.

The next day, Saturday, I was invited to Number Ten and Margaret asked me to serve as Employment Secretary. I took the opportunity to have a long talk with her. I told her that I wished to see her Government, our Government, succeed and I would do all that I could to ensure that success. I said that relationships between us had been strained for a number of reasons, some personal about which we both knew, and some policy, about which everyone knew. The time had come to make a fresh start.

She fully concurred and I left her study a happy man on that score at least although I was concerned about the nature of my job and the likely course of events.

Our determination to bury the hatchet did not last long. During our talk we had discussed who should join me at the Department. I had asked for Barney Hayhoe, who had been my deputy for the whole period of Opposition, who knew the law on industrial relations backwards, had a very good relationship with the union leaders, and had prepared himself for government over a number of years. But I was told that regretfully she had another very important job for Barney: he was a Catholic and she needed him to go to Northern Ireland. I said then, and have had cause to demonstrate it since, that no one can refuse a request to serve in Northern Ireland. So I did not demur. But Barney was not offered the Northern Ireland job, because of worries about possible connections of his mother's family, living around Dundalk and Crossmaglen, with the nationalist tradition. Without doubt Barney was being pushed well away from the centre. In the end he became an Under Secretary of State for Defence where he was a tremendous success.

I was telephoned on the Sunday afternoon by Michael Jopling, the new Chief Whip, offering me Leon Brittan as my deputy. I said that

Leon wouldn't do. Leon has many qualities, but I knew his manner as one of my deputies in Opposition had already upset both the CBI and the TUC, and in any case I felt it was a mistake to have a barrister who had become so closely associated with industrial relations reform. It would look too much like a re-run of Geoffrey Howe's handling of industrial relations in the early '70s. I suggested a number of names, all of whom were either unacceptable or had already agreed to go elsewhere.

In the end Michael asked if I would take Patrick Mayhew. I agreed: though I didn't know him particularly well, I had heard that he was very good.

The Chief Whip reported our conversation to Margaret. She came back on the line herself: if I wasn't prepared to have Leon, I must have Patrick. Then came her punch line: 'I'm determined to have *someone* with backbone in your Department.' It was clear from that remark it was not going to be a smooth passage: the sweet talk of Saturday morning had soon been forgotten. In fact, Patrick was a loyal and first class Minister. It was a happy chance that brought us together and created a lasting friendship.

*

The power of a modern Prime Minister is awesome, particularly when it comes to the power of appointment and dismissal of Ministers. But the Leader of any party in power will know that there has to be some sort of balance in a Cabinet, between right and left, youth and age, different backgrounds and so on.

The balance of the Cabinet looked better for our wing of the Party than I had dreamt possible. Looking round the table at our first Cabinet meeting, I saw that most of us had worked together in the Shadow Cabinet and had managed to restrain Margaret from pursuing her more extreme instincts.

The only major changes from the Shadow Cabinet were the introduction of Christopher Soames, Peter Walker, George Younger and Humphrey Atkins, who had been Chief Whip in Opposition and became Secretary of State for Northern Ireland following Airey Neave's assassination on the eve of the election campaign.

A number of us had experience of Government at the highest level and knew the difficulties and how hard it would be to bring about change. It wasn't that we were against changes which would lead to a free and more dynamic economy; but we were conscious of the need to seek to carry people with us so that the changes we made would stick. We knew as well that our problem would be compounded by a deepening world recession, which was bound to follow the further dramatic increase in the price of oil in 1979, from around $13 per barrel at the start of the year to $23 by February. By May, deals approaching $40 per barrel were being reported.

I thought that we would at least be able to avoid most of the follies which new Governments tend to commit and that we wouldn't be stupidly right wing and doctrinaire about economic policy, as we had been between 1970 and 1972. It is often forgotten that *The Times*' leading articles in 1971 were arguing that the Heath Government was the most right wing government since the Second World War. In the same way, Labour Governments behave in a ridiculous left wing manner for the first two years before settling down and accepting the facts of life.

However, the composition of the economic team at the Treasury and the other economic Departments obviously showed she was going to have her own way as far as she possibly could. Margaret's main supporters at the outset in Cabinet were Geoffrey Howe, her Chancellor, Keith Joseph at Industry, John Nott at Trade, David Howell at Energy, Patrick Jenkin at Social Services, Angus Maude as Paymaster-General and John Biffen as Chief Secretary to the Treasury – not a very impressive bunch, and with little experience at the centre of Government. In addition, the three 'territorial' Ministers, Nick Edwards at the Welsh Office, George Younger at the Scottish Office, and Humphrey Atkins at Northern Ireland, in the early days all generally supported the Prime Minister's line.

I was the only Minister in the economic team with whom she was likely to have any difficulties. In some respects I was surprised to be offered Employment. After all, I had not had a very easy run with the Party in Opposition but I think Margaret felt to have changed me then would have signified too dramatic a shift in policy, and in any case what else was she likely to have offered me? The writing may already have been on the wall, but it did not seriously worry me to start with, because I assumed she would take things gradually, bearing in mind the experience of Ted's Government some five years before.

The dissenters in the Cabinet included Peter Carrington at the Foreign Office, myself at Employment, Peter Walker at Agriculture, Mark Carlisle at Education, Michael Heseltine at the Environment, Norman St John Stevas as Leader of the House, and Gilmour as Lord Privy Seal and Carrington's deputy.

This left a powerful foursome of Willie Whitelaw at the Home Office, Hailsham as Lord Chancellor, Francis Pym at Defence, and Christopher Soames as Leader of the Lords, who were less openly in one camp or the other. This foursome nearly always split equally, with the former two supporting the Prime Minister.

In Cabinet, Quintin Hailsham, the Lord Chancellor, varied from being brilliant to being astonishingly off-beam. He is a man of enormous character, a splendid and convincing orator. He was always unpredictable, except where the judges were concerned: he would always defend them and their pay increases until he was beaten into the ground. I had great rows with him and he got the impression I was anti-lawyer: in fact, I was not against them, but I was against lawyers getting away with things they would never agree to other people getting away with.

Yet Quintin was a great ally in my 'step-by-step' approach on trade union reform. He did understand human nature, unlike Geoffrey Howe and the then Solicitor-General, Sir Ian Percival, who knew nothing about the shop floor and what made people tick.

Christopher Soames was the most interesting of the newcomers. He had not been associated with the liberal wing of the Party, and he was very much of the traditional centre, tending in some ways to be rather to the right. He was a man of very considerable authority and experience who had been in Cabinet at the time of Macmillan and Alec Home, then Ambassador in Paris and a Vice-President of the European Commission. Yet whenever he had an argument with Margaret, or if someone else was stating a policy with which he did not agree, he became in some strange way at a disadvantage. I think he disappointed himself by not being able to put his points as cogently or coherently as he would have wished.

Having wanted Christopher back because she thought that he would give strength and stability to her otherwise fairly inexperienced Cabinet, Margaret was disappointed and very quickly took the line that she could manage without him. No one had as much experience of the people or workings within the Commission of the Community as Christopher yet she deliberately avoided letting him play any part in discussion about it. Having made an inspired decision to bring him back into Government, she then failed to make use of him.

Peter Walker also returned, although he had been a rebel for a number of years. It was a clever appointment, because as Minister of Agriculture has to spend a great deal of time negotiating in Brussels, and Peter had never been a great supporter or admirer of the Community. He therefore found it quite easy to argue the toss with our European partners, and he was also kept away from the centre of Government decision-making.

Francis Pym had taken over responsibility for Foreign Affairs for a short while before the election. But it was clear that Peter Carrington would be Foreign Secretary. He was well versed in Foreign Affairs, had been Defence Secretary for most of Ted's Government, and was a director of Rio Tinto Zinc, which took him all over the world, particularly to Africa.

Peter's great advantage in Margaret's eyes was that he was a Lord, and therefore not a close rival for her job. She had a soft spot for the aristocracy, especially someone with Peter's charm and intelligence. I was delighted when she made him Foreign Secretary. With all his gifts, he proved a great advocate and ambassador for Britain. He was immensely popular with the Foreign Office at home and with his counterparts abroad.

In the early days of Margaret's Cabinet, Ministers often used to pass notes to one another during Cabinet. There were those which were meant to be amusing, or some private notes; there were those which were very private, which said: 'Wasn't he simply terrible?' or, 'She's got it all wrong.'

Peter Carrington was a great note-passer – his were all cryptic little remarks about what was being discussed or how dreadful someone was. I used to pass notes a lot to Peter Carrington, Christopher Soames and Ian Gilmour – although they were right down the other end of the table so it wasn't easy. Geoffrey Howe was also a great note-passer, and it was he who produced the anagram of Mugabe as 'E Ba Gum'.

Perhaps Peter's most celebrated note was the one he passed Margaret when they were having a meeting with the Chinese Prime Minister. It became clear that nothing could stop the latter talking, and Margaret was getting agitated and fed up. Peter sent her a note saying, 'Prime Minister, you are talking too much.'

*

Margaret had little experience of the higher levels of Government. She had always been cold-shouldered by Ted; she sat in Cabinet on his right side, carefully hidden by the Secretary of the Cabinet, who was always leaning forward to take notes. It was the most difficult place for anyone to catch the Prime Minister's eye, and I am sure that she was placed there quite deliberately.

The best position is one of the seats opposite the Prime Minister, which are occupied by the Chancellor, the Home Secretary, and the Foreign Secretary. I also sat facing Margaret, although not directly opposite. In those early days Margaret was better than Ted at allowing everyone to have a say – her Cabinet tended to be far more argumentative – and it was nothing like such a disadvantage to sit on the same side of the table as Margaret and on the far side of the Cabinet Secretary: for example, Peter Walker and Norman Tebbit both sat there.

Margaret found for the first time that she really did have the levers of power in her hands, and my goodness she was going to exercise them. From day one in Cabinet she was very much more determined and gave a far stronger lead than she ever gave in Opposition. The full extent of the power of a modern Prime Minister, who has the support of the Cabinet Office and Number Ten itself, is still not fully appreciated. Nothing

really happens in Whitehall unless the central driving force of Number
Ten or the Cabinet Office has approved it.

In Opposition, Margaret's tendency to the extreme had been tempered
by her need to carry colleagues with her and her need not to frighten
people into believing there would be chaos if she were elected. The belief
then that Britain was ungovernable was never far below the surface. But,
once in power, Margaret turned this belief to her advantage, for it could
then be used to support her argument that strong government was what
the country really needed. I am sure that by 1979 people were looking
for new courage and a fresh determination in tackling Britain's problems.
Margaret showed at once that she was tough and not likely to be shaken
off once she had made up her mind. More than ever I think that has
been her greatest asset.

Those of us in Cabinet who were out of sympathy with Margaret's
views grossly under-estimated her absolute determination, along with
Geoffrey and Keith, to push through the new right wing policies. We
also under-estimated enormously the change in the whole philosophy of
the right and the changes in the Conservative Party which were taking
place. The fact that the Conservative Research Department was reduced
to a nonentity following Chris Patten's departure to become an MP; that
the Centre for Policy Studies was built up to rival and usurp it; and that
the new right had a grip on the Press, with people like Paul Johnson and
Andrew Alexander spouting extreme right wing views.

We didn't appreciate the degree to which the Party was becoming
more and more doctrinaire in its approach and less and less pragmatic.
And the doctrinaire people were in a strong position in that, although
their own policies did not seem to fare particularly well at first, they
were able to say the whole time that they had to be given a fair chance:
after all, the pragmatic approach had been tried for the previous twenty
or more years and could not be judged as an enormous success. Even the
era of Macmillan and Butler was talked about as a disaster.

We pragmatists were on a very difficult wicket, because we could not
prove in a short time that their ideas were wrong. We could not even say
that ours had been particularly successful, because in the 1970s they
undoubtedly had not succeeded. Only the passage of time would prove
our point, but by then a great deal of damage could have been done to
the country, and to our Party.

We made a number of fundamental mistakes in the way that we tried
to deal with Margaret and her allies. We obviously weren't subtle enough;
perhaps we weren't clever enough to take them on at their own game.
But it was very much like the problems that the Conservative Opposition
had when Wilson first became Prime Minister in 1964. He was able to
blame everything on the thirteen wasted years of Tory misrule. The

thirteen 'wasted' years were the most successful years this country has ever had, but that could still not be proved for a few years, until things started to go wrong. But if someone is determined enough they can make anything that has gone before look rather silly for a time.

*

In the early days I think Margaret was worried that we would not accept her authority and would not do what she wanted. I dare say she was right since most of the powerful voices were ranged against her. She decided that in those circumstances she must control economic policy, and in Geoffrey Howe she found someone whom she could both control and trust.

It was really an enormous shock to me that the budget which Geoffrey produced the month after the election of 1979 was so extreme. It was then that I realised that Margaret, Geoffrey and Keith really had got the bit between their teeth and were not going to pay attention to the rest of us at all if they could possibly help it. That first budget also brought it home to me that I was really on a hiding to nothing from the very beginning, as the only economic Minister who was not of the monetarist right.

Margaret's economic policy was dictated by the belief that 'sound money' was the essential requirement for a successful and stable nation. As far as she was concerned, inflation was a much greater social evil than unemployment, and in any case, in her eyes, you could only cure unemployment by controlling inflation. She thus felt free to castigate all post-war governments, Labour and Conservative, because she reckoned their policies had made our problems progressively worse.

The idea of pumping money into the economy to reduce unemployment was anathema. If only a better balance could be achieved between the public sector and the private, with less public spending, the economy would expand in response to market forces. It was a very simplistic approach, a combination of her own instincts founded in the corner shop at Grantham, laid over by a veneer from Hayek and Friedman. In a world increasingly interdependent and with a people used to a welfare state, it looked an unpromising scenario.

It was on the basis of this kind of simple-minded analysis that Margaret and Geoffrey concocted the first Budget, which was to do so much harm. There were absolutely no consultations about the shape of the Budget. A few days before Budget day, I received a phone call from a worried John Methven, Director-General of the CBI. Word had reached him that there was a proposal to put VAT up to 15 per cent; surely this couldn't be right? As Employment Secretary I must know the effect that this would have on wage claims. Similar advice came from Len Murray.

I went to see the Prime Minister, she heard me with sympathy, and I thought she understood. The night before the budget I gave Moss Evans dinner in my flat. He expressed his concern about 15 per cent VAT. I told him of my conversation, and said that I thought it would go up, of course, but I doubted if as high as that. How wrong I was.

We were all prepared for some switch of taxation from direct to indirect; and we were all ready and willing to cut public expenditure as much as we could, although the logic of putting up nationalised industries' prices escaped Ian Gilmour, Peter Walker and myself. What shook us was the scale of the changes proposed, because of the effect this would have on the cost of living and the follow-through on the wage costs and inflation-proof benefits.

To push up costs in this way at a time when inflation was already ten per cent and rising, and with the backlash of 'catch-up' settlements from the previous government's wages policy in full spate, seemed a great mistake. Here, to my dread, was the inexperience of the new Government plain for all to see.

The decision to push up prices was a much bigger mistake than our commitment to honour the wage increases awarded to the public sector workers by Professor Clegg's Commission on pay comparability, which had been set up by the Callaghan Government following the Winter of Discontent. During the 1979 election campaign we had committed ourselves to Clegg. We had been under very great pressure to say whether we would honour the pay awards for the public sector, which had fallen behind as a result of the previous three years of pay policy – it's always easier for the private sector to get round any pay policy.

I am unrepentant about being one of those who said that we should honour Clegg. I fail to see how we could have got through the election, and stood any chance at all, without making the commitment.

But where we erred was in making Clegg very much more difficult for ourselves by increasing VAT from 8 per cent to 15 per cent; by loading more price increases on to the nationalised industries; and by our immediate abolition of price controls. I don't think that the price controls made much difference, but they did matter from the point of view of public perception at the time. We increased the rate of inflation and the cost of living very considerably, and therefore we bumped up the cost of Clegg.

It was not sufficiently appreciated that every time Government revenue was increased, say by putting up VAT, or by putting extra charges on the nationalised industries, at least a third of all the extra charges had to be paid back in increased pensions, in increased public sector wages through Clegg and so on. There was not sufficient understanding of the effect that one had on the other.

In the case of gas, prices were to be increased by 10 per cent above the rate of inflation each year, to meet the new financial target of six per cent real return. This would produce a profit of over £1 billion by the mid-1980s, compared with around £600 million in 1980. The logic that gas prices should be brought into line with those of other energy sources was impeccable: gas from the North Sea was not unlimited; new resources were costing much more to develop; and new consumers ate up capital expenditure at a much faster rate than could be justified.

But economic logic and good managerial practice do not always go hand in hand. To force management to increase prices and thereby generate an even greater profit is not conducive to efficient, tight management. And, with the Prime Minister telling people that their pay rises had to depend on the profitability of the firms they worked for, it certainly did not help in explaining to a more militant union that they could not have correspondingly higher wage increases.

Keith Joseph presided over a sub-committee of the Cabinet Economic Strategy Committee, which vetted all applications by Ministers dealing with public sector pay awards. The monetarists didn't really care too much about Clegg at first. I used to sit in amazement as increases were sanctioned, not because they were acceptable, but because the new theory stated there would be no pay policy, since control of the money supply would force down the level of settlements.

This particular brand of monetarism was known as 'the rational expectations' approach. There was almost a washing of the hands by the 'head monetarist', Keith, who was saying in effect that all these things would right themselves in time. I was arguing that the consequences of this policy were so disastrous that we would never be able to carry them through.

In Cabinet I argued for a public sector wages policy, combined with a form of national economic forum, such as we had put forward in our policy document in Opposition, 'The Right Approach to the Economy'. Geoffrey Howe would have gone along with this, but Margaret simply wouldn't. It would have involved giving too much credibility to trade union leaders.

She told me that one of her great achievements – and this was in 1980 – was that no one talked any more about incomes policy: we had finally killed off the myth that wages could be controlled by anything other than the market. I was flabbergasted by this claim; it was much too soon to be drawing any such conclusions. However, I think that as things have turned out, she was right and I was wrong.

We were attending the Young Conservatives' conference at Bournemouth in 1980. Harold Macmillan came along to deliver a masterly speech as elder statesman and patron. As a disciple of his for some years past, he knew my views on monetarist theory and on my more hardnosed colleagues on the front bench.

I was chatting with him before his speech and asked him what he thought of the monetarists and their theories. He replied: 'It's all rather silly really – in my days we called it stop–go. Every government has to keep control, we used to have credit squeezes and all that, but we never elevated it to a political or economic theory. People quite like inflation really. The poor like it because they've more pound notes in their pocket, the rich like it because they can always sell a picture or something, it's only retired colonels who don't like it!'

That last remark was addressed very much in the direction of Peter Thorneycroft, who had joined us in the Green Room before we went on to the stage. Peter had resigned in 1958 as Chancellor in Harold's Cabinet because he felt that Harold was allowing too high a level of public expenditure.

After Harold had delivered a magnificent speech which had brought tears to our eyes and was so much the authentic voice of the Tory philosophy, with his customary sprinkling of delightful *doubles entendres*, the great man whispered in my ear as we came off the platform, 'Was that what you wanted, was that all right for you, my boy?'

*

All through the early period of Margaret's Government I felt the Treasury team were out of their depth. They were all theorists – either barristers or, in the case of Nigel Lawson, a journalist. None of them had any experience of running a whelk stall, let alone a decent-sized company. Their attitude to manufacturing industry bordered on the contemptuous. They shared the view of the other monetarists in the Cabinet, that we were better suited as a nation to being a service economy and should no longer worry about production. I could not see how this could be reconciled with the employment of a potential workforce of around 23 million people on a small island.

The Chancellor had a rough time with a number of us in Cabinet – myself, Ian Gilmour, Peter Walker and Norman St John Stevas – but the majority went along with the monetarist experiment. The Cabinet did not appreciate that the world was moving into serious recession shortly after we came into office.

The full impact of the big increase in world oil prices in the first half of 1979 was under-estimated. It was thought that this price rise would help our currency, as an oil exporter, and thus protect us from its full inflationary impact: our imports would be cheaper, offsetting the impact of more expensive fuel costs.

But what was not really anticipated was the effect on the rest of the world and therefore on our exports. In fact, we seemed to end up with the worst situation of all – not only did the price of oil go up very sharply, with all the attendant problems for Western Europe and British exports, but the effect on what had become known as the 'petro pound' was to put up the value of our currency well beyond its proper worth, which made our exports more expensive.

We suffered, therefore, a double effect; that of the general recession on British industry, combined with the very high value of the £ sterling. Quite a large part of British engineering and the 'metal-bashing' type of industries never recovered.

A number of Ministers held that there was nothing we could do about the pound. I never took that view myself. In addition to oil the currency was kept artificially high, by having very high interest rates, as part of the new monetary policy – by late 1980, going above $2.40.

With the world already entering recession, this piled agony upon the misery – our exporters were priced out of markets which were already squeezed, while our home market was flooded with cheaper foreign imports. The consequences for our basic industries – engineering, steel, chemicals – and for a region like the West Midlands, were appalling.

The Ministers who said we could not do anything about it were almost always the same Ministers who said that this tremendous shock was what British industry needed: it would sort out the good companies from the bad, or as Keith Joseph used to say 'the lean meat from the fat'. I thought that the policy at the time was much too severe – though I have to admit that British industry took and survived a lot more punishment than I had expected.

But industry was discredited in the eyes of the monetarists: they looked to the City as the fount of all economic wisdom. The danger with this was twofold – first the view from the City can seem a lot rosier than it looks to the businessman or worker: at times it seems that the seriousness of industry's plight was matched only by the optimism in the Square Mile. And, secondly, the City's mood is notoriously susceptible to the Government's own expectations, and so Whitehall and the City can easily reinforce each other's own judgments about the state of the country.

The notion of setting financial targets was popular in the City. The targets introduced in the Medium Term Financial Strategy (MTFS) announced in Geoffrey's second budget in March 1980, might work in a settled world and be an excellent discipline. But, although many companies have five year financial plans, they need to modify them and update them regularly. For the Government to saddle itself with targets in public seemed to many of us, including usual allies of Margaret's, like John Biffen and John Nott, to be putting our heads firmly on the block. So it proved to be.

The Treasury argued that we needn't worry since these targets would be merely 'illustrative'. But they were soon turned into tablets of stone, no small thanks to the Treasury itself. Geoffrey thought he could control three things – government spending, government borrowing and the money supply. But within a year all three were out of control.

The main intrument used to control the supply of money was interest rates. The higher the rate of interest, the more it would choke off borrowing and thus bring the money supply down. But in practice people know they must go on borrowing or go bust, so they borrow. When individuals and companies can set most interest charges against tax it is not, in the short term at least, a very effective weapon for controlling anything.

The MTFS was also based on the assumption that within about three years the nationalised industries would move into profit. In 1980 the MTFS laid down that the public sector borrowing requirement would come right down, from 5$\frac{1}{2}$ per cent of national output in 1978–79 to 1$\frac{1}{2}$ per cent by 1983–4, five years later. This would be almost entirely due to the swing round, from large deficit to a surplus, in the nationalised industries' financial requirements.

The success of the whole medium term strategy thus depended on the planned revolution in the performance of our publicly-owned basic industries. And, according to the Chancellor, about 40 per cent of the improvement in the nationalised industries' performance was expected to come from the coal, rail, steel and ship-building industries: that story still looks sick some five years later.

Yet the rest of our financial and economic policy seemed designed to ensure that they would make enormous losses. They were basic industries, which in recession cannot be cut back by more than a certain amount and therefore the Government had to go on baling them out – trains have to run even though they may be carrying fewer passengers. To keep public expenditure under any sort of control, other programmes therefore had to be cut more savagely – for instance, housing and education.

The cuts in public expenditure continued to fall heaviest on capital rather than current spending, as had happened under Labour since 1976. Construction and building were therefore also badly hit. Unemployment rose, pushing up spending on benefits and basic industries. By 1982–83, the nationalised industries' financing needs were over £1.75 billion more than forecast in the 1980 Budget. Thus the cuts in public expenditure on the one hand were offset by unintended but inevitable increases on the other.

As other factors in the economy worsened, so it became impossible for the nationalised industries to contain even their existing deficits without exorbitant increases in prices. As a result, by 1981 inflation in the nationalised industries was running at three times the level in most private industries. This was well in excess of the level needed to eliminate any 'under-pricing' of electricity and gas charges and telephone bills. Our policies were thus proving counter-productive and provided yet another boost to the cost of living spiral.

*

Margaret's relationship with Keith Joseph while he was Industry Secretary was fascinating to watch. She owed a great deal to Keith, who had supported her leadership loyally throughout our years in Opposition. She admired his intellect and his ability to evangelise, particularly when speaking to young audiences. No doubt he did play a very considerable role in changing people's views on economic policy from the moment we went into Opposition in March 1974.

On the other hand, Keith had never shown himself to be a very sensitive politician nor able to carry through his convictions into action as a Minister. It was because of these doubts that she did not make him Shadow Chancellor before 1979, or Chancellor of the Exchequer afterwards.

Margaret appointed Keith Industry Secretary in 1979, but he simply was not the right choice as he was constantly regaled with tales of woe from industrialists and pleas to be baled out from the state-owned industries. Being a decent, soft-hearted man, he found this unbearably difficult. Margaret admired him, treasured him, looking upon him like a mother who cannot refrain from indulging a favourite son, even though she knows it will do him no good. In the end it all became impossible and Keith was moved to Education.

This thoroughly honourable man was not suited to being a departmental Minister. He made heavy weather of everything he touched from the Health Service in the early '70s, through Industry, to Higher Education in the '80s. He would invariably indulge in a mea culpa exercise, before moving blithely on to adopt some other hare-brained scheme.

The relationship between Governments of both parties and the nationalised industries was never an easy one. Doctrinally we disliked them, we felt they were inefficient, monopolistic and unresponsive to the market at a time of great technological change. But with their trading losses and their insatiable appetite for investment funds, which counted as public expenditure, they were very unpopular with the Treasury, under any Chancellor, whether Tory or Labour. Their managements found themselves being told by Government either to cut investment or to put up prices by more than necessary, and sometimes both.

The nationalised industries therefore not only suffered from constant interference from Government, but their accountability to Parliament

also made the position of the chairmen almost impossible. To find
someone with the qualities of a politician on the one hand and a knowledge of the particular industry on the other was virtually impossible. It
is not surprising that these great industries were for the most part inefficient, badly managed and a ready target for union militancy and were
losing a hatful of money.

Our response to the outbreak of the national steel strike in January
1980 was symptomatic of the Government's resolve to break with the
past. Ministers were to make no attempt to settle the dispute between the
British Steel Corporation and the steel unions. It is inconceivable that
any other Government elected since 1945 would have adopted the 'hands-
off' approach which Margaret took when faced with a major strike in
one of the main public corporations and one of the country's basic industries.

Keith Joseph and I met the unions' leaders, Bill Sirs of ISTC and
Hector Smith of the blast-furnacemen, at their request in mid-January.
A few days later they also met Margaret. But it was always made clear
that these were not negotiations, nor even interventions on our part, but
merely meetings which the unions had wanted and at which we were
ready to listen and explain our position.

I found this non-intervention line contradictory and unconvincing.
Contradictory because during January 1980 the Government's financial
targets for the energy industries were announced, with the result that gas
prices would rise considerably faster than the rate of inflation over the
next few years. Here was a case where the Government was intervening
in the running of a state industry, pushing up prices by more than the
industry would have wished.

Our attitude to steel was important because all the other public sector
unions, including Ray Buckton's train drivers and Joe Gormley's miners,
would watch our response like hawks: any relaxation of our cash limits
for steel to finance an improved pay offer, and they would be next in the
queue. But I was also very disturbed at the severe damage which a lasting
strike could inflict on the steel industry's own future and on the rest of
the economy, particularly manufacturing.

Margaret was more concerned than Keith about the consequences of a
long strike. In the early days she was anxious to know whether the independent arbitration service, ACAS, was involved in an effort to reach a settlement. Margaret was torn between the pragmatic politician wanting an
end to a damaging strike, and the doctrinaire economist, like most of her
advisers at this time, who seemed to feel that a protracted dispute might
knock some sense into people. But as the dispute became more bloody,
the latter, doctrinaire belief began to take hold. After four months on
strike, the steel unions accepted a 16 per cent pay award compared with

the initial 2 per cent offer, but massive redundancies followed and their strength was seriously reduced.

*

British Leyland confronted the Government with a stark choice in 1979 and 1980. BL had effectively been nationalised in 1975 when the Labour Government took a majority shareholding in the company. The company was making heavy losses and had already received billions in state aid.

If we were to be true to our free market credentials, we should allow BL to go into receivership and hope that various bits and pieces would be picked up. Yet it was clear that this policy would result in redundancies running into thousands, which would not only affect the car trade itself, but a myriad of supporting firms throughout the West Midlands.

The public had also come to have great confidence in Michael Edwardes. For us to pull the plug out would undoubtedly have been very unpopular, when Edwardes was seen to be getting some sense into the workforce, taking on the militant union power which had bedevilled the company for so long.

Viewed in the wider context of our aims on industrial relations policy, it was not unhelpful for the Government to have a major concern like BL, which was dependent on Government support but was not a monopoly and which could therefore be given more backbone not to give way to every union pressure. In fairness it must be said that the union leaders in the engineering industry who took the lead in negotiation with BL behaved with remarkable responsibility.

The BL corporate plan was looked at annually by Ministers during December and January. It always presented severe problems for Government. There was invariably some additional reason for the performance to fall below the forecast: the strengthening of the pound against the dollar which hit exports so hard; or the deepening of the recession; or cheap imports from Spain, which helped Ford but which severely penalised BL.

Not one of us believed that BL could survive on its own as a major independent mass car producer. Equally, none of us could see what other policy we could adopt than the one we did. It was based on the hope that the various parts of the company, other than mass car production, could be fattened up for sale. These included the spare parts division, trucks and buses, Rover and Jaguar. We then hoped for a merger between a large car manufacturer and Austin/Morris. Regrettably, the downturn in the world car market made any sale much more difficult, so BL had to struggle on, having achieved some notable and praiseworthy improvements.

This dilemma between doctrine and pragmatism caused Keith Joseph the most appalling agony. In the review of the 1980–81 BL Corporate Plan, he changed his mind completely in the middle of our discussions. Before Christmas he produced a paper for Cabinet Committee giving his full support for the company. A further paper after Christmas contained few changes. But, when he spoke at our next Ministerial meeting, he came out against his own paper and his proposed statement to the Commons, which was attached to the paper. Against his own paper's advice and against his own Departmental officials' advice, he was proposing that the state funding of BL should cease and the company be put into receivership.

He was defeated in the Cabinet Committee. I suspect that in the end he was relieved not to have to carry through the receivership, and I was more surprised that at that late stage he had allowed his more out of touch and extreme friends to persuade him to disown his paper and earlier advice to colleagues.

Margaret's behaviour was fascinating. She was in favour of saving BL, and other interventions by Government to aid industry. But Margaret knew that these decisions did not fit her rhetoric and her image, nor did they reflect what many of her true and fervent supporters wanted. She would therefore conduct a very penetrating cross-examination in Cabinet and Cabinet Committee: poor Keith used to have sweat all over his face as he contorted himself and his conscience.

Then Margaret would publicly dissociate herself from the decision. She would attack the use of public money for such purposes, she would attack the industry for its inefficiency. She would in fact set herself up in opposition to the policy of her own government. She was Boadicea, hammering away at those wicked people who were seeking to carry out policies alien to her own trusted beliefs and nature.

*

Our most controversial appointment in the public sector was that of Ian MacGregor as Chairman of British Steel in 1980, following the dreadful débâcle of the national steel strike. BSC's losses were running at £7 million per week before the strike, which added on average a further £10 million per week during its thirteen week duration.

In January 1980, there had been a very unfortunate attribution to me of remarks about his predecessor, Sir Charles Villiers, made at an off-the-record lunchtime meeting with the industrial and labour correspondents. I had commented that in the view of Ministers the sooner Villiers left the better. This episode sparked off Margaret's remark in her interview later in February 1980 with Sir Robin Day on BBC Television's *Panorama*: 'We all make mistakes. I think it was a mistake and Jim Prior was very, very sorry indeed. He was very apologetic. But we don't just sack a chap for one mistake.'

A variety of names were suggested to take Villiers' place, but none of them was considered to be of sufficient calibre. I suggested Ian Mac-Gregor's name. I knew that he was interested in the job, as he had told me so. He was a senior partner in Lazard Frères in New York and had for a while been on the board of British Leyland. I knew him well because my eldest son, David, was working for him in New York. I told Keith Joseph that MacGregor was one of the world's outstanding managers and he should see him. I took no further part in the negotiations.

Later on I heard that there was some concern over the size of the salary being discussed. The decision was taken to make a clean breast of it in the Commons. I admired Keith Joseph's courage – I doubt if I could have stood up and announced what he did. The terms of the contract were vastly in excess of anything ever paid before. I remembered the row when Lord Beeching was appointed to be Chairman of British Rail by Ernest Marples. At that time the salary was £24,000, about double those of other heads of public corporations. Here we were announcing a salary of £48,000 along with compensation to Lazard Frères of £225,000 for each of the three years of Ian MacGregor's appointment, plus £1.15 million if he could 'turn round' British Steel.

I could not be in the Commons on the afternoon of Keith's statement, but since I anticipated a call from Ian MacGregor I telephoned Michael Jopling the Chief Whip to hear how it had gone. 'Disastrous,' was the reply. 'I don't think we shall get away with it, there was no support at all.'

Ian telephoned me that evening from New York. I played the reception down, but warned him that he had an uphill struggle. We discussed how he should handle the press conference he was to give the following morning. My soccer club, Norwich City, had recently transferred a player, Kevin Reeves, to Manchester City for £1 million. We decided this would be a good line to take. After all, a good manager should be worth as much as any footballer!

A day or two after the press conference I was talking to some hard-bitten journalists. They were full of praise for MacGregor, he was obviously a remarkable man. He looked fresher after crossing the Atlantic than Charles Villiers did after crossing Eaton Square. And how did he know about that player from Norwich City; surely he didn't study English football? In fact, he had made one mistake – he had said Manchester United, not City, but from all accounts Ian's was a virtuoso performance.

He did an excellent job with the steel industry, rapidly winning the confidence of the management and in particular of the excellent chief executive, Bob Scholey, who didn't hit it off with Charles Villiers. From being an industry of low productivity, bad quality and uncertain delivery, it has become one of the best steel producers in the world, and only failed to get back into reasonable profit because of the coal industry dispute.

Margaret and the whole Cabinet were very impressed by this wily, tough, but quietly spoken American Scot. She once went so far as to say he was the only man she knew who was her equal.

I have no doubt that Ian was more than flattered by her attention and compliments. When it was suggested that he should take over the Coal Board he jumped at the idea, though I think he really wanted to run both steel and coal. Generally Ian would ask my view on these things, but on this occasion he was ominously silent. He knew that my strong advice would have been against it.

*

With the gap between rhetoric and practice becoming apparent by early 1981, a major shift was also taking place in the basis of our economic policy. The folly of high interest and exchange rates was now obvious. We began to hear very much less from the Treasury about their money supply target, '£M3', as it is known to the economists. The Treasury's emphasis became more a question of the need to reduce the Public Sector Borrowing Requirement (PSBR), i.e. the Government's own overall borrowing, in order to keep interest rates down. It took a number of years for the full folly of pursuing a policy tied to '£M3' to be recognised.

As the recession deepened and unemployment soared the argument between 'wets' and 'dries' was whether further cuts in public expenditure had become self-defeating. This argument led to the deep divisions over the March 1981 budget. The Treasury had failed in the autumn of 1980 to secure the large cuts in public spending that it had sought.

Amongst the proposed savings was a plan to remove that year's indexation of state pensions – in other words, the basic old age pension would not even have been increased in line with prices. But I went to Cabinet armed – as was Patrick Jenkin, the Social Services Secretary – with copies of Geoffrey Howe's and Keith Joseph's own personal election addresses in their constituencies at the 1979 election, in which they had specifically pledged to protect pensioners against inflation. So that idea was soon thrown out – Margaret was too good a politician to allow that to happen.

Britain was in the depths of recession with unemployment rising at around 80,000 per month. The rest of the world was entering recession and it seemed a safe bet that in due course the policies of Ronald Reagan, the USA's newly elected President, were likely to intensify it.

I argued that this was no time to cut the level of demand and that the Budget should be framed accordingly. I thought that the Treasury's efforts to cut Government spending and borrowing would, in any event, prove largely self-defeating: we would end up having to spend more on paying people to do nothing and inevitably we would receive less in tax payments.

By the same token, if we spent more in an effort to provide more people with jobs, the savings in unemployment benefit and the increase in Government tax revenues would minimise the need for Government to borrow much more. I therefore urged that we could spend more money in the depths of the recession with no fear that it would be inflationary. I was convinced that we could have borrowed more than the Treasury were saying was possible.

I was haunted by the thought that in the future people would look back and wonder what on earth we thought we were up to, cutting public spending with 2.4 million unemployed and our infrastructure and industrial base crying out for modernisation. I did not think that we, as a Party, would be lightly forgiven, and I feared that it would take us as long to live down our latest period of office as it had to recover from the errors which had been made in the 1930s.

It seemed absurd that the PSBR should become the new totem pole of economic policy. It was merely the difference between two huge figures, both immensely difficult to forecast with much accuracy and both prone to substantial unforeseen changes as a result of external events.

It was one thing for Government to try to ensure that its borrowing did not run wildly out of control: but it was quite another matter to make an estimate of this notoriously volatile figure, the be-all and end-all of economic policy. Donald MacDougall, then Economic Adviser to the CBI, and a former Treasury adviser, reckoned that during his time at the Treasury he could change the PSBR by £1 billion in the course of a morning's work.

Whenever I visited the City at this time they would say that they were terribly worried about the PSBR. When I asked them why, they usually replied that it was because Ministers and the Treasury were saying that it looked worrying. And then back in Whitehall I would hear Ministers and the Treasury saying how worried they were about the PSBR, and when asked why they would say that the reason was the views they heard being expressed in the City. The Treasury was being its usual self, creating the expectations and then using these expectations to force the Cabinet to toe the line: all other policies were subordinated to this tactic.

Against my views, Margaret and Geoffrey argued strongly that there was no shortage of demand (after all, there were plenty of imported consumer durables coming in); that any extra public expenditure would be seized upon by the unions, who would push up their wage claims accordingly; and that a lower borrowing requirement would enable us to reduce interest rates, and this had to be the prime consideration of Government policy.

We were regaled in the Press with stories of 'battling Maggie', reporting that there would be no U-turn and echoing Margaret's own remark at the October 1980 Party Conference: 'This lady is not for turning' – an insulting dig in the ribs at the Heath Government, in which Margaret and Keith had been the most voracious big spenders. At a time of rapidly rising unemployment, the Government therefore sought to pursue a deflationary policy in the 1981 Budget. There were no apologies for this: quite the reverse.

In July 1981 the controversy over the Budget was revived at the Cabinet's annual set-piece discussion of the Government's future spending plans. On this occasion, even several of those usually friendly to the overall policy could find little to favour in the Treasury's dismal submission. Only Margaret and Keith backed the Chancellor and his Chief Secretary. The Treasury's critics included, most notably and unexpectedly, John Biffen and John Nott.

Margaret's reaction was to say that the discussion would resume after the summer recess had given the chance for a fresh examination of the problems. It wasn't fresh examination: it was fresh faces. By the time we returned to the discussion, Margaret had reshuffled the Cabinet. She had given ample evidence of the economic policy which she intended to adopt. This reshuffle – in which I was moved from the Department of Employment to Northern Ireland – was interesting evidence of how she proposed to manage her Ministers to ensure they implemented it to her satisfaction.

CHAPTER EIGHT

THE MANAGER

In her early years as Prime Minister, Margaret adhered closely to the traditional principles and practice of Cabinet government. She operated very strictly through the Cabinet committee system, with the Cabinet Office taking the Minutes.

In Ted's Government, Margaret had been left out from the ad hoc committees which were set up. Any Secretary of State for Education is always stuck in rather an isolated department. She had, however, proved herself a disruptive influence on one Cabinet Committee, the Science Committee, where she had complained that Solly Zuckerman and Victor Rothschild were only officials and had no right to speak. They in their turn had complained about her.

I always thought she would stick closely to the official committee system because she had resented being excluded from the small ad hoc groups set up by Ted. I felt that her views were right. After all, if you are a Cabinet Minister with collective responsibility, you ought to know what is going on. Too often Cabinet Ministers don't know, and this causes resentment.

Unfortunately, after a couple of years, the formal Cabinet committees were very much down-graded and she began to operate much more in small groups dominated by her cronies. I suppose this was inevitable, but for all that it was also regrettable. Even before 1981 she had one small group who met her for breakfast and which was kept very hush-hush. It included Nigel Lawson, Norman Tebbit – neither of whom was then in the Cabinet – and John Biffen. I fancy it was disbanded after John proved himself a rather less reliable supporter. This cosy arrangement was later superseded by her close relationship with Cecil Parkinson.

The operation of a small 'war Cabinet' during the Falklands crisis in 1982 also convinced her that it was far easier to settle issues with just five or six people.

In the years since, she has adopted ad hoc groups as one of her main methods of government. This had obvious advantages for those few on the 'inside track', who come to regard meetings with their other colleagues as increasingly unnecessary and time-wasting. But it is not at all good for the many, including Cabinet Ministers, who are on the outside and who believe ad hoc groups can be weighted against them in the way

Cabinet cannot. Keith Joseph and Margaret had become bitter at their sense of being excluded by Ted but Margaret stored up more trouble for herself with colleagues who felt they were never told what was really going on.

Margaret would give as her reason for working increasingly in small groups that she couldn't rely on her colleagues to respect her authority. I regret to say that this was true.

But the coining of the term 'wet' itself hardly presaged an inclination towards teamwork or mutual trust. Margaret was responsible for pinning this name on to her opponents. It was effective for a time and rather unnerving. In due course it became a badge of honour, but it was hardly conducive to loyalty in Cabinet.

We must have been the most divided Conservative Cabinet ever. There was a deep division on economic and social policy, and members were not prepared to be put off from giving their own views.

Norman St John Stevas was regarded by Margaret as the chief leaker and he paid the penalty by getting the sack in her first reshuffle in January 1981. Number Ten let it be known that one of the reasons for his dismissal was these alleged indiscretions or breaches of confidence, an impression which Margaret appeared to reinforce in a television interview the next day. These comments prompted a letter from Norman, in which he sought 'to clarify' the position. Margaret then had no choice but to contradict the Downing Street version in her reply to Norman.

Shortly after this incident I had a long talk with her about the state of the Government. It was one of many efforts to try to get back into a reasonable working relationship. As I was leaving I said to her: 'I know you think I leak things to the Press, and yes I sometimes do, deliberately at times and by mistake on others. But, of course, so do you.'

'Oh no, Jim, I never leak.'

'Well, if you tell me that I must accept it, but in that case your officials and press people certainly leak for you.'

'Oh, that is quite wrong: they never know anything, so how could they leak?'

Either she was incredibly naive, which I have no reason to believe, or she thought I was, and I frankly doubt that. I believe she really didn't think in terms of 'leaks' herself at all – if she said it, then it had to be right: how could there be any question of a leak?

Although on many occasions I have heard her use strong invective against both press and broadcasting, she was undoubtedly the most adept Prime Minister at handling the right wing Press since the war. She had a marvellous press, they kept on her side right the way through in a way which no other Conservative Government had experienced. Both press and people found her new, refreshing and interesting. Her good looks, the fact that she was a woman – absolutely no doubt that women were proud of her – and her candour and directness appealed in a way others have not managed.

I think Margaret was mistaken to hand out honours to so many working broadcasters and journalists, and they were even more mistaken to accept. I cannot believe that it is good for a free and independent press or TV and radio service.

Margaret was very well served by Bernard Ingham, her press secretary. He had been in the Department of Employment, and was a former Labour council candidate. Everyone was surprised and delighted with this appointment. I cannot help feeling though that he was another of the left like Paul Johnson who, having decided to change sides, has moved right across the political spectrum. However, he certainly did not qualify as an intellectual: he was more in the mould of a political bruiser.

Margaret developed a technique of getting the right wing popular press to have a major lead story on some matter coming up for decision in Cabinet that morning. The headline would be along the lines of 'Battling Maggie Under Attack from Wets'. The issue would then be unfolded in terms of being pro- or anti-Maggie. The Cabinet would hold its discussion and everyone would say how shocking it was that there had been a leak that morning, which simply must not be repeated. An edict would go out that no one, but no one, was to give any indication of the decision which had been taken.

But, if the *Standard* didn't carry a headline that evening, the morning papers would certainly do so. In October 1980, at the time of the Cabinet discussion on public spending, the *Sun* proclaimed: 'Premier Margaret Thatcher routed the "wets" in her Cabinet yesterday in a major showdown over public spending. She waded into attack . . .' This was not what had happened. So much for creating a united and cohesive team. When the *Sun* finally reported a month later that the Prime Minister and her Treasury team had not secured the cuts they had sought, its headline typified the view that Margaret was somehow separate from her own Government: 'Maggie At Bay: Tories baffled as the battle for £2 billion extra cuts is lost.'

*

Most of her senior Ministers she treated reasonably if patronisingly, although her treatment of Geoffrey Howe was sometimes really awful – as, for example, when she attacked him after he had become Foreign Secretary and he proposed meetings some years after the Falklands war with the new democratic Government in Argentina.

She couldn't understand why we needed so much support from our civil servants: she reckoned that she could run the Government almost single-handed with fewer Ministers or their officials. This came to light when she hit on the idea of going round Departments to meet people and to have a discussion with senior officials. It was a great piece of public relations and I thought an excellent thing for her to do.

Before she came to the Department of Employment we spent days preparing a brief for her visit. It was to be divided into three sessions, one before lunch with senior officials during which policy issues would be raised, a buffet lunch for her to meet various people, and then a visit round certain groups.

The first session showed her at her worst, as she got into an argument with one of the best and most dedicated civil servants I have ever met, Donald Derx. She insisted on picking an argument without knowing the facts or the legal position on secondary industrial action. Even when Patrick Mayhew intervened in utter frustration she still wouldn't stop. It ended by Donald Derx saying, 'Prime Minister, do you really want to know the facts?'

I suspect that, as a result of this, Donald had a black mark against his name and appeared to be passed over for promotion. It was a pity that she was not able to accept that by standing up to her, he was displaying qualities which a civil servant must have if he is to serve his Minister properly, and which she of all people used generally to accept. Even the two senior women officials present, who were obviously delighted to see a woman Prime Minister taking on the men, became a little crestfallen at the way the discussion went.

On the other hand her afternoon tour was a great success. She was excellent at going round the Department; she talked to people, showed an interest in them and their jobs, thanked them for what they were doing and, if only the morning episode had not taken place, it would have been superb.

At one time the relationship between Margaret and the senior civil servants had become very bad. Willie Whitelaw suggested a dinner for Permanent Secretaries would be a good idea. It would enable a general discussion to take place and, to use the cliché of the day, 'a full and frank discussion'. It was held not long after the SAS had freed the hostages held in the siege of the Iranian Embassy in London.

Sir Frank Cooper, Permanent Secretary at Defence, had to leave the room. As the discussion after dinner became heated, acrimonious and rather one-sided, Frank was seen to disappear a second time. 'Where has he gone this time?' enquired one Permanent Secretary of another. 'To tell the SAS to come and get us out of this place,' came the reply.

Frank was replaced on retirement by Clive Whitmore, who had been the Prime Minister's Principal Private Secretary and was very young to be promoted, although extremely able. One night in the Commons division lobby when Francis Pym, then Secretary of State for Defence, was having one of his interminable rows over some weapon system costings, the Prime Minister turned to him and was heard to say: 'Well, if you can't do it, Clive and I will have to sort it out for you.'

It was interesting that Margaret should appoint Robert Armstrong to serve as Cabinet Secretary and much to her credit, as Robert had got on particularly well with Ted Heath when he was his Principal Private Secretary at Number Ten. That she should appoint him showed her confidence in his ability.

The post of Cabinet Secretary with its great responsibilities to the Prime Minister and the Cabinet is generally one of low profile. The position carries with it the prime responsibility for all matters of top security and intelligence which might affect the State and is the main source of confidential advice to the Prime Minister.

Considering the bumpy ride which a radical, reforming and female Prime Minister has initiated, it is not surprising that his profile has been more public than that of his predecessors. It owes much to Robert that the machine has worked as well as it has, given the nature of the terrain.

In 1986 it was Robert who had to appear in front of the Select Committee on the Westland affair to defend the decision that certain civil servants, who had already been investigated by him, should not have to give evidence to the committee. Even those who were straining at the bit were subdued by Robert's ability to deal with their questions. He made them look rather amateurish.

Margaret was clearly not at all enamoured with the Think Tank which Ted Heath had created to assist Cabinet decision-making. As is the case in many other walks of life, an institution is only as good as its leader, and the Think Tank was never the same following Victor Rothschild's departure in 1974. It had fallen increasingly under the influence of the permanent civil service bureaucracy and since Margaret had no intention of reforming it and restoring it to its former role, she was justified in abolishing it shortly after the 1983 election. By this time she had increased her own team of advisers in the Number Ten Policy Unit. Since they gave advice to her and, unlike the Think Tank, not to the full Cabinet, this marked yet another step in the seemingly inexorable growth in the power of the Prime Minister.

There was no doubt that, on matters of purely personal relationships with Ministers, backbenchers and people generally, she was extremely considerate and took a great deal of trouble. This was very evident when her driver, George, having just retired, sadly died very suddenly. She went out of her way to go to the funeral. It was a gesture of respect and kindness which I liked very much.

She nurtured her relationship with backbenchers and kept much closer to them than Ted had as Prime Minister. She could quite often be seen either in the tea-room or the dining room sitting with a group. She made them feel wanted, and that she was listening to their views – listening not being her strongest virtue, particularly with her Ministerial colleagues.

There had been one notable occasion when we were discussing a cut in the up-rating of supplementary benefit. Peter Carrington had started to say that it couldn't be done, but Margaret kept interrupting. 'Prime Minister,' he retorted, 'I must ask you to listen for a minute, because you cannot do what you want to do, as your colleagues won't let you. Hadn't you better listen to what I have to say?'

The accusation was made that many of us were being male chauvinist in our attitude to Margaret as Prime Minister. Kay Graham, for example, the *Washington Post* proprietor, said as much to me at a breakfast with the *Post*'s editorial team during one of my visits to the States as Northern Ireland Secretary. Kay argued that, although she herself did not agree with Margaret's policies, Margaret had really done a lot better as Prime Minister than we males were prepared to give her credit for, because we did not like a woman being Prime Minister.

I asked Kay how she would have felt, and what she would be saying if she had been treated in the way that some of us had been? The example I gave was the occasion when I had said in Cabinet that I strongly disagreed with Margaret's line of argument. There was then a row, at the end of which Margaret said to me, 'Well, if you feel like that, you had better come and see me afterwards.'

However, I admit that there was something in what Kay Graham said. One of Margaret's great qualities was her ability to challenge people. She would brief herself well and then set about a thorough demolition of the arguments being put by a Minister in Cabinet or Committee. Mind you, she had probably been briefed well on the arguments which the Minister had been given by his Department. Only after she was completely satisfied that the case had been properly prepared and answered would she rest content.

This ability to challenge is very important and very few people can do it. Not only does it require knowledge but in no way can you allow sympathy with, or admit understanding of, the opposing point of view. Margaret not only starts with a spirit of confrontation but continues with it right through the argument.

It is not a style which endears and perhaps even less so when the challenger is a woman and the challenged is a man. I have to confess that I found it very difficult to stomach and this form of male chauvinism was obviously one of my failings.

If that was one of my failings, then perhaps one of hers was trying to give the impression that she was a good deal softer than undoubtedly she is. I don't think anyone could enjoy getting rid of Ministers, it must require considerable toughness to be a 'good butcher', but no one can say she ducked the hard decisions.

But it was not only Cabinet Ministers who found themselves on the receiving end of Margaret's tongue: even the American Ambassador was not spared on an earlier occasion. At the end of one lengthy Cabinet while she was still Minister of Education, Margaret accompanied me to the front door at Number Ten. Walter Annenberg, the American Ambassador, was arriving with Elliot Richardson, a subsequent Ambassador, for lunch with the Prime Minister. I knew Walter well. Either he didn't know Margaret or had a temporary lapse of memory, as he introduced her to Richardson as Mrs Prior. He was put down in icy tones: 'Ambassador, Mrs Prior may be a very clever lady, but she is not a Cabinet Minister yet.'

Margaret certainly had the last word when I pulled her leg one day. The *Guardian* had reported that she had developed a 'sexy' voice in a radio programme. In fact this had not been deliberate on her part, but the result of a slight cold. I had been away and, when I saw her a day or two later, I said, 'Margaret, I read in my paper that you have developed a "sexy" voice.' Back came her reply, 'What makes you think I wasn't sexy before?'

Traditionally, politics has been a male preserve, and I think we did all find it difficult coming to terms with a woman leader. Margaret has always sought to exploit the fact that she is a woman amongst a large number of men. Sometimes she was almost in tears when she was not getting her way – for example over a row on immigration policy in Opposition. Airey Neave was going round before Shadow Cabinet saying he had just come out of her room and how upset Margaret was.

On the other hand she also sometimes takes the line that 'I'm the only man amongst all you lot'. She herself rejoiced in the knowledge that the popular press would quite often take that line.

A few tears occasionally, the odd tantrum, then a bit of coquetry were all permissible. This latter certainly extended to some of her colleagues whom she found attractive. In this category I would include Humphrey Atkins, who was her Chief Whip all through Opposition, and must have had a very difficult time, and Cecil Parkinson.

*

Perhaps one of the best examples of Margaret's style of management was the way in which she handled the divergent financial and economic views of her Cabinet, whether they arose from conflicting philosophical convictions or the annual battles between Departments and the Treasury over spending. It was the intensity of these disagreements and Margaret's response to it that preceeded her first major reshuffle in September 1981.

There has been a lot of criticism of the 'wets' in Margaret's Cabinet in the early days for our failure to work together much more closely. We felt that it would be dangerous for us to form ourselves into a cabal, since we would run the risk of being castigated immediately as conniving together against the leadership.

Geoffrey Howe's deflationary Budget in the spring of 1981 polarised the divisions in the Cabinet. It was the one occasion on which two of the other leading wets and I deliberately made issue together.

Geoffrey asked me to see him late in the afternoon of the Monday, the day before the Budget. When he told me the main outline of the Budget I told him that I thought it was awful and absolutely misjudged: it was far too restrictive, the PSBR was being cut by far too much, and it would add to unemployment. I couldn't say anything bad enough about it.

Geoffrey was cross and said that he was surprised that I had taken this line because he had seen Willie Whitelaw, Peter Carrington and Francis Pym, who had all seemed to think it was quite all right.

I went home and said to Jane: 'Either my judgment has gone totally haywire, or I'm right about this Budget and all the others are wrong.' Next morning we had the pre-Budget meeting, and there was no doubt that Geoffrey received overwhelming support. Ian Gilmour, Peter Walker and myself were critical. Peter Carrington, Francis Pym and even Willie Whitelaw were not very pleased, but they took the line that we had to support the Chancellor and, if he said we had to have tough measures to stick to our policy, that was that.

Peter, Ian and I met for breakfast the next morning and tried to decide what action we could take. The Budget had been announced in the House, so in effect we were already beaten.

I felt so desperately about it that I was willing to chuck in my hand. Although it is enormously difficult to leave a government, with accusations of rocking the boat and letting your colleagues down, I would have been prepared to face all that. But there are other ties of loyalty – a lot of people in my own constituency had supported me loyally over issues which they didn't really think too much of, and they would see their MP, almost at the first whiff of gunfire in Government, quitting to make critical speeches from the back benches. It is not a role I would choose for myself.

I came very close to resigning, and a year or so later regretted very much that I hadn't, but at the time I felt that the resignations of the three of us would not have made much mark. Peter was beginning to recuperate after having been on the back benches for four years, from 1975 to 1979, and was not at that time a very powerful figure. It was also known that Ian Gilmour had been protected by Peter Carrington in the January 1981 reshuffle. Therefore our quitting wouldn't have made much difference. A lot of people also said that I would be sacrificing myself unnecessarily.

Once you think of resignation you have to decide whether you will have more influence from outside than inside the Government. Most experience shows that you have more influence within, although I am now less certain. This was one of the major factors in my thinking, not because I had any major qualms about leaving my Department, as by then my industrial relations reforms, about which I write in the next chapter were on the Statute Book and consultations were under way on the Green Paper on Trade Union Immunities. My concern was to stay in a position to try to influence economic policy.

There were, however, perhaps two beneficial consequences of my row over the 1981 Budget. With support from Ian, Peter and the others who had not been too happy about the Chancellor's severity, we did establish for the first time that Cabinet had to have the opportunity for a full discussion on economic policy in January or early February each year, before the Chancellor goes into purdah to reach his Budget judgment. There would be a further Cabinet economic session in the summer before the start of Whitehall's annual review of public spending. This was at least a concession by Margaret, although its practical value was limited.

The second benefit was that my colleagues were more receptive towards my plans to replace the old Youth Opportunities Programme with a new Youth Training Scheme, to provide at least some basic training for all young people who were unemployed. This was a long overdue reform in Britain, making the first step towards the kind of training provided for all young school-leavers in West Germany.

I had visited Bonn and Nuremberg that Easter to study their scheme at first hand, and in the summer was able to persuade Margaret and the Treasury to boost our spending on tackling youth unemployment and launch the new training scheme from 1982. I doubt very much if I would have pushed these proposals through Cabinet had it not been for the enormous row I kicked up at the time of Geoffrey's Budget.

*

The summer months of 1981 were the most worrying time for the Government during the 1979–83 Parliament. First, unemployment had soared towards the three million mark. Secondly, the inner city riots had shocked a great many people – not least, Michael Heseltine, who had visited Merseyside after the rioting. Margaret was also worried about how to handle the House at Question Time. She didn't like the idea of spending more money, but was relieved that she would have something more positive to say about the Government's efforts on youth unemployment.

Thirdly, there was now also a great deal of discontent in the Party about the growing gap between the Government's rhetoric and the practice of our policies. The rhetoric was trenchant: 'no U-turns', no support for 'lame ducks', the 'market place' had to decide. Yet the practice was to grant considerable Government aid for a whole range of industries, particularly steel and BL. Why should we continue to receive all the odium for being callous, uncaring and doctrinaire, when in fact we were saving hundreds of thousands of jobs through Government intervention? Shouldn't we be taking some credit for doing so?

Finally we were in the middle of a civil service strike. In April, Christopher Soames, who was responsible as Lord President of the Council for civil service pay negotiations, advised Cabinet that he could clinch a settlement at an overall cost of 9 per cent. He was told by Margaret and the Treasury that this was far too high: he had to keep within his cash limit of 5 per cent, with a settlement of no more than 6 per cent. Christopher warned that this was plainly unrealistic and we would suffer a damaging strike, with loss of revenue and extra costs for the Government in financing its heavier borrowing deficit. But Margaret and Geoffrey were adamant, so the civil service strike began.

After about six weeks it became clear that a settlement would be possible at $7\frac{1}{2}$ per cent and this could be met within the prescribed cash limit of 5 per cent with a slightly faster rundown in civil service numbers. Already the dispute was worrying the Treasury and proving very costly. The strong advice of Christopher and myself was to settle. But when the matter came to the full Cabinet, it was clear that Margaret had lobbied intensively. Willie Whitelaw said afterwards she had told him she would resign if she didn't get her way – as if a Prime Minister would go on such an issue, though enough believed her.

The debate was one of the most acrimonious I have ever experienced. The Cabinet was completely split down the middle. In the end, the Prime Minister got her way and the dispute dragged on. The Treasury became even more worried. At the meetings to consider the strike, Geoffrey Howe gradually changed his stance. Eventually, after nineteen weeks the strike was settled – at $7\frac{1}{2}$ per cent, within the 5 per cent cash limit. We could have had the deal after six weeks. Instead we had lost a further £250 million in revenue and finance charges, which we would never recoup.

This did not make it easier for us to go along with the Treasury when they asked for further cuts in public expenditure.

Christopher Soames was sacked in September. Downing Street let it be known that the Prime Minister was dissatisfied with the way he had handled the civil service dispute. This was a travesty of what had actually happened and a shabby way to treat anyone, let alone a distinguished statesman with a wealth of experience. Ian Gilmour was sacked too and I was reshuffled to Ireland.

*

Margaret always seemed far less sure of herself in dealing with foreign affairs than she was in her management at home. To give her her due, she wisely placed herself in the hands of Peter Carrington by appointing him Foreign Secretary, and although she clearly listened to him, many of her early judgments seemed to some of us naive to a degree. Nevertheless, foreign affairs were to provide her with one of the greatest triumphs of her Premiership.

Rhodesia was her first big test in Government. Past experience of the Conservative Party on this issue did not give me much confidence that we could solve the problem. Immediately before the General Election in Britain, Ian Smith arranged fresh elections. In Shadow Cabinet, we asked Lord Boyd of Merton (formerly Alan Lennox-Boyd) to head a team of observers and report back.

Their report arrived during the campaign and was broadly favourable to what had happened. Margaret wanted to make a speech in support of Smith's elections and backing Muzorewa. A number of us were unhappy that we should say anything at all at that stage. It did not seem necessary; we were not fully conversant with the views of other countries, particularly the Commonwealth. It would be wise to wait till we were in Government. We remembered the difficulties we had got into with the Commonwealth with our premature commitment on South African arms at the beginning of Ted's Government. We did not wish to have a repeat performance at the forthcoming Commonwealth Conference at Lusaka.

Already Peter Carrington's influence was very much at work. The temptation to appease the right wing during the election campaign was resisted. A few weeks after the election, Peter, as Foreign Secretary, made clear our determination to bring Rhodesia to legal independence with 'the widest possible international recognition'. Handling the issue in this way was a wise decision, making possible the progress made at the Lusaka Commonwealth Conference, which in turn led to the 1980 Lancaster House Agreement on independence.

Margaret's mind was changed at Lusaka by an intoxicating combination of the Queen, Peter Carrington and the enticing prospect of bringing off a settlement without bloodshed, which had eluded successive Prime Ministers and Governments for the previous twenty years. In the end Margaret became almost too enthusiastic and had to be restrained by the more pragmatic Carrington.

Neither she nor any of us was prepared for the Mugabe victory when it came, and she in particular expressed great concern that this particualr nationalist leader was ever to be trusted. I have been told since that the Foreign Office had a very good idea of the likely strength of Mugabe and Nkomo, and thought Mugabe was bound to win. However, their concealment of those views prevented what might have caused a breakdown in the talks at Lancaster House.

We owe a lot to Christopher Soames, who was appointed Governor-General to handle the transition to independence and dealt with a most difficult situation with great subtlety and competence.

*

Much of Peter Carrington's energies were devoted to patient, and sometimes not so patient, efforts to bring Margaret round to a more balanced point of view. The difficulties over Britain's budget contribution to the EEC was a case in point.

During the transition period after our entry in 1973, the contribution we were expected to make had been fair and worked smoothly. But by 1978 it was becoming clear that our contribution would be far higher than could be justified by our GNP. In fact the Germans and ourselves would be the only net contributors with the French a net beneficiary. Given our bad economic positon and the professed aim of the Community, for a fair distribution of wealth, it was obvious that a re-negotiation of the financial arrangements was required.

The issue of Britain's contributions came to a head at the EEC Heads of Government Conference in Dublin at the end of November 1979. It did not go at all well. Margaret was a fairly new member of the club. She had built up a regard and an understanding with Helmut Schmidt, of whom she would say, 'He may be a Socialist, but his economic views are more sensible than those of the wets.' But with Giscard d'Estaing there was right from the start a coolness and aloofness. He obviously regarded her as a somewhat tiresome woman. There was clearly no way that she was going to separate Giscard and Schmidt. But her tactics only united them more firmly than ever. She hammered away at the inequity of the contribution and talked a lot about 'my money' and 'my oil'. She kept thumping the table to stress her point: her ring made a noise which did not improve her listeners' nerves. The meeting broke up without any decision, but agreed that further talks would have to be held before the next summit in April 1980.

In the meantime, Margaret encouraged anti-EEC sentiment in Britain to grow: the richer countries of the EEC were after 'our money', and she was not going to let them have it. I felt that these tactics were wrong; I doubted if trying to bulldoze in this way was likely to move the EEC partners. They had found little positive benefit in Britain's membership, and it was dangerous to push the anti-EEC argument too far, both at home and in Europe.

I could understand Margaret's sentiments on the Common Agricultural Policy and the problems which it now caused, but this begged the question of which policy we should adopt for British agriculture in its place. When I asked her, she replied: 'We should use the system of tariffs and import controls which we had intended to introduce in 1970.' Regrettably, it was not that easy: we could not go it alone on farming and stay a full member of the Community. And, without being in the Community, our previous trading partners would never have let us introduce such a system: the pressures on us to sacrifice farming again, as had happened in the 1930s, would therefore have become irresistible.

Some progress on Britain's contribution was made at the April Summit. Peter and Ian Gilmour then were able to strike a good bargain for Britain at the Foreign Affairs Council in late May, with a two-year settlement which gave us most of what we wanted.

Peter and Ian arrived back from Brussels after having been up all night negotiating and went straight to Chequers. They were subjected to a dressing down from Margaret which lasted about three hours. The agreement was no good; they had sold us down the river; the backbenchers would never accept it. But Peter and Ian had taken care to brief the press, who duly reported that this was a great triumph for the Prime Minister. By the Monday morning the press were singing Margaret's praises for having taken a tough stand and for the sensible compromise she had then allowed the Foreign Secretary to engineer. It was this which effectively prevented her from torpedoing the settlement. As things turned out, it was better than anyone could have hoped: our first year's contribution was about £15 million instead of the expected £450 million.

The row over the EEC showed Peter Carrington as a superb diplomat, both in representing the interests of Britain and in dealing with Margaret. He was in the great tradition of our Foreign Office. Al Haig might have seen him as a 'duplicitous bastard', but that was the view held of British Foreign Secretaries throughout the last half of the nineteenth century and they were quite successful. Here was a twentieth-century Foreign Secretary achieving the same grudging admiration throughout the world, but with much less power behind him.

Losing Peter from Cabinet at the start of the Falklands crisis was a great tragedy. It is inconceivable for instance that Peter would not have found a way round the difficulty which the next Government subsequently experienced in receiving the PLO representatives had he been around. As it was he was still amongst the first to warn of the dangers our refusal had caused to our standing in the Arab world.

*

If relations with the Community were strained, the same could not be said of those with the new American administration. President Reagan had a naive view of sound economics similar to Margaret's. The vital difference was the immense power, size and strength of the United States as compared with Britain. As Lane Kirkland – the US equivalent of the TUC's Len Murray – said to me, 'Even a Republican administration under Reagan could not damage the economy by more than 10 to 15 per cent, the private enterprise ethic is so strong.'

Reagan and Margaret found they had a great deal in common. Although I did not go along with the economic policies, I welcomed the close relationship which the two leaders were able to create. Margaret was the first foreign leader to be received by the new President, and she revelled in the honour and the limelight. Her visits to the United States were marvellous for her morale, giving her renewed faith. She felt most at home in the US talking to audiences of dyed-in-the-wool Republican businessmen. I don't think this was much to the liking of Nico Henderson, our Ambassador in Washington, and Peter Carrington as they listened to all the extreme rhetoric.

Shortly after her visit, I went to the States to see my opposite number a Minister for Labour, Mr Donovan. He was a building contractor from New Jersey whose claim to high political office was that he had subscribed and raised large sums for Reagan's election campaign. I asked him how he thought the Administration would affect his industry – I admit it was a loaded question. 'I have to tell you,' he replied, 'that about 5,000 of my colleagues will go out of business this year. But they are all behind what the President and the Administration are doing; that's what I call real loyalty.'

The US administration was wrong too, but the USA was rich enough to get over it. But my main criticism of American policy concerned its strategic implications. I strongly favoured matching Russia in terms of nuclear and conventional weapons. There was no doubt that we had fallen behind and great efforts were called for from NATO countries to get back into balance. However, the massive build-up of US defence had to be seen against the effects of US economic policy on the rest of the world.

The deeper the recession, the greater unemployment, the more likely there was to be unrest, particularly in the under-developed nations who suffered most. By the end of 1982, it was clear that the US Government would have to modify its policy or there would be a total breakdown in the world's banking system, with a domino effect starting with the more exposed and shaky banks. All the defence forces in the world will not win the battle against communism if the policies pursued by the capitalist countries push people to desperate measures.

*

The Argentinian invasion of the Falklands in late March 1982 ushered in one of the most remarkable periods in post-war politics.

During the previous year's public spending review, there had been a number of discussions about the withdrawal of HMS *Endurance* from the Falklands. The Foreign Office were strongly opposed to its withdrawal. The Government were given repeated warnings through an active campaign run by Aubrey Buxton about the way in which the Argentinian regime would interpret such a move. I had raised the matter in Cabinet as I knew that Peter Carrington was having difficulty in persuading John Nott, the Defence Secretary, to keep the ship down there. Unfortunately, the Foreign Office lost the day and *Endurance* was withdrawn.

On Friday, March 30 news reached London that the Argentinians had invaded the Falklands. The next day I was on weekend duty in Northern Ireland and listening to some of the Commons debate on the radio, could feel the atmosphere in the Chamber and wondered whether the Commons had taken collective leave of their senses because the expression of reaction on both sides of the House was so extreme and lacking in control. That evening I was telephoned by Willie Whitelaw to be told what a disastrous occasion it had been. John Nott's speech had been dreadful.

Shortly afterwards, John and Peter Carrington appeared before the 1922 Committee. Apparently John put up a better performance retrieving ground lost earlier in the day.

On the other hand, Peter Carrington was very upset by his reception. He had little rapport with the backbenchers: he regarded most of them rather disdainfully and they knew little about him. He was out of touch and realised for the first time the animosity, distrust and sheer hatred on the back benches for the Foreign Office and all its work. It was this as much as anything that persuaded him to resign. There was, of course, also his sense of honour that as the Minister responsible his policy had failed. I still believe that he might have stayed on, had it not been for the disgraceful articles on the Monday morning in *The Times* and other papers: these were the last straw. As it was we lost the services of the best Foreign Secretary this century.

The moral of Peter's experience is that the Minister in charge of every important Department needs to be in the Commons, not only to stamp his authority on the policy, but so that he knows his backbenchers and keeps in touch with them. In the week of the crisis, Peter had been in Brussels and Israel, dealing with matters which had seemed of far greater long-term political and strategic importance. Unfortunately, as far as the House of Commons was concerned the Falkland Islands and their inhabitants were more significant.

Perhaps the most extraordinary aspect of the Commons was the Labour Party's attitude regarding the Falklands. All Parties reflected a wide range of views, but there was nothing to choose between the views of Julian Amery and Bernard Braine on the right, and Peter Shore and Stan Newens on the left. Apparently the more lukewarm Labour MPs were subjected to strong attack in the Labour clubs, which were absolutely behind the Prime Minister. I found incredible support for Margaret in the pubs of Lowestoft.

The Falklands Task Force sailed on the Monday. At that day's special meeting of Cabinet the Lord Chancellor, Quintin Hailsham, took me aside and said: 'Well, Jim, whatever our views might be, because British troops are committed, we've got to stand rocklike together behind the forces.'

I sent a personal, hand-written note to Francis Pym, the new Foreign Secretary, with a copy to Willie Whitelaw, pledging my full support for Francis's efforts to achieve a peaceful settlement. I was not at all sanguine about people's likely reactions once British lives started being lost.

For the most part the Cabinet was worried, looking for some way out, but remaining united. If Galtieri had accepted either the Haig proposals or the Peruvian peace plan, there is no doubt that we would have had to go along with them. This would have split the Conservative Party. There would have been about sixty MPs who would have voted against such proposals and a few who would have resigned the whip.

Margaret had the worry of not only committing British troops, but also of splitting the Party as she tried desperately to achieve an honourable solution. Some would say that all along she was bent on confrontation, but I do not believe that to have been the case. Her stance in the Commons was always more belligerent than in Cabinet.

A small War Cabinet was formed, consisting of John Nott, Willie Whitelaw, Francis Pym and Cecil Parkinson. Margaret of course presided and the Chiefs of Staff were present. Cecil Parkinson was an unusual appointment as he was Chairman of the Party and to have a party representative in the War Cabinet when national unity was imperative seemed odd. I believe John Nott requested him, and certainly Margaret would have wished for someone firmly on her side. It turned out to be an inspired appointment as Cecil's appearances on television and at press conferences did much to give confidence at a time when the Ministry of Defence spokesmen were proving obtuse and inept.

I do not think that we could have got through those three months without the Foreign Secretary being in the Commons. Francis Pym, who took over when Peter Carrington resigned, did a superb job in the most difficult circumstances. His speeches in the House were balanced and well received. He saved Margaret's bacon on countless occasions. He contributed greatly to our subsequent election victory, but he was to reap a very bitter harvest.

The Falklands campaign was one of the few occasions in war when we won the first and all-important battle. The army had for years been toughened up by its experiences in Northern Ireland and this certainly added to its preparedness and professionalism. The recapture of the islands by the services was a feat of logistical brilliance, sheer courage and great professionalism.

The Party, far from being split, was united by a great victory largely achieved by Margaret's resolution: it transformed the political outlook. She took risks which not many of us would have been prepared to accept; there was a large bill to be met, but no one can doubt that she had secured her place in history. The army came home on those great troop-ships to a moment of patriotic fervour. I never doubted afterwards that Margaret would deservedly be re-elected.

*

By April 1983, Margaret was trying to decide on the date for the general election. She consulted Cabinet by summoning us in small groups. I saw her with Peter Walker, George Younger and Nick Edwards.

I went to our meeting thinking that the last thing in the world she would want would be an early election, because it was against all her instincts. I was absolutely amazed to find that she had virtually decided to go in June: she put all the arguments for an early election, and hardly any for an October one.

All of us were in favour of the early election. The discussion then focussed on whether it should be the 9th, 16th or 23rd. It was a question of whether she could afford to be away at the Economic Summit during the campaign. We thought she could. The Social Democrats had failed to get off the ground at the Darlington by-election earlier that year. If they had done well there, it would have put our thoughts about an election in a totally different perspective.

It was quite extraordinary how little our Manifesto was discussed. Geoffrey Howe was in charge of drafting it, but there was almost no discussion outside the small group working with him. The rest of Cabinet were allowed to propose drafts of our own sections. In my draft, I referred to the Republic of Ireland, which caused some objections because a Conservative Manifesto had never previously acknowledged the Republic's existence. But George Younger at the Scottish Office supported its inclusion because it would otherwise have looked as if we were in favour of devolution *per se*, rather than devolution in an *Irish* context.

There was no real discussion on economic or social strategy in Cabinet before the Manifesto was drafted. The only time in the previous four years when we had put our Departmental responsibilities to one side and had any collective, strategic discussion was when Terry Burns, the Chief Economic Adviser at the Treasury, came along in 1980. That had turned into a discussion on when we could expect to see the first upturn in the economy: the forecast seemed to depend entirely on the rate of building new houses, which was a superficial view of how a Government might seek to run the economy. By 1983, of course, the policy itself had changed quite considerably from that first pursued in 1979.

Margaret's concern to bring local authorities under control meant that Cabinet spent more time in acrimonious debate on these issues than on economic strategy. Of the few specific pledges in the 1983 Manifesto, two dealt with local government. Margaret had first pledged to abolish domestic rates in the October 1974 election. Although she had later fudged the issue in the 1979 Manifesto, she knew it was a popular proposal. But Peter Thorneycroft, then Party Chairman, had warned her not to pledge abolition because it would prove impossible to deliver.

After 1979, all the various Cabinet Committees which examined local government finance failed to find suitable alternatives to domestic rates.

In early 1983 Willie Whitelaw reported to Cabinet that the Committee he had chaired had been unable to find any suitable alternative, and we should therefore forget about abolition; but Leon Brittan, then Chief Secretary, said that the right answer was to go for control by 'rate-capping'. This would legally limit the amount by which local authorities could increase their rates, combined with control over the public expenditure element of their revenue. Others argued strongly that this was a further infringement upon local government democracy and would cause a lot of trouble. Michael Heseltine was very much against it. But Margaret said she couldn't possibly go into an election without a pledge of some kind, and in the end the Cabinet consented.

Margaret also believed that the abolition of the GLC would save a great deal of money. Michael Heseltine disagreed with this proposal too, and after the election his opposition led Margaret to deliver to him one of the most violent rebukes I have witnessed in Cabinet. No doubt these issues of local government fuelled the disagreement between Michael on the one

The budding politician

The politician

The Macmillans in support

The Priors in attendance

The farmer

The cartoonist's view, part one

Claret and laughter: Clive Jenkins and Tom Jackson

In Northern Ireland

The Two Faces of Toryism

The cartoonist's view, part two

The politician at ease

With the grain

hand and Margaret and Leon on the other which ultimately led to their resignations from her Cabinet over the Westland affair in January 1986.

I suspect that, when Michael walked out of the Cabinet he was acting on impulse. He had said to me on a number of occasions that he thought he and I shared the same maxim, that it was best 'to stick in there', and not be pushed out. He may have thought about taking such action beforehand, but if so I doubt if he had also worked out the consequences. I feel this because of my own involvement in an earlier, notorious episode in Michael's career.

Following the vote at the end of a particularly acrimonious debate in the Commons when we were still in Opposition and Michael was our front bench industry spokesman, a group of left wing Labour MPs had started to sing 'The Red Flag' – whereupon Michael picked up the mace from the table and, holding it above his head as any good Tarzan would, advanced threateningly towards the chanting MPs on the benches opposite. Some started to shout in mock disapproval, others to get ready for a fight. Soon most of the House was on its feet: there was a lot of noise and some good-humoured laughter.

I had been sitting next to Michael and I now leapt up and grabbed the mace from him. 'You bloody fool,' I shouted, 'give it to me, and get out of the Chamber as quickly as you can.' I put the mace back on the table as Michael departed.

If the event caused him some embarrassment, it also gave him a great deal of publicity. Thanking me a few days later for rescuing him, he remarked that he had made up his mind to pick up the mace. But he hadn't worked out how to get rid of it!

*

The election of 1983 was almost the election that never was. There was no doubt that the Conservative Government would be returned, the only interest was in the size of the majority. Would it be so large as to be unmanageable? – the fear expressed by Francis Pym in his notorious broadcast at the time. If so, how would the enlarged parliamentary Party perform in the House of Commons?

It was an unusual election. Michael Foot filled every hall the whole way through the election campaign. The extreme left and the old Tribune group all loved him, and every meeting he went to he got carried away. But I heard that at Labour's daily early morning private briefing sessions Michael was told that every time he opened his mouth on nuclear deterrence and disarmament, he lost thousands of votes. Michael's reply was that the people in the halls simply loved it; he'd been doing it for twenty-five years and he'd got to go on doing it.

I found people in and around Lowestoft who had never voted anything else but Labour – some indeed had been Labour councillors until a few years previously – who were telling me that they weren't going to do so this time. It was the first time in my political career that I've ever really seen a swing, not necessarily a swing towards us particularly, but a swing away from Labour.

The other odd feature of the election was that Margaret, for all her radical rhetoric and despite her dominance in the Party after the Falklands, was fighting on an ultra-cautious manifesto. She had been frightened by the reception given to the 'Think Tank' documents suggesting radical reforms to the Welfare State which had been leaked the previous autumn. She was certainly most careful to avoid being committed to total review and, by implication, destruction of the National Health Service. That was the one issue on which, if the Labour Party had stuck to it, they might have got somewhere. But, every time they got on to the Health Service, within twenty-four hours either Callaghan or Healey, or Foot himself, made a speech taking the debate straight back on to nuclear defence again. They kicked the ball through their own goal with almost unnerving accuracy and regularity.

During the campaign I was not invited to attend a single Central Office Press Conference. I did only three days' touring and no Party political broadcasts. In contrast to my time in Ted's Government, when I was always touring or on television, I was asked to do practically nothing, and I even had some trouble in getting Central Office to publish my speeches. On one occasion I gave my speech direct to the Press Association, which attracted a lot of publicity.

In this speech I argued that people had suffered in the last few years and they would want to feel that their lost employment and their suffering had some point: it wasn't good enough to show what we'd done to get things better in terms of inflation and the economy generally, we had to carry it forward to show there was some benefit for these people. It was a theme which Francis Pym also took up during the campaign.

*

The June 1983 election resulted in the biggest landslide in terms of a Commons majority since Labour's victory in 1945. We had won 397 seats, giving us a majority over all other parties of 144 seats. Labour had been reduced to 209 seats, their lowest since 1935. The SDP/Liberal Alliance won 23 seats, a mere 3.5 per cent of seats in the Commons, despite having won 26 per cent of votes cast. Such are the vagaries of the British electoral system that our 'landslide' was achieved despite the 2 per cent fall since 1979 in our share of the vote, which fell to 42 per cent.

My own majority in Waveney, as my Lowestoft constituency had been re-named, increased to 14,298. So I enjoyed the security of a comparatively safe seat for the first time – and this despite having lost about 10,000 predominantly Tory voters over the Norfolk border into Great Yarmouth in the re-drawing of constituency boundaries.

Each year since 1979 that we had spent in Government I couldn't see how we could continue to pursue our economic policies without modification. I thought that by the time we got to the autumn we were bound to have a crisis of one sort or another, and would have to trim our sails.

All successful Prime Ministers need luck. Whereas Ted Heath, was denied it, Margaret was extraordinarily fortunate. By far her best piece of luck was the utter feebleness of the Opposition, particularly during Michael Foot's leadership. Even with the disastrous level of unemployment and the effects of deep recession, Labour was unable to make any impact before 1983. Some would ascribe this not to luck, but to Margaret's dynamic personality, which destroyed the Opposition's will. But the plain fact is that the Labour Party was divided and in deep decline and she was Prime Minister when the realisation of this first fully dawned on the world at large.

Nevertheless, Margaret is a Prime Minister of great intelligence, efficiency and determination. They are qualities which have enabled her to accomplish the abolition of the GLC and exemplified her leadership during the Falklands campaign. Undoubtedly it was her leadership which saw to it that in the confrontation with the miners during 1984–85 it was not the Government which fell, as it had done ten years before. I only wish that she had brought the same resolution and management skills to reduce the worst unemployment of the century.

CHAPTER NINE

POWER AND THE UNIONS

I have deliberately refrained from writing about my time as Secretary of State for Employment and then Northern Ireland in Margaret's Government until this point as I wanted to describe first both the framework of her economic policies and her style of management.

Within twenty-four hours of my appointment at the Department of Employment I knew exactly what she thought of me from her remark that she was determined to have 'someone with backbone' as my junior Minister. Neither the Party, the press nor the unions needed a crystal ball to predict that I was going to have a rough passage. With Margaret as Prime Minister and my views being regarded as well to the left of the Party, there were bound to be question marks over my credibility – would I last long on the front bench? Was it really worthwhile for the unions to bother to get to know me?

My first great concern on my appointment in May 1979 was to try to maintain an effective dialogue with the trade unions. I was haunted by our experience towards the end of Ted's Government, when our communications with them and their leaders had been quite inadequate.

Given Margaret's right wing views I was surprised that when she became Leader in February 1975 she had asked me to continue as Opposition front bench spokesman on employment and industrial relations. It was a responsibility which I was to hold for over seven years, the last two and a half in her Government as Secretary of State for Employment.

Throughout my entire time in the job I was having to fight on two fronts – I was striving to impose some form of legislation on the unions while repelling the right-wing demands for extreme measures which were extreme.

As Shadow spokesman for Employment, I used to find myself under attack each year as the Party Conference approached – either by my more right wing colleagues in the Shadow Cabinet or on back benches, sometimes organisations like the Freedom Association and almost always by the popular press – the *Daily Mail*, the *Daily Express* and the *Sun*.

The row over our policy on the closed shop came to a head at the 1977 Party Conference, where a motion on the issue had been selected for debate. The right were organising a vicious campaign against me, which had started in the summer. I was called a 'Quisling' by John Gorst, the Tory MP who had been advising George Ward at Grunwick, a photo-graphic processing company in North London, which had created a *cause célèbre* by refusing to recognise and give bargaining rights to the trade union APEX. Norman Tebbit, using his best invective, made a speech in his Chingford constituency in which he argued that there were people to be found in the Conservative Party, as well as among the Liberals and Labour, with the morals of Laval and Petain, because they adhered to 'the doctrine of appeasement'.

However I was interested that, when he came to address the Party Conference that year, Norman considerably modified his language and found his own inimitable way to back the Party line: 'I am a hawk and not a kamikaze pilot. Jim is a dove but he is no chicken. We are right to disavow any heavy-handed legislation.'

When my own turn came to speak at that Conference, I said that the challenge for the Tory Party was to win the support of rank and file trade unionists who were not socialists, but who had never been able to bring themselves to vote Tory. Some had done so in our 1976 and 1977 by-election victories in traditional Labour strongholds, 'But there are many millions more who long to cross that bridge from Socialism, but who first wish to be sure that we have the strength that comes from unity, the warmth and understanding that is the basis of a caring society. We must provide that reassurance, and that is why I am taking the view in a difficult situation that I have taken.'

I was determined to stick to my own programme: reform of industrial relations became the be-all and, if necessary the end-all of my political career.

I wanted legislation which could work, be seen to work, and would carry support, and which would also form the starting point and foun-dation for many years to come. Basically, Margaret recognised that this approach was right, although there were times when her instincts and impetuosity would get the better of her.

There were, however, advantages in me being seen to hold back the baying hordes of the Party's right wing. It was an uncomfortable stance, but made me look the reasonable man and therefore difficult for the TUC to attack. It fitted in well with my strategy to keep just behind the public's demands for more action and to speak quietly but act firmly.

*

During the winter of 1978–79, the Labour Government's Winter of Dis-content, it became clear that the unions were far exceeding their proper role.

There was strong pressure on the Tory Party to become committed to tough legislation. I was determined to resist in every way possible. I felt that some legislation on the unions would be required, but my overriding concern was that it should not be too extreme. We should wait and then act with caution in Government.

We offered Jim Callaghan's Government our support if he would take reasonable legislative action, principally to control picketing. There was a great prize for us if we could get the Labour Government to introduce such legislation. I was determined that we would not make the same mistake as we had in 1969–70 when we did not back Barbara Castle's union reforms. But Callaghan, who had played a key role in defeating Barbara Castle's plans, could not contemplate legislation to curb the unions. No doubt such legislation would have destroyed the Labour Government, although no more so than the unions' actions during the winter succeeded in doing.

At this time, from late 1977 to 1979, my position in the Party was probably at its strongest. Industrial relations were at the heart of the political battle. We were making sensible although strong noises. I was seen to be holding the line. My reputation was on the up, I played an important part in the 1979 election campaign, although I failed to appreciate the full strength of my position at the time.

As Employment Secretary I was fortunate to be assisted by a first-rate team of Ministers. Patrick Mayhew had been appointed following my refusal to accept Leon Brittan and I used to tease Patrick about being the 'backbone' of my Department. We became good friends and he was to prove a magnificent support to me, arguing the case for my 'step-by-step' approach with clarity and conviction.

Grey Gowrie, my deputy as Minister of State, was one of the best intellects in the Government, a brilliant speaker with a grasp of the English language which reflected his poetic style and his Irish romanticism. Jim Lester was a caring 'One Nation' Tory, excellent at dealing with the problems of the young unemployed and devising the manifold schemes we were developing for training. I was upset when Margaret sacked him in her first reshuffle in January 1981.

*

Trying to keep our channels to the unions open and clear was an almost impossible task. At the Cabinet before the first TUC annual conference after the May 1979 election, Margaret supported Geoffrey Howe's plan for a major speech. I took the opportunity to advise colleagues on the need to exercise the utmost caution over any comments before or during the TUC. Union moderates were having a tough battle behind the scenes to hold the union movement to a reasonable approach. Strident statements by Ministers could only undermine them. I did not want my consultations with the TUC on union reforms wrecked, nor did I want to see the creation of a confrontationist atmosphere on economic policy.

I might as well have saved my breath. On the Friday I travelled up to Swinton College in Yorkshire to address the Conservative Trade Unionists. Late that afternoon I was told about Geoffrey's speech. It was an unrelenting attack on the 'dreamworld' of the unions. My Department had been told by the Treasury's press office that they had been assured that I had approved the speech.

In fact I had not been consulted, apart from the general discussion in Cabinet which had prompted my warning against such a speech. My own speech to the Conservative Trade Unionists that evening was entirely different in its approach. Apart from the political folly of Geoffrey's comments, it hardly seemed sensible for senior Ministers to be delivering such wildly divergent messages.

The TUC's team for the consultations over my proposed reforms was led by Len Murray, the TUC General Secretary, and Harry Urwin of the TGWU, and was drawn from the TUC's Employment, Policy and Organisation committee. I used to sit on one side of the table with my junior Ministers and advisers, and about ten or a dozen union leaders and TUC representatives would sit opposite. They included Bill Keys of SOGAT, Ken Graham and John Monks of the TUC, and Ken Gill of AUEW-TASS. Ken Gill was a great cartoonist and would invariably present me with an excellent caricature of myself at the end of each session.

Len was a tough but sensitive leader. He knew the score – they couldn't ever agree with me but couldn't be seen to refuse to talk. His tactics were to claim that much of what we wished to do was unnecessary and the rest was simply Tory union-bashing.

I liked Len enormously and came to have a great respect for him. Years later when he became a peer, I was very privileged to be asked to be one of his guests at lunch before the introduction ceremony. I sat on the steps of the throne watching him as I had done when listening to the debates on my legislation.

Harry Urwin was not well known outside the TGWU, but he was a powerful advocate. I don't think he realised how much the position and power of the unions had changed. He thought they could defeat or nullify the legislation as they had in 1971 and 1972.

*

During the late summer and autumn, I worked on the detailed drafting of the Bill. This involved innumerable and seemingly endless meetings debating the pros and cons of the many options and how they might best be given effect in the law.

My main purpose in all this was to put the onus on the unions. It would have been easy for the Government to go too far in changing the law and to do so too fast: we would then find that not only the unions but also business and most of the country would unite in saying that we had produced a scheme of law which was unworkable.

I wanted to hold some shots in my locker, so that the unions would know that if they continued to abuse their power tougher measures would follow. A cautious, 'step-by-step' approach would also make it virtually impossible for them to whip up an effective campaign of opposition, since the measures being introduced could scarcely be portrayed as draconian.

We were all agreed that the Labour Government's sweeping extension of the immunities granted to unions to protect them from legal action between 1974 and 1976 had to be pegged back since it allowed industrial action against companies far removed from the original dispute.

There was, however, a chance that the courts themselves would effectively restrict union immunities. The Court of Appeal's judgment in *Express Newspapers v. MacShane* in December 1978 had established that it was not enough for those taking industrial action to believe that their action was 'in furtherance' of a dispute for it to be lawful. Objective criteria also had to be taken into account – e.g. the action might be too remote from, or simply be incapable of furthering, the original dispute.

The House of Lords was due to rule on the Court of Appeal's judgment later in 1979. I decided that it would therefore be wiser to concentrate specifically on picketing in the Bill and to await the Lords' judgment. If the Lords were to overrule the Court of Appeal, I could then consider adding an extra clause to curb other forms of 'secondary' action.

*

The Employment Bill was introduced in December 1979. My purpose was to bring about a lasting change in attitude by changing the law gradually, with as little resistance, and therefore as much by stealth, as was possible. There were also dangers in having tougher legislation which employers might in practice be afraid to use. It would be wrong to pass legislation which the courts could not enforce, as had been the case with the 1971 Act.

In a way, the right wing of the Conservative Party also helped me, because the more they said that the legislation was nothing like tough enough, the harder it became for both the Labour Party and the trade unions to resist it. Neither the Labour Party nor the trade unions were able to get a concerted attack on the legislation off the ground.

While I could not expect the legislation to be fully accepted or be properly effective during the first period of Conservative Government, if we won a second time the trade unions would have to come to terms with it. It was therefore all the more important not to push our reforms too far in our first period of Government, for fear that one might undo everything by re-kindling Labour's and the unions' fighting spirit.

The Bill had four main aims, each of which could be clearly seen as necessary and timely. First, Government cash was to be made available for union elections, strike calls or amending union rules when these were conducted by postal, secret ballots. An objective observer might have thought that this would be relatively uncontroversial, but it took six years for the unions to come to terms with it. Some Tory right wingers were, however, against the use of Government funds and felt we should make all unions ballot compulsorily by post with the unions paying.

The second aim was to limit picketing to a person's own place of work. This was very restrictive and was a reform of far-reaching importance. In the Winter of Discontent of 1979, there had been many cases of lorry drivers picketing at haulage depots other than their own, and outside factory gates and at docks. They had often managed to prevent any goods being moved. By restricting pickets to their own place of work, much of the intimidation and wholesale disruption would be overcome.

The penalties for unlawful picketing would be placed on the person who had organised the picket. This caused further controversy because many people wanted the penalty placed on the relevant *union*. I had fought to prevent this, as once again it would have risked taking us back to the 1971 Act in which unions were made liable for their members' actions: I feared that it could become the cement of union solidarity. In my legislation I was seeking new ways to avoid bringing the unions into the courts, which would quickly bring to the fore emotive questions of solidarity and loyalty.

The third plank of the Bill was to make changes in the way in which closed shops operated. In existing closed shops, the Bill enabled anyone who had been dismissed for refusing to join a union, yet who objected to being a member of a union on grounds of conscience, or other deeply held personal convictions, to claim substantial compensation. This provision would have entitled the forty British Rail employees dismissed in 1977 to claim substantial compensation – a right which the European Court subsequently upheld in August 1981 when it awarded three of those dismissed over £145,000 in compensation.

The Bill also made the introduction of any new closed shop extremely difficult. If a closed shop was set up without the approval, in a ballot, of at least 80 per cent of employees concerned, any dismissals for not belonging to the union would automatically be regarded as unfair and therefore deserving of compensation. The purpose was to deter employers from accepting objectionable provisions in closed shops, and to deter unions from pressing such demands because employers would be able to make them bear their share of any compensation.

Much of the sting of the closed shop and the picket line lay in the fear that a torn up union card could mean a torn up right to work. I therefore also included in the Bill a new right for people to bring a case for unreasonable exclusion or expulsion from their union before an independent tribunal, who could award compensation against the union. Previously, such cases had been referred to the TUC's own appeals committee.

The fourth main plank dealing with abuses of union power tackled the problem of coercive union recruitment tactics. The print union, SLADE, had been compelling people, particularly in small artwork firms, to join the union against their will. Their tactic was to refuse to handle, i.e. 'black', any work by people not in SLADE. Soon after coming to office I had set up an independent inquiry under Raymond Leggatt, QC, to investigate SLADE's recruitment tactics. His report revealed the extent of SLADE's bully-boy methods and justified the measures we took to make coercive recruitment unlawful, a measure which virtually no other trade unionist opposed.

In addition, I included in the Bill some limited amendments to Labour's 1975 Employment Protection Act, which was discouraging employers from creating new jobs.

I had to fight enormous pressure from employers, particularly small businesses, who wanted the Employment Protection Act repealed lock, stock and barrel. Complete abolition would have deprived employees of some much-needed protection to which successive Governments had been committed – for example, protection against unfair dismissal, though extended too far by Labour in 1975, had first been introduced by Ted Heath's Government in our ill-fated Industrial Relations Act.

I amended the Act's provisions on unfair dismissal, maternity leave and the requirement on employers to guarantee payment of wages at a set level during lay-offs. I also abolished the 'Section 11' procedures which could force a firm to recognise a union for collective bargaining, and removed the 'Schedule 11' provision which allowed unions to lodge pay claims based solely on comparability, with no regard to a firm's ability to pay.

In my reforms I also introduced a new right for women workers to claim time off if they were pregnant to attend ante-natal check-ups. This followed the recommendation of the all-party Commons Select Committee on Social Services, chaired by Renee Short, whose report had been concerned to reduce the incidence of infant deformity and disability.

The Bill was introduced and went through the formality of its first reading in the Commons on December 7, with its second reading – the major debate on the principle of the Bill – set for December 19. But on December 13 the Law Lords overturned the Court of Appeal's judgment in *Express Newspapers v. MacShane*. The Lords' judgment re-established the unions' comprehensive immunity from legal action for breaches of contract granted by Labour's 1976 legislation.

In my speech opening the second reading debate I therefore made it clear that I would have to consider further measures for inclusion in the Bill. The Lords' ruling had shown that union immunities, as defined by the 1976 Trade Union and Labour Relations Act, were unnecessarily and dangerously wide. The law gave unions virtual carte blanche for any action they chose to take – it didn't matter what anyone else thought, or what the objective facts were, the sole criterion of the legality of any action was the subjective view of the trade unionists who were carrying out the industrial action.

*

All my calculations were almost upset by the national strike at British Steel which began on January 2, 1980. Since we returned to office I had been walking a political tightrope in my effort to stick to a gradual approach to union reform. The rope started to shake a few weeks earlier with the Lords' judgment on *Express Newspapers v. MacShane*. Now there was a gale almost blowing me off the rope as the action of steelworkers and their supporters led to renewed demands for much tougher measures to curb union power.

Within a matter of weeks the steel unions had expanded their industrial action from British Steel, with whom they were in dispute, to the private steel producers. Mass secondary picketing returned to the streets and TV screens, in scenes reminiscent of the previous year's Winter of Discontent.

Following the Lords' judgment I had been considering how best to tighten up the law on union immunities. The basic issue was whether to restrict immunities solely to the original dispute itself, as we were proposing on picketing with our plan in the Bill to limit picketing to a person's place of work. Or should we allow some scope for sympathetic, or 'secondary', industrial action by unions in furtherance of the original dispute?

I opted for the latter course of action, believing that anything more restrictive at that stage simply would not stick. How could one realistically expect the law to prevent people on strike from trying to black or disrupt supplies to or from their company? I was, however, far from optimistic about the chances of convincing my colleagues. I suspected that they would want to ban all secondary action.

My concern grew when I received a letter from John Nott at the Department of Trade arguing that a radical clamp-down on union immunities would be needed in light of another recent House of Lords judgment, in the *Nawala* case. The shipowners felt that the judgment had left foreign ships coming to Britain particularly vulnerable to the campaign by the International Federation of Seamen's Unions against the use of 'flags of convenience'. It was argued that our union law made it much easier to pursue a campaign of blacking in British ports than in any other West European ports. As a result, Britain's trade would suffer because only high-cost shipping would be prepared to risk coming to our ports.

I heard, however, that the Lord Chancellor, Quintin Hailsham, was strongly opposed to John Nott's argument. I went to see him and discovered the vehemence of his opposition – he feared that too radical a reduction of union immunities would prevent British seafarers being able to protect themselves against an employer who dismissed them merely to hire cheap crews from the Third World, some of whom would go on ships for board and food, with no pay. He was genuinely worried at the likely impact on the British merchant fleet.

At the Cabinet's Economic Strategy Committee, or 'E' Committee as it was known, Quintin supported my line on union immunities against the likes of Geoffrey Howe, who as usual argued that we should return to his approach of wholesale reform, adopted in his 1971 Industrial Relations Act. In the end my approach was backed: I was also given the go-ahead to stick to my process of consultation before drafting the detailed legislation.

I therefore set about preparing my consultation document, with a view to publishing it in mid-February. I would then be able to present a detailed reform of the law to Parliament about four or five weeks later, in the form of a new clause for inclusion in the Employment Bill, then in Committee.

But as tempers boiled over in the steel strike the political pressure quickly built up within the Party for immediate and tougher action. The legal position became even more confused at the end of January. Notwithstanding the Lords' ruling six weeks earlier which had appeared to give the unions carte blanche, the Court of Appeal now ruled that the unions' action against the private steel producers *was* unlawful.

The Party Chairman, Peter Thorneycroft, came to see me a day or two later to say that if the Lords subsequently overturned this latest Court of Appeal ruling, the political pressure for tougher action on union immunities would become irresistible. There was concern on the back benches, and my enemies were doing their best to whip it up.

I was tipped off that a new campaign was being organised against me, and sure enough George Gardiner, the Tory MP for Reigate and Thatcher-loyalist, wrote an article in the *Sunday Express* on February 3 calling for much more drastic action. The *Sunday Telegraph* editorial took the same line.

At 'E' Committee we discussed whether our plans to curb union immunities went far enough and whether emergency measures should be rushed through Parliament to ease the plight of the private steel producers. I managed to hold the line on my 'step-by-step' approach.

On the evening of February 6 Margaret and I met a lobby from the private steel producers at Number Ten. They demanded immediate action by the Government to put an end to the picketing at their works and the blacking of their supplies. But when I left at the end of the meeting the TV and Press reporters were waiting to hear whether we would rush new measures through Parliament. I was able to say that we would not change from our proposed pace of change – we were seeking to make changes which would last.

The next day I was summoned to appear before the 1922 Committee, the regular Thursday evening gathering of Tory backbenchers. Earlier in the day BBC Radio 4's *World at One* asked me for an interview with Robin Day. The officials in my Department advised me not to accept, but with the political pressure against me in the Party I felt that I should. Then my private office received a call from Number Ten. Bernard Ingham was saying that I should not go on. That convinced me that I should appear.

I recognised that there was serious concern in the Party. We had been elected to curb union power and yet here we were, in our first winter, having to stand by as a national strike threatened to erupt; and we were unable to say anything more than some limited reforms were wending their way through Parliament and should be in place for the following winter.

Yet apart from the small number of MPs who took a really close interest in the issues, and who either backed me or were vehemently opposed, the vast majority attending the 1922 Committee would be looking for reassurance that the Government's approach was the right one, that I had my brief under control and that my judgment was sound. They did not want a discursive analysis on the detailed arguments. So I kept my comments short and to the point, and tried to sound as crisp and confident as possible.

It did the trick. There were a few criticisms from predictable quarters, but I had won the Parliamentary Party's support.

There was, however, one hiccup before the evening was over. The meeting had been well publicised, not least by my critics who had expected me to take a beating. The press were anxious to know how I had fared. The job of briefing the Parliamentary lobby correspondents afterwards belonged to Derek Howe, who served as a Special Adviser to the Government. He was duly told what had happened by Edward du Cann, in my presence, immediately after the '22. But, within minutes of the lobby briefing, backbenchers were being asked why they thought that I had fared so badly and had such a rough ride. There was clearly something awry, but fortunately my back bench supporters who had attended the meeting were able to put the record straight, as the press reports showed the next morning.

Even so, I was still not out of the wood. On Saturday evening I was phoned by Peter Walker to ask me what I thought about Geoffrey Howe's speech earlier that day on union law. 'What speech?' was my response. Neither Geoffrey nor the Treasury had let me know about his speech beforehand. In his speech, he argued that 'the whole framework of union law' played into the hands of the militants. This was his usual theme in Cabinet when arguing that we should desert my 'step-by-step' approach and re-launch the wholesale reforms attempted by Ted's Government. Having lost the argument in Cabinet Committee, the Chancellor was now pushing his line in public.

I was due to return to 'E' Committee with the draft of my working paper proposals the following Wednesday and present them to Cabinet the next day. If I was defeated I would resign.

On the Tuesday morning I had to go to the Commons, to deal with the Committee stage of my Bill, but Jane and I discussed my chances beforehand. We were so worried that while I went to the House, she went to the Department to see my political advisers, Rob Shepherd and Robbie Gilbert, and my diary secretary, Joyce Wheeler, who had worked with me in Government since 1970.

They devised a strategy to rally support behind me. Rob duly came over to see me at the Commons. We cancelled my other meetings for the rest of the day and set about identifying which Cabinet colleagues I should lobby. I had recently seen Ian Gilmour and Peter Walker, who I knew would back me. I was already due to see Quintin Hailsham. We arranged meetings in addition with Willie Whitelaw, Peter Thorneycroft, Norman St John Stevas and Michael Heseltine. I also spoke with Peter Carrington by phone.

As I arrived for 'E' on the Wednesday morning, February 13, my resignation was on the cards.

The meeting was touch and go. But in the end my line held. The full Cabinet meeting the next day was more a formality and I was finally given the go-ahead to publish my proposals to curb secondary strikes the following Tuesday, February 19.

But Margaret was under intense pressure from her own supporters to be tougher on the unions. They hated the fact that I had seen off their demands. Her own instincts were to respond to events. At Prime Minister's Questions that afternoon she seized her chance, announcing to the surprise of the Commons and many of her Cabinet colleagues, that plans were in hand to ensure that in future people on strike claiming social security benefits would be deemed to be receiving strike pay from their union. A certain sum of money would be docked each week from strikers' social security benefits.

We had put forward this proposal in our manifesto and it had been discussed by some of us in Cabinet Committee. But it had not been raised at Cabinet, despite the fact that it was a politically controversial proposal.

Margaret hated the fact that she had been thwarted from taking tougher action and was determined to announce an initiative of some kind against the unions. The right wing loved it. I did not dissent from the policy, but disagreed with the way she chose to announce it, upping the 'ante' with the unions when our agreed policy was to try not to inflame tempers in the steel strike any further. The Chancellor duly incorporated the new policy in his 1980 Budget.

Margaret was still itching to take immediate steps to crack down on the unions in the steel strike. Patrick Mayhew and I were summoned to see her at ten o'clock on the Monday night before the publication the next day of our consultation document on secondary strikes.

She wanted to rush through Parliament, in a day or two, an immediate, one-clause Bill to outlaw secondary picketing. I have no doubt her advisers were urging her to take a tougher line, and she wished to respond to them. A provision to outlaw secondary picketing was included in the Bill being considered in the Commons, but would not be on the statute book till the summer at the earliest.

I was totally opposed to her suggestion. Rushed legislation almost always turns out to be bad legislation. Plucking one item out of the Bill would look like a panic response, admitting that we should have acted faster from the outset. It would raise the temperature even higher in the steel strike, cause great anger amongst moderate trade unionists and ruin our attempts to continue talks with the unions.

I argued that it would be much wiser to write to Len Murray, reminding him of the TUC's own guidelines issued the winter before, which were being flouted, and also for the Attorney-General, Michael Havers, to make a statement reiterating the *existing* law which dealt adequately with questions of intimidation and obstruction. In the end Margaret accepted that this would be the more sensible approach.

The presentation of my new proposal to restrict secondary industrial action was no easy matter. Restricting unions' secondary action without banning it altogether was a complex task, fraught with all manner of pitfalls – the precise circumstances in which secondary action would be made unlawful had to be clearly identified.

To assist my presentation at the Press conference my officials prepared a diagram to illustrate how the new law would affect various hypothetical disputes. As I stood at the easel, complete with baton to identify the situations in which unions would still be allowed to take action, I looked like some military strategist, or perhaps more like an old-style school-teacher – an image seized on by *Private Eye* in their cartoon series 'Fifth Form at St Maggie's'.

The next day, the TUC agreed to meet me and discuss the proposal. Despite the heightened tension of the steel strike, I had managed to stick to my 'step-by-step' approach and keep talking with the unions.

We completed the consultations on the plans to curb secondary indus-trial action in time to publish the new clause the week before Easter, a couple of days after the rest of the Employment Bill had emerged from its laborious nine-week Committee stage.

*

The right wing's last effort to unseat me over the Employment Bill came in early July 1980, at the Report stage of the Bill in the House of Lords. They concentrated their attack on the new clause included to deal with secondary industrial action, and fortunately received short shrift from the Lord Chancellor.

The week before the Lords debate, George Gardiner and forty other Tory MPs had written to Edward du Cann, chairman of the Tory back bench 1922 Committee, to suggest the clause dealing with secondary indus-trial action should be strengthened. I spoke with Edward to say that I would like to attend as I knew I could see off the rebels very effectively. But Edward and his senior colleagues felt that they should not allow themselves to be bounced by the right, and so I was not invited.

I therefore prepared an open letter to George Gardiner, which strongly rebutted his attacks on my policy, and timed its release for maximum effect in the following Sunday's papers. And on the Monday I circulated to all Tory backbenchers and peers a detailed answer to my opponents' criticisms.

Shortly before the crucial Lords' debate Margaret held a late night meeting at the House at which Lord Spens and Lord Orr-Ewing spoke for the rebels and I was supported by Patrick Mayhew and my deputy, Grey Gowrie, who led for the Government in the Lords. Margaret made no effort to crack the whip at the rebel peers, who can only have left with the feeling that she would not be too troubled by a sizeable rebellion. Patrick, Grey and I stayed on with Margaret, and we were in no doubt where her true sympathies lay.

But you can never predict how their lordships will behave. The Party whips have notoriously little control over the final outcome of debates, not least because they can never be sure exactly who, or how many peers, will turn up to vote. The rebels were rumoured to be persuading the backwoods-men, who rarely attend from one year to the next, to come in force.

I took up my right as Privy Councillor to sit on the steps of the Throne to watch their lordships debate my proposals and settle my fate. It was an extraordinary afternoon, with the benches packed and many familiar faces and voices from a bygone age, as well as a sea of faces whom I had never seen before.

Peter Thorneycroft argued for the Bill to be given a chance, and I was heartened to win the support of the Bishops. But it was Quintin Hailsham, rising from the Woolsack, who stole the show. He made clear his own convictions: 'If I had thought the Conservative Party in its manifesto had taken the line that it was going to stop all secondary action, I should certainly not have supported the manifesto myself, and I certainly should not have accepted office in the present Government.'

In an impassioned conclusion, he appealed to the rebels: 'Let's not hit out blindly or be misled by over-simplified arguments. Let us go forward clear-sightedly and calmly. Not only justly, but by being seen to be just.' I have much for which to thank Quintin Hailsham.

Almost three hundred peers made their characteristically dignified and unhurried way through the respective division lobbies. At last the vote was declared: 249 peers supported the Government, and only 41 voted for the rebels' amendment – the last serious revolt had been defeated.

*

In their campaign to toughen up my Bill, the Tory right had received strong support in the press. Yet Fleet Street's own industrial relations were a disgrace, the result principally of years of bad management which the print unions had exploited mercilessly.

Dick Marsh, the former Labour Cabinet Minister and ex-chief of British Rail, led a delegation from the Newspaper Publishers' Association to see me at the Department of Employment. Dick launched the meeting with an intemperate demand for much tougher laws against the unions; his principal demand was that the employers should be able to sack people whose wages they had to pay even when they were not working as a result of a strike elsewhere in the company.

I told Dick and his colleagues in no uncertain terms that it was about time they put their own house in order before coming to Government and asking for the law to be changed to suit them. When I said that there was nothing to prevent them renegotiating their own contracts, I was told that this would be quite impossible for them. I understood why – management had been virtually non-existent in Fleet Street for so many years that there was practically no control left.

In Opposition I had visited the *Guardian* newspaper to watch a paper being formed and finally printed. A young, enthusiastic manager conducted me round the plant and explained the new technology being introduced. I asked how this was helping with productivity. 'Not much yet,' he replied, 'but we have just had our first major breakthrough, we've reached agreement to retire people at sixty-five.'

I didn't react much to this as it seemed a rather small change. So, noting my mood, he went on to say that in Fleet Street the unions had complete control over who was employed and who retired, that the *Daily Mirror* had someone of eighty-one on their books and had taken him on at age seventy-six.

On this visit I was also introduced to the practice of the 'blow'. In the bad old days in the printing press room there were a lot of fumes and ink flying about, and the men were allowed up on to the pavement for a ten minute 'blow'. Despite the great improvements in working conditions, however, the ten minute blow eventually became half an hour, then half a night shift, and finally half a week.

A number of years later I again met the same manager at the *Guardian*. He remembered our conversation and rather sadly reported that the retirement rule of sixty-five had in fact never been implemented, and they now had someone of seventy-six on their books. He was a pensioner from the *Daily Mirror* who came to work on a pensioner's concessionary travel ticket and was very well paid.

At least the *Guardian* appeared to know who they paid and employed. It subsequently came to light that the *Daily Telegraph* had 300 more paid men on their books than they realised. None of this has ever stopped for one minute the proprietors, editors and leader writers from giving advice and dishing out criticism to everyone else on how to run their business and how to tackle the unions. But at times even they went too far.

*

In February 1981 the country faced a miners' strike after the National Coal Board responded to the impact of the deep economic recession and the need to cut back production by announcing an accelerated rate of closure of older pits with poor productivity.

I was involved in the Ministerial discussions with Margaret on how we should handle the threat. The NCB had misjudged the situation and the miners were quite ready to strike and give the NUM's moderate President, Joe Gormley, full backing.

The NCB were therefore obliged to withdraw the programme and the Government agreed to adjust the industry's cash limit to accommodate this decision and to meet the cost if the NCB was able to obtain reductions in imports of coal by the electricity and gas industries.

I could not see how else we could play it, but although the decisions were not mine, the blame was soon pinned on me.

On Thursday, February 20, the day after the strike threat was called off, the *Daily Express* ran a front page 'exclusive' story by its Political Editor, Jack Warden, under the headline 'Prior the Plotter: Jim was to blame for surrender'. I was accused of holding 'backstairs meetings' with Joe Gormley over the pits crisis. I was alleged to have met Joe twice in the previous ten days.

There was no truth in the story. I had not seen Joe during the period in question. Jack's report was apparently based on information from sources within the Government, but he had not spoken to me about the allegations or asked for my version of events.

I was in Harrogate that night, and as soon as I heard about the story I issued a statement making clear that the report was not true. It was a disgrace. I demanded an apology from the *Express*, but their response, the following day, did not satisfy me.

In the end, I had to threaten a libel action and settled for a sizeable contribution by the *Express* to a charity which Jane nominated.

*

With my legislation on the Statute Book, I turned my attention to drafting my Green Paper on Union Immunities. I had put forward the idea of publishing a Green Paper to Margaret and the hard-liners in Cabinet at the height of the national steel strike the previous February. My offer had helped persuade them to support my more measured approach to union reform.

I did not feel that I was giving too much away since once the first Employment Bill was passed there would clearly have to be a debate about possible further reforms, and a Green Paper would enable me to present my own philosophy and develop my own thoughts on the various options.

It seemed to me that if Labour's legislation had been unbalanced in one direction, favouring the unions, we had to be wary of not tilting the balance too far back in the other.

I made it clear that the issues which needed to be addressed ranged wider than the narrow question of the unions' position in the law. We also had to consider the 'duties which trade unions and employers owe to the community as a whole', and I posed the following two questions about their role: 'Are they merely pressure groups with obligations to their own members and no duty to take a wider view? Or have they already, by virtue of a very long if informal relationship with the state and their importance in the running of a complex modern economy, become bodies of a different type whose influence and concomitant duties have, however, not yet been properly defined?'

For my own part I am convinced that unions and employers do have a duty to take a wider view. Employers, unions and Government already met to discuss 'questions of the day' in 'Neddy', the National Economic Development Council, and, as I suggested in the Green Paper, 'This practice could be expanded with advantage.'

But there was little immediate prospect of my developing this thinking into practical effect. That would depend on my staying at one of the Economic Departments throughout Margaret's Government.

As the consultations on the proposals in my Green Paper proceeded through the first half of 1981 so the pressures for further legislstive measures mounted. For instance I was urged to take further steps against the closed shop, principally as a result of left wing local councils in the West Midlands dismissing employees for refusing to join the union. In February 1981 Sandwell Council had dismissed Joanna Harris, a poultry inspector, when she refused to join NALGO, which had a closed shop agreement. She refused to claim the compensation to which she was entitled under the 1980 Act, arguing that all she wanted was her job back. In nearby Walsall, where six dinner ladies were dismissed, four of them took their case to an industrial tribunal and were awarded a total of £10,598 under the terms of the 1980 Act.

Later in the summer, in August, the European Court of Human Rights ratified an earlier judgment by the European Commission that the three British Rail employees who had appealed against their dismissal for refusing to join a union had been unfairly dismissed and were awarded substantial compensation. The sizeable compensation awarded certainly increased the pressure for higher payments to closed shop victims.

I was prepared to introduce new measures on the closed shop, including increased compensation and provision for regular reviews, by secret ballot of all those affected, of closed shop agreements. I would also have made it unlawful to refuse to include firms in tenders, or to offer or award contracts to them, on the grounds that they do not employ union members or recognise, negotiate or consult with unions or their officials, as 'union labour only contracts' were a particular problem identified in the consultations.

I would not, however, have curbed union immunities any further than they had already been restricted in the 1980 Act. I wanted to see the main provisions in our first Act given time to be accepted, and not to try to rush ahead too fast.

In my discussions with Margaret during the summer of 1981 I made my position clear.

*

I was not expecting to stay on as Secretary of State for Employment. I had been the Party's front bench spokesman on Employment and Industrial Relations, in Opposition or in Government, for seven years and I knew that, if I did stay there would be some enormous fights with Margaret.

On the other hand I would have been happy to go to the Department of Industry. It seemed obvious to me that Keith Joseph would have to be moved from Industry, and I would have been very interested to take over the work; I was also concerned to maintain a major influence on economic policy and to ensure we pursued a more positive industrial policy.

There was, however, a lot of speculation that I would be moved to Northern Ireland. People were saying that Margaret wanted this, not so much to do good in Northern Ireland as to get rid of me from the centre of Government.

Perhaps a politician should study how to play reshuffles so as to win the posts in Cabinet he wants: but I never could. This was the only time I tried to plan my responses, I was playing for high stakes, and I got it wrong.

It wasn't so much that I was set against going to Northern Ireland; it was more a matter of wanting to stay at the centre of economic affairs. I felt I had to take a gamble and make my views well known if I was to stand a chance.

But I was mistaken in my attempt to lay down what I would do under certain circumstances, going so far as to say at one stage that I would resign rather than go to Northern Ireland, and allowing one of my closest allies and friends in the Commons, Richard Needham, to say as much to Adam Raphael of the *Observer*, who duly gave it front page headline treatment the day before the reshuffle was due.

The colleagues I talked to told me to stand firm: I was in a strong position: if I dug my heels in she would not be able to move me. But when it came to the crunch those who had advised me to dig in were the first to say: 'Well, you'll have to take it, won't you? There isn't much we can do.' The truth is that any individual Minister, unless he is very strongly backed by his colleagues, is in a weak position to challenge an established Prime Minister's appointments.

When I went to see Margaret on the Monday morning she started by telling me that she had always wanted me to go to Northern Ireland and that she had planned it some months ago. To this I replied, rather cautiously, that I felt it was a great pity that as the person involved she hadn't actually told me what she was planning. Didn't she realise how much more difficult she had now made it for me to take the job?

'Oh, but Jim, I want you to do it,' she said. 'I think you're just the person who will bring a fresh mind to this very difficult problem and you can rely on having my full support in all that you seek to do. We really have got to come to grips with this problem.'

Then I went to speak to Willie Whitelaw and Michael Jopling, the Chief Whip. They had advised Margaret on her reshuffle, and they gave me the old guff, as you would expect: how important it was that I should do it, how she really wanted me to do it, what a blow it would be to the Party if I didn't.

I said to Willie, 'But surely it's become almost impossible for me to take it on, because I've said quite openly that I don't wish to go to Northern Ireland.' He blithely replied 'Oh, they don't mind that sort of controversy over there. In fact, they rather like that sort of thing. That will make no difference. And you can take it from us that you will have our full support.'

I knew that I was going to have to accept the appointment once it had been offered to me. Apart from everything else, if you turn it down, you are liable to be branded – and I certainly would have been – as a coward. I should have worked out my position much more fully in advance. It would have been wiser simply to say that I intended to stay at the centre of the economic argument but not get involved in views on going to Northern Ireland.

I discussed all the arguments with my family and we decided that I should accept it. From that moment onwards, Jane and I determined that we would give of our best in every way we could during our time in Northern Ireland.

It was, however, a bad start to my time there and a bad ending to my influence on economic policy. In accepting Northern Ireland I made it a condition that I remained a member of 'E' Committee, the Economic Strategy Committee. This wish was willingly and smoothly granted. But I was partially responsible for the downgrading of the Cabinet committee system as henceforward the committee was denied all consideration of nationalised industries and pay.

The way I played the reshuffle and subsequent events considerably weakened my authority, and also the cause of the moderates on the Conservative back benches. I was out-manoeuvred by the Prime Minister: that is probably why she was Prime Minister and I was certainly never likely to be.

PART THREE

IRELAND

CHAPTER TEN

INITIATIVE

Within moments of my appointment as Secretary of State for Northern Ireland, Jane and I were surrounded by the whole panoply of security – the Special Branch detectives, the bullet-proof cars and a constant watch on our homes.

We flew over the Irish Sea to Northern Ireland the following day. As we approached Belfast above the lough, with a patchwork of small green fields on either side and the docks of Harland and Wolff ahead, we both felt a sense of trepidation, yet excitement. What lay ahead? Was there progress to be made?

I arrived with a determination to succeed where others had failed. I suspect that a number of Englishmen had arrived before me with just such determination and probably with just as little understanding of the problems that run so deep through the history of Northern Ireland.

Our RAF flight landed at Aldergrove, Northern Ireland's main airport, but we disembarked well away from the terminal for civilian passengers. We were whisked off in special cars with our detectives, straight to Stormont.

As we drove through the main gates of the Stormont estate and down the mile-long avenue to the old Northern Ireland Parliament buildings, with Carson's statue in front of them, the imposing complex of grandiose buildings struck me as a folie de grandeur.

We immediately went to my office in Stormont Castle, a few hundred yards from the Parliament building, and met my private office staff. My Principal Private Secretary usually accompanied me to and fro between Stormont and Whitehall, but I had two private offices, staffed by officials and secretaries who were permanently based either in London or in the Province.

I met Ewart Bell, head of the Northern Ireland Civil Service. His staff, who formerly worked for the Northern Ireland Prime Minister and Cabinet before direct rule from Westminster was introduced in 1972, administer the Province-based Departments, including Agriculture and Commerce.

Then we were taken to Hillsborough Castle, which was to be our home in Northern Ireland for the next three years. Hillsborough is the prettiest village in Northern Ireland. The Castle had originally been the home of the Downshire family and more recently the residence of all Governors of the Province. It is more a stately home than a castle: elegant and with a hundred acres of garden and lake. There are wide sweeping lawns, some fine trees and many beautiful azaleas and rhododendrons, including the largest rhododendron in Europe. Each visiting member of the Royal family and each Governor has planted a tree and the grounds are rightly admired by all who visit the Castle.

Our flat was on the first floor in the rooms originally used as the private suite of the Governors. We were well looked after, indeed very spoiled. Junior Ministers were not quite so fortunate as they had to live in bed-sitting-rooms at Stormont House, close to their offices in Belfast, although when they were in the Province for weekend duty they used to stay at Hillsborough.

That first evening, we gave a dinner party for the senior civil servants and their wives. So we could all get to know one another in a much less formal setting than our briefing sessions at the office. With the special challenges and pressures which Northern Ireland imposes on politicians and officials, I was keen to work closely as a team and create as strong a sense of mutual trust and support as possible.

*

My first official visit, on the next day, was to the Maze Prison. The hunger strike by Republican prisoners in the H-blocks at the Maze had already lasted for more than six months. In their campaign to win political status, ten had starved themselves to death and a further seven were refusing food. But in the previous few weeks the relatives of several strikers had persuaded them to start taking food.

I was taken to the prison hospital where a young man, Liam McCloskie, was in his 46th day of hunger strike. We looked at him through the little window in the hospital door. He was sitting up in bed with a dressing gown around him, completely oblivious to us and, as far as I could see, oblivious to the rest of the world, just sitting there, staring into space. There was no great sense of agony, of emaciation, nor any sign of pain.

I was struck by how much this man looked at peace with himself. I began to realise at that moment that Northern Ireland, and perhaps the history of Ireland, has been made up of a number of people on both sides of the religious and political divide of utter determination and conviction, prepared to commit acts of violence and in a stubborn, yet courageous, way to accept the inevitable and to die. This was my first inkling as to what the problem of Northern Ireland was all about.

A day or two later McCloskie's mother asked to see me. At that stage of the hunger strike I judged that it was not possible for me to meet her, but she would be perfectly at liberty to see my deputy, Grey Gowrie, who had moved with me from Employment to Northern Ireland. He was deeply sympathetic to the Irish situation, a Southern Protestant with a real feel for the history of the country. Mrs McCloskie and a friend came to see him. She made it plain that, once Liam went into a coma, she would ask for him to be fed: she did not wish her boy to die. And she summed up her feelings very clearly in these simple words:

'My boy's been a bad boy. He never should have got mixed up with those people, and never should have had that gun. But for all that, he's not a criminal. If he was a criminal I would never let him cross the threshold of my house again. But, Lord Gowrie, he's not a criminal.'

You have to hear those words and seek to understand them; and you have to do so in the context of what Liam McCloskie was actually in prison for – he was sentenced in 1977 to ten years for offences including robbery and possessing fire-arms – to appreciate what drives people to these dreadful crimes and makes Northern Ireland such an unhappy land.

*

My first impression was of an embittered and totally polarised society. Until my first few days in Northern Ireland, I had never realised how deep was the bitterness and division which could exist between Catholic nationalists and Protestant unionists. It was indeed a legacy of hundreds of years of the same old enmities and distrust.

In simple terms 60 per cent of the population were Protestant, and 40 per cent Catholic.

The Protestants were almost all unionists. The Protestant unionists are a hardworking, stubborn people, of great quality, who believe that Northern Ireland is *their* country. They have very strong religious and historic perceptions and wish above all to remain part of the United Kingdom. They hate the idea of a United Ireland, which they believe would subjugate them to what they see as policies that are alien to their way of life and, in particular, to the dominance of the Catholic Church. They cite the fact that, when the Republic was formed, 10 per cent of its people were Protestants and now there are only 4 per cent. They resent the domination of the Church over the State, which has made Ireland a confessional state, particularly as Ireland has probably the most conservative Catholic Church in the Western world.

The Nationalists believe that Ireland is *theirs*, that they have a right to it, and that the Protestant unionists are no more than Scottish settlers who came into the ascendancy from the time of William of Orange and really do not belong to Ireland at all. Of Northern Ireland's dozen parliamentary seats at Westminster, until the number was increased in 1983, at least ten were held continuously by Unionist MPs. Besides being under-represented at Westminster, Catholic nationalists were condemned to permanent opposition in the old Stormont parliament and excluded from office in Northern Ireland governments for fifty years following the creation of Northern Ireland in 1920. Catholics suffered from the gerrymandering of local council boundaries, so that in Londonderry, for example, the nationalists were denied any chance of winning a majority of seats despite the fact that Catholics were in the majority in the city itself. They were seriously under-represented in the police force, having no representation at all in the 'B Specials' which had been established in 1920 to combat the IRA.

In Britain, before the civil rights disturbances began in Northern Ireland in the 1960s, we deluded ourselves that the partition of Ireland and the creation of a devolved government in Northern Ireland had effectively solved the Irish problem. When I first became an MP in 1959, Northern Ireland MPs were almost entirely Ulster Unionists who were not expected to do much more than support the Conservative Party. The responsibility for Northern Ireland itself lay entirely at Stormont with the Northern Ireland Parliament and the Northern Ireland Government.

But this was living in a false world. Looked at realistically, it should have been clear that the one-party rule and sectarian discrimination which had persisted in Northern Ireland simply could not last.

In April 1969, the passion of Northern Ireland politics was brought to the Commons in Bernadette Devlin's maiden speech following her victory over a Unionist in the Mid-Ulster by-election. The civil rights campaign was in full flood and the clashes between the rival sides were becoming bloodier.

Bernadette took her seat on her twenty-second birthday and flouted convention from the outset. The benches were packed and the atmosphere electric as the House began to debate Northern Ireland. Within an hour of her introduction as a new MP she was on her feet, delivering a speech packed with prejudice, hatred and magnificent passion. It was a virtuoso performance.

As she sat down to some cheers, but mostly stunned admiration, I leaned over from the bench directly behind Ted Heath and said what a good speech it was. 'Yes, but it's the only speech she's got in her, she can't make another one,' was Ted's reply. He was right. Bernadette was to make the same speech on many occasions, but it never rivalled that first dramatic entrance.

By now 'The Troubles' had brought out and exacerbated the divisions between the two communities – the Protestant unionist majority, whose wish is to remain inalienably a part of the United Kingdom and the Catholic nationalist minority, whose aspiration is the unification of Ireland.

The divide between the two communities was appalling, deep enough to enable the terrorists – chiefly on the nationalist side, but also on the unionist side – to flourish and maintain campaigns of murder and destruction. Both sides took out their fury on Britain, who after all was largely responsible for the creation of the divide in the community.

During the summer of 1981 these divisions and distinctions had been further accentuated and seemed virtually irreconcilable. As the hunger strike dragged on, violence had intensified on the streets, with disturbances, marches, demonstrations and riots. The police and army were firing prodigious numbers of plastic bullets. A number of innocent people, including children, were killed or maimed, their deaths adding to all the bitterness caused by the deaths of the hunger strikers. More deaths caused more marches: we were in a vicious circle.

There had also been two by-elections in Fermanagh and South Tyrone, following the death of the Independent Socialist, Frank Maguire. At the first, in April, the Republican candidate Bobby Sands, one of the hunger strikers, had been elected to Parliament, winning over 30,000 votes. Sands died less than a month later. In the second by-election, in August, his seat was won by Owen Carron, who had been his agent. The moderate Nationalist party, the SDLP, had not fielded a candidate in either election. The victories for the hunger strikers showed how divided the community had become.

Those months undoubtedly provided a boost for the Provisional IRA. There were people in Fermanagh and South Tyrone who had lived side by side with other Catholics and Protestants all their lives and who to all intents and purposes were good citizens and neighbours, but who went into the polling booths to vote first for Bobby Sands and then for Owen Carron and all that both of them stood for – violence, murder, intimidation, and, quite simply, anarchy. There were other people who voted for the Unionist candidates, Harry West and, on the second occasion, Ken Maginnis, both honourable men, who were firm democrats. But the majority chose Bobby Sands, then Owen Carron, by considerable majorities.

*

As Secretary of State for Northern Ireland I found myself performing a dual role, as a Governor-General representing the Queen and as such the enemy of every Republican in the Province, but also as a Secretary of State acting like a referee in a boxing ring whose authority seemed to be resented equally by both sides.

I was combining two tasks kept separate until the introduction of direct rule by Westminster in 1972. At one minute I was discharging duties previously performed by the Governor-General on behalf of the Queen; the next I was, in effect, the Prime Minister of the Province. I was living at Hillsborough Castle, in the countryside of Down, the former residence of the Governors-General of Northern Ireland, which is why nationalists do not like going there for ceremonial events such as the summer garden parties. I was working at Stormont on the outskirts of Belfast, the traditional base of Government in Northern Ireland and a symbol of the Union for all unionists.

My political role was unique in itself. I was the head of Government, yet my own political base was not in the Province but across the Irish Sea in Britain. On many occasions I felt as though I was a foreigner in another land. In the space of my first few weeks I was picketed by Republicans at Derry, who shouted the same slogan – 'Brits Out' – as the Loyalists shouted at Newtonards a few weeks later. My specially protected official car was attacked and badly dented at Londonderry by some of Ian Paisley's supporters, the very people who pay homage to the Queen, and whose symbol is the Union Jack.

What also made my job different from that of any other Secretary of State, apart from the Foreign Secretary, was the importance of establishing close relations with another Government, the Republic of Ireland. This was essential, because of the strength of the Irish tradition in the North, where around 40 per cent of the population identify with Dublin and because any Dublin Government is bound to be concerned with their interests.

Our two countries have so many things in common. We are part of the British Isles; we share the same language; for many years we were one kingdom; we may have a different mixture of blood in our veins but for so much of our history we have shared one culture and been one people. It seemed absolutely crazy that we should not find means of coming closer to each other when we faced a common threat from terrorism.

I went to Dublin in early November for my first meeting with Dr Garret Fitzgerald, the Republic's Prime Minister, or Taoiseach. We spent a friendly and happy evening at the guest house outside Dublin given to the Irish Government by Elizabeth Arden. Garret was an easy man to get on with, more of a don than a politician, who had once been Dublin correspondent for the *Financial Times*. He tells the story that after he had entered politics and become a Minister, the *FT* phoned him up and asked for a piece on Irish politics, clearly under the impression that he was still their 'stringer' and oblivious to his membership of the Government.

When I returned to Northern Ireland after my visit to Dublin, I was heavily criticised by Unionist politicians. What possible good could come from my talk with the Taoiseach?

After the first few weeks I also had a long talk with Enoch Powell, who has sat in the Commons as a Unionist MP since October 1974. He said that I should never use the word 'reconciliation', because in Northern Ireland it means reconciliation between the two parts of the island as well as between the Irish and Unionist traditions on the island, and it is therefore totally unacceptable to the Unionists. If this had been sound advice, it would have been a chilling commentary on Unionist thinking. In fact, Enoch's advice was wrong because I was to hear many people on both sides talk about the need for reconciliation, none more so than moderate Protestant churchmen who have in many cases, in very difficult circumstances and under great provocation from some of their congregations achieved moderation.

*

I met the main political leaders in the Province within my first few days. My talks with them and their Parties on the scope for progress lasted through the autumn and into the new year.

Ian Paisley is by far the strongest and most powerful leader in either community. He founded the Democratic Unionist Party, and remained its Leader, espousing a harder line Unionism than the old-style Official Unionists and winning more support from working-class Protestants.

He is basically a man who thrives on the violent scene – when he is preaching from the pulpit of his own Free Presbyterian Church, it tends to be the sort of sermon with the text: 'the wages of sin is death'. And, when he talks politics, his aim is to stir the emotions of the Protestant people, crystallising every issue into the need to defeat the Provisional IRA and to stand rock-solid against any question of a United Ireland.

Willie Whitelaw's experience of Paisley had already served as a warning of what to expect. Paisley came in to see him one day to complain, as usual, about the security situation and to call, as the Unionists frequently do, for firmer measures – firmer measures never being carefully or accurately specified, but it is something that the Government ought to do which it isn't doing or prepared to do. In the course of the discussion, Paisley said: 'And, by the way, I understand that you are going to pull down Carson's statue.' Carson's statue is a shrine for the Unionists.

Willie said that he had absolutely no knowledge at all about pulling down Carson's statue, he'd heard nothing about it, and there was no intention of doing so. When Paisley went out to speak to the press, they asked him how he had got on with the Secretary of State. He replied bluntly that he'd had a pretty unsatisfactory meeting with the Secretary of State, who had refused to do anything to help the security situation. He had, however, been able to get one assurance from him – that he was not going to pull down Carson's statue.

In February 1974 Paisley exploited the election called by Ted Heath on the issue of the miners, to scupper the power-sharing initiative launched at Sunningdale by the British and Irish Governments in the previous year. Sunningdale had established an Anglo-Irish Council and a power-sharing Executive in Northern Ireland, comprising moderate Unionists and Nationalists.

Paisley beat the anti-Sunningdale drum at the hustings, playing on Unionist fears of a sell-out by London, and ten of the eleven Unionist MPs returned to Westminster were opposed to Sunningdale, although their share of the total vote was only a little over 50 per cent. Their stance was a severe blow to the standing of the new power-sharing Executive in Northern Ireland.

Paisley and his followers undermined it further that spring through an Ulster workers' strike. In London, the minority Labour administration felt it already had too much on its plate to face this particular problem in Northern Ireland. Rather than stand firm, Merlyn Rees, the then Secretary of State, allowed the Executive to fall.

Paisley is a strong leader, with an engaging personality but his bigotry easily boils over into bombast. He is a hard worker and has a certain charisma, nevertheless I found him hard to trust, and could never be certain what he was going to say or do next. A man of considerable character, there was no escaping doing business with him: I therefore came to the conclusion that I should always listen carefully to what he had to say, despite the many difficulties which he created for me.

Whenever Paisley came to protest about some alleged security lapse or political initiative, he invariably concluded his remarks with the same phrase: 'As a result of your actions today, I shall be following a lot more coffins this year.' There seemed to be a chilling ring to the emphasis he put on 'coffins'.

When Paisley was elected to the European Parliament in 1984 with a large majority, he announced that this was a punch on the nose for Jim Prior and I should resign. The next time I saw him, I said: 'I understand you have given me a punch on the nose thanks to your great victory, on which I congratulate you.' But I added, 'Don't worry, I don't expect to be here for much longer, so you needn't go on calling for my resignation.' To which Paisley replied: 'You mustn't take all that seriously, you've got to stay here for years yet.' He could be wretched to deal with, but I have something of a warm spot for him, though I often wonder why.

Jim Molyneaux, the Leader of the Official Unionist Party, was almost the exact opposite to Paisley: not charismatic, rather quiet, much less of an orator, but quite effective in his own way. I felt the whole time that he was allowing Enoch Powell to make the running. At Westminster he was Enoch's puppet, and it made him a less pleasant man than his nature would normally have dictated.

I never quite knew how to take Molyneaux. He gave me the impression of being devious, but I suspect this may be necessary in dealing with some of the people who form the Official Unionist Party. They were a divided, uninspiring collection and Molyneaux must have had a difficult job trying to keep them in any sort of line.

John Hume, the Leader of the main democratic Nationalist Party, the Social Democratic and Labour Party (SDLP), had the most difficult role of all. The SDLP had suffered a great loss with the expulsion of Paddy Devlin in 1977 and the defection of Gerry Fitt in 1979. Both were warm-hearted, courageous men with traditional labour movement roots and sentiments. They were working to remedy injustice rather than to peddle traditional nationalist views. The SDLP was less of a force without them. John Hume's deputy, Seamus Mallon, was certainly pushing the party in a more nationalist, 'greener' direction.

John is an articulate speaker and made a good impression when he came into the House of Commons at the 1983 General Election. He's most agreeable, a good man to spend an evening with. I doubt, however, whether he has the powers of leadership or the organisational ability to get his Party into a strong enough position from which they can wage a successful fight. It always seemed to me that, whenever I talked with John Hume about what he really wanted, it was rather like punching cottonwool, you could never actually find a hard core to his demands. In what was admittedly a very difficult position, neither the character of the man, his background nor the nature of his party enabled him to be a strong leader.

The Church also have to be reckoned with in the politics of Northern Ireland. The Catholic Primate of All-Ireland, Cardinal O'Fiach, came from Crossmaglen: they say that, if someone comes from Crossmaglen, you should be careful to look at them more than once. Although I found him an agreeable man, I never felt certain about his reliability.

On the other hand, I formed a very high opinion of Bishop Cahill Daley, Bishop of Connor and Down. He always came out strongly against violence, from any quarter, and preached reconciliation between the Churches. He had a very difficult job too, particularly with his re-sponsibilities for West Belfast. He put his views very strongly on behalf of the minority and did his utmost to see that they made progress towards some share in government. I felt that he was a saintly man – rather more so than Edward Daley, the Catholic Bishop of Londonderry, but he too was someone I respected greatly and with whom I got on well. He had an equally difficult task, with a diocese which included both the Creggan and the Bogside.

On the Protestant side, the characters concerned were bound to have a lower profile. There was of course the dear old Archbishop of the Church of Ireland, Archbishop Armstrong, for whom I feel great affection. After the dreadful incident in November 1983 when the Irish National Liberation Army (INLA) attacked the Pentecostal Church on the border at Darkley, he went with the Moderator of the Presbyterian Church, the Leader of the Methodists, and the Cardinal, to say prayers outside the church. He received a number of telephone calls and letters accusing him of the most dreadful things, because he had knelt in prayer, asking for forgiveness, alongside Cardinal O'Fiach. This really upset him. I felt desperately sorry for him, because he was a man of great sincerity, but lacking effective influence since the Protestants are so bound up with the unionist tradition.

I have a great respect for many other Protestant and Presbyterian leaders, who did everything they could to bring the sides together and to preach peace. But their voice of moderation tended to get drowned in the press and on the media by the fiery talk from Paisley's sermons at his own Free Presbyterian church and by his fellow demagogues, the Revs. Macrea and Beattie. It was Beattie who once said in my presence that, rather than tolerate a united Ireland, he would see the Catholic West Belfast razed to the ground.

It is very hard in Northern Ireland for either side to separate religion from politics. I have a great admiration for the many ministers and parish priests who did their best to hold their flock together and not to allow very unchristian acts and thoughts to take hold when members of their own congregation were attacked or murdered.

One of the most outstanding was Canon Barry, the Church of Ireland minister at the village church in Hillsborough. This is a delightful church, in a lovely setting, and had been Canon Barry's home for thirty-five years. The church was always full, the singing good, the atmosphere friendly and warm, never more so than when a christening service was held in the middle of Sunday Matins. The baby used to be taken in Canon Barry's arms and he walked up and down the aisle showing the child to the whole congregation. They were moments of great beauty and affection, and I suppose did much to give me faith in the people of Northern Ireland, and make me come to love them in a way which might seem to outsiders to be difficult to understand.

In a country where religion was obviously so significant and whose people were undergoing such a traumatic time, it seemed appropriate to spend Christmas with them. All our children flew over to join us. I think this helped people to realise that we actually wanted to be there, and that

we wanted to share this special time with them. The hospitality and
generosity of the Irish people are well known, and we received countless
invitations to celebrate Christmas with them. Our four children were
made so welcome and felt so much at home that they spent the whole of
Boxing Day in the Marquess of Downshire pub in Hillsborough village –
licensing hours seemed to evaporate that day. Also at our first Christmas
in Northern Ireland it was characteristically thoughtful that Margaret
Thatcher should phone us on Christmas Day.

*

The goodwill shown to us at Christmas did much to reduce my sense of
being a foreigner and to assuage my distress at one of the most upsetting
experiences during the whole of my time in Northern Ireland. In
November the Provisional IRA murdered the Official Unionist MP, the
Rev. Robert Bradford, along with a community centre caretaker, at his
Saturday morning constituency surgery. This appalling atrocity outraged
the whole Protestant community and others too.

I felt very strongly that I had to attend Bradford's funeral, held at the
Dundonald Presbyterian Church, to express my sympathy for the family,
my commitment to the people of Northern Ireland and my willingness to
share in their anguish. I was advised not to, as the police could not
guarantee my personal safety. But Robert Bradford's family had reserved
a seat for me near the front of the church and I felt it would have
offended them if I had not gone.

As my car approached the church a mob of several hundred angry
unionists surged forward and started banging on the roof. I had to sit
inside with the mob surging round me while the police struggled to clear
a way to the church. I then had to make a run for the church door, with
my detectives shielding me. I just about managed to get through in one
piece.

I was met in the porch by Paisley, who shouted at me, 'You've no
right to be here.' He gave every impression of having stirred things up as
much as he could, although he told me afterwards that he had been
outside to quieten down the crowd. If so, it must have been the only
mild-mannered speech he ever made.

As I walked into the church itself I was greeted by hissing from the
congregation. It was therefore impossible for me to sit near the family in
the place they had reserved for me. I was about five or six pews back.
Immediately, someone nearby told me to have a good look at the coffin,
because it had the Red Cross of Ulster on it, not the Union Jack.

The service eventually began, and we were then subjected to a sermon
from the minister officiating at the service. He was a real fire-brand. In

the middle of his sermon he called for the re-introduction of capital punishment. This was applauded by the congregation. He then went on to say that he was not intending to stir things up. But his words added petrol to the flames.

After the service was over, it was clear that it would be some time before I could leave safely. I spent quite a while in the vestry. But the crowd were still waiting for me, and when I eventually left I was jostled and kicked. There were people at the back carrying umbrellas with sharpened points who started throwing them at me. Many of the so-called unionists were shouting, 'Kill him! Kill him!'

Robert Bradford was a highly respected Member of Parliament. I know that following the terrible tragedy, the desecration of his funeral by this behaviour was a great shock to his relatives. I felt so very sorry for them. Its frequent repetition on the television screens is a constant reminder of that agonising occasion. How I wish they could have been spared both the horror of the event and the reminder of its sequel.

Following Robert Bradford's assassination, Paisley organised a Day of Action and a Day of Marches with the avowed aim of making Northern Ireland ungovernable. On the Monday after the funeral, he assembled all his followers in his 'Third Force,' in various parts of the Province. We thought we would have serious trouble. It was an unnerving experience as I was phoned by various people and told that I would not be able to rely on the Royal Ulster Constabulary to keep the peace, that many of them were utterly dissatisfied with both the Government's policy and the Chief Constable, Jack Hermon, and that they were therefore likely to join forces with Paisley's so-called private army.

These allegations against the RUC turned out to be utterly untrue. I have no doubt that there were a number of people in the RUC who were disloyal to the Chief Constable – maybe still are – and who were passing every piece of information to Paisley. But I believe that this was a small minority.

On the Day of Action extra troops were called in, and they proceeded to seal off the large park around the Stormont buildings and take up positions in Stormont Castle and in Stormont House. Jane remained at Hillsborough Castle where possible trouble was expected.

It was a macabre day. Overnight, armoured cars and a large detachment of soldiers had arrived at Hillsborough and were positioned around the grounds. After an uneventful morning but with the feeling of dark clouds approaching, Jane decided to go for a walk in the grounds. The gardens seemed unusually quiet and she told me afterwards she had a strange feeling of unease, if not nervousness, as she walked by the stream and through the shrubberies.

It was not until she returned to the Castle that she realised that all the soldiers on duty had been told to lose themselves in the bushes whilst she was allowed to enjoy a walk. She had been watched every inch of the way. The silence of the day was increased when the policemen on duty insisted that all curtains should be drawn at three o'clock. In different ways we both spent a bizarre day with a great sense of foreboding.

That evening, which happened, of all days, to be the Chief Constable's birthday, I watched how events were developing throughout the Province in the control room at the RUC headquarters at Knock. It was an uncanny feeling to be engaged in what amounted to a military operation over part of the United Kingdom. As we sat there, we could not be sure whether emotions would boil over and the whole Province become indeed ungovernable. It is not an experience I would ever wish to live through again.

*

Within a few weeks of arriving in Northern Ireland I judged that a fresh political initiative was urgently needed to bridge the gap between Catholics and Protestants. Nothing else would reduce the terrorism and improve the quality of life.

The hunger strike had eventually ended in early October, and though a failure in its declared objective, it had served the Provisional IRA well in other respects: it had increased the divisions between the two communities, added to the flow of funds from IRA supporters in the USA, and had strengthened the Provisionals' hard-core support amongst the nationalist population. The Government had to seize the initiative and try to wrest back the advantage. Some political movement, however uncertain, is required in such circumstances.

My first step in trying to build a bridge between the communities had to be to open a political dialogue. I set about talking with the democratic parties, and made it plain from the outset that there was no way in which a British Government would hand back to the people of Northern Ireland responsibility for their own affairs unless and until it could be shown that both communities were involved. In other words, we were not going to give the Unionist majority the right once more, as they had for nearly fifty years under the old Stormont legislation, to govern the Province entirely as they wished, free from any checks or conditions. I think most Unionists recognised this.

The Unionist Parties, both OUP and DUP alike, made it equally clear to me that they were simply not prepared to accept the form of 'power-sharing' which had been introduced in 1973. They did not believe that it was possible to run an effective government in which some members were unsympathetic to remaining part of the UK. And the Nationalists made it equally plain that they required both a form of power-sharing and a much closer relationship with the Republic of Ireland, often referred to as the 'Irish dimension'. Both of these requirements were anathema to the Unionist Party. Predictably, therefore, we had a virtual stalemate.

I thought, however, that if I could entice all the parties round the same table, I might be able to get some views which I could meet and which could show that, despite their differences on constitutional issues, they could nonetheless co-operate on economic matters. So in December 1981 I invited them all to attend a day's discussion of the Province's economy. This was to be a prelude to the meeting which I would soon hold with my Ministers to settle the detailed public spending budgets for the Province on housing, roads, job schemes and so on for the 1982–83 financial year.

I knew that it was going to be a better year for Northern Ireland on public expenditure, and that I would therefore have some extra cash to allocate. I had exploited the formula by which the Province's share of the whole UK's resources is calculated, and by winning some other battles with the Treasury I had been able to extract about an extra £100 million out of the Exchequer.

As things turned out, the Unionists refused to come because of their protests about security following the assassination of Robert Bradford. Enoch Powell had not wanted them to take part anyway, as this would undermine his 'integrationist' stance. We were left with John Hume representing the SDLP, and the small non-sectarian Alliance Party with Oliver Napier and David Cook, so another attempt to make progress had been stymied.

I spent many days during the autumn weighing up the views of the Parties and the various possible options with my Northern Ireland Office advisers and with my Ministerial team. Margaret had given me the promise of a free hand and I had been able to choose my own Ministers. I had insisted that Grey Gowrie, who had been my deputy at Employment, join me, along with Nick Scott whom Margaret had banished to the back benches when she became Leader in 1975. Fred Silvester, who has one of the most astute political brains in the Commons, continued as my Parliamentary Private Secretary. With Adam Butler, John Patten and David Mitchell, who were already serving in Northern Ireland, we were rated as the strongest Ministerial team since direct rule was introduced in 1972.

I was disturbed that direct rule from Westminster was coming to be seen as permanent. It had brought fair, impartial government to Northern Ireland, and was broadly acceptable to the majority of both communities. It was in fact everyone's second choice, although in a sense there was some virtue in this since everyone's first choice was totally unacceptable to someone else.

Direct rule, however, had only been introduced as a temporary expedient by Ted Heath in 1972. By late 1973, power had again been devolved to Northern Ireland, this time to a power-sharing executive led by the moderate Unionist, Brian Faulkner, and including the then Leader of the moderate nationalist SDLP, Gerry Fitt. But this became another casualty of the February 1974 election as I have already explained. Since then direct rule continued uninterrupted as it has done virtually ever since.

Direct rule in practice denies elected representatives in Northern Ireland virtually any say in running their own affairs. The Province is run by British-based politicians and civil servants in the Northern Ireland Office; and by Northern Ireland civil servants in the various Departments, who had previously answered to the Province's own politicians at Stormont but who now effectively answered to no one. Scrutiny of Northern Ireland at Westminster was lamentable: the usual ration, year-in, year-out, was a monthly forty-five-minute question time on the floor of the Commons, a few poorly-attended debates usually held late at night, and the occasional statement to the House following some particularly awful atrocity.

At the local government level, there was even less for councillors to do than in Britain. Most councils are dominated by either Unionists or Nationalists with no prospect of any change in political control. The overriding need to ensure fair administration of local affairs thus precluded them from responsibility for all but the most mundane tasks. Housing, for example, is the responsibility of a Board appointed directly by the Secretary of State, which has representatives from both communities and which oversees the work of a Province-wide Housing Executive.

The longer direct rule lasts, the less relevant and less responsible Northern Ireland's politicians seem destined to become. How can we ever ensure that the ballot box triumphs over the gun if elections remain divorced from choosing which politicians can take the decisions and be held responsible for their actions? How can we make any kind of progress if elections remain little more than opportunities to express the old tribal loyalties? What pressure can there be on Northern Ireland's existing politicians to eschew extremism for a reasoned and responsible debate? And what hope can there be of attracting high calibre people into the politics of the Province if a political career is limited exclusively to endless posturing, with no prospect of the opportunity to exercise the responsibilities of office?

There were other more immediate reasons for a political initiative. It was not simply that I wanted, in the aftermath of the hunger strike, to focus the political debate on how to build long-term bridges between the two communities. There was also a short-term security imperative. Defeating terrorists depends on co-operation from the community but by late 1981 the Nationalist population were in no mood to co-operate: there was a flood of support for more extreme attitudes. I *had* to win back support for moderation.

The Army's General Officer Commanding (GOC) and the Royal Ulster Constabulary (RUC) Chief Constable impressed upon me that their forces could only be effective if popular support for the terrorists could be drained away: the terrorists could swim far more easily and remain undetected if the pool of approbation was full. There was therefore no time to waste in showing the Nationalist community that the Government did in fact understand them and was genuinely seeking to govern in the best interests of all the people, not just for the Unionist majority.

I was also conscious of the severe time constraint which Westminster politics imposes on any initiative. More than two years had already gone by since the 1979 election with no political progress in Northern Ireland to show for it. The next general election would have to be held by spring 1984 at the latest, and I reckoned that Margaret would almost certainly want to go to the country some months earlier, possibly October 1983. That gave me just two years. At that stage, in late 1981, the Government's chances of holding on to office looked slim. I did not want to see a change of Government in London dash the hopes of a Northern Ireland initiative, as had happened in early 1974.

Although all those reasons for launching an early initiative were clear to me, I was not at all sanguine about the chances of anything ambitious. Whilst the polarisation of the community, the violence and the mood of despair made some attempt at political progress an absolute priority, these same pressures had left too deep a mark to expect very much from it. It was clearly impractical to consider, for the foreseeable future, any return to power-sharing on the lines of 1973–74.

*

One of the options which I had ruled out at a very early stage was the policy of 'integration'. This would entail integrating Northern Ireland fully within the United Kingdom, running it as though it were no different from, say, Norfolk or Yorkshire. Any idea of restoring a devolved administration to the Province would be abandoned and more power would be returned to local councils.

This was the approach advocated by Enoch Powell and some other Official Unionists and about twenty to thirty traditionalist right wing

Conservative MPs including most notably Sir John Biggs-Davison, chairman of the Party's Northern Ireland backbench committee, and Ian Gow, Margaret's Parliamentary Private Secretary.

Conservative policy in Opposition had come close to accepting the integrationists' logic. The 1979 manifesto proposed the establishment of a regional council, effectively a new, upper tier of local government. Airey Neave, our frontbench spokesman, had been assassinated when his car was blown up as he left the Commons on the eve of the election, but I was told that he had already developed reservations about the policy. His loss was a devastating blow to Margaret, and her courage in adversity was quickly noticed by her colleagues.

In office, my predecessor, Humphrey Atkins, soon decided that the regional council was a non-runner and had endeavoured to foster political dialogue with the parties. As a former Chief Whip, he was trusted by the right wing in a way which I could never be, but even Humphrey found after a few months in office that the manifesto was untenable.

The integrationists argued that the surest way to end Northern Ireland's troubles would be for the Government to demonstrate, once and for all, its firm commitment to the Province remaining part of the United Kingdom. This done, the Nationalists would have no choice but to accept it, and terrorism would die away. But as things stood, they argued, London's policy of perpetually treating Northern Ireland differently only served to cause anxiety amongst Unionists as to London's real intentions, and to foster the belief amongst Nationalists that they were pushing at an open door and that, in time, Ireland would be re-united.

I thought that the integrationists talked nonsense. Some were romantics, like Biggs-Davison, a Catholic himself, but a strong Unionist. But I fear that Sir John and the other Tory integrationists underestimated the depth of Nationalist sentiment and the strength of the Irish tradition. They were wrong to assume that once integration had been introduced British-style political divisions could simply emerge in place of the old sectarian divisions.

Enoch Powell's integrationist approach was fine at Westminster, but put him at odds with many in his Party in Northern Ireland, where a return to rule by Stormont was still popular. The Official Unionist leader, Jim Molyneaux, a former Party agent, was no match for Enoch. He always sounded very integrationist in the Commons as he spoke from his place on the Opposition benches with Enoch at his side. But once he had got off the London–Belfast air shuttle and was back on Ulster soil, he sounded much more devolutionist.

The conspiracy theory was always well to the fore in Enoch Powell's speeches on Northern Ireland. He suggested that Ministers in the Northern Ireland Office in conjunction with the Foreign Office were determined to bring about a united Ireland. It was all part of a conspiracy between ourselves and the United States, cooked up by the CIA. Their purpose was to permit a degree of chaos in the North with murder and mayhem, and then for the British Government to announce that the only solution was a United Ireland. This would, in turn, free the way for Irish membership of NATO, which would enable the United States to have bases in the South of Ireland and to guard effectively their Eastern approaches.

Enoch accused me of trying to undermine the political parties, particularly the Unionists. He claimed that I used civil servants to spy on their activities and to seek to promote people we liked at the expense of others. He pointed out that as Minister of Health he never used civil servants to promote political activities, so why should I?

It was beyond his comprehension that in Northern Ireland we were not working in the normal political situation as at Westminster. We were in fact seeking ways towards a new constitution. We were not in the normal party political battle. There was no way for the Government to find out what the politicians at grass root level thought – save by asking them.

I rejected integration because it would have made a bad situation worse. It offered as a permanent solution an approach favoured by only a minority of the Unionists – one section of the Official Unionists. It would have made the position of moderate, democratic Nationalists impossible, and played into the hands of the terrorists. It would have scuppered any hope of co-operation with Dublin. And it assumed that institutional change could have a much greater impact on attitudes and behaviour than Tories have traditionally believed.

*

As my talks developed, I was increasingly attracted to the idea of establishing a framework within which the parties could work towards a return of power from Westminster at their own speed. This seemed to offer the best chance of making some gradual progress, which could lead to devolution at any time whenever the Parties themselves could achieve a sufficient degree of agreement.

I suggested that we should start slowly by setting up an elected Assembly in the Province, which could monitor the Northern Ireland Government Departments and which could serve as a forum for debate. This would help restore the familiar role of democratic politicians and at the same time act as a check on the administration. Initially the Assembly would not be granted any devolved power to legislate for the Province.

I felt that an Assembly, with no legislative power to begin with, was the most likely body in which some common agreement might emerge on a number of non-constitutional subjects. The Assembly would have a system of specialist committees, each covering the work of the main Departments of Government in Northern Ireland (Agriculture, Industrial Development, Health and Social Services, Education, Environment, Finance). The chairmanships and deputy chairmanships of the committees would be shared between the parties according to their overall representation in the Assembly. I hoped that sitting together in specialist committees, cross-examining Ministers and officials, the parties would find enough common ground on a number of specific issues for them gradually to get used to the idea that they could work together.

In time, if sufficient agreement emerged between the parties to form a Northern Ireland administration, they could seek a return of legislative powers from Westminster. But it might be that they could agree on policy in perhaps two or three areas – say agriculture, environment and industry – but not on the rest. In that event it would be sensible to devolve powers for the areas of agreement, but to retain powers over the remaining areas at Westminster. Clearly, responsibility for defence and foreign policy, and also for some time security policy, could not be devolved. It would also be laid down that there had to be widespread support throughout the community if any powers to legislate were to be handed back by Westminster.

My proposals thus became known as 'rolling devolution'. It was the same step-by-step approach that I had applied with some success to the changes in industrial relations legislation. I rated the chances of success much less high, but it was worth a try – at least it would improve the checks on the Northern Ireland administration and provide a new democratic focus and forum for debate.

When I put these views to the Parties, the Unionists did not show any great enthusiasm for them. But the DUP decided that this was at least a step towards the return of devolved government in Northern Ireland and were therefore prepared to give the proposals some support. The Official Unionists, however, were very lukewarm. Their leadership tried to argue that there must be either a return to majority government or total integration of Northern Ireland within the United Kingdom. In reality the OUP were divided, with Powell at one extreme doing his best to make them all 'integrationists', and a number of others on the other wing of the OUP saying that Northern Ireland needed its own government.

While the Alliance Party went along with the proposals, the SDLP were bitterly disappointed. They felt that the proposals did not go far enough to guarantee a sharing of power.

A problem with the SDLP was that at one point during my talks I had said that I was considering an approach more akin to the American

Cabinet system, whereby Ministers would not need to be members of the legislature. The Secretary of State might choose his own Ministers: they would be part of the Secretary of State's executive and, as such, answerable to the Assembly, although not necessarily members of it. This might have made possible a more balanced executive, representing Nationalists and Unionists.

I think this, together with the committee system in the Assembly, might have proved acceptable to the SDLP. But it would not have been acceptable to the Unionists. It would mean the Secretary of State again choosing who was to be a member of the Executive. The Unionists felt that any member of the Executive must be a member of the Assembly, and answer to the Assembly for his or her responsibilities.

Unfortunately, when I told the SDLP at my next meeting with them that I had to drop this idea, they appeared to be tremendously upset and virtually accused me of having acted in bad faith. It had been no more than one of a number of suggestions, at a time when we were all trying to think of ways which would meet both the rights of the minority, as well as the obligations and rights of the majority.

By February 1982 I judged that both the main Unionist Parties and the Alliance Party would fight elections to an Assembly. But I had no guarantee that I could persuade the SDLP to fight an election, although I suspected that, at the end of the day, they would. They were very nervous of elections – they had very little organisation and lacked strong candidates. They had done themselves a great deal of damage by not participating in the Fermanagh and South Tyrone by-election, leaving the way open to the hard-line Republican H-block candidates. This action had been strongly condemned by many, including the SDLP's own former Leader, Gerry Fitt.

*

I drafted a White Paper, based on the proposed framework for devolution which I had developed. My draft went first to a small Cabinet Committee, which was not enthusiastic.

The Prime Minister, a natural sympathiser with the Unionists, was very much against the whole idea. At that stage, a little over midway in her first Parliament, there was no prospect that she would put Ireland at the top of the agenda. She felt that the chances of getting a settlement were too remote and had the Unionists, particularly Enoch Powell, breathing down her neck.

During my predecessor's two years, Margaret was determined to run Irish policy from Number Ten. But she knew little about it. There was the occasion when Garret Fitzgerald was trying to get her interested in assisting the SDLP, and kept pointing out that failure to help them

could result in Provisional Sinn Fein becoming the majority Catholic
party. Margaret replied: 'Oh, but they're not a Unionist Party.' She relied
almost entirely upon Ian Gow, who gave her hard-line Unionist advice,
which was utterly disastrous.

She was worried about any form of, or even any suggestion of, devolution, for fear that this would give an opportunity once more to the
advocates of devolution in Scotland and Wales to revive their campaigns.
And, although the suggestions which I had made for greater co-operation
with the Republic of Ireland fell well short of the arrangements which
had been agreed at Sunningdale between the British and Irish
Governments in 1973, they were too much for her. She insisted that the
separate chapter on Anglo-Irish relations in my draft should be scrapped,
and a less positive version incorporated at the end of the chapter on 'The
Two Identities' in Northern Ireland.

However, I had good support from Willie Whitelaw, Francis Pym, and
Humphrey Atkins, the Cabinet's three former Northern Ireland Secretaries, and from Leon Brittan, Quintin Hailsham and of course Peter
Carrington; but no support at that stage from Geoffrey Howe, who was
still at the Treasury, and not much from other colleagues.

By the time of the Cabinet Committee discussion, there was already
intense press speculation about the proposals. We agreed that we would
say nothing. But I found it necessary to say to the press that at least I
had been given a reasonable reception. If I had not said that, I do not
think I would have got any plans off the ground at all: all the reports
would have been so negative that the initiative would have been killed
stone dead. The fact that I said my plan had had a reasonable reception
was then taken by the Press as meaning that I was likely to be able to
make progress. When I came back to Cabinet with a revised White Paper,
I was able to get it through.

The revised White Paper was less supportive of the Irish dimension. I
knew that it was therefore unlikely to be as well received by the Nationalists in the North or by the Irish Government as I had hoped. This was
probably our great mistake. But I could not push either Margaret or
Quintin Hailsham into a better position, and the others felt that I had
got as much as I was going to achieve.

*

My statement to the Commons and publication of the White Paper were
set for Monday, April 2. As events turned out, it could not have been a
more inauspicious time. On the Friday before, the Argentinians invaded
the Falklands. Saturday's special debate in the Commons had ended with
the Government in disarray.

Willie Whitelaw phoned me on the Saturday evening to say that the Northern Ireland White Paper should not be published: the Party was in such a mood that they were simply not interested in it and would not accept it; it would merely prolong the row which was already building from the right wing.

On the Monday morning the resignations of Peter Carrington, Humphrey Atkins and Richard Luce from the Foreign Office were a further setback. But I was determined that we should go ahead. What would be the reaction in Northern Ireland itself if, yet again, the British Government was seen to shelve its new policy for the Province? It was agreed, in the end, that we should proceed.

When I announced publication of the White Paper in the Commons that afternoon, the mood was sombre yet excitable. The Tory right wing and the Official Unionists were tetchy. Critics of my approach, like John Biggs-Davison and Julian Amery, were joined by a number of others who had old axes to grind against me personally over the industrial relations legislation, like George Gardiner, and also by others, like Michael Latham, who just felt that the whole situation in Ireland was hopeless and the best we could do was to try and sit on the problem and do nothing. Although the Chief Whip, Michael Jopling, felt that the statement went reasonably quietly, it was to be the start of a very difficult passage for my proposals in the Commons. As the subsequent legislation was going through at the time of the Falklands War, there was added tension between the right wing and the rest of the Party.

I had to give an undertaking that the Bill giving effect to the White Paper's proposals would not be published until the White Paper itself had been debated. As I knew the Bill was still not ready, this was not a particularly difficult undertaking to give. What was onerous was the fact that the delaying tactics of people like Julian Amery and John Biggs-Davison were designed to stop the Bill being published at all. They came up with all manner of arguments for the delay . . . Why bother to go for legislation during the summer? It's a bad time to introduce legislation, it's towards the end of the Parliamentary session, and everything is stacked against you. Leave it until the next session, and then let's have a properly thought out and discussed Bill.

My problem was that I knew that, if it was left until the next session of Parliament, we would be running up against a general election. Elections for a Northern Ireland Assembly could then only be held perhaps just before a general election and, as we had learned with bitter experience in 1974, a general election could overturn the whole apple cart and ruin any chance of getting the Province settled down.

On this basis I secured the Cabinet's permission to go ahead with the Bill. As a constitutional measure, its committee stage was taken on the floor of the House. We soon ran up against filibusters, which were organised by Enoch Powell and Conservatives like John Biggs-Davison, Nick Budgen and Robert Cranborne: the latter two had only recently been appointed Government Whips, but both resigned in opposition to the Bill, illustrating vividly the difficulties for the Government.

The Bill itself was comparatively short, but we made little progress with it. Before long we faced the inevitable question of whether to introduce the guillotine procedure to limit the amount of time to be spent on the remainder of the Bill. This had to be discussed by the Cabinet. The vast majority of colleagues backed me wholeheartedly. The Prime Minister, however, was opposed. She made her views abundantly clear, saying that she thought it was a rotten Bill, and that in any case she herself would not be voting for it because she was off to the USA. But the guillotine went through and the Bill then completed its passage.

I am glad to say that at least when it came to the third reading Margaret was present to vote for the Bill, and alongside her in the voting lobby was Ian Gow, her PPS. No one should be under any illusions about the part that Gow played in trying to undermine the Bill and all that I was seeking to do. He was seen to be conferring with the right wing of the Party and tipping the wink to the Official Unionists that the Prime Minister was not in favour of it. I regard it as a disgraceful episode and not one which had helped towards the peace in Northern Ireland that he and we were seeking. Ian subsequently resigned from the Government over the Anglo-Irish Agreement of November 1985. His position at that time was wholly honourable, but the damage in the intervening years was immense.

I am certain that the Northern Ireland Assembly would have got off to a far more promising start if the Government had shown itself strong and united during the passage of the Bill. We should have been seen to take on the Official Unionists and rebut some of the ridiculous claims that they were making. And, at the same time, we should have been more generous to the Nationalists. As it was, the Official Unionists felt that they had the Prime Minister's backing for their opposition to the Bill, and the SDLP obviously felt that the Unionists were getting the upper hand.

However, the SDLP's former Leader, that engaging man Gerry Fitt, was amongst my strongest supporters during the passage of the Bill through the Commons. He was the only MP from Northern Ireland who gave me credit for making an effort to find a solution which was acceptable to all the people of the Province and he was a constant source of inspiration.

I do wonder whether the SDLP ever understood fully the implications of the White Paper and the Bill. But they felt isolated and unloved and thought that their views were not being considered. Right up until August, after the Bill had passed through Parliament, they had not reached a decision on whether to fight the Assembly elections. Eventually they decided to stand, but to abstain from taking their seats. They continued their opposition to the Assembly for the rest of my time as Secretary of State, a decision which I regard as another of the many tragedies which have beset that poor and unhappy country.

*

During the late summer and the autumn of 1982, terrorist activity increased. The Unionists blamed me for every murder that took place. They argued that the uncertainty caused by the passage of the Bill and the setting up of the Assembly had led the IRA to believe that they had only to make one last effort and they would achieve their goal, a United Ireland. They stubbornly refused to recognise that the IRA always try to wreck any move towards political peace and stability because it is the last thing which they wish to see.

The Assembly elections on October 20, 1982 did not surprise me as much as they seemed to surprise others, particularly those in mainland Britain who did not take a very close interest in Northern Ireland. Provisional Sinn Fein, in its first Stormont election, won more than 10 per cent of the first-preference votes (the election was conducted under the single transferable vote system). This gave them 5 seats in the Assembly.

In fact the Sinn Fein vote was only 2.5 percentage points higher than the share won by pro-H-block candidates in the 1981 local council elections. It was this level of support, plus those who had previously abstained, whom Provisional Sinn Fein were able to attract. Yet when the results were declared most of the press reported it as a great blow for me personally and a serious setback for the Assembly.

But what the voting figures showed, unmistakably and unequivocally, was that there *was* a considerable degree of support for Sinn Fein, even allowing for large numbers of votes rigged by personations in West Belfast and Londonderry.

The SDLP did lose out to Sinn Fein, winning 14 seats, 5 fewer than in the 1973 Assembly. However, the SDLP made a small recovery in terms of first-preferences compared with the 1981 local elections.

On the Unionist side, the Official Unionists won a 7 per cent lead over Ian Paisley's DUP, thus reversing the DUP's slight lead in the 1981 local results. The composition of the 78-seat Assembly, with the share of each Party's first-preference vote was as follows: OUP 26 seats (30 per cent); DUP 21 seats (23 per cent); SDLP 14 seats (19 per cent); Alliance 10 seats (9 per cent); Provisional Sinn Fein 5 seats (10 per cent); and 2 seats for other Unionists.

The Assembly was set up at the end of November 1982 and I was asked to attend and to make a statement and answer questions on the security problem. It was a very difficult occasion as it was a constitutional novelty for a non-elected person to go in front of an elected body. When I walked in I was anticipating a barrage of vocal hostility. My speech was deliberately slanted to try to be as helpful as I could to the Nationalist community, without inflaming the unionists. It contained the blunt warning that there would be no devolution unless and until there was widespread acceptance *throughout* the community.

To my surprise my speech was received for the most part in silence. It was remarkable how calm the atmosphere was. Afterwards various Assembly Members came up to me, saying: 'Didn't we behave well? Aren't we much better than the House of Commons?' There were indeed signs of hope in what happened that day, but, in the strategy to bring peace to Northern Ireland, the creation of the Assembly was only the first of the battles in my three-year campaign.

CHAPTER ELEVEN

BATTLES TO WIN

On the morning of Tuesday, December 7, 1982, I was woken up at six o'clock by a phone call from my Principal Private Secretary. A bomb had exploded at eleven o'clock the night before at a bar and dance hall, the Droppin Well Inn, at Ballykelly, near Londonderry. Sixteen people were dead, eleven of them British soldiers from the nearby barracks. Sixty-six were injured.

It was the worst outrage during my time as Secretary of State. The Irish National Liberation Army, a rival offshoot from the IRA, claimed responsibility. I was furious that I had not been told about the massacre as soon as the news had come through late the previous night. My officials saw no useful purpose in disturbing me, but that was not the point. I insisted after this that I should be told immediately of any serious incident.

I set out for Ballykelly by helicopter at nine o'clock. It was an awful day, with a gale blowing. We were thrown about in the sky as we crossed the Province, and had to stop more than once to refuel.

I went to see the mayor and chairman of the local council before going to the disaster. As we flew in, the white ribbons cordoning off the area marked a scene of total devastation. The bar and dance hall had been reduced to smouldering remains, completely flattened by the bomb.

The bomb had been placed against one of the stanchions supporting a flat, concrete roof. When it exploded, blowing out the stanchion, the whole roof collapsed on to the crowded dance floor. It is a miracle that more were not killed. Most of those who died were crushed rather than being killed by the explosion itself.

The Droppin Well Inn and its dance hall were used by British troops when they were off-duty from the nearby Shackleton Barracks. At the time of the attack, the Cheshire Regiment formed the garrison.

The dead and injured had been removed by the time I arrived. The young soldiers patrolling the scene looked desperate. They had used the pub themselves, and had spent the night trying to rescue their colleagues and friends and then having to recover their bodies. There was real sorrow and despair, though little anger.

I then flew to the hospital at Altnagelvin to visit the survivors and the staff who had been nursing them. I talked with the clergy who had been at the scene of the bombing through the night, and with the doctors and nurses who had immediately rushed to the hospital.

There has been an enormous advance in medicine in Northern Ireland. They now lead the world in micro-surgery and have achieved wonders in dealing with the most terrible injuries. The quality and standard of nursing is very high and one can detect a special pride in the unusually difficult work they do.

Where possible, I visited the injured. Their morale was astonishingly good. But some of the families refused to let me see their relatives. I could feel their hatred for me, as a representative of the British Government. They felt that we were not doing enough to defeat the IRA, that all we were interested in was an 'acceptable level of violence', and that none of us really cared about them and their relatives.

Of course that was not true. I never did get used to the violence in Northern Ireland and was particularly distressed by what I saw that day, although every murder profoundly affected me. Even though I wrote letters in my own hand to the relatives of members of the security forces who had been killed, and comforted the widows of murdered RUC men, I realised how powerless I was to lessen their grief. Nevertheless I wanted desperately to re-assure them of our sympathy.

On the day I visited the Droppin Well wounded in the morning I had to get to the House of Commons by 3.30 p.m. to make a statement about the bombing. It meant another dreadful helicopter flight to Aldergrove Airport, where the only plane available was an old Andover which took a lifetime to get to RAF Northolt in West London. A police escort from Northolt took me to the House of Commons just as John Patten, one of my junior Ministers, completed the statement. This was a typical example of how difficult it is both to deal with emergencies and to answer to the House of Commons.

After taking Press, radio and television interviews, I then returned to Northern Ireland for the evening to speak at a Chamber of Commerce dinner. It was important to maintain as great a sense of normality as possible, but the strains of travel and pressure were considerable.

*

I quickly realised that terrorist atrocities of this kind could only be finally reduced and brought to an end with the help of economic as well as political measures since high unemployment inevitably fostered conditions in which terrorists thrive and recruit.

Northern Ireland is one of the most depressed regions of the British Isles and one of the poorest in the European Community, comparable with parts of Italy. In 1981, average weekly income was £8 less than in

Great Britain and more than 20 per cent of average family income came from social security benefits.

The principal cause of Northern Ireland's economic plight was the unrelenting decline in its four major traditional mainstays – agriculture, shipbuilding, textiles and clothing. Employment in these four declined by half over the three decades from 1950.

Unemployment in Northern Ireland remains a good deal higher than in the rest of the United Kingdom. This has always been the case, but it was one thing when unemployment was 2 per cent in the rest of the United Kingdom and 4 per cent in Northern Ireland, but quite another matter when it is 12 per cent in the rest of the United Kingdom and 21–22 per cent in Northern Ireland. The unemployment is not evenly distributed. There are certain areas where it is even higher, for example Catholic West Belfast, where up to 35–40 per cent are unemployed, and in the Catholic areas of Londonderry and Strabane and other places in the West unemployment runs at similar levels.

Not surprisingly the relative level of public expenditure in Northern Ireland is much higher than it is for Great Britain. Northern Ireland's economy has become too much dependent on public spending, a substantial share of which is now provided by British taxpayers. The Province receives about £1,300 million more from the Exchequer than is collected in taxes and other revenues in Northern Ireland itself: twenty years ago, this Treasury subvention stood at £52 million. As a proportion of Northern Ireland's Gross Domestic Product, the subvention rose from between 2 and 5 per cent in the 1950s to between 20 and 30 per cent in the 1970s. This is much too high for the good of the community, but it very difficult to reduce.

There are constant calls for more money to be spent on everything under the sun. People, who criticised my performance as a Minister one minute, would come to see me the next, forgetting their animosity and demanding more money. I found it hard to blame them given the appalling economic, social and security problems.

I first met John DeLorean just before Christmas 1981. He was a tall, very smooth, good-looking man, self-confident and in total command. When I visited the DeLorean factory, he arrived late. It was clear from his subordinates that nothing could be said and nothing could be done until he arrived: he was the one person who counted. It was equally obvious that he did not mind keeping the Secretary of State waiting. I could not help feeling that he was a tricky man, and he certainly was not my type, but on the face of it he was doing a lot for West Belfast. I was later accused by the unions of being prejudiced against him. I do not think I was, although subsequent events would certainly have justified it.

The DeLorean venture had been launched during a Labour

Government, when Roy Mason was Secretary of State. The Labour Government was pouring money into Northern Ireland at the time, which helped sustain Unionist support for the Government, when Labour lost its overall majority in the Commons. Roy was sent to Northern Ireland in 1976 with two instructions: first, to spend whatever money was necessary to keep everyone quiet; and secondly to be very tough on the terrorists. This made him popular with the Unionists, who regarded him as the best Secretary of State they had had.

When I arrived in Northern Ireland the DeLorean motor company was apparently going strong. They had started to produce cars in the spring of 1981 and supposedly because of the demand had very quickly built up to a day and night shift. In many ways, the DeLorean exercise had been a brilliantly carried out operation – from a green field site to the production of motor cars with a totally untrained workforce in the space of two and a half years. I doubt whether this has been accomplished so quickly before.

By the end of 1981 the factory appeared to be working smoothly. Cars were being produced, although not to a high standard of finish, and sales seemed to be going well. They were working three shifts, with over 2,000 people employed.

DeLorean wished to talk to me about further Government investment for another model, a sedan. Already it was quite apparent that the company could not exist on the one gull-wing sports car, which was their sole product. He wanted the Government to give him a further £40 million. I was much more interested in reducing the company's £25 million overdraft, which carried a Government-backed guarantee, and seeing some return on the other cash we had invested. He made it plain that he did not like a Conservative Government, he objected to the company being cut back and not getting his own way. He became abusive and made it clear that he much preferred Roy Mason. Again and again he repeated that if we did not give him the money he would move either across the border to the Republic, or would go to Puerto Rico. I do not think any of us who heard him talk took this seriously. No promises were made. I made it plain that there would be no more money, and we asked to see the forecasts by the company and by McKinsey, the analysts, of cash flow and sales for the coming year.

Within a few days I had to go to Cabinet Committee to renew the overdraft guarantee which the Government had given. Leon Brittan, then Chief Secretary, fought very hard to have the total guarantee withdrawn. I asked for it to be approved at £15 million, a reduction of £10 million. Given the circumstances, I felt that I could not ask for more. I believed we were under an obligation to go on supporting the company, although we should take steps to reduce the Government commitment as and when it was possible. Most of the people employed came from poor West Belfast. It was a boost for the Catholic community. As regards terrorism and vandalism, there had been some damage, which had occurred the previous summer during the hunger strike, but the company had come through the difficulties of 1981 pretty well.

The company's troubles began after Christmas. Early in the new year there was a short dock strike, which prevented ferries from docking at Belfast. I was telephoned whilst on leave to be told that this had meant the DeLorean factory had to go on to a three-day week. I was immediately suspicious. How could a dock strike lasting no longer than two days cause the factory so much difficulty? It soon became evident that the problems had nothing to do with the dock strike at all. The real reason was that sales were practically nil in the USA, and money was running out.

The answer may have seemed fairly simple from the point of view of my Government colleagues: when the money runs out, you just close the thing down. But in Northern Ireland nothing is quite that simple. First of all, the Government had already committed a great deal of money, and therefore there was going to be considerable criticism about closing the plant down. Secondly, one could never tell what the reaction of the local workforce would be. It offered the only chance that many would have of finding employment in West Belfast.

There had been other occasions when Harland and Wolff, and Short Bros., had received Government loans or grants. They were predominantly Protestant workforces so why shouldn't the Catholics be given some help, it would be argued. It clearly had all the makings of a very nasty crisis and I knew that I would have to approach it with extraordinary care.

My first action was to try to find out exactly what the facts were. DeLorean arrived with an immediate demand for £15 million. He maintained that this was owed to him as compensation for the damage and loss of production resulting from the riots which took place during the summer. That was the first claim that had to be beaten back.

He then made other demands, claiming that we had not backed him with the resources which we had promised. I refuted this and said that I could see no alternative but for the company to go into receivership. I hoped that it could be a constructive receivership, which might either enable someone else to buy the company and put money in it, or at least ensure that there could be some orderly run-down.

By this time I was being assailed by creditors of the DeLorean Motor Company, who sought to maintain that it was the Government who was responsible. It at once became obvious that, if I had allowed more money to be put in after I had discovered its true state, I would be accepting a liability for the creditors.

The creditors alone at that time must have been owed well over £20 million, one of the biggest being the French Renault company. So apart from the Government money involved, which was some £70 million, it looked as if a further £20-odd million might also be lost. The Government had no intention of getting involved in further losses. It was bad enough as it was.

I saw DeLorean again towards the end of January. I told him that it was my intention to appoint Sir Kenneth Cork as the receiver of the company, in the hope that he would be able to run the company whilst it was being sold to someone else, or until DeLorean had found the money necessary to continue. First of all he begged me not to appoint Sir Kenneth. DeLorean said that he was known as an undertaker and, once his name was associated with the company, no one would have anything to do with it.

I made it clear to DeLorean that I thought Kenneth Cork was the best man in the business. He had very generously agreed to give a great deal of time and effort in trying to save the company. I was determined that he should be brought in. At that stage, however, I would defer announcing that Kenneth Cork would act as receiver. I announced instead that we would have an immediate inquiry, which would be carried out by Cork Gulley. This gave DeLorean two to three weeks, while a proper look at the books could take place, and we could see how the future was likely to unfold. In the meanwhile, work at the DeLorean plant continued on a three-day week, part-time basis.

When the preliminary report arrived, it was quite clear that not only was the company insolvent, but that the cars were not selling and money had been misappropriated. I now made it plain that I could now see no alternative whatsoever but to put the company into receivership at once.

DeLorean asked to be given a further twenty-four hours to raise the necessary money. He told me that there were three definite interests in the future of the company. I asked him who they were. He said that the first was an Arab interest; the second was Lord Weinstock of GEC; and the third was a company in California. When he told me that Arnold Weinstock was supposed to be interested, I merely laughed: it seemed so improbable. When I checked with Arnold, he had a hearty laugh too: he had never met DeLorean and knew nothing about him. DeLorean finally pleaded to have the decision put off until early the next morning, so that his Californian interests would have a last chance to come up with the cash. That deadline was missed as well.

Kenneth Cork and Paul Shewell were eventually appointed as receivers. I told them to manage the company as best they could, and either sell or try to ensure an orderly run-down. One of the first facts to emerge was that 500 cars had been shipped to the USA from Belfast and yet no payment had been made to the Belfast company. This was in direct contravention of the agreement which had been signed, which said that all cars had to be paid for, before leaving Belfast.

But the receivers soon reported to me that the set-up at the American end was in a terrible state and that there was no likelihood of any money from the 500 cars ever coming back to Belfast. Then there was a sum of £14 million which they could not trace. As Kenneth commented in his inimitable way, the money seemed to have gone 'walkabout'.

Kenneth Cork very wisely took his time in running down the company. He allowed much of the steam to be dissipated and was able to explain to the unions that there really was no hope of the company surviving if he could not find someone to take it over. As a result, the employees co-operated in finishing the cars on the production line with available components: these were subsequently sold off and at least saved a bit from the wreck.

As Kenneth rightly proceeded with caution people in London, including Margaret, became impatient. I think she became suspicious that I was trying to cook something up. Nothing could have been further from the truth. Obviously if Kenneth could have found someone to take over the company, that would have been fine, but the slow run-down was essential to maintain peace in the streets.

Gradually the whole operation came to a halt and only a few men were retained for maintenance of the plant. By September, Kenneth was reporting that there were still one or two people who might be interested in buying. These included DeLorean himself, who was now talking of raising some £20–30 million to re-open. I doubted whether this was acceptable but I told Kenneth that, as receiver, he could follow it up if he felt it might be in the interest of the creditors.

In October 1982 I heard for the first time through intelligence sources, that DeLorean was likely to be charged with an alleged drugs offence. I was given no details, but it obviously made it impossible for Kenneth Cork to carry on negotiations with him. I therefore phoned Kenneth to say that the time had come to put up the shutters and stop any further talks.

He was very cross with me: 'But I thought you wanted someone to take over! I'm within an ace of getting DeLorean to buy back his business, and you're telling me that I can't go ahead. As a receiver, I take a very poor view of this. This isn't the right way to protect creditors' money.' I told him that I would give him a further twenty-four hours, but if he couldn't bring it off during that period, it was all over.

Forty eight hours after my conversation with Kenneth, the news broke that DeLorean had been arrested. Kenneth rang me up to ask if I had known in advance and to say how lucky it was if I did know. I told him of the warning I had received, although I had been given no idea when the story would break or whether DeLorean was likely to be arrested.

I do believe that DeLorean was trying to raise money to save the company although he was also hoping to save his own skin too. But I think he had a genuine attachment to the Belfast factory and wished to help Belfast people.

Looking back with the benefit of hindsight, the factory should never have been started: for a small company to begin from scratch and depend on only one model of car was asking for trouble. To make matters worse the car came into production in the middle of the great recession not only in the USA, but in the rest of the world.

The company had no reserves to pull it through and was therefore bound to go under, unless the Government kept putting more and more money in. There was a limit to what the Government could be expected to do. One of the tragedies of Northern Ireland is that it attracts so many risky businesses, those which perhaps do not go elsewhere because they can't get the cash. This led to several other industrial mishaps.

The Commons Public Accounts Committee looked into the DeLorean affair, but its report had to be postponed pending a lawsuit. It was predicatably critical of the way that Ministers and civil servants had behaved in giving money to DeLorean without taking enough care. Some of the criticisms were no doubt justified, but it is all too easy to be critical until one thinks of the unique circumstances in Northern Ireland.

*

One of the reasons I felt so strongly I had to help the young in Ulster was that unemployment was a breeding ground for terrorism in the Republican IRA and INLA, and the loyalist UVF or UFF. I was particularly keen to do what I could to help young people get some training. We were able to introduce the youth training programme for sixteen-year-olds who had left school and could not get a job, a year ahead of the rest of the United Kingdom.

One of the more imaginative schemes was to provide Government aid for the centre in West Belfast, which helped young people to learn how to drive and maintain cars. There had been a great deal of trouble with stealing cars and joy-riding, with several young people driving straight through roadblocks and being shot at, and killed, by soldiers and the police. This scheme gave these young people an opportunity to pursue their interest in cars without having to resort to crime.

We ran by far the greatest public works scheme of any part of the United Kingdom. The Housing Executive was building about 5,000 houses a year, which was out of all proportion to the number of council houses being constructed anywhere in Great Britain. A hundred years ago Belfast had probably the best housing of any major city in Europe. By 1960, with the exception of Naples, it probably had the worst. There is now hope that by 1990 it will once more have the best. A great deal of effort has been put into good housing. Because the new housing programmes were started later than in Britain's cities, Belfast has very few high-rise blocks: the village communities of Belfast have very largely been retained. Efforts have been made to see that the two communities can be kept separate, but many of the old corrugated iron barriers covered by their dreadful graffiti have been pulled down.

Harland and Wolff, once one of the world's greatest shipyards which only a few years ago produced over one per cent of the world's new shipping each year, had become only a shadow of its former self. It had a history of bad management and delayed deliveries, and everything else which characterised British industry at its worst. I managed to persuade John Parker to come back from British Shipbuilders to run it. The Chairman of British Shipbuilders, Sir Robert Atkinson, was extremely loath to let him go. In the end I had to appeal to the Prime Minister, who gave me her full backing, to persuade Patrick Jenkin, the then Industry Secretary, to agree.

I had to fight very hard in Cabinet to keep the yard open. Each worker was being subsidised to the tune of £7,500 a year by the taxpayer. Although it has been loss-making, Harland and Wolff is an essential part of the economy of Northern Ireland, not just for the jobs and skills it provides, not only for the sub-contractors who get their living from the yard, but also because of its symbolic importance.

A few days before Jane was due to launch a large ship built for British Steel at Harland and Wolff's yard, Paisley had accused me of treachery.

An American correspondent had quoted me as saying I was in favour of Great Britain and the Republic exercising joint sovereignty over Northern Ireland, which was quite untrue. Paisley was demanding a special debate in the Assembly, with his accusations echoed by banner headlines in *The Newsletter*, Belfast's fiercely Unionist daily newspaper.

John Parker told me subsequently that he wondered what sort of reception we should get, and whether he ought to call off the launch. But, when we arrived for the ceremony, there were cheering crowds in the yard. The whole event was wonderfully heart-warming. It was one of the great occasions of our time in Northern Ireland.

John Parker remarked to me afterwards, there was in fact a great deal more common sense and stability in the Province than you would ever guess from some of the antics of Northern Ireland's politicians or its media. Recently there has been some decline in the high standards shown at that time.

Like Harland and Wolff, Short Bros are right at the heart of industrial and emotional Belfast. Shorts succeeded in winning orders from the US Air Force, but the Americans examined their hiring policy in detail and made it clear that more Catholics must be employed before any further orders could be made.

I was told by one garage proprietor that on the night Shorts announced that they had won the order from the US Air Force for the Sherpa and Harland and Wolff announced another big ship order, people were calling at his garage and ordering new cars, in a new spirit of optimism and hope for the future. This is an interesting sidelight on Northern Ireland: the spirit of optimism is never far from the surface. Given any chance at all, people wish to break out from the terrible barriers and restrictions which terrorist activity has placed upon them.

*

The toughest, bloodiest and most urgent of all our battles in Northern Ireland was of course the struggle to combat terrorism in the streets and the countryside. The level of violence in Northern Ireland had been ratcheted down from its peak in 1972, but the problem remained awesome.

There are probably not more than between 300 and 500 active terrorists operating within Northern Ireland at any one time. But the tragedy is that as one wipes out, or at least puts behind bars, a particular gang there are always a number of others ready to take their place.

The republican terrorists, the IRA and the INLA, were concentrated in West Belfast, on the west bank of the river Foyle by Londonderry, and along the border with the Republic. Their attacks on the Protestant communities along the border amounted to genocide, fuelled by the centuries-old sense of grievance that the Protestant settlers had been able to secure the best land.

The Ulster Defence Association is the largest loyalist paramilitary group. Its membership in 1983 was around 13,500, some of whom were reckoned to have links with the smaller, proscribed groups, the Ulster Freedom Fighters, the Ulster Volunteer Force and the Red Hand Commandos. During my time in the Province, the loyalist terrorists concentrated their attacks on the nationalist community, killing individuals merely because they were Catholic. These murders often involved the most appalling acts of bestiality on the victims' bodies.

Both republican and loyalist terrorists were heavily engaged in bank robberies, blackmail and extortion. They shared out the territories for their protection rackets between them: there were cases of construction sites which did not bother with nightwatchmen because they were under the protection of one group of terrorists or another. Their involvement in criminality meant that eradicating their organisation and sources of support was bound to be a protracted and painstaking task.

How could we win the security battle? I had tried to set out my answer to this in my first address to the Northern Ireland Assembly.

> We cannot balk the fact that terrorism survives through its ability to manipulate and exploit abiding divisions and mutual suspicions in the community, and it is the responsibility of all of us to help heal these fears and so create conditions in which terrorism withers. This means that we have to operate on several fronts simultaneously. There are no panaceas – weapons alone cannot be successful against paramilitary violence and public disorder. In spite of the great hunger of many people for a simple solution there is no easy or clear-cut way. This is because paramilitary crime as a phenomenon is not remotely comparable to the threat from, say, the uniformed army of an invading foreign power. It cannot be countered as though it was an assault from without . . .

> Progress has a political and social aspect but it also depends on the extent to which the security forces themselves can win the support of the community and act with sensitivity as they go about their difficult task . . .

> We will apply the law even-handedly to all sections of the community, and the law will apply equally to those whose task it is to impose it. However tempting it may seem, we must not fall into the trap which terrorists bait for us: we must not be tempted into using the methods of the terrorists themselves. We will not resort to measures outside the law.

At its worst during 1971 and 1972 the security situation had demanded the presence in Northern Ireland of about 21,000 British troops. This followed the disbandment of the B-Specials and was at a time when the police force in Northern Ireland, the Royal Ulster Constabulary (RUC), was at very low strength. The Ulster Defence Regiment was established in 1970 and now consists of about 6,500 men and women, some full-time, with the majority part-time. They are for the most part engaged in guard and static duties, which enables the regular British troops to play an active role in the more difficult areas, such as the border and parts of Londonderry and Belfast.

The RUC has expanded from about 3,000 and now has some 8,500 regulars and 4,500 reserves. Unfortunately, both the UDR and the RUC have lost most of their Catholic recruits because of the intimidation against them and their families by the IRA. When the UDR was first formed, it was nearly 20 per cent Catholic, and the RUC used to be 15–16 per cent. Now both percentages are down to low single figures.

The Army's General Officer in Command (GOC) when I first arrived was General Sir Richard Lawson, a politically sensitive soldier who did much to cool the rows between the Army and the RUC which had almost come to boiling point before he took command. Dicky Lawson did a great deal to strengthen the authority of the Chief Constable and, quite rightly, to put the RUC into the front line against all forms of violence. Under him, the Army began to reduce its numbers and its presence. I am certain that this was the right policy, and it was continued by Dicky's successor, General Bob Richardson.

During my years in the Province, there were around 9,000 British troops in Ulster, which is only 3,000 above the normal garrison strength. By 1986 the total had risen to 10,500, but the hope must be that the number of troops can be reduced, for in many ways they are an incitement to violence and an invitation to the IRA to try to shoot them if they possibly can.

The security policy proposed by successive British Governments has produced results. This is not to minimise the scale of the problem still remaining, but I believe that some credit is due, particularly when the alternatives of hard-line critics would in all probability have created much greater violence.

In 1972 terrorist violence killed 467 people and injured 4,857. During the 1970s the number of victims fell steadily. In 1981, the year of the hunger strike, 101 people were killed and 1,350 injured. In 1982, 1983 and 1984, there were respectively 92, 77 and 64 terrorist murders; and 515, 510 and 866 people were injured. In 1981, 918 people were charged with terrorist offences, in 1982, 686; in 1983, 609: and in 1984, 528.

I was determined to resist the demands from Unionist spokesmen to increase substantially the number of British troops in Northern Ireland. Their view that smothering the Province with British soldiers would finally eradicate terrorism is a dangerous delusion.

The truth is that however many troops we brought in, the problem of discovering terrorists and their supplies would still be like searching for a needle in a haystack. In fact, the task would become even more difficult because an effective anti-terrorist campaign depends crucially on information, which in turn depends on winning the trust of the Nationalist community.

Combatting terrorism by militarising a society is to play into the terrorists' hands. The sight of vast numbers of British soldiers on the streets would lend greater credibility to IRA and INLA propaganda. Equally important is the need to ensure that the RUC itself does not become transformed into a military-style force. This was a difficult position to hold, but over the past decade the pressures to militarise the RUC have been resisted. The force's professionalism has reached the highest standards, and its evenhandedness is increasingly plain for all to see.

In West Belfast there is a battalion of troops, divided between several barracks. They live in very poor conditions, in close proximity to the police. When police go out on foot, patrolling in pairs, they are generally accompanied by four blocks of four soldiers – not with them, but perhaps a group of four about 200 yards in front, followed by another 200 yards behind, with two blocks guarding other street entrances, in case of trouble. The fact that sixteen soldiers are needed to guard two police is indicative of the tension on the streets of that area. On the other hand it does enable police to be seen once more on the ground doing their job in West Belfast. I sometimes wonder whether they are not doing a better job than perhaps in the so-called good old days before the Troubles, when I very much doubt whether much patrolling was ever done in that area by the RUC. It was always a very difficult part of Belfast and for a time it did become a no-go area. This could not be permitted, and was one of the reasons why in 1969 the troops had to be brought in.

Most of the British troops are now concentrated in the border area, trying to prevent terrorists from crossing, coming up from the South and returning after the crime has been committed. The exercise is subject to constant criticism from the Unionists, who believe that in some way it is possible to seal the border. They also believe that there should be a shoot-to-kill policy – if anyone is suspected of being a terrorist at any time, then shots should be fired and questions asked afterwards. I spoke to a Chief Superintendent about this on one occasion, and his reaction was instructive: 'As far as people who make those sort of comments are concerned, it would be fine just as long as we are killing Catholics. But it would be a very different matter if we started to kill Protestants.'

One of the most difficult problems for the security forces active in the border area is the mining of, or placing of explosive charges in, culverts. To some extent this has prevented our security forces from moving around by wheeled transport – they either have to go on foot, or by helicopter. Not only does this seriously constrain their activities, but it also means that the local public do not see anything like so much of the troops as they would if they could move around in landrovers or armoured cars. This often leads to unfair comparisons between our efforts and those of the Republic, who do not face the same difficulty.

The explosives can easily be made from a mixture of diesel oil and ammonium nitrate fertilizer. Nowadays there are some very sophisticated techniques for letting off these explosives, either by a radio wave or by means of a cable. In many instances explosives are placed under a bridge and the terrorists set themselves up at a fairly safe distance, under cover, and watch for troops or the UDR to arrive. The terrorists have generally staked out their ground very carefully, so that they know at exactly what time, and in what manner, they can best blow the bridge to achieve the most devastating effects. They have their escape route well planned, either back across the border or sometimes to a safe house in the North.

In the autumn and winter of 1983–84 we suffered a resurgence of IRA violence, which raised the question of whether we should close a further number of border crossings. The Republic's Government and the Nationalists hate any crossing being closed, because they consider that this puts up a further dividing line between North and South. The Unionists love to take the opposite view, because they consider the border not to be a border at all, but a frontier: ideally they would like to seal off the North from the South in any way possible, in order to emphasise and reinforce the difference between North and South.

So I was faced with Paisley's demands on the one hand: 'Close border crossings'. He was saying this ostensibly on the grounds of security, but with a deeper motive. At the same time the Nationalists were saying to me: 'Keep the border crossings open, they are necessary for the free flow of people from one side to the other.'

The Chief Superintendent in South Armagh once told me, when I asked him how things were going on his patch: 'Well, down there they are nearly all Nationalists: so they wish to see a united Ireland, just so long as they can keep the border.' The existence of the border, with the excise regulations, ensures the profitability of smuggling!

We did close two or three crossings in the spring of 1984 by placing concrete barriers across the road. But within forty-eight hours, two of them had been re-opened owing to "irresistible pressure" from the local population on either side – i.e. bulldozers.

This particular exercise was not carried out very sensibly. It made life extremely difficult for me and was a highly embarrassing incident. It is simply no good closing border crossings unless you are certain they can be kept closed. After this incident I asked the Army about our future policy on border crossing. They told me it was impractical to close crossings right on the border, because in many cases it separated two parts of the same farm. Closing a regular crossing on the border line often merely encourages people to remove the obstacle or simply go round them. They therefore suggested that we should consider more road blocks set well back from the border.

When I put this idea to Paisley and Molyneaux, Paisley reacted immediately, said that it was now quite clear that the Army was not prepared to defend Northern Ireland, and that hundreds of square miles of territory were to be given over to the terrorists.

*

Although the overwhelming majority of the Nationalist community will have nothing to do with terrorism, many are not keen to give information to the authorities. The result is that it is not difficult for a terrorist to remain undetected. Once they escape across the border, to places like Dundalk, they join a considerable number of others lying up, waiting perhaps for a year or so for things to quieten down before another attempt – 'sleeping' as it is called. There is always a reservoir of such men who can be brought back into action after losses have been sustained.

The surest way to catch terrorists is through effective intelligence, so that it is known where they are operating and where they can be dealt with, either by straightforward police measures or, on occasion, by undercover methods. The intelligence operation has improved enormously over the past few years, as a result of highly professional advice and better co-ordination of the intelligence efforts of the Army and the RUC and of the intelligence services themselves.

The introduction of the SAS into the security operations in Northern Ireland by Harold Wilson initially introduced some confusion between the various forces. But over the years the SAS have performed an invaluable role. With their special training, they can 'lie up' in a city attic, a farmyard loft or on an open hillside, for days at a time, watching a terrorist haunt or arms cache, and ready to take the terrorists by surprise.

In 1982 and 1983 a number of informers, both Protestant and Catholic, came forward to give evidence about terrorist activities and to implicate the culprits. As a result of these informers – who became known as 'supergrasses' – a great many people were rounded up and charged with murder, carrying arms and membership of an illegal organisation.

Allegations were made that this was another form of internment because we were locking up the accused before trial on very flimsy evidence. In fact the evidence was good, but it was not easy to corroborate other than through the police because witnesses were reluctant to come forward: they feared that they would be got at, and frequently were. This lack of corroboration was highlighted by lawyers, usually but not exclusively acting on behalf of the republicans.

Allegations were also made that the police were paying vast sums of money to bribe people to give information and were granting informers parole, and even immunity from prosecution. Exception was being taken to a judge sitting alone without a jury, even for capital offences.

Of the cases which came to trial, some were dismissed. In the cases where the proceedings continued, a number of those charged were convicted, but others were set free. I could find no fault with the conduct of the supergrass trials, and I believe that the judges showed themselves to be totally impartial and upholding the highest traditions of judicial behaviour in all that they did. The very fact that known and self-confessed criminals and terrorists were freed despite the evidence given by the supergrasses is I think an indication of how careful the judges were in interpreting their own rules.

Great efforts were made to infiltrate the terrorist organisations. This could be done by seeking to plant people within the organisation, or, where there was an opportunity, of bribing someone already there.

On occasions it became clear that some of our agents were in danger and they would have to be got out, resettled, given new names and a completely new life either in other parts of the United Kingdom, or perhaps in other countries. This was not cheap and it was thought that we were offering great sums to people to become supergrasses. This was not true. Most of the money, which amounted to a few hundred thousand pounds in one or two years, was paid out to those who were already working for us, or had to be resettled.

One of the good results from the supergrass trials and arrests in '82 and '83 was the spread of consternation within the ranks of the terrorist organisations. They did not know who their friends were and who they could rely upon. They became very jittery with each other. This obviously aided the security forces.

When you are dealing with a ruthless group of people who will bomb or shoot on sight, and have no scruples at all about their policy of murder, you have to be prepared to adopt covert methods. It ill became some of the Unionists to complain about the manner in which we were using supergrasses when at the same time they were asking us to take even more stringent defence and military measures to contain and stamp out terrorism.

*

Apart from the political, economic, military and intelligence measures available to me, I also had to initiate diplomatic progress with the Republic on the question of extradition. This was one of the most contentious problems between the Province and the Republic Very often a terrorist, having committed a crime in the North, would escape across the border to the Republic. The police in the North would know who it was, and the police in the Republic would know where he was. But because there was no automatic extradition, it was impossible to get the Irish Government to return them to the North to stand trial.

In my speech on security to the Assembly, I had expressed the Government's deepest regret and concern that the Republic had not felt able to accept the European Convention on the Supression of Terrorism. This measure is designed to ensure that terrorists are not able to plead the alleged political character of their crimes as a means of avoiding justice. Subsequently, I was naturally delighted by Garret Fitzgerald's statement during his visit to London in February 1986 that the Republic would become a signatory to the Convention, thus opening the way for the extradition of terrorists from the Republic to the United Kingdom.

Garret's statement followed a shift in the judges' interpretation of the Republic's Constitution. Up to 1983 the judges in the Republic for the most part maintained that the offences which were committed in the North were political, and there could not be extradition for the commission of a political offence, however heinous. This belief, however, began to break down and judges were now prepared to say that, although the offence committed was political, the person in question should nonetheless stand trial in the North.

This happened in the case of Dominic McGlinchy, a notorious terrorist regarded as responsible for murders in Northern Ireland, who escaped to the Republic, committed a number of offences there, and was at last captured there in a shoot-out. Overnight the judge decided to extradite McGlinchy to the North. He was delivered back to us, subsequently stood trial, and was convicted of murder. But he appealed successfully and was then immediately re-extradited to the Republic. He was a known, self-confessed terrorist, but the evidence was not sufficiently strong finally to convict. Who can say that our system of justice is not scrupulously fair? He has since been convicted of offences in the Republic.

*

There was one further battle to win. This was the propaganda campaign which I realised would have to be fought and won in America. The IRA's terrorist campaign had to be funded from somewhere. We knew that they were heavily involved in bank robberies, blackmail, extortion and protection rackets, all of which were being tackled by the security forces. But the IRA were also being funded by sympathisers in the USA, and it was to meet this challenge that Nick Scott, my junior Minister, and I gave urgent priority to getting our message across in the States.

During my time as Secretary of State I made three visits to America to try to improve the understanding of the British position in Northern Ireland. IRA sympathisers were raising around $600,000 a year in the USA, ostensibly for widows and orphans, but much of the money was financing terrorist activity.

To many Americans it appears that the British retain colonial control over Northern Ireland and that, if only we would remove the colonial yoke, the Province would gratefully become part of the Republic of Ireland. However hard one tries, many Americans simply refuse to accept that the majority of people of Northern Ireland wish to remain part of the United Kingdom, and will not under any circumstances be part of the Republic of Ireland. The most difficult people are those congressmen and senators, like Senator Edward Kennedy, with large numbers of Irish constituents who still harbour views which originate from the potato famine of the 1840s and the ghastly oppression to which the British subjected them.

The Irish Government was always helpful in the USA on the subject of terrorism. Garret Fitzgerald's utter condemnation of violence was particularly effective. His campaign enabled me to emphasise that people in the US who might be sceptical of a British Minister's statements on the subject only had to listen to what the Taoiseach was saying to find out the true nature of the IRA.

But there was also a very active campaign, particularly amongst US public opinion-formers, to convince the Administration and Congress that the only solution to the Irish problem was the unity of the island. When people like John Hume of the SDLP visited the States, he spent a lot of time condemning terrorism, but naturally making it quite clear that he felt the only solution was a United Ireland. John and politicians in the Republic used to tell me that I should leave it to them, because they were much better able to make the case against terrorism than we were. We were said not to be credible in the USA because we would always be seen to be putting a British, colonial point of view.

But this would have left the field completely open. The difficulties faced by the British Government and an understanding of the Unionist position would never be properly explained. Nick Scott and I therefore made great efforts through frequent visits to the USA to try to change the prevailing impression all along the East Coast, and in Minneapolis and San Francisco, where it was perhaps stronger than anywhere else.

Our visits to the United States were extremely hard work. They used to start with a number of breakfast TV programmes, beginning at 7 am, continuing with constant media interviews most of the day. These would be interspersed with meetings in Washington, with members of the Senate, the House of Representatives, and the Administration. There were also a whole series of meetings with industrialists and bankers to try to persuade them to invest in Northern Ireland.

Wherever we went in the United States, we were very carefully guarded and protected by the police force. But once in a Boston hotel I could not sleep, and opened the wrong door in the middle of the night. I found myself in the corridor. The policeman on duty outside was fast asleep! And, as this was Boston, I have no doubt that he was Irish.

On one occasion I was in the ludicrous position of attending a meeting in Harvard, arranged for me to discuss the British Government's policy, and being confronted by Danny Morrison, one of Provisional Sinn Fein's leading figures. He had entered the United States illegally, had been sent home, but then had been called over again to stand trial. While he was waiting to stand trial for illegal entry, he was spending his time following me around the USA, at the expense of the US Government!

As a result of a fresh appreciation of the Irish problem the US administration became far more co-operative in the efforts made to prevent the passage of arms, either through the Republic of Ireland or direct to Northern Ireland itself. The FBI had restricted the supply of weapons, but it was much more difficult to stem the flow of funds.

I used to spend hours with congressmen on Capitol Hill, trying to convince them of the error of their ways. Tip O'Neill, the Speaker of the House of Representatives and the leading Democrat, was perfectly rational about terrorism. He was utterly against violence in any sense whatsoever, but felt the only solution was a United Ireland. His thinking did not go any further. He just wanted us to get out of Ireland as and when we could and allow the island to be united. The only problem is that he did not seem to understand that the Unionists would not agree to it.

I must admit that I could never really come to terms with Senator Edward Kennedy. He was very civil, but I felt that he just did not want to listen to the facts. It was much more convenient for him to be able to indulge in rhetoric, rather than actually to get down to the details of what was happening in Northern Ireland, or to consider the difficulties of the sort of solution which he favoured.

This was not true of Senator Moynihan, whom I found to be very co-operative. On one occasion he said to me, 'I guess you're telling me to keep quiet.' I hope he did not find this difficult, because he is a very articulate gentleman. He was in a particularly difficult position as the Senator for New York, with a large Irish-American population, but he behaved in a most statesmanlike way. A number of congressmen who formed themselves into the Friends of Ireland followed his example, in particular the Congressman from Washington State, Tom Foley.

I was in the United States in 1982 when the IRA bombed the Green Jackets band in Regents Park and the Household Cavalry near Knightsbridge Barracks. The slaughter of the horses had a curiously powerful effect, symbolising somehow the IRA's utter callousness. These atrocities had a marked impact on opinion in the USA. I was able to appear on a large number of television programmes that day and get coast-to-coast coverage, pointing out exactly what support from US citizens for the IRA was in fact doing.

The murder of an American in the IRA's bombing of Harrods shortly before Christmas 1983 also shifted US opinion against them. These serious misjudgments by the IRA enabled us, and Garret Fitzgerald's Government, to have some impact in explaining what the IRA really want – the destruction of democracy, and its replacement by a

Marxist Irish state, which in time might threaten the whole of Western security.

*

I hoped that the IRA's activities on the mainland of Britain would take some sting out of Paisley's frequent over-reaction to violence in Ulster. His response all too often played into the hands of the terrorists. Following a terrorist attack, Paisley and his cohorts would come rushing in to Stormont Castle to see the Secretary of State, demanding that further measures were taken on security, and stirring up everyone's emotions.

There were a number of occasions during my three years when I thought that events would boil over and get out of control, but they never did. Maybe it was because the troops and the police were much more active in the subsequent days, both working at an unsustainably high level. Or it may simply have been that the IRA felt they had brought the mood in the Province to fever pitch and did not wish to provoke it any further. I was never able to fathom which, but was always thankful that the ultimate crisis never erupted.

Throughout my time in Northern Ireland I tried to anticipate and combat the tactics of the terrorists as effectively as I could, while using the minimum of force and making the minimum of fuss. Although this sometimes laid me open to the charge of complacency I felt that the calmer the atmosphere and the more normal the appearance of everyday life, the better were our chances of deterring further recruitment into the terrorist groups. It may have frustrated those who expected exciting leadership and more dramatic action, but I am convinced that my approach served the best interests of Northern Ireland.

Despite Ian Paisley's frequent criticisms of my attitude to the violence, after my first two and a half years there was evidence that his reaction to me and my policies had moderated since the funeral of Robert Bradford in November 1981.

In early 1984, the Provisional IRA murdered another Official Unionist politician, Edgar Graham, a young member of the Northern Ireland Assembly. This was a terrible tragedy. He was shot as he stood talking in the street outside Queen's University, Belfast, where he was a law lecturer. Jane and I attended his funeral service, just as I had insisted on going to Robert Bradford's.

This time instead of leaving the church to a barrage of abuse and even physical violence, I was accompanied by Jim Molyneaux, Leader of the Official Unionists, and other members of the OUP who gathered round me to escort me out. Ian Paisley went across to Jane and remained protectively by her as they walked out of the church.

This was heartwarming and generous. I felt that despite the differences and disagreements between us and the Unionist leaders, Jane and I were now accepted by the community.

CHAPTER TWELVE

FEARS AND HOPE

I realised that there must be something seriously wrong the minute I heard that my Permanent Secretary at the Northern Ireland Office was on his way to see me. I was spending a few days at the 1983 Party Conference at Blackpool, and it is almost unheard of for civil servants to turn up – certainly not the head of a Department.

The Press and everyone else at the Conference seemed to be talking about nothing except whether Cecil Parkinson would have to resign and what Sara Keays would say next, but I knew that my Permanent Secretary's mission must concern something much more serious.

He had come to tell me that there was an imminent and carefully prepared plot to assassinate me. Intelligence sources had discovered the plan, which was to be carried out in Northern Ireland. I discussed the threat with Margaret. Although it was clear that Cecil's future was in the balance it was also clear that she would not contemplate switching me back to a Whitehall-based Department, so I agreed to soldier on.

The intelligence service was worried that rearranging my engagements in Northern Ireland could compromise their source. One suggestion was that Richard Needham, who had succeeded Fred Silvester as my Parliamentary Private Secretary, could take my place at some risky engagements – an idea which horrified me and which I dismissed outright. Poor Richard must have wondered who had it in for him. Once the alarm had passed, however, Richard and I used to joke about it all being in a PPS's line of duty. We were able to come up with a convincing excuse for rearranging my planned engagements.

During my three years as Northern Ireland Secretary, I was only informed of one other direct threat on my life. Again, the plan was to kill me in the Province. For a time Jane and I therefore had to return to London secretly every night and fly back unobtrusively to Belfast early every morning to maintain the pretence that we were leading our normal lives in Northern Ireland. After a while we stopped going back to London but would sleep randomly at Stormont House or Hillsborough, instead of returning regularly to our flat at Hillsborough.

The threat to a Northern Ireland Secretary places considerable demands on the protection squads, the ordinary police in Britain and Northern Ireland, the army and UDR, and the intelligence service. Intelligence had the task of sifting the various threats to decide which were made by cranks and which were real. The protection continues for all former Northern Ireland Secretaries, a tedious necessity but one which we have to accept – although I have a suspicion that one or two quite like all the attention. But our problems are nothing compared with those faced by anyone who has served in a senior position in the security forces in Northern Ireland itself and who will need the strictest protection throughout their retirement.

The emotional strains of the Northern Ireland job are the hardest. It isn't the amount of work, but the knowledge that at any time something may go wrong, that lives are going to be lost, that tragedies are going to happen, and that at the end of the day you are ultimately responsible for them. Sometimes an outrage such as the Droppin Well bomb leads to a great upsurge and protest from people about the level of security; the accusation that all the British Government is trying to do is to contain things – that there is 'an acceptable level of violence' – and that we are not serious in defeating terrorism. And then you have to listen to interminable lectures from Paisley, the Official Unionists and the Orange Order, the Churches on occasion, and just about everyone else. If there was an easy and simple way of dealing with terrorism and defeating it, we would have taken it. But unfortunately there wasn't.

We have to operate under very difficult circumstances in a comparatively free society, although not as free as it is in the rest of the UK, which in itself is a matter for yet more criticism. The RUC, the Army and the Northern Ireland Department in fact do an exceptionally good job, but when things go wrong it is always their fault. No wonder at times the job of Secretary of State seemed weary and lonely.

Immediately after the 1983 general election I had told Margaret that despite the pressures of the office I wished to carry on in Northern Ireland and complete a term of three years. The Unionists were always speculating and hoping for my replacement by someone more sympathetic and compliant. My continuation as Northern Ireland Secretary did at least show that the Government would stick to a consistent policy. I was also delighted that Chris Patten joined my Ministerial team. He is outstandingly gifted, and Margaret had recognised that, despite his liberal views, he should be given his chance in government. I was able to persuade her that he should work with me and he proved an outstanding success.

Inevitably with their huge new majority many in the Conservative Party were going to agitate for the return of capital punishment. Certainly it was wanted by the Unionists. And when I opposed this for terrorist murderers, it was seen as yet another sign of my lack of intent to root out terrorism. This was, however, one issue where Enoch Powell and I were at one – he too was opposed to bringing back hanging.

Since the abolition of capital punishment in 1965, Parliament had voted against the restoration of the death penalty on three occasions, the last in July 1979 shortly after we returned to office. Margaret had always made clear her own wish to see hanging restored and had promised during the election that Parliament would be given an early opportunity to vote on the issue.

There was very little discussion in Cabinet beforehand. It was thought better that we should take the debate on hanging early to get it out of the way before the Party Conference in October, so that the new Home Secretary, Leon Brittan, could go to the Conference and say that Parliament had made its decision, one way or the other. If it had been left over until after the Party Conference it would have been much more difficult for him, and for Members of Parliament generally, who would have been exposed to months of emotive campaigning from both the pro-and anti-hangers.

We thought that it was going to be quite a close vote. The nearer we got to the day of the debate the more worried Margaret became. Although she had been much in favour of obtaining a positive vote for hanging, she began to appreciate both the dreadful difficulties this would cause for the Government's legislative programme and the wider effects on public opinion of introducing such controversial legislation. On the one hand, her strong personal prejudice meant that she wanted to win, but on the other her reason told her that she would be very happy to lose.

In Cabinet I made it plain that under no circumstances could I do other than advise Members of Parliament to vote against hanging for terrorism. To hang Irish terrorists would be a disaster.

Cabinet agreed that I should make my position clear in advance of the debate, and that only Leon Brittan, the Home Secretary, would speak from the Government front bench. I made my own views public in an open letter to my constituency chairman. There is no doubt that my statement had more influence than if I had spoken in the debate itself.

I reproduce below the text of my open letter, originally published the weekend before the 1983 parliamentary debate:

As you know, I have opposed the re-introduction of the death penalty over many years with the one exception that in 1975 I voted for its re-introduction for terrorism. I recognised within a short time that this was a mistaken and emotional response and long before I was closely associated with the affairs of Northern Ireland, I had reverted to my former position.

Having changed my mind myself, at a time of terrorist brutality, I do appreciate the strong feeling that many people have and they, like me, may not have fully appreciated the true position as far as Irish terrorism is concerned.

I hope that my experience and the reasons I give now why there should be no return to capital punishment and in particular for terrorism will help to convince my constituents and others that one does not take these decisions lightly or without a great deal of thought . . .

Parliament, in taking its decision must give the greatest weight to Northern Ireland considerations for it is surely clear that a matter such as this cannot simply be decided for Great Britain and that we must have a uniform law for the United Kingdom as a whole.

It is, of course, technically possible for Parliament to legislate to restore capital punishment for terrorist murder in Great Britain but not in Northern Ireland. I recognise that many people who have thought about this have directed their minds mainly to Great Britain and might well conclude that rather different arguments apply in Northern Ireland.

It would, however, to my mind, not be possible to single out terrorist murder for capital punishment and then to exclude the area where the main terrorist threat exists, let alone execute Irish extremists who killed in Britain but not those who killed in Northern Ireland.

The statistics show why Northern Ireland considerations are so important. In England and Wales during the six years from 1977 to 1982, four people were convicted of what would be called terrorist murder and seven of the murder of police officers. All but one were aged 18 or over.

In Northern Ireland, in that same six-year period, 221 people were convicted of terrorist murder; 34 of them were under 18 years of age. Assuming that people under 18 would not be subject to the death penalty, these figures mean that if capital punishment had existed for terrorist murder during the last six years there would have been 19 cases in Northern Ireland for every one in England and Wales. The Home Secretary would have to consider the question of a reprieve in rather less than two cases a year, whereas there would have been a continual flow of these cases being considered in Northern Ireland. These figures must be set against a Northern Ireland population of $1\frac{1}{2}$ million and an England and Wales population of 50 million.

These statistics demonstrate that Northern Ireland is subject to a terrorist threat of a different dimension from that which has been experienced in Britain. Though international terrorism is a growing anxiety, most recent terrorist activity in Britain has been an extension of IRA terrorism from Northern Ireland.

It is therefore sensible, when assessing the likely impact of capital punishment on terrorism generally, to test the arguments in relation to the main form of terrorism we face in the United Kingdom.

In the long history of terrorism connected with Irish affairs, executions and deaths in prison have played a prominent part. The IRA have been skilful in turning terrorists into martyrs and drawing strength and support from executions and deaths.

Such considerations could be set aside if capital punishment were likely to deter the terrorist and prevent murder. There is, however, ample evidence that the IRA are not deterred in this way. They are so committed to their cause that they are prepared to risk their own lives as well as to destroy the lives of others.

Up to April of this year (i.e. 1983) more than 307 have been killed in the course of the present terrorist campaign, some by the security forces, many blown up by their own bombs.

Most terrorists believe they will not be caught. The defeat of terrorism depends upon arresting and convicting the terrorists. As I shall explain below, capital punishment is likely to make it more difficult to secure evidence and less likely that those who can be brought before the courts will be found guilty. If capital punishment had applied at the material time it is likely that a significant proportion of the 331 convicted adult murderers (nearly all terrorists) now serving life sentences in Northern Ireland, would still be at large to commit further crime.

In Northern Ireland intimidation has made the jury system inoperable for terrorist offences. Trials are conducted by a single judge who, in a contested case, must alone decide whether the accused's guilt has been proved.

The removal of the accused's protection of jury trial is justified in the special circumstances of Northern Ireland, and Parliament has been content to renew the arrangement year by year. But it could not easily be defended if the judge's decision involved the death penalty, nor is the onus of deciding, in effect, the issue of life or death one which the judges should, in my view, be asked to bear.

On the other hand, a restoration of jury trial in present circumstances in Northern Ireland could only increase the probability of terrorists escaping justice – the more so if the jury were looking for a scintilla of doubt in order to avoid conviction for a capital crime.

I am particularly concerned about the effect of capital punishment on the work of the police, especially as regards evidence-gathering. Before finalising my own views, I sought the opinion of the senior officers of the RUC.

It is the considered professional judgment of the Chief Constable of the RUC, after consultation with his chief officers, that the reintroduction of capital punishment for terrorist murders would make the task of the police in Northern Ireland substantially more difficult. I appreciate that the Police Federation take a different view but I must be swayed by the assessment of those with command responsibilities.

The RUC are largely dependent upon information from members of the public, confessions from the criminal himself and information provided by former terrorists. They have made remarkable progress in overcoming the ruthless intimidation and exploitation of community loyalties by the terrorists in Northern Ireland. Senior officers believe that if those possessing information about a terrorist crime knew that the consequence of passing it to the police was likely to involve the execution of the terrorist concerned, they would be more inclined to remain silent.

They are concerned that in practice the death penalty would adversely affect the co-operation which security forces receive not only in Northern Ireland itself but also elsewhere. Though, as I have said, the motives of the terrorists are difficult to predict, the existence of the death penalty would surely make confessions less likely and might well increase the reluctance of the courts to accept the uncorroborated evidence of such confessions.

The valuable information and evidence which has recently begun to flow from converted terrorists (sometimes described as 'supergrasses') would be jeopardised if people knew their former colleagues might hang. And even greater pressure would be put on the families of those who did come forward to persuade them to withdraw their evidence.

The police would not only find their task of dealing with the terrorists more difficult. They would have to devote more resources to dealing with public disorder. One of the advances of recent years is that the violent street demonstration or riot is very much rarer than a decade ago. The exception was for a period during the hunger strike. Executions, however well justified, would lead to violent disorder.

Over recent years the RUC have been able increasingly to rely on greater community acceptance, or at least greater community opposition to the presence of terrorists. This progress would be set back both by the executions and the measures which the police would be obliged to take to deal with the disorders which would follow them.

Nor might it stop at disorders. So far from deterring terrorism, executions could very well lead to more acts of vengeance, killings and atrocities against members of the security forces and others on a substantial scale.

I have concentrated on Northern Ireland considerations and terrorism because of the profound effect which capital punishment for terrorist murder would have upon the part of the United Kingdom where my responsibilities lie.

But I should not want, by silence, to appear indifferent to the more general considerations which persuade many, as they do me, against the restoration of capital punishment in any form: considerations such as the risk of hanging someone who turns out to have been innocent; the effect on our society, from the prison officials and their attendants who conduct the execution, to the public, whether waiting outside the prison gates or reading the details in the press; and, to my mind, the impossibility of defining categories of murder in a way which public opinion would not think unjust when confronted with individual cases.

But for me the crucial test is a simple practical one: whether bringing back capital punishment for terrorism is likely to lead to more or fewer policemen soldiers and civilians being murdered in Northern Ireland. My considered judgment is that it would make it more difficult to bring terrorists to justice, strengthen their support and destabilise society in the Province. Like a number of eminent historians, I believe that executions of terrorists in Northern Ireland would serve not as a deterrent but as a new inspiration for the IRA and other extremists. I am not therefore basing my argument on the moral one that it is wrong to take life, but on the practical effect that the policy would have.

Leon Brittan had circulated a copy of his speech to me before the debate. When my civil servants in the Northern Ireland Office saw it – and most of them were former Home Office Officials – they thought it was extremely ill-advised.

In the actual debate Leon put all the arguments against hanging and then ended up by voting for it. It was a strange performance. Roy Jenkins said to me that he thought it was the worst speech he had ever heard from a Home Secretary.

Leon appeared to have made the mistake, which he was subsequently to repeat, of doing and saying what he thought Margaret and the right wing of the Tory Party would wish. In so doing, he spoiled his tenure of the Home Office and probably his chance of becoming one of the political leaders of his generation.

I sat with Margaret on the front bench when the Commons vote was declared. I expected her to be pleased or at least relieved, as before the vote she had seemed worried that it might go her way. But as soon as she realised that the vote was lost her populist politics got the better of her. She shouted at Gerald Kaufman, Roy Hattersley and Peter Shore across the dispatch box that they didn't know what the people wanted, and that on the council housing estates the Labour leadership would get stick for turning down hanging.

By October and the Party Conference, Leon still seemed worried at the pressures from the right wing. He therefore decided that he would introduce a minimum sentence for murder, which would be 30 years if

committed by terrorists and 20 if committed by others. I objected vehemently. There was no one in prison in Britain for terrorist offences who
would be released during his period of office, whereas in Northern Ireland
I had people who were about to be released. If they were then retrospectively
to be tied to a minimum of 30 years, it could cause tremendous unrest in the
prisons. I could not vouch for what would happen.

I was simply not prepared to go along with this. It would not be a
problem for him, but it would be a real problem for me. I persuaded
him therefore to reduce the minimum to 20 years for terrorism in Britain,
though I would not have dreamed of committing a Northern Ireland
Secretary to follow that advice. When I was asked almost immediately in
the Commons whether I would follow the Home Secretary on his sen-
tencing policy I made it clear that I would not.

In the case of a number of young men, I believed that probably eight
or nine years was a long enough sentence: it must depend on the circumstances of the offence and on the judge's summing up at the time and his
views later.

The Conservative Party did not emerge from the hanging debate and
the policy change on life sentences with any great credit. Although everyone had been told that the new intake would vote solidly for hanging,
they split in just about the same proportion as the rest of the parliamentary Party.

The true significance of the vote was not immediately apparent. While
some were prepared to go along with Margaret because they had got into
Parliament on her coat-tails, others rather resented any such suggestion
and a lot did not like being branded as right wingers.

They soon realised that the confrontationist stance may be all right for
dealing with General Galtieri, but it was not necessarily right the whole
time when dealing with the most sensitive issues in our own community.
As time went on we have seen a subtle change in the new members, and
perhaps amongst some of the old ones too, as they recognise that confrontation is not always the answer. Political fashions are constantly
changing and very soon after the 1983 election we began to leave behind
us the confrontationist phase.

*

Although I felt that I had made a genuinely important contribution to
our handling of the Irish problem on the issue of hanging, I quickly
found myself held responsible for two major setbacks.

On 25th September 1983, a Sunday I happened to be on duty in
Northern Ireland. Jane and I had just been walking round the garden at
Hillsborough at about 4 o'clock when I noticed a helicopter in the sky. I

commented to Jane that I hoped it did not mean something was wrong.

Within ten minutes Noel Cornick, my private secretary, was on the phone to tell me that there had been a break-out by thirty-eight Republican prisoners from the Maze; a prison officer had been killed; ten prisoners had been quickly recaptured but the rest were still on the loose.

The prisons in Northern Ireland are always simmering with trouble. This is understandable if one recognises that of the 2,300 prisoners, over 800 are in for life. There are many more 'category A' prisoners in the Northern Ireland prisons than there are amongst the entire 45,000 prison population in Great Britain. And not only are the 800 men utterly ruthless, but they are for the most part Catholics and Republicans hating the Protestants, who form the vast majority of the prison officers.

The treatment of these prisoners created a unique problem, for although they regard themselves as political prisoners, they are convicted criminals, whom some people regard almost as prisoners taken in a war. Were they prisoners-of-war in an ordinary sense they would be confined in a foreign country without friends or sympathisers, but to take them to the British mainland would exacerbate the political situation. It would also create enormous difficulties in arranging visits by families and friends, quite apart from the extra burdens it would place on the overstretched prison service.

Some people have advocated the creation of an Alcatraz-type prison on an island, but this is logistically impossible. In the circumstances the Maze was the best solution which the prison service in the Province could devise.

Over a time, the prisoners' friends and families had smuggled into the Maze a number of weapons or parts of them, sometimes by concealing them in their rectums or vaginas. After each visit the prisoners were made to walk from the visitors' block back to the cells, some distance away. For prisoners concealing weapons it was a pretty uncomfortable walk and, although it sometimes exposed the prisoners' weapons when frisking did not, it was far from foolproof as a means of detection.

There was no doubt that over a period of time the Republican prisoners had very cleverly managed to acquire a lot of privileges they should not have had. No doubt emboldened by their secret armoury they used threats of violence further to strengthen their hand against the prison officers. Furthermore there was always a good deal of collusion between loyalist prisoners and republican prisoners, although they were both always trying to secure total segregation from each other.

During the August Bank Holiday just before the break-out, an inflammable situation was made more dangerous still when we received a threat from the prison officers that they would all go on strike, and refuse to enter the prisons.

Once the guns were in the Maze it is not difficult to see how prisoners could obtain command in a cell block.

On the afternoon of the escape, they had overpowered the officers, and put on the officers' uniforms. They had then forced the driver of a prison meal van to drive them to the main gate, where they fought with the guards before making their escape. Besides those re-captured immediately, a further nine were caught over the next few days, leaving nineteen on the run.

Immediately after the break-out I of course offered Margaret my resignation. She refused to accept it. She was naturally as furious as I was, but felt that the escape was a risk that was inherent in the unique conditions of Northern Ireland's prisons.

The discussion with the Prime Minister, with whom I agreed the lines of a statement I would make to the House, convinced me that it would be wrong for me to press my resignation. My statement included the broad terms of reference of the full report which I commissioned on the break-out from Sir James Hennessy, the Chief Inspector of Prisons. For me to have resigned straightaway would have played into the hands of all the troublemakers. It would have been seen as again giving way to pressure from irresponsible Unionist MPs. Above all it would have added another immense boost to the already heightened morale of the IRA.

The question of my resignation was one of many I had to answer in the House. To what extent is a Minister responsible for everything that happens in his Department, even down to the day-to-day operation of the prisons? I took the view that I should not resign unless it was clear from the Report, which would take some months to complete, that a policy change or directive had been the direct cause of the escape – for example, if we had denied resources to the prison or given ill-advised orders about the way in which discipline should be enforced.

During the course of the inquiry, we were criticised by the prison officers on the grounds that the prime cause had been new rules introduced at the end of the hunger strike on the wearing of prison clothes and allowing prisoners to associate more freely within the block. But the accusation was quickly refuted, as owing to the prisoners' intransigence we had refused to relax the rules on greater association at that time.

A much more serious charge was that the reforms that we had granted at the end of the hunger strike had undermined the authority of the prison staff. They alleged that this was a moral victory for the republican prisoners which had sapped morale so seriously that their own discipline had suffered to the point of permitting the break-out.

Apart from the accusations of inefficiency in the prison service, every charge under the sun was laid against the RUC and the Army for not capturing more of the prisoners who had escaped. In the circumstances of Northern Ireland there are always people who will hide terrorists on the run and then in time get them safely across the border to the South, where they can lie low; as indeed most of them have done ever since – although a few have returned to terrorist activity.

When the Hennessey Report on the break-out was finally published in January 1984, it showed that no policy decisions contributed to the escape. But it was extremely critical of many aspects of security at the Maze, and I therefore had to decide whether to take action against the Governor, who must carry ultimate responsibility for the state of the prison. If I had done nothing, undoubtedly I would have been told that the whole inquiry was a whitewash. On the other hand, when I asked him to resign and leave the service early – although we fully safeguarded his pension – I was accused of trying to push the blame on to him when it properly resided with me. Politicians in the Province were particularly quick to do this. It is much easier for them to blame British Ministers and the Northern Ireland Office than to accept any responsibility for what goes wrong within Northern Ireland themselves.

The Maze break-out had, once more, created tension in the Province. Regrettably, public figures, the press and TV thrive on this kind of excitement. It is the kind of unhealthy state which Northern Ireland needs to avoid. What it needs above everything is not always to be the centre of publicity. The image of the Province as being *continuously* subject to violence and murder, explosions and mob-rule is contrary to the reality, and yet it is the image which most people in Britain hold.

Of course the public wanted to be assured that a gaol-break of this kind would not happen again and that the escaped prisoners would be recaptured as fast as possible. It was understandable that they felt an example should be made of whoever was responsible, whether it was the prison Governor, a junior Minister, or me. But I still think that both in principle and in practice my decision to remain was right, although I was certainly not unaware of the constitutional dilemma.

*

Although I had done my best to try to reduce the degree of support in America for the IRA, it was a visit by an American which caused a further major crisis for my administration.

An American, Martin Galvin, one of the leading figures in Noraid, the organisation which raises funds for the IRA, decided to come over to Ireland. Over recent years, Noraid had taken to organising a summer excursion for American supporters, both to the Republic of Ireland and to the North. Their visits were generally accompanied by riots and disturbances in the Province.

In view of Galvin's excitable and insurrectionist comments in previous years, I had thought it advisable to forbid his entry into the Province. I therefore asked the Home Secretary, Leon Brittan, to ban him under the Prevention of Terrorism Act. The Foreign Office, however, on the advice of our Embassy in Washington, thought that this would be a great mistake. A series of letters – subsequently leaked to the *Guardian* – duly passed between all three Departments. But in the end the Home Secretary agreed with me and the ban was imposed.

When Galvin arrived in Dublin it became clear that he would make an effort to cross the border. This was only to be expected, and it was left to the RUC to tackle the problem.

Nevertheless Galvin duly turned up in West Belfast. What was more, Provisional Sinn Fein organised a major march and provided an occasion for Galvin to make a speech. There was mounting tension and when Galvin appeared, the police attempted some strong-arm tactics to arrest him, this ended in a riot and brawl. In the mêlée one man, Sean Downs, was hit by a plastic bullet at very close range, and subsequently died. The incident occurred in front of the television cameras and inevitably it was repeated on news and current affairs documentaries for some days.

The event was a very serious setback for the RUC who had been building greater acceptability within the Catholic community. To add irony to the occasion, the Commander of the RUC that day was himself a Catholic.

I felt that in the circumstances all that I could do was to take full responsibility. The decision to ban Galvin had been mine. But, had I allowed him in, might not some Unionists have tried to shoot him? Either way, Galvin's determination to enter Northern Ireland was almost certain to cause trouble.

My objective in taking responsibility was first to protect the RUC and at the same time to defuse the situation quickly – I was following my usual policy of trying to damp down strong feelings, which are inevitably aroused in tragic and difficult circumstances and which could easily spark off worse violence.

I think I did to some degree succeed in my objective. But although there was considerable praise from the Nationalists for my acceptance of the responsibility, and indeed from moderates throughout Northern Ireland, I was roundly condemned by the Unionists for conceding that things had gone wrong. An English Secretary of State is never going to win.

*

The need to concentrate on the immediate consequences of sensational events like the Maze break-out and the Galvin incident did not distract

the Administration from our more fundamental and longer-term efforts
to establish peace in the Province.

From my earliest days in Northern Ireland, I was convinced that developing closer relations between the United Kingdom and the Republic
of Ireland was essential to help bring peace.

Furthermore, both Governments were aware that beyond the issue
between Catholics and Protestants, and their respective attachments to
the Republic and the Union, lay the spectre of Marxism.

On security grounds there was obviously a clear need to seek better
cross-border co-operation. But there were also compelling political and
economic reasons to build closer links between London and Dublin, not
the least being that we shared a lengthy land boundary and had similar
interests on a range of agricultural, industrial and social issues. What is
more, we were both new members of the European Community.

The Provisional IRA are not simply working for a united Ireland:
their objective is a Marxist workers' party state, with all which that would
imply not only for the people in the Province and the Republic, but also
for the wider security of Britain and Western Europe. The Marxist
danger from the Provisionals was more acute to the Republic than to the
United Kingdom. If Provisional Sinn Fein and the IRA were ever to
gain a foothold and a real recognition in the North, the consequences for
democratic politicians in Dublin would be devastating. The Marxists
would have a base from which to subvert democratic politics in the
South.

If true progress was to be made in developing collaboration between
London and Dublin much would depend on the personal convictions and
relationships of the two Prime Ministers.

When Margaret came to power, Charles Haughey was Taoiseach – he
was Leader of the Republic's largest party, Fianna Fail, and generally
regarded as more inflexible on the question of the North than the leader
of the principal Opposition party, Fine Gael, Garret Fitzgerald.

I recall that Willie Whitelaw said he preferred Charlie Haughey to
Garret Fitzgerald. The only possible logic for this remark was that we
knew Charlie disliked England and felt that the only answer was a united
Ireland. On the other hand, although he had more sympathy with the
republican cause than Garret Fitzgerald, he was prepared to take just as
stringent action against terrorism.

In December 1980, Charlie Haughey hosted the first Anglo-Irish
Summit in Dublin, at which he and Margaret discussed a proposed
structure for closer relations. It was apparently a great love match. The
problem was that Charlie put one interpretation on what was agreed, and
Margaret put an entirely different one. The outcome was that, having
been at first very much in favour of Charlie, she then became very

disillusioned about him – and this subsequently coloured her view of the Republic as a whole.

In the early days Margaret's reaction to Charlie also affected her views on Garret Fitzgerald to his considerable disadvantage. Fortunately, this had changed by the time that Garret became Prime Minister in 1981.

Garret Fitzgerald is an exceptional man. of great honesty and integrity, and has always done his best to try to find common ground which would enable both the North and the South of Ireland to live together in peace. Of all the Irish politicians that I know, I have perhaps greater respect for Fitzgerald than anyone else.

He emerged as the strongest advocate of a more pragmatic approach to the problems of North, explicitly acknowledging in his Dimbleby BBC lecture in May 1982 the need to recognise the Unionist tradition and to seek political progress on the basis of consent from both Nationalists and Unionists. While moves by London to impose total integration would clearly provoke Republican terrorism, equally moves by Dublin to impose 'unification' would provoke bombings and murders by loyalist terrorists.

When Garret and Margaret met for their first summit conferences, in November 1981, my only worry was that Garret has a reputation for arguing his case with great articulateness and courtesy but with never a pause and that Margaret would not get a chance to talk herself. Luckily this didn't happen. They made a reasonable start and have got on better and better ever since. They respect each other: she recognises that he is trying to find a solution and is prepared to be courageous in accepting the Unionist position in a way that other leaders in the Republic have not been prepared to do; and I think Garret respects Margaret for being forthright, determined and positive.

It was therefore something of a disaster when in January 1982 Garret lost a vote on the budget and his Government fell, which brought Haughey and Fianna Fail back to power.

This meant that, at the time when I was preparing my White Paper on the creation of the new Assembly designed to return as much responsibility as possible to the people of Northern Ireland, Charlie was Prime Minister in the South. He made it absolutely plain that he wanted to have nothing to do with my proposals. He was only interested in a United Ireland, became as obstructive as he could, and encouraged the SDLP, particularly its 'greener' wing, to follow suit.

This in itself was extremely damaging, but the relationship between Great Britain, Northern Ireland and the Republic was made a good deal worse by his attitude towards the Falklands Islands dispute. It appeared that he was going out of his way to do everything to make Britain's position difficult, not just by abstaining in votes at the United Nations, but by arranging to get motions put down drawing attention to Britain's position.

This resulted in a very strong anti-Irish feeling in Britain which was meat and drink to the Unionists, who were showing great loyalty to the Government and to the United Kingdom. At the same time they were not slow to point out that if we could send troops to protect 1,400 Falkland Islanders, who wished to remain part of the United Kingdom, we should certainly do absolutely everything we could to help the million or so Unionists in Northern Ireland, who also wished to stay in the United Kingdom.

*

There was little progress in Anglo-Irish relations till the spring of 1983. By this time Garret Fitzgerald was back in power, and John Hume, Leader of the SDLP – hoping to win a seat in the coming British general election – persuaded Garret that the time was right to set up a 'New Ireland Forum'.

This Forum consisted of representatives of all the democratic Nationalist parties of the island of Ireland – the Unionists were invited to participate, but they predictably declined. Its aim was to thrash out an agreed blueprint, or at least a suggested way forward for the future political development of Ireland, North and South.

Setting up the Forum would give John Hume and the SDLP a good platform on which to fight the general election, which was expected in the autumn of 1983, by which time the Forum would have been well on with its work. But, as the election was called for June, Hume could only say that the Forum had been set up and had started meeting. This was sufficient to help get him elected to Parliament. He was returned as the sole member of the SDLP, but sadly Gerry Fitt, the former SDLP Leader and now an Independent Socialist, lost West Belfast to Gerry Adams, the leader of Provisional Sinn Fein.

I too was disappointed that the Forum was not further forward in its deliberations because the time when a government really needs to move on Northern Ireland affairs is in the early days of its life. With the prospect of four or five years of Conservative government ahead, and with the reasonably secure position of Fitzgerald's coalition, it seemed that 1983 and 1984 provided the best period for a long time in which we might make progress.

In this case the Government's hand was particularly strong as a result of its overwhelming majority. We were in no way beholden to the Unionists, who had since 1974 always tried to play one side off against the other in Parliament to win an advantage for themselves. We were therefore in an excellent position to take a fresh initiative, except that we were held up by the deliberations of the New Ireland Forum.

To add to my impatience was my awareness that, when I had spoken to Margaret about my future at the time of the 1983 general election, I had told her that I would like to complete three years in Northern Ireland. This meant I had only about a year to go.

To be honest, I hoped very much that I might be able to move to one of the major Departments of State. However, it was clear to me that Margaret had no intention of offering any of them to me, for she had appointed her people like Leon Brittan to the Home Office and Nigel Lawson as Chancellor of the Exchequer; Geoffrey Howe had gone to the Foreign Office and when Cecil Parkinson had to resign in the autumn of 1983 she had given Trade and Industry to Norman Tebbit – although I knew that my name had been suggested to her and it was a post I would have very much liked to have held.

My frustration at the delay in the Forum Report and my awareness that there was little likelihood of being offered one of the major Departments by Margaret meant that when GEC approached me in the spring of 1984 to find out if I would be interested in becoming their Chairman, I was in a receptive frame of mind.

I was still determined to see out the three years in Ireland to which I had committed myself, but accepted the GEC offer as a gateway to a new career which greatly appealed to my entrepreneurial feelings that had always run close to the surface. I had been in Parliament for twenty-five years and on the front benches for about twenty, but I still felt young enough to take on a career outside politics.

I went to see Margaret and told her that I thought there was a good chance that I would be offered the GEC job. I wanted to assure myself that she would approve because of GEC's position with the Government as one of its major suppliers. I also wanted to find out whether she had any other proposals for my future.

I was not surprised when she jumped at the idea. It seemed an easy way out for her, and she covered herself brilliantly by saying: 'But of course, Jim, there will always be a job for you in my Cabinet.' She did not go on to say what job.

The Forum Report was finally published in April 1984 – not long after the approach from GEC. It was an extremely disappointing document which I felt could have been written very quickly in the previous summer. But we had to make the best of it.

The opening chapters were grossly unfair about what Britain had sought to achieve in Northern Ireland. What is more, the three principal proposals were at variance with our declared policy: the first was a United Ireland; the second was a federal system, within a United Ireland; and the third they termed 'joint authority'.

Although the concept of joint authority was not fully developed in the

Forum Report, they referred to joint authority as meaning 'an equal share in the executive control of Northern Ireland'. This concept, and the terminology and limited explanation provided arose, I suspect, because I had warned them that under no circumstances would it be possible for us to contemplate 'joint sovereignty' for Northern Ireland. Yet, as it turned out, that is precisely what the phrase 'joint authority' seemed to mean.

The one hopeful part of the document was its recognition that we could look for other solutions besides the three proposed in the Report – that nothing was ruled out.

Unfortunately, the line taken by Haughey and Fianna Fail was considerably tougher than the Forum Report. Haughey made it perfectly clear that all he was interested in was a United Ireland. But there was a positive consequence of this, for the more Haughey said he was interested only in a United Ireland, the more conciliatory Fitzgerald became.

I felt very strongly that if the opportunity offered by the flexible paragraphs of the Report was not to be missed, the Prime Minister herself would have to be fully involved and committed, so that her authority would add impetus to the new initiative.

In Britain, the *Daily Telegraph* had consistently supported the Unionist hard-line against any collaboration, but I now noticed that their leading articles on Ireland were beginning to change in tone. It seemed to me that Peter Utley, their leader writer, was beginning to understand that we had to reach some accommodation with the Republic and that he was not quite so fervently Unionist as he had been. I thought it would be a good idea if we had a talk.

I told him what was in my mind, how I believed that we had to work towards some solution and outlined to him, as I had done to many others, the way I thought this might possibly come about. I asked him whether he would be prepared to go to talk to Margaret about it. In due course he wrote me a note, setting out what he thought we agreed about. I found the note entirely accurate.

He then sought an interview with Margaret. He told me afterwards that she really had not come to grips with the problem at all during the course of the interview. It had not been a productive meeting. She had wanted to talk about other things rather than Ireland. He seemed disillusioned about her views, which did not augur well for the future.

The Forum Report was debated for two days in the Commons in July 1984, and I was glad that we treated it as a major debate. It seemed to me that the ground had never been better prepared for politicians on both sides in Ireland to take account of all the relevant factors: hitherto they had refused either to recognise or discuss the basic principles which seemed all too obvious to detached observers.

My speech was designed to make it quite clear on the one hand that the Unionists could and should remain part of the United Kingdom; that I saw no possibility of any change in the constitutional position of Northern Ireland without the consent of the people; and, since I did not foresee that consent coming, we had to look for solutions within Northern Ireland itself.

But on the other hand, Unionists had to recognise that, while their position was protected by these guarantees, the new solutions had to be acceptable to the Nationalist community in the North *and* to the Republic of Ireland, which had a legitimate interest in Northern Ireland affairs because of the security position and because Nationalists in Northern Ireland felt alienated and otherwise unrepresented.

Perceiving Garret Fitzgerald's own readiness to be accommodating, I felt that we had to do all we could to be accommodating too. My statement represented a considerable step forward in the Government's approach. It was accepted by the House of Commons, and gave some pleasure in Dublin, without at the same time causing any major problems in the Unionist camp.

My last few months at Stormont were spent in trying to ensure that the concepts outlined in my speech could be translated into practice before the mood changed or the political merry-go-round turned on.

The route opened up by my statement in the House did not seem to me to raise any of the problems over sovereignty which 'joint authority' automatically raised. My hope was that, by moving to closer consultation, the needs of the Catholic minority would be met and that gradually they would feel able to take their part in the Northern Ireland Assembly, for the members elected from the SDLP and Sinn Fein had so far refused to sit.

As the representatives from all parties developed their role in the Assembly, with the powers that could be given to them both in the committees and subsequently through a devolved executive, I hoped that in turn the Republic's Government would need to play a smaller part, and there would be less need for London–Dublin consultation on Northern Ireland.

But I knew that, until that time was reached, we would have to accept the Republic's Government playing a bigger part in the consultations. A number of suggestions were therefore put forward as to how these consultations might best be organised.

The first possibility was that there should be some form of consul, or representative, of the Irish Government in Belfast, who would be able to consult the Secretary of State at all times, and who might make up a triumvirate, with a Northern Ireland politician and one from Westminster, to advise the Secretary of State.

A second or perhaps additional possibility was to set up a joint security committee on which the Secretary of State and the Minister for Justice in the Republic could take part together. Matters which affected the security of the island as a whole, could be brought to the committee. It was suggested that below this committee there should be some form of working arrangement. Possibly the Chief Constable of the RUC in the North, with the Commissioner of the Garda in the South, together with perhaps the Army from both countries would play some part in it.

A third suggestion was that there should be a border patrolling area, about ten to fifteen miles wide, where joint forces should operate. The reasoning was that a large number of (although by no means all) terrorists were operating within that corridor. But we were told by the Republic that it was quite impossible for them to allow any British troops or RUC to cross into the Republic, and they doubted very much whether there would be any desire for the Garda operating in the North.

John Hume put forward the proposal that the Catholic areas of the North, such as West Belfast and Derry and one or two others, should have a separate Catholic police force, preferably drawn from the South rather than the North. But this seemed to me to be impractical and to fly in the face of sovereignty and the question of whose responsibility it is to govern the country.

I myself suggested that there might be an Ombudsman appointed by the Republic Government, to whom cases of Nationalist intimidation or persecution in the North could be taken, and who would then have a right to make representations to the Secretary of State.

I had to make clear throughout our talks on the various suggestions that the Secretary of State would eventually have to take the full responsibility; it was not possible to have divided responsibility. The Secretary of State was responsible to Parliament, and Parliament was sovereign in all these matters.

Sovereignty is a difficult concept to keep in perspective. I could not, for example, ever get the Unionists to accept that throughout history there were occasions when the powers of a nation to control its own destiny were diminished in the interests, perhaps of others, but also of the nation itself. For example, I quoted agriculture and the European Community's Common Agricultural Policy. It is no longer possible to say that Britain has sovereignty over its agriculture, since we have effectively given it over to the European Community; it could be argued likewise on NATO defence matters, through NATO, and in practice in many other areas. It seemed to me perfectly logical that in the desperate search for peace in Northern Ireland, and throughout the island of Ireland, we should be prepared to pool sovereignty in certain matters where it was in the greater interest of the people as a whole.

An amusing, and perhaps enlightening, ray of light was shed on
Unionist attitudes to sovereignty in practice and their view of whether
they were more British than they were Irish, through the row over milk
production which was going on at the time of the Forum debates. Garret
Fitzgerald had managed to achieve very favourable terms for the Republic's milk producers at a time when the rest of Europe was required
to cut back production. I did my best to see that the terms available to
the Republic were also made available to Northern Ireland. The Prime
Minister fought hard for that equality of treatment for the whole island
of Ireland at the EEC negotiations, both in Athens and later on in
Brussels.

Yet, at the same time that Margaret and I were fighting hard for
Northern Ireland's milk producers, some Unionist MPs were busy saying
that they would rather have *worse* terms in Northern Ireland: the outcome
had to be similar to that in Great Britain, not the same as the deal which
was available to the Republic. If ever there was a case of cutting off
one's nose to spite one's face, this was it.

*

In the weeks when we were working on these plans there was considerable
pressure on Margaret to change her mind and try to hold me in Cabinet.
But she did not attempt to do so and it was quite obvious therefore that
she preferred to have me out of harm's way. It was equally obvious that
the sooner I got out the better.

It was in this mood that I appeared early one Monday morning on
BBC Radio Norfolk, and in the course of a conversation about my future
said I was not expecting to stay in Northern Ireland a great deal longer
and that perhaps I would not stay in the Government either. I suppose
this was a characteristic indiscretion on my part, but all I was doing was
saying in public what I had been saying in private and to lobby correspondents 'off the record' for some time.

It led to a few days of intense misery for me and speculation among
others, with politicians in Northern Ireland saying that I was simply
giving up, that I was a 'lame duck', and that the sooner I was replaced
the better. Lobby correspondents at Westminster were being questioned
on programmes like *The World at One* about what had caused me, as one
of the last of the so-called Wets, to make this decision.

In Northern Ireland, Jim Molyneaux went as far as to say that, since I
was now a lame duck, it was important that someone should take over in
Ulster, and that he was therefore going to take over: he did not explain
precisely how he planned to achieve his coup. And, with that, the OUP
walked back into the Assembly again! As I remarked at the time, if my

planned resignation was having this kind of effect on people, perhaps I should have announced it sooner.

I was pleased when Margaret told me that she had appointed Douglas Hurd to succeed me, though I would have been very happy to see her promote Patrick Mayhew. Having got used to me and my style, the Unionists found it more difficult to know how to read and react to Douglas's calm, reserved and apparently intellectual approach.

The morning after his appointment I had a long talk with Douglas in which I tried to brief him on the most significant issues and personalities – not only the politicians in Westminster, Belfast and Dublin, but also the civil servants in the corridors of Whitehall and Stormont.

I followed this personal briefing with a 4,500 word letter to Margaret, which I copied to Douglas. In this, I set out both my appreciation of the present situation and the opportunities for action which were immediately open to us.

I was convinced that things could not be left as they were. There was a moral obligation on all of us to make every possible effort towards the restoration of peace. Secondly, I told both Margaret and Douglas that I believed there was an opportunity, which would never come again, for them to take the decisive steps towards a political settlement. I was in a much better position than anyone else to see this after my three years in the job.

I made a strong, direct appeal to Margaret for her full personal involvement. Any progress needed the committed authority of her office and she more than any other British politician was trusted by the Unionists as being rock-solid on Northern Ireland's position within the United Kingdom. These two factors, combined with her own personal influence, I felt might render palatable measures which would otherwise be rejected outright by the Unionists..

I believed that the Government had to seek to move on three fronts: establishing a new relationship with the Republic of Ireland primarily on a London-to-Dublin basis; continuing to search for an internal system of government which would command cross-community acquiescence; and taking action to indicate our recognition of the legitimacy of the 'Irish identity'.

The trick was not to be perceived to be rewarding one community at the expense of the other. If progress was likely on the Anglo-Irish front, this would have to be balanced by a genuine attempt to bring about some devolution of power in Northern Ireland. We could not afford to swap the alienation of the minority community for the alienation of the majority. A middle course had to be found.

Garret Fitzgerald's Fine Gael-Labour coalition Government in the Republic wanted progress in Northern Ireland even if on a basis which fell short of a united or federal Ireland. Even so, their bidding was far too high, but I felt that an agreement might prove possible, both because of Fitzgerald's personal commitment to exorcising the constitutional issue, and because of his fear of the impact of Sinn Fein in the South.

The level of violence in the Province had, in general, been reduced to its lowest for fifteen years, although the situation in some border areas remained tense. The line could be held, probably indefinitely. But I warned Margaret that, in the absence of measures to reduce the alienation from authority of many in the Nationalist community, there was greater potential for deterioration and considerably increased casualties in the security forces.

In the short term, however, a political breakthrough could make the violence worse. Terrorists of all colours who were deeply involved in organised extortion and robberies would be determined to undermine any initiative before the political progress which it created became firmly rooted.

Unemployment would be running at 25 per cent by the next general election. Unless a political breakthrough could be made, facilitating a new push to attract investment, the annual UK Treasury subvention, then running at £1.3 billion, would have to be further increased.

Most worrying was the real danger that Provisional Sinn Fein could yet become the leading Catholic Party. The SDLP had held their support fairly solidly outside West Belfast, although this had been partially at the expense of the non-sectarian Alliance Party. Sinn Fein's support was drawn chiefly from hard-line Republicans who had previously abstained, from young voters and from those who had benefited from their involvement in community politics.

Given determination on our part, I believed a package might be constructed. We would need to contemplate devolving the Departments of Health and Social Services, Economic Development, Environment (excluding Housing) and, perhaps, Agriculture.

The essential elements of any devolutionary package like this would have to be: first, acceptance in Northern Ireland that there could not yet be a return to full Government by a Northern Ireland Executive or Prime Minister; secondly, that there would have to be a genuine sharing between the parties; and thirdly, areas of traditional sectarian dispute would have to be reserved to Westminster.

Agreement on any such development would be fragile and would need to be buttressed in several ways. First, a method would have to be devised whereby boycotts were not rewarded by allowing any one Party to destroy the whole edifice of agreement. Second, a mechanism would need to be instituted providing for a right of appeal from minorities in the Assembly to either a panel of Ombudsmen or to the Secretary of State. This might, at least in the beginning, help filter off those decisions upon which the parties would find it impossible to agree. Third, there would have to be some form of judicial co-operation with the Republic. In short, I felt it was necessary for us to give the Unionists some greater form of devolved power, while reassuring the Nationalists by giving Dublin a right of consultation.

The Nationalists often say that British policy towards Ireland has always been one of doing too little too late, and I fear that they have history on their side.

If we did not try strenuously to reach a breakthrough, I warned Margaret and Douglas that we could be sure of two things. First, the price of involving the Irish Government and accommodating the Nationalist minority would rise; and second, in years to come the extent to which a window of opportunity had existed in 1984–85 would be exaggerated and we would find ourselves once more charged with dereliction of duty.

As far as I could see we were facing the best opportunity for progress internally and with the Dublin Government for a decade. Many Unionists were concerned by the rate at which able young middle class Unionists were migrating to England; and some remained convinced that their best guarantee against English perfidy was to take greater control of their own affairs.

On the Nationalist side the SDLP and the Dublin Government saw their cause misused by Sinn Fein and control slipping from their hands.

Having grappled with the problems for three years I remain convinced that Northern Ireland is different from other parts of the Kingdom. Englishmen, while they can know the situation, can very rarely understand it.

Northern Ireland must remain part of the United Kingdom as long as that is the wish of the majority of voters in the Province. But peace will only be possible if three conditions are met. First, if the Nationalists are allowed a closer identification with their sympathisers in Dublin, otherwise they will identify with more malign sponsors. Second, if the Unionists can be persuaded to broaden their society to accommodate constitutional Nationalists. And third, if Northern Ireland's elected representatives themselves are required to shoulder greater responsibility for the affairs of the Province as a whole, rather than solely for the affairs of one community or the other.

*

I left office finally on Monday evening, September 17 and started work with GEC the following Friday. I had neither time nor inclination for

regrets before I was plunged into the new world of industry, with a greal
deal to do.

Conventionally, a Secretary of State is there one day and gone the
next. In my case there were at least three months when people knew that
I was going, a situation which had certain advantages. It not only gave
Jane and me the opportunity to say goodbye, gratefully and without
haste, to a great many people, but there were also some very moving
moments when they said goodbye to us. We were most generously and
royally entertained; the kindness bestowed on us was deeply touching.
The RUC, the Army, the Chambers of Commerce, the CBI and many
other organisations arranged farewell parties and presented us with extremely handsome gifts.

The kindness shown to us in those last few days made me feel that
perhaps the previous three years had been rather better spent than they
had appeared to be at the time, and certainly the warmth of the many
friendships we had made will remain with us always. Once Northern
Ireland gets into your system, I doubt if you can ever be free of it. I still
live the problems, think about the people, and will always be prepared to
do everything I can to help them.

Until the time came to leave, I did not realise how unhappy I had been
in the Government during those last few years. Although I was totally
committed to its Irish policy – and was indeed its architect – and although
Margaret now backed it wholeheartedly, I was also a member of Cabinet
responsible for British policies. But over these I had no control and less
and less influence; what is more I felt distinctly uncomfortable about
some of those policies.

Anyone feels when they decide to end a career, certainly if it means
leaving the Cabinet, that they are closing a very big door in their life and
that a painful reaction will follow. I am lucky: the withdrawal symptoms
I expected have never come.

PART FOUR

CONCLUSION

CHAPTER THIRTEEN

WITH THE GRAIN

Thirty years after we bought the farm at Brampton as a base for my political life, Jane and I still live there.

Today, however, there are no longer black swans on the moat round the house. We did not replace the pen that was killed by the fox in 1974, as swans mate for life. We handed the old cob over to Peter Scott at Slimbridge, since it would certainly have killed the new young pair which we brought to the moat. We have watched several broods of swans and geese grow up. Some we have given to friends; the rest have flown away.

Our own children, too, are fully fledged and although they too have taken wing I am glad they frequently return to the farm – in fact, Simon, our second son, now runs it in partnership with me. Our eldest son, David, joined British Steel where he worked under Ian McGregor: he is the only one with political aspirations. On the other hand both Sarah Jane and Jeremy have inherited my entrepreneurial strain and started businesses of their own.

Many new MPs have asked Jane and me for advice about how best to rearrange their lives to cope with the pressures of Westminster, constituency and family life. Should their partners and their children stay in the constituency or come to London? What should they do about the children? And so on.

Our advice, drawn from our personal experience, has never wavered. In school holidays, which to some extent coincide with Parliament's, the children must be given priority; if that means husband and wife being apart during the week, so be it. But, during term time, husband and wife should spend the week together in London and go home at the weekends, taking the children with them if they are not at boarding school. For a male MP to leave his wife at home in the constituency, dealing with the chore of coffee mornings, whist-drives and angry constituents, while the husband is either living it up in London or more probably getting bored and lonely, is courting disaster.

It takes a strong marriage to survive a long political career. We have been lucky. Divorce is rightly no longer a bar to Parliamentary success, but I have witnessed the trials and agonies of too many colleagues and friends to leave me in no doubt that it is an ordeal which both partners in a marriage should make every effort to avoid.

Our children have grown up in a fairer and more affluent society than I experienced. In all my years of moving about the constituency I have never once seen a single case of deprivation, poverty, eviction or distress to equal those I witnessed when my father took me round with him during the foreclosures of the thirties.

But the improvements made in many aspects of our lives have not been balanced by sufficient progress in others. Whereas many of the standards of living – food, clothing, houses, motor cars, working conditions and holidays – have risen dramatically for most people since those days, I doubt very much whether education has improved to anything like the same degree, for all the increase in University places. Certainly the way in which schools have been funded and managed seems to have reduced levels of learning and the sense of professionalism among the teachers. The really dramatic and dangerous shortage of maths and physics teachers will have a severe effect in a few years' time on the skills of people entering industry and on our industrial performance in the future.

I think that our recent treatment of hospitals and staff in the National Health Service has had similar results. Despite the dedication of so many doctors and nurses some professional standards have declined since my mother used to go round the wards in those years between the wars.

I sometimes wonder what my old headmaster, Robert Birley, in his wisdom and with his experience of the resurrection of Germany after the war, would have made of our efforts to modernise Britain in the last fifteen years. He would certainly have been saddened about the lost opportunities in education and I'm certain he would have shared my profound disappointment at Britain's failure to make the most of our membership of the European Community. When we were negotiating British entry in the early 1970s my future continental colleagues often used to say to me that they wanted Britain to become a member, because we would bring political skills and democratic institutions to strengthen the economic success of the Common Market.

But we have failed them. We have scorned Europe and concentrated so much on the smaller issues that we have totally neglected to put ourselves in a position from which we could radically influence or lead one of the most powerful political groupings in the world.

The right wing of the Tory party, just as much as the left wing of Labour, have shown themselves to be Little Englanders. In particular our failure to join the European Monetary System is symptomatic of the lack of enthusiasm for Europe. If British spirits were raised by our victory in the Falklands, we should not delude ourselves into thinking that this display of national independence was any substitute for a true vision of Britain's role in a modern world. I am glad that, throughout my political career, successive British Governments have at least remained firmly committed to a defence policy based on membership of the North Atlantic Treaty Organisation.

At a purely personal level it amuses me to speculate on Robert Birley's reaction to some of his pupils' achievements. He was not surprised by Simon Raven's success as an author; he might have found it improbable that William Rees-Mogg and I should sit together on the GEC board; but I think his eyebrows would have risen at the idea that one day Simon and I should have a book coming out in the same season and from the same publisher. They would have shot up even further had he heard, as Simon assures me is the case, that the studious William also has a contract to deliver a book to the same publishers but has failed to meet his deadline!

Robert would have been as proud as I am that the Test team selected by Peter May and his colleagues in 1985 should have defeated Australia and as mortified by the subsequent disaster which befell the team chosen for the West Indies in 1986. He would have been equally regretful of the decline in editorial standards at *The Times*, when William Rees-Mogg ceased to be its editor.

On the other hand, Robert was a pragmatist and knew that Britain had to move with the times if she was to keep afloat in a world where our defeated enemies Germany and Japan, and our demoralised ally France, threatened our survival as a manufacturing society with their newly reconstructed institutions and driving ambitions. We need more vision, energy and self-reliance in breaking through some of the old shibboleths. This kind of determination has helped change the old Fleet Street pattern of weak management and union restrictive practices. The misprints of *The Times* and vulgarities of *The Sunday Times* are a price we should be prepared to pay for ending decades of appallingly weak management and restrictive union practices in Fleet Street.

It is sometimes said that people in this country do not like to see others succeed, but I do not believe that is true, as long as people feel the success is justified and the rewards have been deserved through hard work. This is why it is important that the Conservatives do not allow themselves to become identified solely with the interests of the wealthy or with the financiers and money men in the City. If we do, then we cannot expect to be supported by those who work long hours, often at monotonous jobs, for comparatively small reward.

Ted Heath realised this when he compared the different attitudes towards those who had made vast sums of money overnight in the property boom of the early 1970s and towards the Sainsbury family, whose company went public at the same time. In the latter case, people felt that the company and its management were working hard and were doing a good job to serve the public. They deserved their success. There was no sense of unfairness, no feeling of bitterness.

I see no contradiction for the Conservative Party in expressing a philosophy which emphasises the importance of individual self-reliance wherever possible, and which at the same time values the concept of people working together harmoniously. The Conservative Party must appeal to all those who have a natural distaste for bureaucratic control and interference, who believe in lower taxation and who want greater opportunity to build up their own savings and buy their own homes. But these aspirations go hand in hand with a wish to feel comfortable in society: most people like the idea of working together and their leaders trying to work with the grain and not against it.

Too often we are told that we should seek to emulate the success of the United States and to adopt their philosophy of laissez-faire. But this is to misunderstand the deep difference between the history and the culture of the United States and Britain.

It is one thing to admire the enterprise ethic of the United States, but the belief that we can emulate it is wide of the mark. A new society with all the challenges of a young vigorous economy in a country of great natural resources is very different from the likes of Liverpool and Leeds, or for that matter Wiltshire or Worcestershire. We are an old nation scarred by war, the effects of the industrial revolution and the competition of the technological revolution which has followed it. Our roots are deep, we depend heavily on one another, and we are not motivated by the need to prove ourselves in the world.

When I hear my former Cabinet colleagues claim that we must look to the United States to see how jobs are created, I really wonder if they understand what they are saying. During a recent visit to South Carolina, I was speaking with the state official responsible for economic development. He told me that after a few years of considerable expansion in industry and employment it was much more difficult to attract new industry and create new jobs. In contrast, the old industrial state of Massachusetts had much higher education standards and was therefore turning out the graduates that industry needed in large numbers consequently, unemployment was falling.

About 35 per cent of young people go to college to read for a degree in the States, compared with 15 per cent in Britain who attend university or polytechnics. We need to increase our numbers and not reduce them, as is planned at present. However, we shall not be able to increase the numbers significantly if we retain the current system of student grants. We need, therefore, to introduce a loan system, which works well in the States, and be more flexible about the time taken to obtain a degree by those who are also doing a job while attending university. The savings made in Government spending through a loans scheme, together with additional resources, should be used to increase substantially the numbers of people able to obtain a university education. Not only would this raise general education standards and hence be of benefit to industry, but it would also help to reduce unemployment in the 20–24 age group.

We need to develop a more positive and coherent industrial policy in Britain. Keith Joseph's attempt to have no industrial policy whatsoever was short-lived, but since then we have staggered on with a piecemeal approach because of the doctrinaire beliefs of those with no experience of industry and because of the Treasury's dominance of Whitehall. We should have been prepared to follow a more expansionist, yet controlled, policy to restore the country's infrastructure and to provide considerably more help for those who through no fault of their own have been the sufferers during this economic recession. It is very little compensation that the level of provision for those without jobs is now better than it was in the 1930s. I am deeply concerned that mass unemployment over such a long period is creating a listlessness and a fecklessness in society.

We must do more about unemployment. It is not enough to produce schemes which cope with some of the worst cases and to keep on saying that all a government can do to help is to stick to the same economic policy. There is no reason why our unemployment should be three or four percentage points worse than France or Germany, and with our natural resources of energy we ought to do better.

Many of the schemes for helping the unemployed which have been introduced since the late 1970s were short-term, based on the optimistic view that the economy would come right and unemployment would fall. It now looks as if the problem could still be with us for a number of years and we need positive long-term plans to deal with it. Those plans must include full-time education or training for all up to 18, and a much enlarged higher education sector. At the other end of working life, there should be a massive increase in the job release scheme whereby those over 60 can retire if their place is taken by an unemployed person.

Equally we must not turn our back on the low-paid. Some of my colleagues in Government were constantly seeking to abolish the Wages Councils, which provide a form of protection for some of the low-paid. If there is a case for restricting Wages Councils' powers and their scope so that they do not destroy jobs, there is an equally strong need to recognise that the weakest in society do need some form of protection against exploitation, and it is the Government's task to perform this role.

The Conservative Party is at its best when we seek to unite people, understanding that not everyone aspires to greatness and that we have no monopoly of patriotic sentiment.

The bedrock of our society is the countless thousands of people tucked

away in the terraced houses of Bradford or on the council estates of
Birmingham who are intensely loyal to their country, who take pride in
their work and the dignity of family life. Doubtless many of them do not
vote Conservative and would never think of doing so. But we have a duty
to provide them with the opportunities which their parents, or perhaps
their grandparents, never had and to help them sustain their pride and
sense of dignity.

Since 1959 I have been fortunate to represent Lowestoft – or Waveney
as the constituency is now called. It includes a strong, traditional working-
class community, and the range of people from different backgrounds
and with different attitudes has strongly influenced my view on what the
Conservative Party should stand for. I have been much happier dealing
with problems like pensions entitlements or maternity allowances and the
other basic difficulties which people experience, than I would have been
representing a plush seat in the stockbroker belt where the postbag con-
tains letters about the current state of the money supply or the public
sector borrowing requirement.

It is not easy for a Conservative MP, representing a suburban tree-
lined area or a constituency in the shires, to understand the problems or
the motivations of the loyal and intensely patriotic working class communities. They are the people, not unlike the Dagenham family who
taught me so much in the fifties, whom I tried always to bear in mind
when negotiating with the unions and preparing the 1980 Employment
Act.

*

Whatever regrets I have about the failure of both parties to make more
of our Education and Health Services and, far more seriously, to seize
the opportunities offered by Europe, I have a real sense of regret that I
was not able in Government to do more to bring down the highest rate of
unemployment since the war.

On the other hand I shall always be grateful for the chances I had in
Government to contribute something, however little it was, to the reform
of agriculture, the legislation regulating industrial relations, the introduction of improved training for young people, and our attempts to find
solutions to the problems of Northern Ireland.

My days at the Ministry of Agriculture were largely spent introducing
reforms which were due anyway, but which by happy coincidence
dovetailed with the requirements of our entry into the Common Market.
If agriculture is no longer the Conservative power base that it was –
owing to mechanisation, there are far fewer people working on the land
than in 1959 when I entered Parliament – farming is one of the success

stories of the last thirty years. Our farmers have had no problem in withstanding the competition within the European Community and, although they now face new pressures as prices have fallen over the past year or two, it is economically and strategically desirable that we should grow as much of our food as possible. It should be perfectly possible to strike a reasonable balance between this objective and the conservation of the countryside.

I approached my task at the Department of Employment with certain convictions: that in looking backwards rather than forwards the unions were restricting production and thereby were diminishing rather than improving the employment opportunities and standards of living of their members; that the laws governing union rights and immunities had become an anachronism and produced a further constraint on production; and that the majority of the British people now resented the damage that was thereby being done to the nation as a whole.

On the other hand I was equally convinced that many managers simply had no idea of how to lead and handle their work forces; that investors, financiers and banks too often failed to appreciate the rights of human labour invested in industry vis-à-vis the rights of the shareholders; and that it is impossible to coerce employees and their unions with threats of fines or imprisonment if they wholeheartedly believe in the justice of their cause or if unreasoning anger gets the better of them.

It was these convictions which guided my efforts to pursue a balanced policy and dictated my step-by-step approach to union reforms. In a sense the problem of Britain's industrial relations has not been that the unions have been too strong, but that because of a combination of their weakness and of bad management in too many companies, who allowed shop stewards to usurp power, British industry has been more vulnerable than most to frequent stoppages and short-term disputes.

I often felt that if unions had been better organised at the centre and had been able to offer their members more advice and more support, their officials would have been better able to counter the growing strength on the floor of shop stewards and the small groups of militants who have done so much to disrupt British industry. For years I think the Conservatives made the serious mistake of not spotting the more responsible union leaders: we should have been doing everything in our power to back them in their efforts to persuade their rank and file to accept and co-operate in the introduction of the modern technology and working practices needed to keep Britain competitive.

Len Murray, for whom I have high regard, told me before the 1983 election that if the Conservative Government won a second time the unions would have to come to terms with the legislation.

The following autumn when mass picketing broke out during the dispute at Warrington between the printers' unions and Eddie Shah, Len Murray went on record saying that the unions must obey the law. It was a courageous statement, representing a volte-face from the TUC Wembley declaration in 1980 of non-co-operation with the new laws. From that moment on the left were out to get him.

Insensitively, the Government provided the opportunity by announcing in January 1984 that no more union members or representatives would be permitted at the GCHQ security headquarters at Cheltenham. All unions would be banned and people were offered £1,000 to leave their union.

The decision had been prompted by the unions' actions at GCHQ during the civil service dispute in 1981, which had caused dislocation to our security services and had very much upset the Americans. There may have been heavy pressure on the Foreign Office or Ministry of Defence to take action, but incredibly the Government made its announcement without any consultation with those who understood what was going on in industrial relations.

The Government's decision caused uproar throughout the union movement. It struck at their very heart: the right of people to join a trade union. Even the most rabid right-wingers in the union movement were appalled.

Only a few days before, Len Murray had been telling trade union members to respect the laws passed by a Tory Government and now that same Tory Government had done this. Len tried desperately to reach some compromise, even going as far as to offer a non-strike agreement at GCHQ – precisely the type of agreement which we had been saying for years we wanted to see in the public sector. Yet this, in an act of further stupidity, was turned down. Len Murray was lost. In the short term this may not have hurt the Government, but in the longer run a strong and wise leader like Len Murray is invaluable to any government or society which is seriously concerned to promote better industrial relations.

Generally speaking, I believe that the terms 'win' or 'lose' should never be used in relation to an industrial dispute. The miners' strike of 1983–84 is, however, the exception which proves the rule. In this case, Arthur Scargill's motives seemed to be concerned with inflicting defeat on the democratically elected Government as much as they were with the issue of pit closures. Neither the National Coal Board nor the Government were left with any alternative but to fight it through to the bitter end.

I did feel, however, that earlier use should have been made of our reforms to the law on picketing and secondary action, particularly after the Nottinghamshire miners, who broke away from the NUM, had resorted to legal action. The hope now must be that the NCB remembers the Churchill maxim of 'magnanimity in victory' during the aftermath of the miners' strike, and that Rupert Murdoch will do likewise following the clash with the print unions over his decision to move his newspapers to the new plant in Wapping.

I would not claim that the present laws on industrial relations are necessarily perfect or that they may not still be open to abuse by employers or by unions. However, I think we have proved now that organised labour does not require laws to give it that special protection which was seen to be necessary in 1906.

Perhaps the next step is to place employers and unions on exactly the same terms. In other words, to make all agreements between them enforceable at law. Legally enforceable agreements place much more responsibility on both sides to make sure that those agreements are properly constructed. They might help to bring a greater professionalism into the trade union movement.

I believe that the introduction of such enforceable agreements could play a vital part in sustaining industrial peace after we have begun to eliminate the scourge of mass unemployment.

*

The political and constitutional problems of Ireland were a major issue in British politics during the nineteenth century and have continued to bedevil the peace of the British Isles for much of the twentieth. It is therefore unlikely that they can be quickly resolved. Nonetheless, I went to Ireland in the belief that every new government is beholden to make the utmost efforts towards the establishment of a lasting peace in that unhappy island.

After looking at all the possibilities, I felt I only had two opportunities for moving towards a long-term solution: the first was to return as much autonomy as we could to the Province, and the second to invite the Republic to join in close consultations with the North in order to reassure the Catholic minority that their democratic rights would never again be disregarded.

I was therefore delighted that, after I left, Margaret committed her full personal authority to the Anglo-Irish Agreement and have nothing but praise for the enormous courage she has shown in giving Ireland top priority. In Douglas Hurd and Robert Armstrong we had two extremely skilful negotiators. Douglas was an admirable choice for Northern Ireland; he was far more intelligent than any of his predecessors and clearly impressed the Province.

It is a very great pity he was moved to the Home Office after so short a time and only a few weeks before the Agreement with the Republic was signed in November 1985. Tom King is an honourable man but Douglas's replacement was read as a signal to the Province that their

affairs and their interests were again being down-graded. How could
they believe that we were really giving them the highest consideration
and fully understood their anguish, when we were prepared to withdraw
the key man at the key moment – even if we were in need of a strong and
able new Home Secretary after Leon Brittan was shuffled to the Department of Trade and Industry?

One of the problems in conducting the negotiations was that Dublin
invariably keeps John Hume, the Leader of the SDLP, closely informed on
the progress of any talks with London or Stormont. This in itself raises
Unionist hackles because they object to someone who leads a political party
inside the United Kingdom, and who is a member of the United Kingdom
Parliament, having such close contacts with a foreign government.

What is more, it is impossible for the British Government to consult
the Unionists or for that matter the Nationalists as closely as the Dublin
Government seems to think it is wise to consult John Hume. If the
Unionists had been consulted, they would have raised every objection
under the sun about the very concept of any sort of agreement or deal
with the Republic of Ireland.

We therefore had to press ahead and try to reach the best judgment of
what would be acceptable while also staking a great deal on the Prime
Minister's personal authority. I am convinced that the risk was well worth
taking. As I said in the Commons debate on the Anglo-Irish Agreement,
there is no other way but to take some chances in the interests of peace in
Northern Ireland.

A strong reaction from the Unionists the moment the Anglo-Irish
Agreement was announced was only to be expected. As a professional
diplomat Douglas Hurd would have been ideally qualified to handle the
delicate situation. Apart from his transfer at the critical time, the other
mistake was for the two Prime Ministers to meet and sign the Agreement at Hillsborough Castle. Hillsborough is very much the symbol of
Unionist loyalty to the Crown. It is treated with the same respect and
care as Buckingham Palace is by the English – or even more. The
Unionists do not really like the fact that English Secretaries of State
now live there, and to hold the signing ceremony at the Castle, whatever Garret Fitzgerald may have wanted, was an act of quite unnecessary provocation.

However angry and frustrated we may feel at the way in which the
Unionists have reacted, and however inexplicable and unreasonable their
opposition may seem, it would be equally wrong for us on the mainland
not to recognise the strength of their opposition and their bitterness.

What can the Government do next in Northern Ireland? To scrap the
Agreement now would be to ring the death knell of peaceful, constitutional nationalism and, indeed, of the present Irish Government. Yet to

proceed with the Agreement as if Unionist objections could be simply brushed aside is equally impossible: we have to try to find a balanced approach which takes account of their objections.

Perhaps there is a way forward, if both sides, the Unionists and the Nationalists, could each be encouraged to make a major concession: the Unionists to acknowledge that the Agreement would continue, and the Nationalists to accept that there could be a return to devolved government for certain departments of state in Northern Ireland. The Nationalists would need to enter the Northern Ireland Assembly after fresh elections, and then be prepared to allow majority rule to be restored and a new Executive established for certain Northern Ireland departments. In return, their reassurance would be the continuation of the Anglo–Irish Agreement, which could monitor the decisions reached within the Assembly, until both sides felt able to work together in a normal democratic arrangement.

In the longer run I hope that we can build on the Anglo–Irish Agreement. For my own part I would like to see the courts in the Republic and in the Province working together. For example, one judge from the Republic could sit with two judges in the Northern Ireland courts, and a Northern Ireland judge could sit with two judges in the Republic's courts. Certainly the constitutional theorists and the lawyers always raise objections to proposals of this kind, but the fact of the matter is that we need to establish much greater confidence in the system of justice among both traditions on the island of Ireland. We should be searching for practical solutions which will help Ireland to rid itself of terrorism and return to peace, and not remain hidebound by a narrow, legalistic interpretation of the concept of sovereignty.

I know there are people who, in moments of exasperation, feel that we should pull out our troops and our resources from the Province. It is argued that we should threaten to withdraw in order to call the bluff of the Unionists when they play the 'Orange card'. But I utterly reject that approach. Such talk would merely reinforce the view that we neither care nor understand the problem. It also encourages the terrorists to believe that, if only they carry on their campaign, they can eventually succeed. There should therefore be no suggestion of us reneging on our commitment to the people of Northern Ireland for as long as the majority in the Province wish to continue to be a part of the United Kingdom.

The resolve shown by the Prime Minister and her Cabinet colleagues, and the response of the British public, at the time of the Brighton bombing, demonstrate that neither the British Government nor the British people will be intimidated by terrorists. Whatever the magnitude of the cost we should continue to do our best to bring peace and stability to

Northern Ireland, which is what the vast majority on both sides of the sectarian divide wish to see.

*

In this book I have tried to do more than simply give an account of the political events in my life. I have tried also to show why I believe that politics should be not so much a matter of doctrine but of personal judgments and of balancing the available powers to apply them. My overriding desire has been to work with the grain of society, to plane down the causes of conflict and to create amongst people a sense that they matter and that their wishes are being taken into account by their government.

Looking back I feel that, when I was knocking on doors and canvassing for votes in my first election in 1959, society was more content and less divided than at any other time since. We are of course better off now than we were then in the sense that our living standards have risen. But the conflict and confrontation which characterise our industrial and political affairs compared with many more successful nations with whom we have to compete for trade and jobs have if anything become worse over the years.

Of course the British party system gives people the opportunity to express dissatisfaction with whomever is in power, but if influential elements in both the Conservative and Labour parties are bent on extremes and confrontations, as has been the case in recent years, the voter may simply find the options are between a frying pan and a fire. Perhaps this is precisely why there seems to be at least a temporary swell of support for the Alliance, the Liberals and the SDP.

The Conservative party has been through two distinct phases over the last forty years. It has swung from Harold Macmillan's and Rab Butler's concepts of One Nation and The Middle Way to the more right wing laissez-faire radicalism of Margaret Thatcher and Keith Joseph.

This swing to the right has been accentuated by a number of factors including the failure of previous governments of all persuasions to tackle inflation satisfactorily, the split and gradual disintegration of the Labour party in the 1970s and '80s, and the incidence of increasingly undemocratic trade union leaders and practices. All these have led to intellectual arguments and gut feelings favouring the radical right over socialism. In 1979 the country was ready for the strong leadership which Margaret Thatcher was offering.

With the new leadership came a change not only of personality but also of philosophy – the abandonment of paternalism and the adoption of rigid monetarism with a harsh rhetoric to go with it. Under this régime the Conservatives have presided over the control of inflation, have introduced legislation to inhibit the abuse of trade union power, have embarked on the privatisation of enterprises which are likely to prove more efficient if set free, and have found a way to curtail the extravagance of municipal councils.

But despite all the rhetoric it is clear that it has not been possible to make many of the fundamental changes which the more doctrinaire monetarists would have liked. Part of their problem is that Margaret Thatcher herself, despite her leanings to the radical right and her combative style, is a much more cautious politician.

For instance a drastic reduction in government spending has not been possible; important nationalised industries have not been brought into profit; when Keith Joseph was at the Department for Industry, he found it necessary to give government aid to a number of enterprises, particularly BL, which otherwise would have gone bust; similarly, the level of unemployment benefit and other social security benefits has had to be increased in line with the cost of living, resulting in very little difference between the incomes of those out of work and a large number of lower-paid workers.

I therefore do not regard the swing to 'Thatcherism' – as it has been called – as more than a passing phenomenon in the evolution of the Conservative party. The art of leadership is to change the mood so that the unacceptable becomes possible. To some extent Margaret Thatcher has achieved this, as is demonstrated by the electorate's acceptance of very high levels of unemployment and their manifest support for trade union reform. But the fact that Margaret herself has had to trim her policies and not always live up to her own rhetoric shows that in a country like Britain it simply isn't possible to go against the grain for more than a very limited period.

If the Conservative Government is to win a third term of office in the 1980s it will have to come to terms with this reality and change the language of its argument. On too many occasions it sounds as though it is hell-bent on pursuing some harsh doctrine even when it is doing nothing of the sort.

My own conviction is that in politics it is much better to speak softly and to act firmly when absolutely necessary. Some of the Prime Minister's most ardent supporters on the backbenches have confessed to me that, when they return to their marginal constituencies, they moderate their tone because they recognise they must seek a broader appeal.

One Labour MP, Joe Ashton – a staunch but by no means extreme member of the party – once told me that Labour had to stir things up and to produce stories which would create jealousy and bitterness to be successful. This seemed to me to be a curious philosophy for a Party which once aspired to be the natural party of government.

Many Labour MPs look with admiration at the way in which neither the day-to-day difficulties nor the Whitehall machine have been able to shake Margaret Thatcher from her fundamental beliefs. In their eyes she has not done a Harold Wilson or a Jim Callaghan, by which they mean winning an election on a party manifesto but quickly deserting its principles and resorting to a series of short-term compromises.

They want a Labour Government to be as strongly committed to doctrinaire socialism and nationalisation as the Prime Minister is to red-blooded capitalism. This belief has driven them further and further from the realities of political power.

In 1980 when Michael Foot was elected leader of the Labour Party one of the older Labour MPs, Douglas Jay, commented to me that Michael's victory was a vote for safety. Denis Healey was regarded as being far too risky, and would have led to an even deeper split in the Party.

Yet the election of Neil Kinnock as Leader in 1983 was a much bigger risk because of his total lack of experience in Government. To have any chance of becoming Prime Minister, he has to fight and be seen to fight the hard militant left in his Party. The more he fights the more the country will respect him. Kinnock therefore faces a taxing dilemma. To win power he has to distance himself from socialism and from the unions. Yet the more he does so, the more he alienates so many of his own supporters.

The Alliance between Liberals and the SDP has been the beneficiary of the extremists and confrontationists in the other two main parties. The problem for the Alliance is that inevitably they have only a very limited number of senior politicians with any experience of government, and most of those are former members of the right wing of the Labour Party.

Few Liberals in or out of Parliament look impressive as potential members of a government. The Liberal Party increasingly seems to represent a very broad coalition of people whose main concerns are local issues rather than running the country.

The Alliance have found it hard to make a breakthrough in the industrial areas because of their difficulty in attracting the traditional Labour vote. In the south of England they are now very often second to the Conservatives. In an attempt to achieve the breakthrough, the SDP Leader Dr David Owen has therefore become more and more right wing to attract more dissident Conservatives. But he still has to contend with the fear of people in the south of England that by voting Alliance they will merely let in a Labour Government. And, since people are much more consistent in voting against what they dislike rather than voting for what they like, I suspect that this will save many southern England seats for the Conservatives.

I admire the way that David Owen has stuck to his guns and forged for himself a place at the top of British politics. He has proved himself a very good performer in the House of Commons, extremely good on television and very adept at judging the political mood. But his toughness can come across as arrogance. The epitaph, in the Government chauffeur service, on his days as Foreign Secretary during Jim Callaghan's Government was that David Owen had got through more drivers than London Transport.

Not long after the SDP was founded, Denis Healey and I were having our usual battles with our respective Parties when we happened to bump into each other at the House of Commons. Denis flippantly remarked: 'You know, Prior, you and I should set up our own party.' But Denis is too conservative to leave 'this great movement of ours', just as I am too Conservative to leave the Tories.

Many people have, in fact, asked why I and other like-minded Conservatives did not join the SDP, although none of their founder members was so blatant or tactless as to approach me. I have never been tempted to change my Party allegiance. Whatever the contemporary mood of the party, one is a Conservative because of certain instincts and beliefs about society, about life and about change. Conservatism itself has evolved slowly and the prevailing mood or ethos of the party may take years or even a generation to alter. But if you have a view of society, as I do, then you do not suddenly up sticks and leave your party merely because you are at variance with the approach and style of those who are temporarily leading it. We are witnessing shifts in the political loyalties of the electorate and it seems to me probable that at the next election we will again see a three-way split in the vote.

In the long run I believe that it will be the Conservative Party which will survive as the dominant political force because its traditions can best accord with those of an island people steeped in history. But, to succeed, it must adapt as it has always done, and continue to appeal to all sections of the community.

*

Even if the people of Britain now have three main parties to choose from, and even if the Conservatives once again address themselves to the needs of all sections of society, one cannot spend thirty years in politics without questioning whether the system itself is best designed to serve the needs of the nation.

As a Conservative I do not believe in reform for the sake of it, but I feel that the time has come when we should adapt our Parliamentary and electoral systems so that they are more in tune with the country's needs and people's wishes.

Looking back I feel that in Britain we have sometimes been willing to sacrifice a higher standard of living for the sake of perpetuating old battles and settling old scores. I do not believe that most people any longer want this state of affairs, yet our political institutions help preserve it. I am now convinced that reforming the electoral system could play a major part in making Parliament more representative and reducing the confrontational element in our party politics.

The most fundamental reform which I favour is the institution of proportional representation along the lines of the system in West Germany; 300 to 350 MPs would be directly elected in single-member constituencies. This would enable us to retain the link between the MP and his or her constituency, which is important because it gives people a direct line to a particular MP and also gives that MP a specific responsibility for people and their communities. The new constituencies would be larger than at present, but, with improved help for MPs and the benefit of modern communications, I see no reason why the average size of each constituency should not be increased from its present 65,000 electorate to around 120,000.

In addition to these MPs directly elected by constituencies, between a further 100 to 150 should be elected from national lists prepared by the Parties. The MPs elected from the Party lists would be used to top up the number of MPs elected for each Party in the single member constituencies, so that the overall strength of each Party in the Commons after an election would more recently represent their level of support in the country. This would be of special value in Northern Ireland.

One of the main objections to introducing reform along these lines is that proportional representation is more likely to deny any single party an overall parliamentary majority and will therefore lead to coalition – which might mean a weak – government. But no one could seriously claim that West Germany, for example, has been unstable over the last forty years, and they have had the benefit of much greater continuity in policy than Britain has enjoyed. Britain's problem has been the constant chopping and changing of policy as the Governments have alternated, and the uncertainty as each new Government goes through its learning curve and eventually discovers that many of its more extreme policies planned in Opposition are simply not practical.

Secondly, in order to reduce the dependence of the Labour Party on funding from the unions and of the Conservative Party's links with private industry – both of which aggravate controversial issues – I would like to see the introduction of a degree of state funding. This would help provide more professional advice and support to parties in opposition.

The use of state funds should be confined to spending on the parliamentary Party, long-term policy advice and research, with some cash

available for general Party organisation. But we must not make the
funding so generous that there is a disincentive for Party supporters to
go out and raise funds from individuals. One possibility would be for the
Government contribution to be limited to 25 per cent of the money
raised otherwise.

There is a third means by which we could, I believe, reduce the
acrimony of party politics in the process of parliamentary debate without
in any way diluting the force of questioning and argument without which
democracy would die.

When Winston Churchill stood in the ruins of the House of Commons
the morning after it was bombed during the war, he made it clear that
the new House should be built to resemble in every detail the one that
Hitler destroyed. It is understandable why, at that moment in history,
one of the greatest of all English parliamentarians should feel as he did,
and should also wish to recreate the historical pattern of the chamber
inherited at Westminster and admired as a cradle of democracy throughout the world.

But in late twentieth-century Britain I do not believe that the arrangement of the Chamber, with the parties sitting opposite each other and
engaging in confrontation day in and day out, is any longer satisfactory.
The parliamentary confrontation spills over into our political life and our
industrial life and gives an impression of conflict and an edge to relationships which we can ill afford.

When people of strong conviction and passion sit opposite each other
in the small Commons Chamber, there is bound to be fierce argument
and the creation of a sense of drama and theatre. This can be entertaining
and exciting. It may have been suitable a hundred years ago when there
was little ideological difference between the main parties, when the issue
of the day was whether Gordon was to be relieved in time at Khartoum,
and when Government did not yet feel obliged to intervene in almost
every aspect of our daily lives.

Today I would like to see us adopt the European or American style of
seating arrangements for the Chamber of the House of Commons – in
other words, to move away from the Opposition and Government benches
facing each other and replace them with a semi-circular arrangement.

In the existing House it is impossible to resist the pressure to reduce
debates to the crude level of being either for or against the Government
of the day. The result is that while controversial but comparatively trivial
issues are magnified and become pure theatre, debates on crucial issues
which are not likely to threaten the Government's immediate future are
reduced to being so dull as to be practically meaningless. It is a scale of
values we can no longer afford.

If we need to reform the nature of Parliament to avoid the extreme swings of the pendulum and the confrontations, which at present inhibit the formulation and pursuit of any long-term policies for foreign relations, defence, industry, the social services and even private investment, we also need to reform the workings of Parliament to improve its efficiency.

We should look first at the sittings of the House of Commons itself. The present organisation of business, the hours it keeps, the pressures it imposes on the work of Ministers, civil servants and ordinary members, and the frequent occasions when the Chamber is virtually empty because most MPs are attending committees, party meetings or constituency work, are clearly undesirable. I should like to see meetings of the full House of Commons limited to two days a week. Business on those two days would be confined to question time and major debates, perhaps on the second reading of a Government Bill, or on some major issue of economic policy or foreign affairs.

To restore and promote the Chamber of the House of Commons as the forum for national debate in this way would entail a further major reform.

I would introduce a system where the bulk of Parliamentary work is conducted through the system of Select Committees. At present their effectiveness is hindered because their membership is determined by the Party Whips, and MPs are not allowed to serve long enough on any particular committee to develop sufficient expertise and gain real authority.

We should develop a system of seniority on a Select Committee along the lines of the US House of Representatives and Senate, and pay the chairman a salary in addition to his or her salary as an MP.

Parliamentary traditionalists will object that these reforms would detract from the authority of the Chamber of the House of Commons itself, but of course the committees would not sit on the two days in the week when the House itself was in session. Furthermore it should be remembered that the House of Commons itself introduced the Select Committee system, because the old Westminster model of debate was no longer enabling Parliament to act as an effective check on the Government. A further objective of the present Select Committee system was to enable serious and expert analysis and discussion of issues free from domination by party politics and confrontation. I believe that the reforms that I have set out would help take this a significant step further.

During my time in Parliament the workload on the backbencher has grown out of all recognition. Thirty years ago an MP would have to look for work and go and search for the problems in his constituency. Today the burden of constituency surgeries and the many cases which come to an MP's attention through his post are enormous.

MPs therefore need to be provided with permanent staff on the lines of American Congressmen, and also be given increased pay. MPs would then be much better able to serve their constituents and to develop a professional expertise as Parliamentarians.

With improved facilities we would also be able to cut down the number of MPs in the Commons. I believe that the total should be reduced from its present 650, which is unnecessarily high, to around 450 or 500. I hope that one result of these reforms – together with increased pay – would be the encouragement of people from a wide range of backgrounds to become MPs. In particular, I think women would find it easier to make their mark and have more effect in a Parliament which was less dominated by heated arguments in which the noisiest MPs can make all the running.

It should also encourage more people with industrial experience to enter Parliament and Government. If they realised that they would not be humiliated by their lack of knowledge of the curious procedures and customs of the present House of Commons. I witnessed Frank Cousins on the Labour benches and John Davies on the Conservative benches being crucified by a House of Commons which was more concerned with destroying the reputations of people who had succeeded outside politics than listening to the arguments drawn from their experience.

At present few industrialists of any stature would be prepared to sacrifice their careers to take on the drudgery and the long hours of work which is the lot of the backbencher.

Any reform of the legislative machine would have to be accompanied by a review of the executive, from the Cabinet downwards and outwards. This assumes that we still want a Cabinet in its present form. In fact too much power is probably now concentrated at Number Ten, which does not make for good government. This centralisation of political power is mirrored in Whitehall, where the Cabinet Office and the Treasury are dominant. So much power in so few hands almost invariably leads to misjudgements and bad government.

Cabinet Ministers are often too over-burdened, both with their Departmental work and also their parliamentary responsibilities, to contribute effectively to Cabinet Government. This may suit the Prime Minister of the day and the civil service, who are more easily able to get their way with the Minister.

In these conditions, when you get a Prime Minister who knows her own mind and is determined to get her way, and Ministers who are either equally determined or at odds with each other, the cohesion of the Cabinet can crack under the strain. It did so in the affair of the ailing Westland aircraft company, when the Minister of Defence, Michael Heseltine, favoured its rescue by a European Consortium while the Minister for Trade and Industry, Leon Brittan, apparently supporting the Prime

Minister, preferred an American bid. When one of the Ministers was the impetuous mace-brandisher, and the other his adversary on the issues of municipal government, the formula was explosive: both went, and a number of senior civil servants were showered with the debris.

I have enormous respect for the integrity, loyalty and professionalism of our civil service, but I believe that Ministers should be able to recruit more outside help and specialist advice. Indeed, I believe that senior civil service posts should be open to competition from outside the service. We should move towards short-term contracts for senior civil servants and look to a much greater interchange between industry and the public sector. These changes would gradually enable Ministers to participate more effectively in collective Cabinet decision-making, which would be further helped if the Government 'Think Tank', set up by Ted in 1970 and scrapped by Margaret in 1983, was re-created in its original guise.

At the heart of every Government's policy and planning lies the economy. Any programme of political reform should look at the procedure for the formulation and presentation of the Budget. It is absurd that the Government's spending decisions and its decisions on taxation and revenue should be announced so peremptorily each year. These announcements should be incorporated and presented as a Green Budget some months before the presentation of a final Budget allowing a process of consultation involving the Select Committee on the Treasury and the National Economic Development Committee.

Finally, I would introduce the televising of parliamentary proceedings. It was a great disappointment that the Commons voted against this, particularly following the success of the experiment of televising the House of Lords.

I can understand the qualms of some MPs about the editorial power which would be given to TV producers. I favour setting up a new channel, which would be devoted to parliamentary broadcasts. On the two days of the week when the Chamber was in full session the broadcasts would be entirely devoted to the business in the Chamber itself. On the other three days the broadcasts would be able to concentrate on the various Select Committee hearings.

I do not imagine for a moment that large numbers of people would watch such broadcasts, but if our parliamentary system were reformed to reduce the worst partisan excesses, to ensure that the best-attended and most passionate debates were confined to major issues, and to conduct the more detailed business in well-run and effective committees, the processes of open and democratic government could be visible to every voter in the country.

I have suggested these changes because I believe they accord with the country's needs and with the nature of the society which we have become.

Conservatives do not propose institutional reforms derived from abstract theory, but the record of almost every Conservative administration since the days of Peel in the 1840s shows that we do not fight shy of change where we believe it will best serve the national interest.

*

It would be futile and misguided to suppose that somehow we can eliminate all controversy: it would also be profoundly undemocratic. That is certainly not my intention: my objective is to ensure that the controversy and debate which lie at the heart of democracy are not continually distorted by short-sighted party political battles, which at the moment can spill over from Parliament into our national life instead of going to Parliament for effective resolution there.

I welcome the fact that we now live in a much more open and questioning society. Old party allegiances and class loyalties have broken down and people are now much more ready to judge policies and politicians on their merits. But people, mercifully, have many other interests in life besides politics and therefore they entrust politicians with the power to make the difficult decisions for them. The politicians may not always get the answers right, indeed there is often no 'right' answer to a social, economic, political or diplomatic problem. For these reasons it is vital in a democracy that the choice of our Government and the way in which it exercises its power should be approved and watched over by as many people as possible.

This is the basis of democracy and all governments need to be aware of it – both governments in which I served certainly were. As time has moved on, I look back with great gratitude that I was permitted to serve in two Cabinets under two Prime Ministers, both remarkable people and curiously similar in their background, their characters and determined approach to the problems we faced. Ted had the wider and longer-term vision, but he was ahead of his time and the Country was not ready to respond to him. Even if he had been the best communicator in the world, which he was not, I doubt if he would have succeeded at that moment. Margaret caught the mood exactly right; her vision was blinkered by her new-found belief in the dogma of Friedman and Hayek, but her powers of communication enabled her to appeal to popular opinion on those issues which she instinctively knew were worrying people. However, as these memoirs must reveal, I was happier under Ted and was never really comfortable as a member of Margaret's team.

Perhaps my own approach to politics has been too paternalistic and reserved, but then my roots are deep in the English countryside where change does not come quickly and where today we enjoy the fruits of what our ancestors planted hundreds of years ago. It is not easy though from the stance of the middle ground to capture the public imagination for policies and reforms which may not seem dramatic, but which I believe are important to sustain a fair and involved society.

These memoirs simply set out to describe what happened in my time as events appeared to me. They are an attempt to give an account of successes and failures which may help to guide others. I hope too that they will give encouragement to those who seek personal fulfilment in a public career and to reassure them that even if they do not achieve all their aspirations there will always be other things to do with their lives, other frontiers to cross, other hills to conquer, other people to help. I hope also that by working with the grain they will find, at the end of the day, that satisfaction which comes from a sense of understanding the moods and strains of a society and its people whom they have set out to serve.

INDEX